The Phoenix

Girls

Book II - The Crimson Brand

By
Brian Knight

JournalStone
San Francisco

JOURNALSTONE
YOUR LINK TO ARTISTIC TALENT

JournalStone books may be ordered through booksellers or by contacting:

JournalStone
www.journalstone.com
www.journal-store.com

ISBN: 978-1-940161-37-2   (sc)
ISBN: 978-1-940161-38-9   (ebook)

Library of Congress Control Number: 2013956491

Printed in the United States of America
JournalStone rev. date: March 14, 2014

Cover Design: Denis Daniel
Cover Art: M. Wayne Miller

Edited By: Dr. Michael R. Collings

To my muse, as a bribe to come back and visit more often.

If that's not enough, then come for the coffee and pizza.

Acknowledgements

I owe thanks to a lot of people, too many to fit between the covers of this volume, let alone the very limited space allowed for acknowledgments.

Here are a few.

Amanda Richards, Lauren Doll, M. Wayne Miller (Mr. Eye Candy himself), Frank Errington, Karen Bryant Doering, Susan Matute, Lost Lenore, Debra Lobel, Rhonda Cash, Norman Rubenstein (Godfather of The Phoenix Girls), Carol Weekes, Dr. Michael Collings, Christopher Payne, Robert Fleck, Rob Miller, Sharon Fitch, Geoff Guthrie, Scott Tyson, Jamcat Cook, Judi Wutzke, Judi Key, Ellen Knight, Christopher Kennedy, Kecia Serene, Shawna Knight, Judi Snyder, Rocky Snyder, Nshara Key, Dave Lancaster, and really just too many to list.

Most of all, thank *you*.

The Phoenix Girls

Book II - The Crimson Brand

PART 1

The Circle of Friends

Chapter 1

Relics

When Ronan stalked, he moved with all the stealth and grace of any other, any normal fox. It was something he'd perfected in the past few years, as much practice as instinct, because Ronan was not a normal fox. In fact, Ronan was not normal in any sense of the word.

He got around, wandering far away from Aurora Hollow and learning the countryside. During his solitary years before the girls had come, there had been nothing else to do, so he spent his time pretending to be normal, and he'd gotten quite good at it. Mostly he moved about with his body dimmed so that others couldn't see him, but even when he crossed paths with one of the very few people who could see him, they hadn't seen him for what he was. To them he was just like the other wild foxes that occasionally roamed close to town. He'd been shot at a few times, though never hit. Extraordinary or not, it might take him some time to shake off a bullet wound.

He had also learned to hunt, an unfortunate necessity during his extended stays in the area. He had no objection to the occasional taking of life. It was, after all, how natural foxes survived, but he had always preferred to take his nourishment in more enjoyable and less messy ways.

He was not hunting rabbits or field mice today. The objects of today's hunt were much more important than simple nourishment, and the longer they remained unfound the greater the danger they posed. It was only a matter of time before someone found one of them and opened a door best left closed.

* * *

Dogwood's landfill was several miles beyond the border of the town in an arid scrap of valley too dry and stony to produce anything but weeds. The man who ran it was youngish, with a long dark mane of thinning hair and a love of shooting anything that moved on four legs. Ronan had seen him at it, sitting on an old patched recliner on the front patio of the little camper where he lived and worked, a .22 rifle with scope pressed to his shoulder, scanning the junkyard for rats and rabbits, stray cats and dogs, and, on two occasions, Ronan himself.

Unfortunate luck, really, this unpleasant guardian of Dogwood's garbage being one of the very few who could see beyond the purely physical world, could see Ronan even when he didn't want them to.

He'd missed both times, which Ronan counted as *good* luck. Ronan had watched the man at work since late that previous fall, and he rarely missed. The place stank of his kills, the carcasses rotting among Dogwood's garbage.

It was not the carcasses or the garbage Ronan had come for, but a half-collapsed structure standing at the far end of a labyrinth of old sofas, refrigerators, and other human castoffs.

Leaning against a ruined and charred trailer was a partially burned false front in the shape of the monster that had terrorized Dogwood's children last fall during the annual autumn fair. Only his girls (for that was how he thought of Penny, Zoe, and their new friend Katie) remembered the monster as it truly was.

The leaning false front, now damaged by both fire and the elements, was a giant effigy of The Birdman, who had come to town in the guise of a magician, one of The Reds who'd frequented the annual fair in years past. When the monster had abandoned his burning house of horrors, he had left behind some very dangerous toys. Those toys, those potentially dangerous relics, were what Ronan hunted.

* * *

Ronan crouched low in the tall grass across the putrid little valley, waiting for the man to go inside. The sun had fallen low in the sky behind him while he waited, painting the wasteland below him with its surreal, deepening orange until the place was almost beautiful. Ronan was patient. He had to be. He'd found some of them already, along with a few other unexpected surprises, but if the girl's description of that strange door-lined hallway was accurate, there were still three to account for, and if something happened to him, if he was unable to recover them all, the results could be disastrous.

The Phoenix Girls always attracted a certain amount of trouble. It was unavoidable, but the new Phoenix Girls came with extra complications. The crow had almost certainly talked when Penny and Zoe had sent him back to his world unarmed and helpless, so chances that their return had gone unnoticed were slim. They were not ready for the trouble that was sure to come their way, and though Ronan had kept a careful ear to the ground and heard nothing telling, he feared that trouble was coming soon.

Then of course there was Penny herself, perhaps the biggest complication of all simply because of who she was. It was a complication he'd have to reveal to her in detail someday, but not yet. She wasn't ready.

If she knew the whole truth, it would break her heart.

First things first, Ronan reminded himself, and refocused on the job at hand.

The last thing any of them needed was for some unwitting person to find one of the doorway relics and open the way for new trouble, so when the man finally rose from his seat, slinging his rifle back over his shoulder as he climbed inside his camper, Ronan didn't waste a moment.

Lesser quadrupeds—the rats, cats, and dogs too clever to be picked off by the garbage man's bullets—fled before him as he raced down the barren slope toward the junkyard's bordering fence. They couldn't see him now. Like most humans they were blind to him when he made himself dim, but they could smell and hear him. He moved slower, stealthier as he approached the rusted barbed wire fence, and then crossed beneath the lowest strand and into the wasteland beyond. He knew his way to the burnt-out husk of the trailer well enough that he could have run there in his sleep. He'd been there many times already, and a minute later, he stood before it again.

He spent a long moment studying the leaning false front and the fire-blackened siding, then the open front door, mostly blocked by charred rubble and broken glass, looking for any sign of recent exploration other than his own. Vermin and strays had made this place home, their scents and tracks everywhere, but he wasn't worried about the animals. The rubble piled inside the open door had not been moved or shifted since his last visit, and no human could have entered these ruins without disturbing them. He chuffed with satisfaction and scanned the length of the trailer to where the exit for the House of Mirrors had been. This portion of the structure had remained partially intact during the search following the fire but had collapsed when the authorities had brought the trailer here.

The collapsed walls and roof changed that end into a claustrophobic maze of broken glass and charred wood. Many of the twisting paths were too dark and narrow even for Ronan. These were the only places he had yet to search for the remaining Relics.

Tonight he would have to dig.

Might as well get it over with, he thought, and with a very unfox-like sigh, leapt up onto the threshold of the open doorway.

The stink of old smoke and decay filled his sensitive snout, and he sneezed several times before crouching low to pass beneath a large shard of smoke-blackened mirror.

The structure was mostly gutted, only a few warped and half-burned struts remained where walls had once stood, and the sagging ceiling had split in many places. Ronan navigated the dangerous debris by memory and moonlight until he reached what had been the back hall, the short corridor where the troublesome Birdman had kept his handy doorways.

The thing that troubled Ronan most about the girls' story, a story he'd confirmed during his explorations of this ruined place, was how a lone avian had accumulated so many rare and dangerous items. It simply wasn't possible. The Birdman's operation was small, though effective, and no rogue flier just appears in an ordinary, sleepy little town with such a trove of rare and powerful magic.

The Birdman's dangerous tools, his specialized knowledge of this world, and the sheer number of children he'd taken—all of it pointed to something much bigger than a lone, wandering avian snatching children for the open slave market. Much, much bigger.

That monster had been the tip of some unseen sword, but who or what was holding that sword's hilt?

Trouble coming on this side, something big happening on the other.

Ronan could feel the fragile peace of this once-safe place shivering, about to shatter, like The Birdman's House of Mirrors.

He worked well into the night, burrowing through the wreckage until something shiny revealed itself in the ash and rubble. Despite his discomfort, Ronan managed a brief grin before pulling the dirty brass object from the debris with his teeth. He backed carefully from the rubble and emerged into the clean night air a minute later.

He peeked from around the cover of the false front to the camper on the hill. The chair was still empty.

Again, Ronan took quick advantage of the garbage man's absence and sprinted from the wreckage, through the maze of human junk, with the etched brass doorknob between his teeth, slinking low to the ground to pass beneath the barbed wire, and was halfway up the hill and the start of his long trek back to Aurora Hollow when he scented something that stopped him in his tracks.

Ronan's sense of smell was superb, much stronger than his hearing or vision, and his memory for unique scents was eidetic. If he smelled a fire from far away, he almost always knew what was burning: the sharp, poisonous preservatives in processed lumber; the heavy tang of pine sap; the rich, pleasant smell of wheat grass.

His favorite scent was clover in spring, a wild, sweet scent unlike any other.

He could identify each of his girls, his only companions in this place, by their individual scents, and could tell if they were happy, sad, angry, or scared.

The scent that stopped him was a familiar one, and unexpected. It raised his hackles and made him want to shrink into the grass. He resisted the urge and stood alert, scanning the countryside for the source. Hoping he was mistaken but fearing he wasn't.

The scent, and the thing it belonged to, didn't belong here.

Cursing his luck, Ronan dug a shallow pit in the stony earth and dropped the relic into it. He swept the loose dirt back over it, marked the spot in his memory, and moved back in the direction of the landfill.

Stalking, again.

He didn't cross the fence, just skirted it, moving away from the trail back to Aurora Hollow and toward the low hills and the darkness beyond the landfill's security lights. The scent was strong, and as he passed the boundaries of the landfill and into air undiluted by the sour stench of human rubbish, it grew stronger still.

He settled into the grass, nose in the air, and waited. After a few minutes something moved toward him, soft footsteps padding in the dirt and rustling the dry grass.

Footsteps?

That wasn't right.

Nothing to do but wait. He would see for himself soon enough.

And soon enough, he did.

A man's silhouette appeared on the top of the hill: head and shoulders, torso and arms, then legs carrying him forward in an easy stroll through the deserted darkness. The scent was all around him, but he was not the source of it. His weaker human scent, sweat, old onions, and some acerbic cologne that burned Ronan's sensitive snout diluted the alien scent. He stopped at the top of the hill, hands on hips, and paused for a long moment before continuing toward the landfill.

Ronan stayed put, moving only his head as he tracked the stranger.

The man moved at his steady but unhurried pace until he stood at the fence, then shielded his eyes as a security light turned on, spotlighting him against the backdrop of last year's dead grass and tumbleweeds. Soon the new green would appear, as it had everywhere else, but here it wouldn't last long.

The man was tall, stout, bald, with black trousers and a dark overcoat covering a crisp white shirt. He held one hand in front of his face, shielding his squinting eyes, and the other in the pocket of his jacket. He waited almost a full minute before speaking.

"Joseph, hurry up, boy. I don't have all night." The ease of his posture and the calm in his voice belied his words. A moment later the long-haired killer of rats, cats, and dogs hurried into view on the other side of the fence, unarmed, Ronan was relieved to see.

"Pa." The garbage man stopped on his side of the fence and nodded toward the dark man. His accent was unfamiliar, thick and slow. He wasn't from around here. "I waited up, but you didn't come."

Without his gun, Joseph didn't seem to know what to do with his hands. They twisted around each other for a few moments, then he shoved them deep into the pockets of his jeans.

"I'm here now," the man said, betraying for the first time a hint of impatience and a trace of his own accent. It was lighter than his son's, but there. "I've got a full plate right now, son. Multiple irons in the fire and only two hands to juggle 'em, so you'll just have to excuse my tardiness."

"I know, Pa, I know that."

The silence that followed made Joseph fidget again.

"Don't ask," Joseph's pa said. "You know how this is."

"Yeah, I know how it is," Joseph said, his own irritation finally breaking through the brittle civility between them. "I just don't trust how it is ... and I don't trust *them*."

"Do you trust me?"

"'Course I do, daddy ... you know I do ...."

"Then just relax and do your job. I'm taking care of everything else."

The two faced off, glared at each other through the old rusting fence for a moment, then Joseph sighed and nodded.

"It would be nice to get out of here every once in a while though. Been stuck here for months." Joseph cast a look over his shoulder and frowned at the landfill. "This place stinks."

His father smiled, clearly pleased his son had brought that subject up. "Then I have some good news for you."

"We finally done here?"

"Not even close to done here, but you've got some help on the way. You can start keeping normal hours soon."

"Who?" Again, there was worry in his voice.

"No one you know," his father said. "No one you need to know either. You won't see them and they won't mess with you. Just think of them as a silent night shift."

"Whatever," Joseph said, casting another look over his shoulder, this time toward his camper on the hill.

"Trust me, son, you don't want to meet these guys."

"Anything else?" Joseph said. "I'd like to get a few hours of sleep before I have to stand guard again."

His father shook his head. "Nothing else, unless you have something to report."

"Come on, Pa, this place is too far out of town for kids to come playing around, and no one else gives a fart about that stupid carnie trailer."

"And you're sure no one can get to it without you seeing them?"

"No way," Joseph said. "I moved it right into the middle and spent two weeks building a junk maze around it. I have security lights at the front gate and at the entrance to the maze. No one is getting through without me knowing."

No humans at least, Ronan thought from his low place in the tall grass. This was all news to him, and all very troubling.

The labyrinthine arrangement of old furniture and appliances made more sense to Ronan now, as did the wrecked trailer's placement at its center. Fortunately for Ronan, he was small enough to slip through gaps that no human could have.

"What's so special about that wreck anyway?" Joseph asked.

"Even I don't know that," his father said, then laughed. "And I don't care. All I care about is no one getting into it."

"No worries then," Joseph said and sighed again, casting another longing look at his camper.

"Alright, go get some rest," the man in the black suit said, and Joseph turned to face him again, content, if not happy.

"Thanks. How about next time you're going to be this late we just wait until morning?"

His father backed a few steps away from the fence, then stopped and frowned. "Joe, you know I love ya, but don't tell me how to run my business." Then he was off without another word, setting the same unhurried pace away from the fence and back up the hill.

Joseph watched him for a moment, then went his own way, back into the maze he'd built around the burned-out trailer and out of sight.

Ronan sat still for a few minutes, watching the stranger in black climb the low hill and drop down the other side. As stealthily as he could manage, he followed the man.

* * *

Once on the other side of the hill, the man produced a flashlight and followed the gently bobbing beam over the barren terrain. Ronan followed, staying only close enough not to lose the man's scent, and perhaps a mile later stepped onto a narrow and rutted dirt road. The man's scent veered off to the right, and Ronan followed. A few minutes later another camper came into view, much larger and cleaner than The Garbage Man's. As he approached it, the man's light illuminated a large black truck, a small shed, and a bulky propane tank.

Ronan waited until the man was inside, then investigated.

A generator hummed inside a small shed, feeding power to the strange man's mobile home. The alerting scent was no stronger now; the thing that made it had been here but was gone now. Slowly, keeping outside the large circle of light cast from the camper's windows, Ronan circled the spot. He didn't know what he was looking for, but was sure he'd know when he found it.

And he did, in a second, smaller shed on the other side of the camper. The shed was empty except for the gas fire pit in the center; a scratched marble basin filled with crushed lava rocks. There were no flames, and the lava rocks exuded only a low, residual heat. It had been cooling for some time. Scattered among the rocks were the brittle remains of a clutch of mottled gray eggs, small sharp shards of shell that looked like stone. There was no sign of the creatures that had hatched from them, but Ronan thought they must be close. A dozen or more he guessed.

Amid the hatched eggs lay a whole one, its stone shell unblemished and intact.

It was worse than he had thought.

Someone on the other side knew The Phoenix Girls were back, and was taking a personal interest.

Ronan crouched just inside the partially open shed door for a moment, then slunk inside and leapt up onto the marble surface and put his ear to the egg. Something moved inside.

Runt of the litter, he thought, *but still alive*.

Ronan picked the egg up between his teeth and leapt back to the ground, stepping carefully outside. When he was sure he was still alone in the night, he bolted into the darkness again and sprinted toward town.

This is not good, he thought again.

The girls would have to work harder if they were going to be ready for what was coming, and Ronan had to convince them of that without telling them more than they strictly needed to know. They weren't ready for the whole story yet, especially Penny and Katie. Their friendship was too new, too fragile. It might not survive.

Sometimes the truth didn't set you free. Sometimes it destroyed you.

Chapter 2

Birthday Girl

Penny Sinclair awoke the morning of her fourteenth birthday with tears on her cheeks and the feeling that she'd fallen back in time, all the way to when she'd last seen her mom out the door of their apartment in San Francisco to her taxi ride out of Penny's life. It was to have been a one-and-a-half-hour flight to Los Angeles. Diana Sinclair never returned. Her company's jet had lost its engines and fallen out of the sky, crashing into the ocean just in sight of LA. With no other living relatives, Penny had ended up in a children's home in San Francisco before her mother's old friend and her godmother, Susan Taylor, brought her to the small town of Dogwood, Washington.

Penny had dreamed about that day a lot in the past few weeks.

The one-year anniversary of her mother's death had passed a month ago without mention, though Susan had treated her as if she were especially fragile and had not commented when Penny went to bed that night hours before her usual, and usually enforced, bedtime. Zoe Parker and Katie West, her best friends, hadn't known that there was anything special about the day, other than that it was a Friday, and had been irritated when she'd told them she didn't feel like doing anything after school.

At the time it had seemed right to ignore the day until it just went away, seemed like the only way to handle it, but now, the day she was supposed to celebrate her birthday with her friends and

Susan, her new mom by default, it felt wrong. Not as if she'd simply tried to forget that day but actually *had* forgotten it.

Penny remembered that she wasn't alone in her attic bedroom and wiped the moisture from her eyes and cheeks before Zoe could see it. Zoe was new in town, too, living with her grandmother, Margery White, while her parents, Dana and Reggie Parker, drove around the country in a semi-truck. Margery, who was one of the crankiest people Penny had ever met, kept company with a pack of similarly cranky old women Susan called The Town Elders.

Zoe's time in Dogwood was supposed to have been temporary, so her parents could save money to set up a new home. More than a year had passed since they left Zoe in Dogwood, however, and the arrangement was beginning to look more and more permanent.

Zoe's grandmother was not happy about it. She hated Reggie, whom she referred to as *That Indian,* and seemed less than fond of Zoe, who favored her Native American father more than her Caucasian mother.

When Penny's eyes were dry and it felt safe to face another human being, she sat up and found Zoe in her usual haphazard sprawl, half beneath the sheets of her attic bedroom's second bed. Zoe was an active sleeper, and any morning that she woke up still on the bed was a lucky one.

As Penny watched her, Zoe snorted loudly and flopped onto her stomach, kicking tangled sheets to the floor. She seemed only one flop away from joining them.

I should probably wake her up before she breaks something, Penny thought, but lay back and closed her eyes instead, wanting another fifteen minutes of dreamless sleep before she had to begin the day but not daring to hope for it.

Penny dozed but could not shut her mind down. She thought about the past few weeks of drama and complications as her eyes slipped shut, and the memories followed her into sleep.

* * *

Zoe's birthday had come three weeks before, and her grandmother had surprised everyone by throwing her a party. She'd made a real effort to be nice to Penny, whom she didn't approve of, and absolutely doted on their other best friend, Katie, whom she obviously did.

For three hours, Zoe's grandmother had preserved a neutral face as a handful of Zoe's school friends milled around the little house, ate cake, and watched Zoe open presents. There was Penny, Katie, Jodi Lewis, Ellen Kelly, a girl in their grade who'd played Dorothy in the school production of *The Wizard of Oz* that winter and could still be seen wandering the halls between classes singing "If I Only Had A Brain," and Trey Miller, a tall, muscular ninth-grade boy with olive skin and a smile that made the girls walk into walls and forget how to talk.

That both Trey and the normally aloof Ellen had come to the party was the talk of Dogwood school the next day, and many sullen looks followed Zoe through the halls.

Ellen was friendly and well-liked, and though she usually rebuffed most attempts at anything beyond casual friendships, she seemed determined lately to ingratiate herself into Penny, Zoe and Katie's little gang.

Half the girls from the eighth to tenth grades were crushing on Trey, and it was becoming painfully obvious to them that he was interested in Zoe. Zoe appreciated his kindness, and understood her classmates' jealousy but denied that Trey had feelings toward her.

"He's just happy to find someone with a little color in this town," she insisted, making it clear that she considered him a friend who just happened to be a boy and not in any way a *boyfriend*. Trey's family was new to Dogwood, too; his was father a dentist in Centralia, the closest thing to a real city within easy driving distance.

The party had ended abruptly with a call from Zoe's mother, the former Dana White, who, unknown to Zoe, was supposed to be a surprise guest, along with her father. After a brief shouting match with Zoe's mother, during which it became clear that the birthday party was also supposed to be a farewell party, her grandmother sent everyone home. Reggie and Dana Parker had changed their minds about returning to Dogwood and were now headed for the East Coast.

As far away from her *as they can get,* Zoe opined a few days later at school.

For the next week, Zoe had been sullen and standoffish, and Penny had resolved to lighten her own dark mood and try to cheer

Zoe up. Penny didn't know if her attempts had anything to do with it, but Zoe's mood eventually lifted just in time for Katie's to take its place in the dumps.

Katie's father, whose fourteen-year-old grudge against Penny's mother and long lost and recently discovered aunt seemed to have expanded to include Penny herself, was becoming more outspoken against their new friendship, which unfortunately included controlling the time Katie spent with Penny and Zoe. These limits were proving to be very *untimely*, because they also restricted the time the three could spend at the secluded canyon grove, Aurora Hollow, near Penny's old family home.

Katie's frequent absences were beginning to raise their fourth, secret friend's hackles, both figuratively and literally. Ronan, the strange talking fox who haunted Clover Hill, where Penny now lived, and Aurora Hollow, was increasingly insisting that they spend every free moment they could at the hollow for much needed magic practice. Though being constantly bossed around by a creature that shouldn't even exist was beginning to get on her nerves, Penny knew he was right.

Aurora Hollow wasn't just special because it was the one place that Rooster, Penny's closest neighbor and least-favorite person in Dogwood, never managed to find and torment them, though that was one of its major attractions. Aurora Hollow was also where they'd discovered something even stranger than Ronan, and even more fantastic. Aurora Hollow was where they'd discovered magic and were learning, too slowly it seemed, to use it.

Unfortunately for Penny and Zoe, who had almost a half-year head start on Katie, there was nothing else for them to learn until Katie caught up to them. *The Secrets of The Phoenix Girls*, a curious old book that was much more than *just* a book, refused to show them anything more until Katie learned what Ronan called the Elementals. She had learned her first three quickly—water, earth and air— seemed in fact to have a particular knack for water spells, but she'd developed something of a block on the last, fire. As hard as she tried, she just couldn't master it, and her diminishing practice time wasn't helping. So until Katie broke through her block, Penny and Zoe were mostly reduced to practicing stuff they already knew. The few new things they had learned had been without the book's help, but were still pretty neat.

Zoe had a particular feel for making stuff grow. The lush canopy of braided willow limbs that covered Aurora Hollow was her handiwork. Penny could do really interesting things with fire, though whenever the creative spirit took her she had to constantly remind herself they were surrounded by flammable trees. Katie was also good, not to mention *shrill*, about reminding Penny to *be careful*, so these days Penny only played with fire when Katie hadn't come with them. No need to be a showoff, especially with Katie's persistent failure in that area.

What Penny, Zoe and Katie really wanted to figure out was the Birdman's trick with doors, the one that had allowed him to enter the children's rooms through closets and kidnap them. Though Penny had no urge to drop in on random people, it would be a handy way to get to and from Aurora Hollow without the tedious hiking. They even had their own door right there, a leftover from the Birdman's visit.

"That is a bit beyond you three at the moment," Ronan had said when she'd asked him how to do it, something she didn't often resort too. Ronan preferred for them to figure stuff out on their own while he lounged around and offered droll observations. "You have to learn how to walk before you can fly."

Flying ... now that *would be fun*!

*   *   *

"Hey, Penny?"

Penny heard the voice and recognized it, even in the nearly perfect blankness of her half-sleep, but ignored it. It was a part of some emerging new dream, had to be since Katie wasn't allowed to visit her house.

"Pssst ... are you there?"

If it was an important dream it would start making sense any time now. No need to worry.

"Hello ... hello ... *helloooooo ....*"

Penny groaned and rolled onto her side so she could slap the snooze button on her alarm clock. Instead, her hand fell on the mirror next to it, a small oval in a pewter frame.

"I see you," Katie said, her voice muffled, and began to giggle.

Not the alarm clock, and not a dream, which could mean only one thing. Penny was awake.

She groaned again and closed her fingers around the small mirror. She fought a brief urge to chuck it across her room and steal a few more minutes of sleep and sat up instead. No need to break irreplaceable magic mirrors just because they sometimes interrupted perfectly good sleep.

One of the useful things she and Zoe had been able to learn while waiting for Katie was how to use the mirrors Tovar had left behind. The big one, which Penny kept shoved under her bed reflective side down, could see through any of the smaller ones anytime the viewer wanted. If Penny spoke Zoe's or Katie's name into the small one she carried with her, they could hear and respond through theirs, which was great, because there was no cell-phone signal at Penny's house, much to Katie's irritation, and electronics in general didn't work in Aurora Hollow.

Penny forced her eyes open, blinking against the sun, risen higher since her last experiment with wakefulness and now stabbing its too-bright light all over.

"Penny, hurry up."

"Alright."

She rubbed the last of the sleep from her eyes and flipped the mirror over. Staring at her from inside was not her groggy reflection but Katie's bright and cheerful one.

"Kat, just because you're a morning person doesn't mean you have to try to turn me into one." Penny was tolerant, not one to judge another's imperfections, but even she had her limits.

"Morning person?" Katie sounded slightly offended. "It's almost noon!"

She seemed to realize how loudly she was speaking and looked furtively over her shoulder.

Penny checked her bedside clock and noticed that Zoe's bed was empty.

"Ten thirty is not almost noon."

But it was time to rise and shine … if she had to.

"I'm coming over today," Katie said, then looked over her shoulder again to be sure no one was eavesdropping.

"Your dad changed his mind?" Penny somehow doubted it. A man who can nurse a fourteen-year-old grudge against a dead woman took his grudges seriously, and Katie's continued glances over her shoulder confirmed her suspicions.

"Are you kidding?" Katie's buoyant mood seemed to slip a notch, but she brightened again almost at once. "Michael's covering for me."

"Michael?" Penny knew Michael by face but had never spoken to him. He was Katie's brother, five years older and something of a town hero. Star quarterback in a championship game against Oakville, a town to the west that Dogwood hadn't been able to beat before he joined the team, or in the few years since he'd graduated. The Dogwood varsity football team had one thing in common with Katie's dad; it knew how to hold a grudge. Oakwood was smaller, but seemed to contain the right genetic pool to produce good football players, and they consistently crushed Dogwood.

Instead of making his play for football stardom, however, Michael had joined the sheriff's department as a deputy. Katie didn't hold that against him though. Just because the sheriff was next to useless didn't mean that Michael was.

"Kat, if you don't start making sense I'm going back to sleep."

"Dad thinks Michael's going to Olympia today and that I'm going with him."

Penny understood, and smiled. "You're going to be in so much trouble if you get caught."

Katie gave Penny *the look*, a thing Penny had first experienced at Dogwood School last fall, when Katie had shared her father's long-held grudge. It was withering, and when directed at you it made you feel about a foot tall. "Fine. If you don't want me to come over I can find something else to do."

"No, I want you to come. I just don't want you to get grounded."

"Oh come on, who's going to tell him?"

Penny did a quick mental checklist of people she knew were coming to her birthday party, not that many really, and had to admit Katie had a point. Still …

Penny shrugged. "It's a small town."

Katie rolled her eyes. "You don't have to tell *me* that."

Despite the risk, Penny was happy Katie was coming over. "I'll see you later then."

There was a muted knocking at Katie's door, and she peered over her shoulder a final time. "Gotta go."

And just like that Penny was staring at her own reflection in the strange little oval of glass. To her surprise, she was smiling.

It was beginning to feel like a birthday.

* * *

Penny arrived downstairs to find Susan putting the finishing touches on her birthday breakfast. Penny simply stood in the kitchen doorway for a moment, goggling at this unexpectedly domestic scene.

"Susan, you're late for work."

Susan turned in surprise, a momentary look of guilt on her face, then she smiled.

"Look who's awake!" She scooped the last of the freshly cooked bacon onto a plate, then dropped her tongs into the sink and rushed toward Penny with open arms. "No worries. Jenny's covering for me."

Penny had to brace herself, the urge to retreat from Susan when she swooped in almost too strong to deny without her morning coffee. She'd lived with Susan, her mother's childhood friend and Penny's godmother, for almost a year now, but she still wasn't used to Susan's open and outspoken affection. Penny and her mother's small household had been a quiet one, where love was an assumed thing, never openly exhibited. With the late Diana Sinclair, public displays of affection were limited to hand holding when crossing a busy street and the occasional, almost businesslike, *love ya kiddo*.

Penny accepted her morning hug with good grace, even offering a clumsy return pat on Susan's back.

"Honestly, Penny, you're so spoiled," Zoe said. "She was about to bring you breakfast in bed."

Penny tried to picture Susan climbing the ladder to her attic bedroom one-handed, with a heavily laden breakfast tray, complete with the usual morning cup of black coffee, balanced on the other, and was glad Susan hadn't tried.

"Actually I was hoping Zoe would take pity on me and volunteer," Susan said, and when Penny reached for a plate of waffles on the counter next to the stove, Susan blocked her path. "No you don't."

"Seriously?" Penny asked when she tried to step around Susan and found herself blocked again. "I can help."

"You sit down," Susan said, pointing at the table, where Penny's coffee waited.

"Come on, Susan, I know how to feed myself."

Zoe slipped behind her and hauled her back toward the table. "Just go with it, Penny. It'll be over before you know it."

So, you're in on it too, Penny thought, glaring as Zoe forced her into her seat.

"Don't be such a baby," Zoe said, interpreting the look. She pointed at the steaming coffee. "You know that stunts your growth don't you?"

"Ha-ha-ha," Penny said, though without much feeling. Zoe loved her short jokes.

Penny didn't think quitting coffee would help her gain height. She'd been born prematurely, an emergency roadside birth after an automobile accident, and was pretty sure she was forever doomed to a life of the vertically challenged. Zoe, on the other hand, was a budding Amazon, the tallest girl in their grade. Penny had tried her hand at tall jokes, to which Zoe was unfortunately immune. They only made her smile smugly.

Before Penny had half-drained her cup, the table was set and Susan was lighting a single candle in the center of a stack of waffles.

"Please don't sing," Penny begged. It was bad enough she'd have to sit still for a round of "Happy Birthday to You" at the party. She didn't need it at breakfast.

Susan watched her for a second, her smooth brow wrinkling as she frowned. "Okay, Penny. I better get to work anyway."

She swooped in for a quick, one-armed goodbye hug and patted Zoe's head before marching out of the kitchen. A few seconds later the front door creaked open, then closed.

Zoe kicked her under the table.

"Ouch ... what?"

"You are so rude! What's your problem?"

"I don't ...."

Zoe interrupted her. "She was just being nice and you hurt her feelings."

"What ... no!"

"Yeah, you did," Zoe said, but she sounded less angry than confused now. "She tries really hard, and she's so sweet to you."

Penny said nothing, only stabbed at her waffles. Suddenly she wasn't very hungry.

Zoe finally dropped her penetrating stare from Penny's face and started to eat. "Aren't you happy here?"

"Yes," Penny said, finally looking at Zoe. "I'm just not used to all the attention."

"I could get used to it," Zoe said and laid her fork onto her plate, as if her appetite had gone off to look for Penny's. "I could *so* get used to it."

Penny's face flushed with embarrassment, both for Zoe, whose disastrous birthday party was obviously still fresh in her memory, and for herself. Zoe was right, she had been rude. She didn't want to hurt Susan.

"Well ... what am I supposed to do?"

"You don't have to do anything. Just stop being so ...," Zoe searched the kitchen's ceiling, as if looking for the right word. "So skittish. Every time she hugs you, you look like you want to run away. Just let her be nice ... and try to be grateful."

"I am grateful," Penny protested again, now cutting even more furiously at her waffles.

"Then show her you are." Zoe spoke this last in a small voice, as if afraid of angering Penny again but determined to make her point.

Penny didn't reply for several seconds, couldn't reply. She knew the right words, but saying them would be too embarrassing. Thankfully, Zoe seemed as ready to change the subject as she was.

"Grandma said I could spend the night again if I wanted ... if it's okay with you and Susan."

Penny thought this was Zoe's way of asking how much trouble she was in.

"That would be great," she said, and when Zoe looked at her again, she smiled. "Guess who's coming over later?"

Zoe's expression leapt from cautious to curious at once. "Who?"

"Kat," Penny said, feeling a little better about herself when Zoe broke into a grin. "Michael's bringing her over."

Zoe's chin dropped and her already deeply tanned skin flushed almost bright red.

"He is so cute!" Zoe flushed a little darker before turning her attention back to her breakfast, seeming determined to keep her mouth busy with breakfast until she could trust it not to say anything else embarrassing.

Penny faced her own breakfast and found her appetite returned. She'd forgotten to blow her candle out, and it was burning low, the wax spreading to fill the closest squares.

I'll make it up to Susan, she resolved.

She blew out her candle and began to eat.

* * *

Michael West's old Jeep climbed the steep driveway to Penny's house just before noon, throwing up a rooster tail of dust in its wake.

"There she is," Zoe said, standing on her tiptoes on the top step of the porch and shading her eyes. A moment later she was shrinking back toward the wall and looking like she wanted very much to melt into it. Penny took her place on the steps and walked down to meet Katie when her brother pulled to a stop.

"Hi, Red!" Michael grinned and waved from the driver's seat. "Hi, Zoe!"

Penny waved back and turned to see Zoe give a feeble little wave of her own. There appeared to be something very interesting on the floor between her feet.

He leaned close to Katie, spoke to her for a moment, then straightened up behind the wheel as she climbed out. He made a loop at the end of the driveway and gave another wave as he drove away.

"Happy birthday!" Katie shouted over the roar of the departing Jeep and ran to meet Penny.

The moment Michael's Jeep was out of sight Zoe joined them, the bag with their book and wands hanging from her shoulder. "We ready?"

Katie looked from Zoe to Penny and smiled. "Yeah. I've been ready."

"And about time too," said a voice from behind them, and they turned in unison to find Ronan scrambling out from under the porch. "You've been away too long, young Miss West."

He emerged and shook the dust off his fur, then ran on ahead of them, pausing only once to turn around and give them an impatient bark.

"Has he always been such a creeper," Katie asked, "or just since I met him?"

Chapter 3

Making the Circle

Ronan shadowed the girls all the way to the hollow but kept his nagging to a minimum. He stuck closest to Katie, extolled the virtues of self-confidence and positive thinking. His pep talks had become increasingly manic, and when Katie's father finally put his foot down and forbade her from coming to Penny's house, Ronan had lost his temper and shouted in a language Penny had never heard before. Even without knowing the language, Penny got the gist of his rant and was pretty sure it wasn't nice.

Now that Katie had returned, he seemed more determined than ever to help her get past her block. Penny was intent on helping her as well. Part of it was simply craving to learn more, to do more, but most of it was the growing certainty that Ronan was preparing them for something. He had said as much after their fight with the Birdman.

This isn't a game. You have a serious purpose.

He still wouldn't tell them what that purpose was, but his changing demeanor brought his warning back to her mind.

Penny had been off in her own little world, not paying attention to where she was walking, and nearly tripped over Ronan.

He barked in irritation or humor, sometimes it was hard to tell the difference. Zoe and Katie had drawn ahead of them while she was daydreaming.

"How much longer until you have to be back?"

"We have a few hours," Penny said. "Susan's picking up stuff for the party after work."

"Yes ... your birthday party," Ronan said. "Happy birthday, Little Red."

Penny groaned and rolled her eyes, but it was a show. The nickname didn't bother her like it used to. She didn't think she was fooling him, either; Ronan was very good at reading their moods.

"Do you still carry the mirror around with you?"

The question caught Penny by surprise. She'd been expecting more of his grumbling about Katie's lack of progress and her, Penny's, responsibility to make things right with Katie's father so she could resume her practice on a more regular basis. The last time he took this line she'd reminded him, a bit shrilly as she recalled, that she'd never even met the man and that his grudge was against her dead mother and an aunt she'd never even knew existed until the previous summer.

That had shut him up. Temporarily at least.

It still seemed weird to her that her mom and Katie's aunt used to be friends, but she was getting used to the idea. That old connection had raised other questions in her mind and a suspicion she hadn't dared to bring up with Ronan yet. She knew what his answer would be: more infuriating silence.

She patted her pants pocket. "Right here. We all carry them."

She expected more words of caution from him, and he surprised her again.

"Good," he said and actually nodded approval before resuming his trot. "Keep them with you at all times. It's important for us to stay in contact, especially with Kat in trouble."

Penny jogged to catch up. "Have you got them all now?"

She knew he'd been snooping around Dogwood since last fall, trying to track down all of Tovar's missing mirrors.

"It's impossible to know without another look in the Conjuring Glass."

"You know where it is," Penny said, catching up to him. She could see the top boughs of Aurora Hollow's willows ahead. As always she looked for the crown of the big tree, the strange one growing at the edge of the creek that ran through the hollow, but she didn't see it. After some botanical research Zoe had identified it as a *Fraxinus excelsior*, a type of ash common in Europe but certainly not in Washington State. She had no idea how a European ash had ended up in Dogwood. From inside the hollow, that tree seemed colossal, reaching into the green canopy toward the sky.

"Tonight maybe. I would like to be sure."

"It'll be like a slumber party," Penny said, and laughed when Ronan turned back to her and rolled his eyes.

A few seconds later they were at the downward path into the narrow canyon that hid Aurora Hollow from the rest of the world, and Penny followed Ronan.

* * *

Zoe and Katie already had their wands out and pointed into the fire pit when Penny joined them.

"You're too tense," Zoe said, grabbing Katie's wand arm and giving it a little shake. "You gotta relax a bit."

"And what," Katie asked sourly, "let The Force flow through me?"

"What's *The Force*?" Ronan asked, pausing at the creek's edge.

"I'll tell you what The Force is," Penny said, "if you tell us what we're preparing for."

Ronan didn't respond to Penny's bait. He leapt across the creek to the stone ledge on the other side and vanished into his cave.

"Way to go, Little Red," Katie said, wrenching her arm free of Zoe's grip with a look of irritation. "You pissed him off."

"*You're not relaxing*," Zoe snapped.

"He'll be back," Penny said, unconcerned.

She kind of hoped he was annoyed though, at least a little. Ronan was still keeping stuff from her, stuff *about* her, and she was beyond annoyed about that.

"Why do I need to relax?" Katie asked, turning her irritation back on Zoe.

"Because it'll help you face your fears," Ronan answered from the mouth of his cave.

All three girls turned to face him, startled by his sudden reappearance.

"I've let you fight this alone for too long, Kat," he said, and he sounded almost mournful. "I didn't want it to happen like this."

"Didn't want what to happen?" Definitely exasperated now. Definitely not relaxing.

"I hoped you would be able to conquer your fears alone," Ronan said. "But you haven't, and you won't ask for help. I didn't want to be the one to drag them into the light."

It was a long moment before Katie could speak. She regarded him with something like horror.

Penny met Zoe's eyes and saw her own confusion mirrored in them.

"Don't," Katie whispered. "Please."

"What is he talking about, Kat?" Zoe tucked the black wand into her pocket and walked to Katie's side.

Katie flinched when Zoe put a hand on her shoulder, but her eyes never left Ronan. "How can you know?"

"I know," Ronan said, and he sounded regretful, ashamed of himself. "But I don't know *what*."

Katie watched him, her cheeks glowing in embarrassment. Penny saw the wand rise in her shaking hand, and for a moment she though Katie was about to attack Ronan. Instead she held it over her shoulder and Zoe took it from her.

"You have to tell us, Kat." Ronan stepped to the edge of his stone shelf and dropped onto his belly. "Tell us what happened."

"It's nothing," Katie said. Her astonishment seemed to have evaporated. Her voice was brisk now.

But Penny saw that it was something. It was hurting Katie to even think about it.

"Tell us, Kat."

"Ronan, why are you doing this?" Penny marched forward and stopped between them, so Ronan would have to look at her. "You're upsetting her!"

"Because I have to," Ronan said, and stood again. "Because she shouldn't have to face her fears alone. It was wrong of me to let her try for so long."

Zoe's stunned expression was slowly hardening, her mouth pulling into a thin line of disapproval. "Leave her alone."

"No. I won't ... I can't." Ronan paced further down his stone ledge, peering around Penny to catch Katie's eyes again. "And Kat knows I can't."

Penny turned to face Katie and saw her anger slipping away as quickly as her astonishment had. In the past minute she had run the emotional spectrum from shock to anger and now to embarrassment.

Katie looked skyward. Penny thought she was struggling not to cry, but when she faced forward again, her eyes were dry.

"He's right," Katie said. "There's something I need to tell you about."

* * *

They were sitting around the fire pit, Penny across from Zoe and Ronan across from Katie. The wands lay atop the book in an open chest at the roots of the big ash tree.

Katie stared into the dead fire pit, seemed to search for something there. Whatever it was seemed to elude her, and after a minute of expectant silence she sighed and looked up at all of them in turn. Her eyes finally settled on Penny.

"You're kind of a firebug aren't you?"

Penny's first impulse was to deny this—this wasn't supposed to be about her!—but the expression on Katie's face stopped the denial before it left her mouth. Her words may have sounded like a question, but they had been a statement of fact. Her expression said so. Her unblinking eyes, the defiant set of her jaw allowed no doubt.

Penny gulped, then nodded.

"I knew a girl like you a long time ago," Katie said, talking to them all but still watching Penny. "Her name was Samantha ... Sam. She lived down the street from me, and she had the coolest tree house. Her dad built it for her, and we used to play in it for hours. We even spent the night in it a couple times."

Katie looked down at her hands, folded in her lap. She seemed to have made herself smaller as she spoke. Even her voice got smaller. The others had to lean closer to hear her clearly.

"She was a firebug, like you, Penny. I used to think it was funny ... how she'd just go quiet if someone lit a match or a candle in front of her. She'd stop doing whatever she was doing and watch the flame. One night we were in her tree house. She had a candle and a book of matches she stole from her father's garage. It didn't seem quite as funny that night, because it was just us up there and she was lighting matches and watching them burn down to her fingers."

Penny thought she knew where this was going and, more importantly, why. It explained a lot, and though Penny really didn't want to hear the rest, she knew that didn't matter. Katie needed her to hear it. Even if Katie's comparing her old firebug friend to Penny was unfair—Penny was always careful ... always—it was how she felt.

Zoe had stood up and moved closer to Katie, very slowly, a step at a time.

"I made her promise to put the matches away and go to bed, but she started again after I fell asleep."

Now there were tears.

"She fell asleep with the candle burning in her hands and set her sleeping bag on fire. Her screams woke me ... her bag was burning and her hair was burning and her face was mostly gone."

Tears were falling faster now, words coming in a rush.

Zoe slipped beside her and wrapped an arm around her shoulders.

Penny couldn't move.

Ronan jumped from his rock and trotted over to Katie, climbing onto her lap. He had once allowed Penny to hold him in a moment of great stress, but she knew he didn't like it. When Katie wrapped her arms around him and buried her face in his thick fur, Penny felt a surge of affection for him.

For several seconds Katie wept into Ronan's fur, still apparently unaware of Zoe's arm around her shoulder.

This was the memory, the fear that she'd been fighting alone, struggling and failing to overcome. Though it hurt Penny to see Katie like this, she knew Ronan was right to force it out of her.

Penny joined them, standing on Katie's other side and adding her embrace.

Some things you shouldn't have to face alone.

Katie lifted her face from Ronan's now-damp fur, and, though her eyes were red, the tears had stopped. She looked at Penny, then Katie. She hugged Ronan even tighter for a moment, then released him.

He leapt down at once and resumed his perch across from her.

Penny and Zoe stayed at her side.

"I tried to beat the flames out with my sleeping bag, but that only made things worse. It caught fire too, and then the floor and ceiling were burning, and my clothes caught." Her voice was foggy but strong. "I was so scared I just jumped. I broke my leg, but I rolled in the grass until my clothes were out. Then Sam's dad was there. He kept trying to climb up to her but the fire was too hot. When the firemen arrived the whole tree was burning and he was kneeling beside me and screaming her name. Her mom was outside too, just watching the fire with her mouth hanging open."

"Was she ...?" Zoe couldn't finish.

"She died," Katie said. "I broke my leg when I fell and I was burned, but she died."

Then she turned to look up at Penny. "You scare me sometimes. I see a look in your eyes when you're playing with that wand, and I think of Sam."

Penny felt a blush burning in her cheeks.

"I promise to be more careful," Penny said, and she meant it. Katie's fears and constant cautions were understandable now, reasonable.

"We're here with you, Kat," Zoe said. "We won't let anything happen to you."

"You girls should get back now," Ronan said, sounding unusually subdued. "You can practice another day."

"No, I think I can do this now." Katie took hold of Penny and Zoe's hands. "If you'll stay with me."

Zoe nodded. "We got your back, Kat."

"We'll be right beside you," Penny said.

Ronan considered them for a moment, then nodded. "Very well, young ladies. You'll stand together … just as it should be."

* * *

Katie held Penny's wand in her right hand and Penny's hand in her left. Zoe stood by her other side, a comforting hand on her shoulder. Katie raised the wand, pointed it at the fire pit, and closed her eyes.

"Relax, Kat," Zoe said, lowering her face to hide a small smile. She held her black wand at her side, ready to respond with water if Katie called for it.

Katie's answering smile was less restrained. "I am."

Penny squeezed her hand, and Katie squeezed back.

Then she opened her eyes, her face hardening with determination and concentration. "I can do this."

But for a long time nothing happened.

Penny felt a subtle shift in the air around them, an energizing, and cast a covert look at Katie.

Katie's focus was on her target and nothing else. She looked fierce but calm.

Penny turned her attention to the wand's crystal tip and watched.

It began to glow very dimly, then to smoke. A short tongue of flame licked from the end, died.

Then it happened. The wand tip flashed and Penny watched a sliver of bright red light leap from it, striking the cold ashes at the heart of the fire pit.

Flames erupted, dancing high for a second before dying down, then dying out.

Penny felt like leaping into the air and shouting for joy; the triumph of Katie's face was the most satisfying thing she'd seen in months.

Zoe finally spoke.

"Excellent, Kat! I knew you could do it!"

"The book," Katie said. Her eyes were still red and puffy, but she grinned at them. "Do we have time?"

Probably not, Penny thought.

"Yes," Penny said, returning Katie's grin.

They ran to the chest together, Zoe and Katie standing aside with their wands in their hands while Penny bent down and lifted the book. Beneath it were pieces of broken wands, untouched since the day Penny discovered them almost a year before, and a tarnished brass cup. Penny stood and carried the book back to the fire pit, laying it on one of the boulders.

"Here," Katie said, passing the wand to Penny.

"No." Zoe put her hand over Penny's and pushed it away. "Kat should do it."

Penny resisted the urge to push Zoe's hand away and grab her wand away from Katie, but a glance at Katie's face, the surprise on it, killed Penny's irritation.

After months of struggling, after everything she'd had to share that morning, the pain she had to relive ... for them.

"Yeah," Penny whispered. "You're right."

Penny stepped back from Katie and nodded at the book. "What are you waiting for?"

A slow grin bloomed on Katie's face, erasing the last of the morning's stress. She turned the grin on Zoe, then looked down at the book.

The Secrets of the Phoenix Girls.

Katie touched the wand tip to the large Phoenix coin inlaid in the book's thick, aged leather cover, and it sprang open. Her left hand hesitated over the open book, then thumbed through the first pages, turning them until she looked down at the page detailing the making of the circle. They knew from previous experience that though Penny and Zoe could see the writing on that page, Katie couldn't.

Again Katie hesitated, looking over her shoulder at Penny and Zoe. Zoe nodded her encouragement. "Go on."

Katie tapped the first blank page, and they waited, breathless.

Nothing happened.

They waited, and nothing continued to happen.

"Ronan!" Penny bellowed, her temper breaking. "What now?"

Zoe faced Ronan, her own frustration barely held in check. She bit her lips to keep her anger from surging out, but her face expressed it clearly enough.

Katie continued to stare at the open book, her excitement ebbing slowly into disappointment. "What did I do wrong?"

"Yeah, Ronan ... gives?" Penny said.

Ronan jumped from his rock, sauntering over to Katie's side.

"How would I know," he said, rising up onto his rear legs and placing his front paws on the rock for a closer look into the book. "This is all new to me."

"What?" Penny realized she was on the verge of shouting again and forced herself to calm down ... a bit anyway. "Haven't you done this before?"

"Yeah," Zoe said, stepping up behind Penny, and as usual towering over her. "What about the ones before us?"

Ronan dropped back to the ground and chuckled darkly.

"I'm almost as much a newcomer to this as you are. I only knew the others ...," he paused, seemed to consider his next words carefully.

Penny recognized this behavior in him and knew he was withholding something, but she knew better than to press him. If she wanted answers, and she did, she'd have to get them herself.

If she only knew how, or where, to start.

"The ones before you," Ronan continued. "I only knew them briefly, but from the little I do know of them, there is always someone here to help out and guide them when they need it."

"Who?" Katie asked, and Penny was peripherally pleased to see she wasn't letting herself get angry. Penny wished she knew how to turn her temper off like that.

More silence from Ronan.

"Come on," Zoe urged. "You're always keeping stuff from us. Why shouldn't we know?"

Ronan flashed a quick, guilty look at Penny, then turned away from her.

Not from us, Penny thought. *From me.*

Ronan sighed, then spoke. "The Phoenix Girls always end. They grow up and go their own ways, but one always stays behind to shepherd the next generation. To help them when they need help, but *only* when they need it."

"Then where is she?" Penny watched Ronan tense at the question, and thought she'd come close to asking one of the questions he was unwilling to answer, for whatever reason.

"Things ended ... badly last time," he said. "I was only here at the end, but I knew when it was over that I'd have to be the one to stay behind, for when you finally came."

For a second Penny found it hard to breath, and she thought her heart may have missed a beat.

For when you finally came.

He might have meant them, the next Phoenix Girls, but she didn't think so. She thought he had meant her, Penny, specifically.

Almost like he'd been expecting her.

And then she remembered something else he'd said to her the day they first met, and felt stupid for not having guessed it sooner.

I wondered when you'd make it this way.

He had been expecting her. He'd known she'd return to her mother's childhood home someday, and he had waited for her.

My mother's childhood home, Penny thought again, and knew something she'd only suspected until then. Something so crazy she had not dared ask about it.

Penny forced herself to breathe, tried to keep her expression as blank as possible, so Ronan wouldn't know how badly he'd just slipped up.

Penny knew who the last Phoenix Girls were.

She knew where to start looking. Now she only had to find out *how*.

"Bad deal for you, I'm afraid," Ronan said turning to include Zoe and Katie in the statement. "But you three are smart. You've learned much on your own. I know you'll figure this out too if you work together."

A long silence followed this declaration, which Katie finally broke.

"Together," she said.

"What?" Penny and Zoe said.

"Come here, you two," Katie said. She placed the wand in Penny's hand, then laid her hand over the top of it. Zoe caught on and laid hers over the top of Zoe's. "Worth a try."

Penny was sure Katie was right, it felt right, so she wasn't surprised when the book responded to her wand's touch.

How it responded, however, surprised them all.

Flames burst from the open pages, then from between all the other pages, blowing them around like a strong, hot breeze.

They jumped back, Penny barely holding on to her wand in her haste. All three shouted in surprise, Katie the loudest of all. Even Ronan shouted in alarm. But when Penny pointed her wand at the book to try to put the fire out Ronan stopped her.

"No, Penny! Let it burn!"

"What?" Penny kept her wand pointed but didn't use it.

"Are you crazy?" Zoe shouted. "Put it out!"

"No," Ronan repeated. "Look at it. The fire isn't hurting it."

And Penny saw he was right. The flames poured from the leather of the cover, from the creased binding, from between the fluttering pages, but didn't consume anything. And the heat that should have poured up from the inferno wasn't there.

Penny moved closer to the book, extended a hand toward the raging flames.

"No!" Katie rushed past Zoe and grabbed at Penny, but not before Penny had plunged a hand into the heatless inferno, then retracted it. She held her hand out, open palm up, and stared with her mouth agape. Flames danced in her open hand, but did not burn her skin.

Katie and Zoe watched in stunned amazement.

"Phoenix Fire," Ronan explained. "It'll only burn what its maker wants it to burn."

"Come on, Penny," Katie groaned. "Put it down!"

"Cool," Zoe said, grinning broadly now.

Katie glared at her.

Penny closed her hand, and the fire in her palm vanished.

When they turned their attention back to the book, they saw the flames were lower, and the book itself ....

Katie moved closer, her fear departing now that the flames seemed to be dying down, and stepped beside Penny. "What happened to it?"

"It is made new in the flames, like the Phoenix itself," Ronan said, and Penny heard wonder in his voice.

And it *was* newer. The heavy, yellowed paper was bone white now, the aged leather cover lighter, suppler. The brass at the corners of the thick cover was no longer tarnished with age but bright and shining.

Then the flames died, and Katie stared down at the previously blank page. First the strange, runic writing appearing, then danced across the page until the markings reassembled themselves into words Katie could read.

"Does this mean we're all on the same page now?" Katie looked at Ronan, raising a sardonic eyebrow.

Ronan barked laughter.

"Yes, I suppose it does, and if there is still time, I suggest you get on with it." He trotted to the water's edge and leapt, clearing the stream and landing on the stone ledge before the entrance to his cave.

"Hey, where are *you* going?" They had all waited a long time for this moment, and Penny thought Ronan should stick around for it.

"This isn't for me," he said. "I'm not a Phoenix Girl, am I?"

He winked and disappeared through the cavern opening.

Zoe watched him depart with a half-smile on her face, then turned to her friends.

"Let's do this."

* * *

The Secrets of the Phoenix Girls lay closed on the rock, the girls surrounding it. Penny placed her right hand over the brass Phoenix and nodded at Zoe. Zoe regarded her for a moment, looking nervous now that the time had come, then placed her right hand over Penny's. A moment later, Katie followed suit.

"You start, Penny," Katie said.

Penny considered for a moment. The instructions that had seemed so easy when they'd first read them now seemed too simple, too vague, to have any power. It called for a declaration of loyalty, a dedication to your friends.

Penny had filled the brass cup with water from the creek as the book instructed and now regarded it a little dubiously.

"Shouldn't we boil that water first or something?" Katie asked, frowning at the cup as Penny reached for it.

Penny picked it up, and began.

"I promise to be loyal to my friends, Zoe and Katie." Somehow that didn't seem enough. "I dedicate myself to learning with them and promise to help them whenever they need me."

Penny drank.

The moment the water passed her lips she felt an energy gathering and spreading through her. Her hair began to rise, as if it were charged with static.

She passed the cup to Zoe.

Zoe took it, regarding Penny with mild alarm. Katie was watching, too, her eyes wide.

"I promise to be faithful to my friends." Zoe watched Penny for a second, then turned to Katie. "I'll be here for you whenever you need me."

Zoe drank, and Penny saw her long black hair begin to rise and flutter around her head. Her skin became slightly radiant. If it had been night, Penny thought she might start glowing.

Katie was next. She took the cup and spoke.

"I promise to be loyal to you ...." She seemed to become tongue-tied, then finished in a quick burst. "No matter what my old friends or my father think, you are my best friends."

She drank, and her hair began to dance around her head. The strange luminescence lit her face and spread down her arms. Then it reached her right hand, placed over the top of Zoe's and Penny's.

Suddenly their hands were bound by light, welded by their shared energy. The book beneath them seemed to vibrate with it.

For a moment, Penny thought it would burst into flames again.

Then Zoe and Katie were gone.

"Hey!" Penny spun in place, but the others were nowhere in sight. "Kat? Zoe?"

No one answered.

Penny ran to the chest to get her wand, but the chest wasn't there either, and when she turned back to the center of the clearing, toward the ring of stones surrounding the fire pit, she realized that she wasn't alone anymore.

It wasn't Zoe, or Kat, or even Ronan, but a strange face, wreathed in flames, rising from the fire pit. The face was featureless, just red coal eyes, a mouth, and the suggestion of a nose. The flames dancing around it looked like wind-tossed hair.

"Who are you?" Curiously, Penny felt no threat even though she was unarmed and alone, only a growing sense of strangeness.

"I am you, and I am me," the face said, rather unhelpfully, Penny thought. "I'm your part of the whole."

"Where are Zoe and Kat?" Penny scanned the clearing again.

"They are here," the face said simply. "With you."

It turned its gaze from Penny to the trees surrounding them, then to the clear water of Little Canyon Creek. The water was higher and swifter than she had ever seen it. Something seemed to be moving within, almost visible, just under the surface. Around her, the trees seemed to shift, to whisper in the wind, to reach for each other with limbs full and green.

"What you seek is a gift," the face said, once more facing Penny, more distinct now, more face than flame, and whatever it said, it looked nothing like Penny. It was old. Wild. Beautiful.

"But it is also a burden," it said. "If you wish to accept The Phoenix's gift you must do so with a whole heart. It is a bond that only death or treachery can break."

"I know," Penny said. Her voice trembled, and her legs felt unsteady as she stepped closer to the beautiful face in the fire. "I don't want to turn back."

A fresh breeze blew through Aurora Hollow. Penny's hair danced in the wind, almost a reflection of the thing she faced.

The flames rose, and a body appeared under the face. A lean body clothed in fire. It raised an arm and reached for Penny.

Without realizing she meant to do so, Penny reached back.

Fingers of flame, hot but not painful, touched Penny's.

Then, abruptly, Penny was standing in the circle with Zoe and Katie, their hands still joined over the book. They regarded one another, eyes large with shock.

They found they could move again, and did, stepping away from each other and from the old book.

"It's over," Penny said.

"No," Katie said. She didn't smile. She seemed almost frightened now. "It's only started."

Chapter 4

The Party Poopers

The girls stowed the book and wands in the chest and ran back to Penny's house, arriving in time to find Susan struggling through the front door with one of the kitchen chairs under each arm. The other two were already set out on the porch, next to what looked like a battalion of folding chairs.

"How many people did she invite?" Penny asked, alarmed.

Zoe took hold of her arm before she could start down the hill. "You should go make up with her."

For a moment Penny only looked up at Zoe, confused. The strange events in the hollow had driven most of the mundane events of earlier that morning from her mind. Then she remembered … the lavish breakfast, the special attention, Susan's enthusiasm, and her own less than grateful reception of it. Susan's hurt expression as she stepped through the front door for her short Saturday workday.

Penny felt her cheeks flush with shame, and nodded.

"Yeah, I better. I was kind of a brat to her."

"Birthday girl needs a head start." Zoe dropped an arm over Katie's shoulder and slowed her down while Penny broke into a trot down the trail they'd beat through the grass. "Is Michael coming to the party?"

Penny smiled as she left them behind. If Michael did show up, Zoe would probably hide in the attic until the party was over. She wondered if Katie knew about Zoe's crush and decided she wasn't going to be the one to enlighten her if she didn't. Zoe would die of embarrassment.

Susan dropped the chairs, wiped sweat from her forehead, and watched Penny approach.

"I thought I'd have to send a search party after you girls. Much longer and you'd have missed your own party."

Penny didn't respond as she crossed the yard and climbed the steps. It took all her nerve to not stop an arm's length away, to cross into what her mom always referred to as *personal space*. Even Susan looked a little startled when Penny, who was still as short standing up as Susan was sitting down, leaned over her almost to the tipping point and wrapped her arms around Susan's neck. As Susan returned her embrace, Penny wondered again if her new suspicions about Susan could possibly be true.

"Thanks," Penny said. It didn't feel like enough, but she couldn't say the words she felt without sounding stupid. She said what she could and hoped it would be enough. "Thanks for everything, Susan. I'm really lucky to have you."

When she disengaged and stepped back into her own comfort zone, Susan was smiling as brightly as Penny had ever seen, and there were tears in her eyes.

Oh no.

She looked down at her feet before she could catch Susan's bout of emotion. She hated tears, her own most of all.

"It's okay," Susan said after she'd gotten her emotions in check. "I'm happy to do it, Little Red."

Penny looked over her shoulder and saw Zoe and Katie halfway down the hill. The awkward moment was over, and things with Susan were good again. When Zoe and Katie joined them a few seconds later Susan's eyes were dry again and she launched herself back into party prep.

It was time to help Penny celebrate another year of managing to stay alive.

More important than her birthday, to Penny at least, Katie had overcome her last obstacle and they'd be able to move on to new stuff now. Now that was something to celebrate!

* * *

Susan enlisted Zoe to help bring the small kitchen table out to the porch while Katie hung a large banner Susan had printed in the copy center of her shop – *Happy Birthday Penny!* – from the eaves over the front steps. Penny sat on the steps, since Susan wouldn't allow her to help with anything, and tried to fake enthusiasm for Susan's sake.

At least the banner doesn't say *Happy Birthday Little Red*, she thought.

The first guest arrived just as Susan brought the cake out. It was Trey Miller, dropped off by his father, a huge gray-haired man in a black Mercedes that looked far too rich for Penny and Susan's gravel driveway.

The second was Michael.

Zoe blushed bright red as his old Jeep topped the driveway and parked at the far side. Zoe didn't retreat to Penny's room but did find an out-of-the-way seat and attempted to make herself as a small as possible. It was a wasted effort. Zoe was simply too tall *not* to stand out.

Jodi Lewis showed up a few minutes later with Chelsea, a friend of Katie's who had quit hanging out with Katie's old crowd when the group's new queen bee started getting them into trouble. Penny was surprised Chelsea came; she'd only asked her for Katie's sake, and Penny had a feeling Chelsea still didn't like her much, only tolerated her.

When Katie had broached the subject of letting Chelsea in on their secret a few weeks back, Ronan had reluctantly agreed to tail her for a while and find an opportunity to let her see him, if she could. She couldn't, so Katie dropped the idea, though with a few hard feelings. They had since agreed to let Ronan make the call on any future memberships to avoid the drama.

Last to arrive was a surprise guest.

"I didn't know she was coming," Katie said, pointing down the driveway to the approaching figure of Ellen Kelly. She pedaled her bike up the top of the rise, a bag swinging off her shoulder and her long blonde hair blowing back behind her.

Katie waved at Ellen, and Ellen returned the wave.

"I didn't know she was coming either," Penny said, but she smiled and walked to meet Ellen in the driveway. The others ran to catch up, Katie and Zoe falling in on Penny's right, Jodi and Chelsea on her left.

Chelsea brightened for the first time at Ellen's approach, shouting loudly to be heard over the others. "That blouse is so *cute*! Where did you get it?"

Ellen paused for a moment, wobbling a little on her bike, to regard her rather plain teal blouse, then looked at Chelsea with raised eyebrows as if to say *seriously?*

Zoe coughed discreetly into her fist, and Penny though she heard a muffled *suck-up* buried in the noise.

Ellen Kelly was a bit of a puzzle to Penny. She was popular, but not part of any school cliques. She had a variety of friends but no best friend, no one you could count on seeing her with. She seemed comfortable enough on her own but lately seemed curious about Dogwood's new, inseparable trio.

"Yeah, she just kind of showed up at mine too," Zoe said. "Just to say happy birthday. I asked her to stay."

Chelsea looked impressed against her will.

"Hi, girls!" Ellen slid from the seat of her bike while still in motion and coasted it to a stop in front of them. "Not crashing your party. Just wanted to bring you this."

Ellen thrust her hand into the bag on her shoulder and handed Penny a card.

Penny caught Jodi and Chelsea watching her with narrowed eyes, as if daring her *not* to invite Ellen to stay. She sensed an uprising in the making and was determined to head it off. "Thanks. You should stick around."

Ellen accepted with a grin and followed them back to the house.

Penny was beginning to feel pleased about the turnout; it was nice to know she was liked, or at least tolerated in some cases, until a familiar old white VW Bug pulled up next to Michael's Jeep driven by Miss Riggs, Susan's older sister and Penny's least-favorite teacher. She, like Katie's father, had a long-standing grudge against Penny's family that now extended to Penny herself.

Beside her, Zoe groaned.

Miss Riggs climbed from the car and approached the porch in a stiff-backed march, as if someone held a gun to her back and was forcing her to be there. She was dressed more casually than Penny had ever seen her, crisp new blue jeans and a pink western-style shirt, but her hair was pulled back into its customary, painfully tight bun. She carried a small package under one arm, which shot down Penny's hope that she was only there for something quick and entirely unrelated to Penny's party.

Susan saw her and excused herself from conversation with Katie's older brother, who then turned his attention to Trey. Trey, looking All-American with his crew-cut hair and football letterman jacket, was trying unsuccessfully to flirt with Zoe.

Zoe, already rather red in the cheeks, went even redder and slid down a few more inches in her chair.

Susan smiled and waved at her sister, but the smile was considerably lower-wattage than usual. "Hi, June."

When her classmates saw the dreaded Miss Riggs approaching, their enthusiastic chatter became subdued, as if they were afraid of being told off for talking too loudly out of class.

Susan offered her standard hug, which Miss Riggs accepted with obvious bad grace and broke too quickly, then, seeing her sister's effect on the party, led her inside.

Nervous eyes watched the two pass, and obvious relief filled the crowded porch when the door closed behind them.

"What is she doing here?" Katie and Ellen flanked Penny, Katie looking darkly amused, Ellen a little startled. Chelsea stood next to Jodi, her arms crossed and looking as if she were planning her escape route.

"She's here to lead us in a chorus of 'Happy Birthday,'" Michael said, sliding in smoothly on Katie's other side.

Zoe flicked her nervous eyes from the closed front door to Michael and giggled.

"Penny's just lucky I guess," Chelsea said, favoring Penny with a look that was *almost* sympathetic.

Katie ignored them. "Seriously ... who invited that killjoy?"

"Shhh ... not so loud," Jodi moaned. "She'll hear you."

"I can hear them fighting," Zoe said in a low voice, and made room for Penny to stand beside the kitchen window and listen. Katie and the others kept a distance from them, but waited with curiosity.

Whatever the fight was about, it was a short one. Penny heard only retreating footsteps from her side of the kitchen window, and a moment later Miss Riggs was striding past them again, toward her car, and without the package.

"What...?"

Zoe cut Penny's question off with a quick shake of her head, and then Susan was behind her.

"Everyone ready for some cake?" Susan carried a knife and a short stack of paper plates, but not her sister's package. Her good cheer was definitely forced now.

Later, Zoe mouthed at Penny, and jumped up to help serve cake.

Afterward, Susan led them in a single, lackluster chorus of "Happy Birthday," and Penny opened her gifts. There were only two on the table, one from Susan and, though Penny had told her friends *no gifts*, one from Zoe and Katie. Penny was relieved that Miss Riggs's mysterious package wasn't on the table. She had no idea what Miss Riggs would consider an appropriate gift for a fourteen-year-old, and didn't want to find out.

Susan's was a laptop computer, the tiniest one Penny had ever seen.

"I'm having internet installed this afternoon," she said as Penny tore open the box. "I'm always thoroughly sick of computers by the time I leave work, but I thought you might like to join the twenty-first century."

Penny liked it so much she gave Susan another hug, which seemed to cheer Susan up a bit. Her smile as Penny moved on to her second gift was less brilliant than usual, but also less fake than the one she'd offered after her sister's quick exit.

Zoe and Katie's gift was a pair of CDs, from the new/used music store in Centralia, Penny guessed, since Dogwood didn't have one. They had been trying desperately to introduce Penny to more modern music. Her taste in music, old rock 'n' roll and classical, quite frankly disturbed them.

Jenny, Susan's only employee at Sullivan's, arrived just as Susan was loading one of Penny's new CDs into the living room stereo. She parked and approached the house slowly, shading her eyes with a hand and scanning the growing crowd around the front of Penny's house. As if unsatisfied by her brief search of the partygoers, she turned her scrutiny to the cars and bikes parked around the edge of the driveway.

Penny waved and stepped down to greet her.

She was young, only a few years out of high school, plump, with brown hair and thick glasses that magnified her wide eyes. She reminded Penny of a cheerful owl.

"Who are you looking for?"

Jenny gave up her search with a shrug and a grin at Penny. "I thought Susan's boyfriend might show up."

Boyfriend? Penny thought, then said. "Boyfriend? Susan doesn't have a boyfriend."

"Well, not *yet*," Jenny said. "Is that Adele?"

Jenny danced her way up to the porch, depositing her gift into Penny's hands before going inside to dance to Zoe and Katie's attempt at bringing Penny's music collection into the twenty-first century.

Jenny's gift was, of course, a book, but still one of the biggest surprises that day. *The Aikido Student Handbook*, a volume Penny had owned a few years before when she still lived with her mother in San Francisco and her runty size had made her a favorite target of neighborhood bullies. Her brief lessons had not turned her into the Karate Kid, but she'd learned to defend herself, and more importantly, as far as her mother was concerned anyway, to control the hot temper that would never let her walk away from a fight. She supposed that Susan had known about the lessons and told Jenny.

"Aikido," Chelsea said, almost sneering at the book in Penny's hands, then at Penny. Her expression seemed to say, *right … as if.*

At Chelsea's words, the others gathered around to see what was up.

"You never told me you were a kung fu master," Katie teased.

"Aikido," Penny corrected, blushing all the way from her neck to her forehead. "I was a novice."

She'd never mentioned it to Zoe or Katie because it was a part of her past life in the city and not something she'd planned taking up again. Her learned skills were rusty now, and the self-control she'd gained had gone out the window after her mom had died and Child Protective Services stuck her in that lousy children's home.

"Oh yeah, I knew that," Zoe said, tipping Penny a not-so-sly wink. "She beat Rooster up in the park the day I met her."

"Fun, isn't it?" Trey said, and nervous laughter filled the awkward silence that followed Zoe's fond reminiscence. "I shoved him in a trashcan once."

They were gathering trash and seeing off the first of her guests—Trey, Jodi, and Chelsea—when Penny felt the little mirror in her front pocket begin to warm and vibrate slightly, someone trying to speak to her through it. She wondered who other than Zoe and Katie, standing only feet from her and perfectly able to speak directly to her, would try to reach her through the mirrors, then remembered Ronan's advice to always keep one handy.

Penny excused herself, ducked into the downstairs bathroom, and answered it.

"Ronan?"

Ronan's face swam from a brief, obscuring mist, grinning his foxy grin at her.

"Didn't have time to give you your gift before you ran off," he said.

"What?" Of all the people, or non-people, she expected a birthday gift from, Ronan was not one. Not that he wasn't a giving or generous … uh, whatever he was, but he couldn't just trot into the Centralia Mall's *Hot Topic* and buy her a gift card.

Ronan rolled his eyes, which was quite something to see a fox do, no matter how many times she'd seen him do it. "I believe it *is* human custom to give the birthday girl a token of one's friendship, is it not?"

"Well … yeah, but…."

"Then when you have a chance to get away, go to your back porch and reach under the bottom step. No one but Kat and Zoe are to see it. I had to leave somewhat precipitously when I brought it over." He wrinkled his upper lip, showing teeth. "I think Kat's brother spotted me going around the house."

"*Michael can see you*?" She didn't realize she'd all but shouted until he shushed her. "Does that mean what I think it means?"

It hadn't occurred to Penny that any of the boys in Dogwood might have the same latent abilities that she, Zoe, and Katie had, but now that the idea was in her head, it seemed kind of silly that she'd never thought of it before. After all, Tovar the Red, who had actually been the Birdman in disguise, had been able to see Ronan. She was pretty sure that even without his human disguise, the monster had been male.

"That depends," said Ronan shiftily. "On what you think it means."

Then the mirror clouded over, and he was gone.

* * *

If Ronan's short surprise appearance had been a pleasant one, then the surprise that waited outside for Penny certainly wasn't. She hadn't thought there was a person in the world she wanted to see at her birthday party, or anywhere else really, less than Miss Riggs ... well, maybe Rooster ... but the scene she found on the front porch after her chat with Ronan made Miss Riggs's visit seem almost jovial.

Katie's father, red-faced and arguing, stood at the foot of the steps with Michael. Katie was between them, her face bright red, staring down at her feet. Michael had a hold on her left arm, her father her right. She looked like she wanted to find a deep hole to fall into.

"You knew she wasn't allowed," her father boomed at Michael. It was an impressive shout; Zoe jumped back at the sound, her back thumping against the wall behind her. Ellen looked appalled. Penny felt like slinking back inside. "You went behind my back ...."

"Father, you're being stupid!" Michael was in full voice too, he leaned protectively over Katie. "You're punishing Katie because ...."

"Because she disobeyed me!"

"Stop it, both of you!" Katie shrieked, pulling free from both of them. She rounded on her father, and Penny thought that if they were giving out prizes for loudest shouts, Katie would have taken second place at least. Her father reached for her but Katie slapped his hand away and ran for Michael's Jeep. "I hate you!"

The silence that followed was perhaps more excruciating than the high-volume discussion had been.

Michael glared at their father, unblinking.

Mr. West stood where he was for a moment, perfectly still, staring at the place where Katie had been, his hand still hovering as if to grab the air in front of him. Then he turned and watched Katie climb into the passenger seat of the Jeep. At last, his gaze settled on his audience on the porch.

Michael snorted in disgust and stalked off toward his Jeep, leaving his father standing alone.

Zoe was wide-eyed and angry, chewing on her bottom lip as if afraid of what might happen if she allowed her mouth to open.

Jenny's mouth was open, but she seemed beyond words. Her jaw worked up and down for a moment, as if she were trying to force speech, but nothing happened so she closed it and, a little weak in the knees it seemed, stepped to the nearest chair to sit.

Susan's face was unreadable, but her brow was creased with deep lines that looked alien on her usually smooth face. Penny thought a storm might be brewing behind those lines.

At last, Mr. West broke the silence.

"Didn't you even think to ask me if she was allowed to come over?" His voice was hoarse from shouting. He gave Penny the shortest of glances before ignoring her again. "You know how I feel about ... them."

"She never did anything to you!" Zoe shouted and advanced on Mr. West, but Ellen stopped her with an outstretched arm.

Of them all, Susan alone seemed calm, but Penny had seen the expression on her face before, just once, when she'd caught Penny sneaking to see Tovar the Red's show the year before.

Susan's still face was a thin mask, barely hiding her wrath.

"Honestly, no. It never occurred to me that you would be childish enough to hold on to your ridiculous grudge this long."

Mr. West seemed about to reply, but Susan pointed a single finger at him, and he held his tongue.

"You had your say. Now you get to shut up and listen to me."

His eyes went even wider, and the flush began to drain from his cheeks.

"I also never thought you'd be childish enough to punish two innocent children, one of them your own daughter, because of a bit of foolishness that happened fourteen years ago. Something neither of them was a part of."

Michael's Jeep growled as he tore down the driveway, throwing up a rooster-tail of gravel and dust. Mr. West seemed to be grateful for the diversion. He watched his children until they dropped out of sight.

When he faced his audience again, he avoided Susan. His eyes fell on Penny instead.

Penny had no words. She felt tears pushing at her eyes, prickly and hot, but resisted them. She wouldn't let herself cry in front of this … this man!

Again, he seemed about to speak, and again Susan stopped him.

"The only two words you're allowed to say to Penny are *happy* and *birthday*." She stepped next to Penny and put an arm on her shoulder. Penny had never been so grateful for an invasion of her personal space. "But I think you've already ruined any chance of that for her."

A moment later Zoe was on her other side, almost vibrating with anger, her arm on Penny's other shoulder.

Mr. West regarded them for another moment, then stalked away.

* * *

Most of the happy *had* left Penny's day.

When the party was over, Susan had no objections to letting Penny help clean up and put things away. Not much later, a van arrived and a uniformed man installed their new satellite internet. Afterward they all seemed content to continue the afternoon's silence while watching a movie that had been on Penny's wish list for weeks. A phone call from Zoe's grandmother broke the trio up before the movie ended. She'd changed her mind about Zoe spending a second night at Penny's, and Zoe mumbled moodily under her breath while she hurriedly packed to leave.

Penny paused the movie while Susan drove Zoe home, taking advantage of the unexpected alone time to reacquaint herself with *The Aikido Student Handbook*, remembering her old lessons and exercises, and missing them. Maybe she could start again; Dogwood didn't have any dojos or Aikido instructors, but she could try to do it alone.

Susan returned home just as she was putting her book down, and they finished the movie in near silence, exchanging only a few words for the remaining hour.

Susan seemed upset, too. Her cheerful manner, usually quick to bounce back, was absent for the rest of the night.

Penny excused herself to her room, considered trying to read again, but decided to wait a while and try to get Katie on her mirror. She fell asleep while she was waiting and didn't wake again until well after dark.

Her first panicked thought upon waking was that there was something important that she was supposed to have done and forgotten about, and while she pummeled her half-awake brain in search of the forgotten thing, she remembered Ronan's brief visit with her before the party ended and the unexpected present waiting for her under the back-porch steps.

Penny jumped out of bed and lowered the ladder to the hallway. It descended smoothly and silently; she'd made a habit of keeping it well-oiled to cover her nighttime jaunts. She walked as quietly as she could down the stairs to the bottom floor, not wanting to wake Susan.

But Susan was already awake.

"Who else could have done it? Who else would have?" Susan kept her voice low, obviously not wanting to wake Penny, but all the calm was out of her voice now. The one person who could make her lose her cool, apparently, was her sister. After a few minutes of silence on her end, Susan spoke again.

"You weren't looking out for anyone. You did it to cause trouble. You and that ...." It seemed she couldn't find the right word or simply wouldn't allow herself to use it. "That *man* has had it in for her since the day she showed up. You never gave her a chance either."

More silence, then Penny thought she could actually hear Miss Riggs shouting from her end of the line.

Susan forgot about keeping her voice down. "You narrow-minded ...."

She called her sister a word Penny had never heard her use before, then hung up.

Penny stayed put on the landing between the second and third floor as Susan stomped from the living room into the hallway, where Penny could see her shaking with barely contained anger, then onto the front porch. She closed the door quietly behind her.

Penny waited a few moments to make sure she wasn't coming right back inside—she didn't want Susan to know she'd heard the argument—then crept down the steps to the hallway and hurried to the back door.

The night beyond was silent, moonlit, cool, and Penny let herself enjoy the peace of it for a few seconds before dropping to her belly in the grass and reaching into the darkness under the steps in search of some unknown, and likely exotic, item.

She found it quickly and was relieved when her hand was back in sight.

Ronan had left her a stone, mottled gray and strangely textured, shaped like a large egg.

Marveling that just when she didn't think Ronan could get any weirder he always somehow managed it, Penny crept back inside, and, after checking that the hallway was still empty, hurried up to her bedroom.

In bed, she examined the strange egg by the light of her lamp. It was heavy, felt solid, and when she shook it nothing rattled inside. It was too rough to be soapstone and too bland to be valuable.

Trying unsuccessfully to stifle a yawn, Penny put the egg in the drawer of her bedside table and nestled under her sheets.

She'd be able to ask Ronan about the weird egg the next day, and maybe he'd even give her a straight answer or two, though with Ronan you could never count on straight answers, only hope for them.

She'd also have to talk to Zoe about the argument she'd overheard through the kitchen window before Miss Riggs had stormed out of the party and, if she had time, start trying to confirm her suspicions about her mom and Susan.

It seemed unlikely in some ways. If Susan and her mom had been Phoenix Girls when they were younger—probably her aunt and Katie's aunt, too—then Susan would know what she was up to when she left the house for hours at a time to visit Aurora Hollow. She would have said something, let Penny know she was a part of the secret, wouldn't she?

With that question in her mind, Penny finally drifted to sleep.

Chapter 5

Memories

Penny awoke with the rising sun the next morning, a plan of action swirling around in her sleepy head. She was looking for her past, her family's past—and where do people store all the old stuff that no longer fits in their day-to-day lives?

In an attic, which was not an option in this case because that's where Susan stored Penny and her things.

Or the basement.

This house had one; she knew that because of the furnace grate in the living room floor, but she had never explored it.

She checked her clock. It was just after six, so Susan would be sleeping. Sunday was the one day she could sleep in, so she usually took advantage of it.

Penny dressed quickly and put her mirror in her pocket. Bright sunlight outside or not, the second floor hall was always dark; the fixture on the landing between floors only ever succeeded in throwing long, creepy shadows. Penny descended quickly and quietly, peeking first into the kitchen, then into the living room for signs of life from Susan.

Both were empty, but something in the living room caught her eye. Sitting on the end table next to Susan's chair lay the package her sister had dropped off during the party the day before. It was open, the flaps sticking up at jaunty, inviting angles.

Come here, Penny. See what's inside. You know you're curious. You know you want to.

Penny was curious but turned her back on the package and walked to the mostly unused utility room. It was one thing to search the basement of her own home, her mother's childhood home, even if she wasn't sure that Susan would approve; but she had no right to see what was in that box. That was Susan's business, not hers.

The utility room was narrow, running almost the entire length of the house. At one end sat an old washer and dryer, with an odd assortment of soaps and arcane laundry-related products on a shelf above them. A door opposite the hallway led to the back steps. At the other end stood a second door, one that she had never opened. If it turned out to be a closet, then she'd have to search the rest of the house for clues to her past.

It wasn't a closet.

There was a small, square landing with a light switch and a set of steep, narrow steps that led downward. Penny tried the light and, almost to her surprise, found that it worked. A weak, dusty glow filled the narrow staircase.

Penny closed the door behind her and descended.

The basement felt like a dungeon. Air ducts ran overhead like thick metal snakes, and the hot-water heater huddled in a far corner, next to an ancient, unused wood-burning furnace.

The walls weren't concrete or brick but stone and crumbling plaster. The floor was ancient, with creaking planks, some sagging slightly under Penny's light frame. A heavy man might fall right through. Who knew what might wait beneath the old boards.

Rows of sturdy wooden shelves covered one wall, and perhaps a hundred old boxes—some cardboard, some wood—filled every inch. The top two rows were too high to reach, but a quick search revealed an aluminum ladder leaning against the wall next to a small army of rusty garden tools.

Penny walked along the shelves, inspecting the lower rows. The thick dust covering most of the basement was disturbed in places, a sign, she thought, that some of the boxes had been moved fairly recently. Susan, maybe digging up a few old photos of Penny's mom.

No way to know until she looked for herself; and there was time probably to check a few of the lower boxes before Susan woke.

She scanned the row before her. None of the boxes seemed likelier to yield answers than any of the others, so she chose one at random and slid it from the shelf. It was big and heavy. She was able to lower it to the floor without dropping it, but there was no way she'd be able to lift it back up to the shelf.

It contained old paperback books and mason jars full of rocks, from exotic to ordinary: crystals of different colors, agates, chunks of common brown and green opal, fools' gold, and more. Penny remembered the old guy at the rock and jewelry shop telling her that her mother used to buy rocks from him.

Must have had quite a collection of pretty rocks, all the time she spent here.

And it was quite a collection.

Penny screwed the lid off one of the jars and tipped a handful of stones into her open palm.

She could name a few of them—a brown opal, one that was either jade or jasper, a piece of white quartz—but most were alien to her.

"Zoe would know them," she said aloud and smiled. She dumped them back into the open jar, then hesitated before screwing the lid back on and plucked out a white quartz. It was tear-shaped, translucent, smooth but not polished.

She held it up, letting the glow from the unshaded bulb shine through it. It seemed to capture the light, the milky interior shining like clouds in a bright sky.

Was this yours, Mom?

She expected no answer and got none.

She pocketed the stone and returned the jar to its box.

The next box was considerably lighter. She slid it out and set it on top of the first.

More books and some old magazines. She fingered through them, found a few she might have considered interesting under other circumstances, and with some effort lifted the box back into place.

The third box was more of the same, plus an old photo album. She opened it and found pictures of her mom, her aunt, and a lot of people she'd never seen. She dropped the photo album into its box and shoved it into place with a growing sense of frustration, realizing that she had no idea what she was really looking for and would probably not find it even if she did. There were no amazing revelations to be found here. Only a lot of dust and junk.

After a moment's consideration, she slid the third box out again and took the photo album. She doubted she'd find any answers, but she could find something of her mother's mysterious past inside. Still images of memories she'd never shared with Penny. It was better than nothing.

She thought about pulling out a fourth box but realized that she had no idea how long she'd been there. It could wait for another time. With the piece of quartz in her pocket and the photo album under one arm, Penny hurried back to her room.

She tucked the album under her pillow and checked the time—a little past seven—thought about calling Zoe or Katie up on her two-way mirror, and decided it was a little early.

So, what now?

That was the problem with going to bed early. She always woke way too early the next morning.

She put the mirror back in her pocket and walked to her wardrobe, a new addition to her room. A Christmas present from Susan, she and Penny had to carry it up the ladder a piece at a time and assemble it in her room. It was small, the left side containing half a dozen narrow drawers with a shelf above them, the right a space to hang clothes. It stood beside her old dresser, which no one had wanted to take apart and carry down a piece at a time.

Penny selected a change of clothes.

A nice, long shower and a cup of coffee were in order if she was going to be useful for anything at all.

* * *

A half-hour later, showered and fully awake, Penny sipped her coffee and cooked breakfast for Susan. As the eggs fried and the bacon sizzled, Susan walked in and greeted Penny with a wide, languid yawn.

"Morning, Susan." Penny was feeling uncharacteristically cheerful. Probably the second cup of coffee; she'd gulped her first while Susan slept.

Susan yawned again to signal exactly what she thought of mornings in general.

"You're up and at 'em awfully early." With both hands, as if it were a lifeline, she took the cup Penny offered.

Penny shrugged and flipped bacon. "Went to bed early."

Susan looked at her, eyes still half-closed. "I thought you'd be up half the night playing on the internet."

"Nope. Didn't feel like playing after the party." Penny had forgotten all about the new internet connection but decided not to tell Susan. She didn't want her to think the money had been wasted. "Just wanted to go to bed."

"I could have strangled that man," Susan said. She sipped her coffee, lingering over the cup for a moment to enjoy the aroma. "I'm going to have a talk with Katie's mother. Maybe she can reason with him."

Penny somehow doubted it but nodded. Couldn't hurt to try.

It wasn't the argument with Mr. West she was interested in at the moment, though; she knew why he hated her. The argument Penny wanted to hear about was the one she'd had with her sister. She didn't think she was brave enough to ask about it straight out though.

"So, what did Miss Riggs bring you yesterday?"

Susan stiffened at the mention of her sister but recovered quickly. She even managed a small smile.

"Let me finish this ...," she said as she sipped her coffee, "and I'll show you."

And perhaps her smile had been genuine, because it stayed in place while Penny finished cooking and Susan sipped her coffee.

At last Susan's cup was empty and she went to the living room, returning with the box just as Penny set the table and pushed a fresh cup of coffee toward her.

"Thanks!" She accepted the fresh cup and half-drained it in one swallow.

Penny sipped at hers, savoring it for as long as she could. With Susan awake she wouldn't be able to sneak another cup.

Susan pushed down the top flaps of the little box and reached inside with both hands. They emerged holding a silver tree, about ten inches tall, with five small, clear spheres hanging from its branches. She brushed the box aside and set the tree down between them.

"That's pretty," Penny said, and she meant it. The little glass balls turned and swung, throwing light in dizzying patterns across the table. She pushed her plate aside, breakfast forgotten, and leaned closer. There were shapes in the spheres, shapes that she couldn't quite make out.

Susan pushed it closer to her. Her smile was gone, her face somber but serene. "Look closer."

Penny did, and gasped. Inside one of the spheres, the small face of a much younger Susan smiled at her. Penny shifted her gaze to another. The second face was unfamiliar, as was the third, but the fourth and fifth....

They were identical but with slightly differing expressions. They were faces she knew and missed.

"Which one is my mom?"

Susan pointed without taking her eyes from Penny. She knew them well, it seemed. "You know who the other one is, right?"

Penny nodded. Her mom's twin, the aunt she'd never met.

"Those are Austrian crystal, laser engraved." Her hand stretched out and set one of the little spheres rocking again. "Katie's aunt Tracy had this made a few months before you were born. It belonged to all of us, but ... well."

Susan left it at that.

Penny didn't really need her to finish. There had been the crash, her father's abandonment, and soon after that all of Susan's friends had left Dogwood forever.

"After a while I just couldn't stand to look at it anymore," she said. "I was nineteen, the youngest of our little circle of friends."

Circle of friends, Penny thought and suppressed a shiver of excitement.

"I felt like they all just abandoned me here." She prodded another of the spheres, setting it in motion.

"I asked June if she could take a few of my old things and keep them in storage with our mom and dad's old stuff, family heirlooms she keeps tucked away in her attic, and she *graciously*," she put a slight, sarcastic twist on the word, "agreed to do so."

Penny dropped her eyes from Susan's face to her younger representation in the crystal sphere. She preferred the smiling Susan to the sour one.

"Obviously she never looked in this box when I had her put it away. I think she would have thrown it in the trash if she'd seen it, but she looked when I called her up and asked her to bring it back."

"Was that what you two fought about?" Penny asked without thinking. She regretted it the moment the words were out.

Susan only chuckled. "Yes. This is what we fought about, among other things."

That was all she offered on the subject, so Penny let it go. She could always ask Zoe what she'd overheard later, if the curiosity was too strong to deny.

"Why did you ask for it back?"

"For you," she said. "And for me too. It's something for us to share. My friends and your family."

Penny took hold of Susan's crystal sphere, removed it from its hook, and lifted it so she could see the face within, backlit by the bright kitchen light.

"You're my family now," she said, again speaking with no premeditation. Not knowing that she meant to say it aloud until it was out.

Susan's smile returned, the big one her younger self wore in the crystal. She reached across the table and took Penny's other hand in hers. "I know this isn't easy for you, Penny. You're a very reserved girl, so that means a lot coming from you. You remind me a lot of your aunt Nancy that way. Your mother, Di, she was the outgoing one."

That struck Penny as odd. If her mother, queen of long silences and personal space, had been the outgoing one, her aunt Nancy must have been as fun to have around as cramps. Maybe when she was younger her mother had been the joyous young butterfly Susan often reminisced about, but Penny had never seen that side of her.

Susan squeezed Penny's hand and let it go.

"I think of you as my family now, too. I have since the day you walked in the door."

The silver tree drew Penny's eyes back to it again and again.

Susan, Penny's mother, and their circle of friends.

And another unanswered question entered Penny's wandering mind.

"Susan, do you have a new boyfriend?"

Susan looked momentarily startled but recovered with a smile and a snort of laughter.

"Jenny is such a blabbermouth," she said. "He's just a man I see around town sometimes. Sweet and charming, but nothing serious."

There was something in Susan's smile that suggested *Nothing Serious* might already be shifting toward *Slightly Serious*.

"I'd like to meet him," Penny said, a little hurt that Susan had been keeping such a big secret from her, though she knew that when it came to keeping secrets, she had no right to complain.

Susan regarded her somberly for a moment, and nodded. "Okay ... if you want to. I just didn't want to throw any more new stuff at you when you're finally starting to settle in."

"I'm a big girl," Penny said and smiled. "I can handle it."

Susan nodded again, tapping a half-eaten piece of bacon against her plate as if trying to decide whether or not to finish it. "I guess I'm being overly cautious, but I've never had a kid before. I'm still learning."

"You're doing fine."

They passed the rest of breakfast in a companionable silence. One her mother would have appreciated.

* * *

After breakfast Penny went back to her room and sat on her bed to look through the photo album. She didn't know what she might learn from it, but it was a treasure trove of memories, and now it was hers.

The first page displayed a single large black-and-white portrait, too old for her mother to be in it. The setting was familiar, though. It was her house, with a large group of strange people posed before it. An extremely old woman, her remaining wisps of gray hair blowing about her, stood frozen. She wore a straight black dress, bore a tired expression, and had her arms folded across her scrawny chest. She was flanked by two younger women, both in white dresses, their hair tucked up into wide-brimmed hats. Standing before them in two rows of six were a dozen young girls ranging from toddlers to teens, all rather shabbily dressed, but most smiling.

Penny pulled the photo out and flipped it over.

A scrawled, faded note at the top identified the house as *Clover Hill Home for Girls*, and dated it 1938.

Home for girls?

Below was a list of names in three rows, three on the top row, then six each on the second and third. She read through them. She hadn't expected to recognize any of them, so wasn't disappointed.

She slid the old photo back into place and turned to the next two pages.

Four photos, all black-and-white except for the last, filled the second page, all four the same girl at different stages of her life. The first was a cropped and enlarged picture of one of the girls from the first photo, around age ten, Penny guessed. She was pixyish with short-cropped dark hair, the exact color impossible to tell from the black-and-white representation. A short note on the back named her: Penelope Johnson, age eleven.

The second was Penelope as a young woman, standing in front of the ocean. She was still pixyish, but her hair was much longer. It blew out behind her like a sail in a high wind. In the third she stood next to a rugged but cheerful-looking older man. Penny slid it out and checked for more helpful notes. Penelope Johnson-Spruce and Billy Spruce, 1950.

Penny slid the picture back in, bewildered, and examined the fourth more closely.

It was in color, but old, faded, and grainy. Billy Spruce was not in this one, but two figures held eternal poses in the background, caught midstride, walking hand in hand. In the foreground, an elderly Penelope, her dark hair now mostly gray, held a child in her lap. The child was plumper than the young Penelope but had the same face and the same hair, short and dark auburn. A second, identical child stood next to Penelope, holding her aged, boney finger in a plump fist.

Penny slid this last photo from its sleeve with shaking fingers and read the back.

Penelope Johnson-Spruce with granddaughters Diana and Nancy Sinclair - 1984.

In the background, behind the walking couple, was a familiar rise of land, a hill with a winding trail leading to the top. Not far beyond the crest of that hill, Penny knew, was Aurora Hollow.

This was her home, her family. Penny did some quick, rough mental arithmetic.

Penelope Johnson-Spruce was her great-grandmother.

The couple in the background ....

Penny slid the photo back in place and moved to the next page, a short pictorial life story of her grandmother, Betty Spruce-Sinclair. The last picture on her page showed her with a thin, balding man. Thomas Sinclair. Her grandfather.

She turned to the next two pages and found her mother and Aunt Nancy.

Aunt Nancy's page held four photos, but her mother's only three. The last sleeve was blank.

Numb from the shock of finally meeting all of her long-lost family, Penny first closed the book, then her eyes.

* * *

The rest of the photo album was an uncategorized and unorganized series of snapshots. A few featured great-grandmother Penelope and grandmother Betty, but most were of Penny's mom, aunt, and an assortment of friends. She recognized some of the faces from the laser-engraved spheres on Susan's silver tree, and she recognized a few from her own memories of the last year in Dogwood.

There was one of her mom—or maybe it was her aunt, it was impossible to tell one from the other—and Susan in the park, the Chehalis River rushing by behind them. There were other figures in the background, and for a moment Penny thought one was the intensely red-haired figure of her father. Close scrutiny revealed it to be a scowling man who only looked a little like her father. There was a definite resemblance, but the man was older, more rugged. The one photograph Penny had of her father showed a smooth-faced man with wild hair that seemed to dance like flames on his head. This man had a few shallow wrinkles, a long scar marring one side of his face, and hair that was forcibly tamed and slicked back against his skull. Penny flipped it over to see if the red-headed man was named but found no clue to his identity, and when she looked at the front again, he was gone.

Penny blinked, studied the photograph, decided it had been her imagination, and put it back.

Another showed Susan laughing, her eyes squeezed shut and a few tears of laughter rolling down her cheeks. This younger Susan had thick, blonde hair, so long it flowed down beyond the edge of the picture. Behind her was a much younger, but no less ill-tempered, Miss Riggs. She regarded the photographer with a forbidding look, her lip curled into a scowl. Of course, in those days she was still probably just plain old June Taylor. She'd married in her twenties and divorced only a few years later, Susan had once told Penny. Susan never told her who had done the walking out, but knowing Miss Riggs as she did, Penny could guess.

One featured an intense-looking young woman that Penny thought must have been Tracy West. She could see much of Katie in the face. The woman was looking over her shoulder at Susan and a man Penny almost recognized. Both were bent over in gales of laughter. She was used to seeing Susan like this, but the man ... and then she knew who he was. She hadn't recognized him because the few times she had seen him in real life there had been no smile or any hint that he ever did anything as friendly as laugh. It was Katie's father. He was older than the others, but still young-looking compared to the man she knew. He wore a black tuxedo and had draped his arm casually over a younger Susan's shoulder. His other arm was wrapped around the waist of his new bride, dressed in lacy white, her veil thrown back over her head. All three were laughing, as if at a shared joke. The back of the photo read *Susan Taylor, Markus West, Lynne Davis-West – reception.*

Another was taken right outside Zoe's favorite shop in Dogwood, the jewelry and gem shop, Golden Arts. Not that Zoe was at all into jewelry. Penny didn't think she'd ever seen Zoe wearing so much as a ring or necklace—Katie was the girly-girl of the group—but Zoe loved the displays and bins of rocks in the back room, as, apparently, had Penny's mother. Standing on the sidewalk in front of the display window, comically protesting the need to be photographed with one upraised arm, was the old proprietor of Golden Arts. He looked exactly the same to Penny. Despite the raised hand and posture of retreat, he too was grinning.

Penny found the two that interested her most on the last page.

The first was of a girl whose name Penny didn't know, though she had been one of the five on Susan's tree. She had brown hair and thick glasses that made her equally brown eyes seem small. She wasn't smiling but somehow looked serene. She had a narrow face with high cheekbones. Though not what Penny might call pretty, she was cute. Over one arm she had a slung bag with something sticking out of one end that might have been the handle of a wooden drumstick.

Penny knew it wasn't a drumstick. Penny knew exactly what it was.

The other picture was of her mom and aunt, now in their late teens or early twenties. This time she could tell them apart. Her aunt looked unhappy but willing at least to hold still for the photo. Her mother, on the other hand, looked positively radiant, grinning more broadly than Penny had ever seen her do in life. She was also very, very pregnant.

Penny studied this picture for a long time, taking in every detail of her mom's face, of her hair, which was thick and flowing and glowed like a garnet in the sunlight. After a long while, two things in this picture snagged her attention.

The first was a ring, a narrow band of gold on the third finger of her left hand.

A wedding ring.

Penny had always assumed her parents had never married. Her mother had retained her maiden name, and though she had never, would never, confirm or deny Penny's suspicions, Penny had always assumed it was because she was not married.

The second thing was a tattoo, small and indistinct in this photograph, on the inner wrist of her mother's left hand.

Her mother had never had a tattoo.

Chapter 6

Temptations

Penny didn't think Susan would miss the old photo album, so she stowed it in her middle dresser drawer under some shirts and decided to take a walk.

"Home before dark, okay?" Susan knew Penny's tendency to dawdle when she went for her walks, but since Penny always came back home in one piece, she never made too big of a fuss.

Maybe it's because she knows where I'm going.

But Penny didn't believe that. Not with all the weirdness of last fall, or Penny's great liking for long walks on her property, often disappearing for hours at a time with Zoe and Katie.

But Penny had already made up her mind about one thing. Susan, her mom and aunt, their friends, had once all been Phoenix Girls.

Had she simply forgotten?

How *could* she have forgotten?

Penny decided she'd had enough alone time for the day. Once she topped the hill and put the house at her back, she pulled her mirror out.

But who to call?

There was Zoe, who she still wanted to talk to about Susan's argument. There was Katie. Penny wanted desperately to know how things had gone for her after her dramatic exit yesterday. There was Ronan, and his odd present.

"Ronan?" Penny peered into the mirror, waiting for the fog to come, bringing Ronan with it, but nothing happened. "Ronan, are you there?"

Nothing.

Continuing toward the hollow, Penny moved to the next on her mental list.

"Kat?" Several seconds passed. She was about to try again when the familiar swirl of fog appeared, then disappeared just as suddenly, leaving Katie's unhappy face in its place.

"Hi," she said. Penny could see the stack of pillows propping her head and guessed she was still in bed, moping or grounded. Probably both. Katie settled it for her a second later. "Dad grounded me. Two weeks, and I'm not allowed to go back to your house ... *of course.*"

Penny had guessed that already too, but it was still disappointing to hear her fear confirmed. "Are you okay?"

Katie rolled her eyes. "Oh yeah, I'm just wonderful. I feel good enough to scream."

And to Penny's surprise, she did.

"I'm so pissed right now!" She glared away for a moment, then looked back at Penny. "I'm sorry about your party."

"It's okay."

"No, it's not," she shouted again. "He was a total jerk!"

Katie's eyes flicked away from the mirror, and she groaned. "Crap, he's coming. Probably thinks I'm on my cell phone. Grounded, you know."

"Later, okay?" Penny asked.

Katie nodded and was gone.

She tried Zoe next.

"Hey, babe!" Zoe greeted her cheerfully. Penny hoped her good mood was genuine. *Someone* should be happy today. "You need to talk to Kat."

"Already have." Penny had reached the edge of the canyon trail to the hollow and, given her past near-tumbles down it, decided to wait until she could give it her full attention. She sat, her feet hanging over the drop. "She's in big trouble."

"I know," Zoe said, actually smiling. "But not as much trouble as her dad."

"What?"

"Michael told their mom about his total freak-out at your party. That guy is feeling no love right now." Zoe seemed to be taking a lot of pleasure in his predicament. "They all hate him."

"A lot of good it'll do Kat," Penny said.

"It will if she stops losing her temper. Michael says it's only a matter of time before their mom wears him down, and Michael won't even talk to him now."

"Wait ... you talked to Michael?"

Zoe blushed and turned her face so a curtain of hair hid it.

"He called. Wanted to let me know what was going on."

"He never called me," Penny teased.

"Well, he's embarrassed. He feels like he ruined your party ... and Kat thinks you're mad at her."

"What? That's just stupid!"

"I know. I told them the same thing. But you've already talked to her ...."

"Not long I didn't." Penny said. "She started yelling and I had to go."

"Oh ... well, temper runs in that family I guess."

"Can you come over today?"

"Naw," Zoe said. "Stuck at home."

"Why? You're not grounded too, are you?"

Zoe hadn't done anything to tick off her bad-tempered grandma lately, at least not that Penny knew about, but sometimes it seemed like Zoe spent half of her time grounded.

"No, nothing like that." She was silent for a moment, and Penny's perspective changed as Zoe turned.

"Grandma had a spell yesterday and called the ambulance. So now her doctor has her on new heart medication and she needs *me* to stay at home today to make sure it doesn't kill her." Zoe rolled her eyes. "She's so paranoid ... and I hear her calling. Gotta run, Little Red."

Then Zoe, too, was gone.

Looked like Penny had a little more alone time whether she wanted it or not.

She pushed the mirror into her pocket and began descending into the hollow.

Time for a little therapy, she thought.

Nothing cheered her up quite like setting stuff on fire or blowing it up.

* * *

Penny worked out her frustrations with a round of target practice, levitating large rocks onto the ledge on the other side of the creek and blasting them with her wand. She was getting good, too, hitting her targets almost every time. Of course, she was getting a lot of practice, much more than Zoe and Katie. It wasn't fair to them, her easier access to the hollow and its secrets. She wished there was something she could do to help them.

She avoided opening *The Secrets of The Phoenix Girls.* She thought the next time should be an occasion for all of them, not just her.

When pummeling unoffending rocks grew boring, she sat on one of the big ash's large, arching roots, kicked off her shoes, and cooled her feet in the water. She thought about the day before, Katie's revelation of and victory over her fears, the bizarre forming of their circle, and the even more bizarre vision she'd had before it ended.

And there were the warm but painless flames, what Ronan called Phoenix Fire.

Phoenix Fire. It'll only burn what its maker wants it to burn.

Penny remembered the feeling of it burning harmlessly in the palm of her hand, how Katie, near panic, had asked her to put it down. But she hadn't put it down or even put it out. She'd simply done what came naturally to her. She'd closed her hand and put it away.

As she thought about it, she could feel the familiar tingling warmth rising in her chest, as if the flames were hiding inside her and waiting for her to call them.

Penny laid her wand on her lap and raised her right hand, not forcing the warmth to flow down her arm toward it, but *letting* it. The tiny hairs on her arm stood on end as the warmth flowed through it, then settled again as it concentrated in her palm.

She could feel it now, just beneath her skin, and realized she was the only thing stopping it. Her will was the only tether holding it back, so she closed her eyes, took a deep, steadying breath, and let it go.

When she opened her eyes, the flames danced from her cupped palm, licking up her fingers. For a long moment she simply marveled.

Then she panicked.

The flames began to spread along her arm, to her elbow and beyond.

"Whoa!" Penny jumped from her seat and waved her arm through the air, but the flames only spread.

She dropped to her belly at the creek's edge and plunged her arm up to the shoulder in the icy water.

"I don't think it's working," a voice from across the creek said, and she looked up to see Ronan standing at rigid attention in the mouth of his cave.

"What do I do?" She cried out, thrashing her arm through the water, though Ronan was right. The flames danced as energetically under the water as they had done out of it. *"What do I do?"*

"Calm down!" Ronan leapt into the creek, and as he swam toward her, she saw her wand washing away in the current.

"My wand!" Penny screamed and lunged for it but missed by several feet and fell headlong into the cold, rushing water. When she had managed to push herself out of the water and back onto the shore, she saw Ronan paddling toward her, the wand clamped between his teeth. She relaxed for a moment, then remembered that she was on fire and panicked again. "Help me, Ronan!"

Ronan scrambled ashore and shook the water from his thick fur, drenching Penny once again, then spat the wand out next to her.

"Calm yourself and get control of it," he shouted, now near panic himself. "It can't hurt you."

Penny closed her eyes and tried to slow her breathing. She couldn't shake the image of the flames, harmless to her or not, spreading until she was completely engulfed, running around and flapping her flaming arms through the air and screaming like a lunatic.

"Calm," Ronan urged. "Just remember, it's a part of you. You called it out and you can put it back just as easily."

Penny recalled closing her fist and not extinguishing the fire but simply putting it away. How the lovely warmth had settled into her, not dying but going into waiting.

Putting the fire back *was* more difficult than letting it out; it was like willing herself to calm down after a fit of anger, but she felt the warmth decrease by slow stages.

"You're doing it," Ronan said, sounding calmer himself. "Open your eyes."

Penny did and saw the flames guttering on her arm, then dying. As they died, her arm began to sting with cold. She pulled it from the creek and watched as the flames retreated toward her hand, and, with a regretful little *poof*, puffed out.

"That was intense," Penny said. She regarded her dripping wet arm with suspicion, as if it might burst into flames again. "I'd better learn to get that under control. If I start bursting into flames during class people will definitely know something is up."

Ronan settled next to her and began to laugh. "I'm sorry, little lady, but that's the funniest thing I've seen in a long time. You have no idea ...."

Losing complete control, Ronan rolled onto his side and wheezed laughter. "... how ... much I've needed this."

Penny dropped onto the ground beside Ronan, scowling at him for a moment before the giggles took her, too. There was just no way to watch a large red fox rolling on the ground in gales of laughter without the image tickling your funny bone.

At last Ronan's wheezing chuckles died out, and he could look at her without being overcome by them. "You should have seen yourself. It really was amusing."

Penny rocked forward with another quick burst of giggles. "I'm happy to have brightened your day."

She picked herself up off the ground, grabbed her wand, and resumed her seat on the tree's arched root. Ronan jumped up beside her.

"I've never seen any of the others do that," he said, sounding impressed. "In fact, I've never seen *anyone* do that."

Penny looked into his upturned, grinning face, and decided that this was as good a time as any to try to press a few answers out of him.

"Not even my mom or Susan?" Penny waited for a moment, but he didn't reply. "What about Kat's aunt?"

His smile did not fade as she'd expected, but he did turn away from her. She crossed arms and prepared for more of his artful dodging.

"Not even them," he admitted. "Of course, Susan never had the affinity with fire that you share with Diana and Nancy. Her element was always air. She was the first of their generation to learn how to fly."

Penny didn't know which stunned her the most; the fact that Ronan was giving her a straight answer about her mother for once, or that Susan could fly.

"Susan ... can fly?"

Ronan shook his head. "Not anymore, but back in her day she was like a bird, that one."

Ronan appeared lost in reverie, looking back on the old days when Penny's mother and all of her friends had called Aurora Hollow their place and had done amazing things which Penny couldn't begin to imagine.

"You know, I'm not surprised you figured it out," he said. "I'm not disappointed, either. You're inquisitive, persistent and intelligent ... your mother would have been pleased."

"Why didn't you just tell me?" Penny felt her familiar frustration with Ronan rise, and squelched it. She had learned to trust him in the past year. His advice had never led her wrong, so he must have good reasons for withholding. "Why hasn't Susan said anything? She has to know what we're up to."

"It's ... complicated," he said. "And not all of it is nice."

"Well," Penny said, feeling nettled again. "Maybe if you use small words and talk ... real ... slow ... I'll be able to follow it."

Ronan made a small barking sound—she couldn't tell if it was a sound of amusement or frustration. "There's not much to tell, honestly."

Penny could sense another dodge coming and determined to prevent it.

"I already know my house used to be an orphanage for girls, and that my great-grandmother grew up there." She paused to enjoy the effect of her words on Ronan. "I don't know when she bought the place, but I do know my grandmother grew up there, too. Were they all ...?"

"Yes," Ronan said. "They were. That's as far back as my knowledge goes, but you're right. I suspect what you're interested in is a little more recent, though."

Penny nodded, waited.

"Your mother and aunt, Susan, Kat's aunt, and their friend Janet ... they were the last, and your grandmother was their teacher." He rose, stretched, jumped to the ground, and began to pace. "Your grandparents were both dead when I entered the picture, but I've gleaned that much from ... other sources."

"And on the night I was born?"

"On the night you were born," he paused, as if considering his next words carefully. "That was the night everything went horribly wrong for them."

"What happened?"

Ronan stopped pacing and fixed her with a stare. "You must know by now you girls aren't the only ones who can do what you do."

"Like Tovar?"

"Yes," Ronan nodded. "Like him. The others are from another place, far away, but they come here from time to time; and when they discovered your mother's circle of friends, these others determined to stop them."

Penny felt herself grow cold and wasn't sure if she wanted him to answer her next question.

"What did the others do?"

"They sent representatives here to watch and to learn and, when the time was right, to sabotage."

"How?"

Ronan took a deep breath, exhaled slowly. "They befriended your mother and the rest of them and destroyed them from within."

Penny waited, arms crossed.

"Only hours after your birth, one of your mother's friends betrayed the rest, and when the circle broke, she stole something from them."

Penny was beginning to feel the chill from her dunk in the creek. That was what she told herself, at least. She had begun to shake slightly. "What did she take from them?"

"Their memories," Ronan said. "Of everything to do with Aurora Hollow."

Penny's arms dropped into her lap and she sagged against the ash.

"Mom would never talk about her past with me," she said. "And the one time Susan did … it was like there was nothing in the world she wouldn't rather do."

"It can be painful," Ronan said, "when you have to think past holes in your memory. It can also be dangerous. They will never know what they're missing, but for them the past is a book they never want to open again."

"Which one was it?" Penny leaned closer to him, one hand on her knee, the other gripping her wand. "Which one of them was it?"

"No," Ronan said, and shook his head, twice, firmly. "I won't tell you that. No good could come from you knowing."

Penny shot to her feet. "Why not? You can tell me the rest of it, but not that?"

"Penny, you needed to know the rest of it." He paced back and forth in front of her. "Those others know about you now. They know the Phoenix Girls are back, and they'll try to stop you, which is why you three need to learn as much as you can as quickly as you can. You have to be ready!"

Penny's agitation grew.

"How? How are we supposed to fight off people who have been doing this their whole lives?"

"You did okay against Tovar."

"That was luck," Penny said. She hated to admit it, probably because she knew how true it was.

"Some of it was," Ronan conceded, but he remained unperturbed. "Most of it was courage and intuition."

"He underestimated us. He thought we were a couple of silly little girls, and he underestimated us."

"Well," Ronan said, his hackles rising, "the others won't. They will come, and they will *not* underestimate you. They take you seriously. If you don't start taking *yourselves* seriously, then they *will* beat you, easily. You three need to learn."

"Then we might as well snap our wands and just give up!" Penny told Ronan what had happened at the party and that Katie was banned from her house.

"Well, that certainly complicates things," Ronan said, sounding only mildly concerned.

"*Complicates?*" Penny nearly shouted. "She'll never be able to come here again."

"Never say *never*," Ronan advised. "The situation with her father may work itself out sooner than you think."

"But …."

"And in the meantime …." He rose and sprinted to the door wedged between two scrawny willows. "Bring that wand of yours over here."

Her irritation turned to excitement as she realized what he was about to do. It was one of the things he had always steadfastly refused to help them with in the past. Today, however, things seemed to have changed.

"This is risky," he warned her. "You can never know who might be standing on the other side of a distant door, so you must promise me never to take unnecessary chances."

"Okay," Penny said, nearly breathless with anticipation. "I promise."

"I'm not sure if this is a good idea. The temptation to use tools like this might prove too much some day."

"We'll be good," Penny assured him.

Ronan nodded in the direction of the door.

"Come here then."

It was so simple that Penny felt stupid for not having figured it out herself.

* * *

By Sunday night things at home were pretty much back to routine, Susan curled up in her favorite living room chair with a book before making dinner, Penny helping in the kitchen when Susan would allow, homework, and finally some time playing on the internet. Penny had had internet in her apartment in the city and had spent much of her days back then either playing online or watching television. After almost a year of small-town life, with the freedom to go just about anywhere she wanted without constant adult supervision, she didn't particularly enjoy idle time spent in front of a screen.

Sunday night routine was all about mental preparation, Penny thought. For the coming school week, or work week in Susan's case. It was an early-to-bed night.

But not that night.

She already had it planned out. First Zoe, then together, they would surprise Katie and maybe give her one thing to be happy about.

"Bedtime, kiddo," Susan said on her way past the kitchen to the stairs.

"Okay." She closed the laptop and slid it into the recently emptied top drawer of the kitchen buffet.

Better not to have the temptation of the internet in her bedroom on school nights, Susan had explained. Penny was fine with that, since the internet wasn't high on her list of temptations anyway.

"G'nite," Penny called as she climbed the ladder to her attic room. She heard Susan's reply, something about bedbugs.

She waited for a quarter hour, making sure Susan was done roaming the house for the night, then used her mirror to call on Zoe.

"Hey Penny." Zoe looked surprised but pleased. "What's going on? Something wrong?"

"Nope," Penny said, almost giddy with excitement. "Is your grandma sleeping?"

"When isn't she sleeping?" Zoe sat up and Penny saw her perspective shift, giving her a good view of her small closet's door.

"Good. We'll talk again in a few seconds." Penny slid from her own bed and approached her new wardrobe. "Just try not to scream, okay?"

"Uh, sure … okay." Zoe looked beyond puzzled now.

Penny said "goodbye," and Zoe's face faded from her mirror.

Penny stopped in front of her wardrobe and considered.

Zoe's closet door opens outward, so ….

She opened the door and stepped inside, pushing a few coats and hanging shirts aside. The good thing about being a pip-squeak, she decided, was being able to fit easily into a small wardrobe.

She closed her eyes, although the complete darkness inside the wardrobe made it unnecessary, and touched the tip of her wand to the door. She visualized the room on the other side of this door, not as her own, but Zoe's. She imagined Zoe sitting on the edge of her bed on the other side at that very moment, waiting for something strange to happen. She could almost hear Zoe grumbling about it now.

Penny shoved on the door with her free hand, but it stayed shut, resisting Penny's attempt to push it open.

What?

Then she understood what was wrong, there was a doorknob on Zoe's side of the door, but not hers, and knocked instead.

There was indeed a short squeal of surprise from the other side of the door.

"Come on, Zoe. It's me. Let me in."

A moment later the door swung open, and Zoe stood on the other side, mouth gaping and eyes wide.

It had worked!

Penny grinned hugely at her and stepped from the inside of her wardrobe into Zoe's bedroom.

"You figured it out?" Zoe bounced up and down in place, and Penny thought she was resisting the urge to scream with excitement.

"No, Ronan showed me," Penny admitted. "And don't scream … you'll wake your grandma."

"A little warning would have been nice, you know," Zoe said, but her smile remained, belying any real anger. "The last time something came out of my closet it was ten feet tall, had wings, and tried to kidnap me."

Penny hadn't thought about that.

"Maybe we should give Kat a heads-up before we step through?" Penny made the suggestion, but it took a bit of the joy out of her.

Zoe considered this for a moment before shaking her head. "Naw. That's no fun."

A minute later Zoe was talking to Katie.

"You alone right now?"

"I was sleeping," Katie grumbled. Penny heard her yawn. "Everyone's in bed. Well, technically my dad is on the couch."

"Good," Zoe said. "We'll talk to you again in a minute."

Katie said goodbye and Zoe tossed her mirror onto her bed.

"You ready?"

"Wait, does Kat's closet door open in or out?" Penny didn't know how much this mattered, strictly speaking, but didn't want any screw-ups.

"In, I think," Zoe said. She'd been to Katie's house a few times, but Penny had never gone. Katie didn't think it would be good for her father to arrive home early from work some day to find *that girl* sitting in his living room. "It's a walk-in."

Penny passed her wand to Zoe and told her what to do.

They stood outside her closet door for a minute, Zoe's eyes pinched shut, visualizing for all she was worth, then Zoe said, "Okay, lets go."

Penny turned the knob and pulled the door open.

Katie greeted them with a barely stifled shriek.

Chapter 7

Unfinished Business

Morgan Duke strolled down Dogwood's Main Street, enjoying the inquisitive looks from the townies, enjoying the clear sky and mild spring weather even more. Although his almost daily visits with the lovely Susan Taylor were strictly business, he found he enjoyed playing the part of the smitten older man with her much more than he usually did. Her answer was the same that day as always, but he found that after every new application of his charm her eyes softened a bit and her smile came more naturally.

He couldn't fathom why that piece of ground was so important to her. At the price he was now offering, double fair market value, she should have been leaping in the aisles of her little shop while visions of dollar signs danced in her head, but she persisted in her polite refusal to sell, at any price.

This was outside his experience. Everyone had their price.

On the other side of the two-lane street Morgan saw the town preacher changing letters on his quaint little church's reader board, saw the preacher noticing him, and paused in his stride long enough to give the man a smile and a wave.

The preacher returned both.

Even that man had his price, Morgan knew. The magic number for which he would sell his own offspring. Greed was simply human nature.

Except for Susan Taylor it seemed.

This didn't trouble Morgan. He liked a challenge. If he kept raising the numbers and pouring on the charm, he would find Susan's magic number. Whatever the price was, it would be worth it.

A honk startled him out of his wandering reverie, and he turned to find a sheriff's cruiser swinging into opposing traffic—well, there was no traffic at the moment, but the wrong side of the road was still the wrong side of the road. The window lowered, and the flushed face of Sheriff Avery Price poked out as the cruiser pulled to a stop.

"Good day, Avery." Morgan put two fingers to his head in casual salute. "Joey's not causing more trouble is he?"

Beyond general complaints of poor service at the town-operated and Price-owned landfill, bad hygiene, and general creepiness, Joseph had behaved himself much better than usual. Not that he had much of an opportunity for real trouble cooped up almost continuously in his camper at the dump. Still, the good Sheriff Price had taken an immediate and strong dislike to Morgan's son.

It happened a lot. Joseph Duke had not inherited his father's easy charm.

"Nothing new," Sheriff Price said, his ruddy face growing slightly redder at the mention of Joseph. A large beat-up pickup approached at well over the posted speed limit, saw the back end of the Sheriff's cruiser occupying its lane, and swerved at the last moment to avoid a collision. The Sheriff seemed not to notice. "Ernest was looking for you. Said you weren't home when he stopped by and that you won't answer his calls."

Morgan sighed. Ernest Price had been growing somewhat irritable since Morgan's arrival in town. It seemed he preferred his silent partner more when they were separated by a continent. Morgan felt much the same way.

"I've been occupied," Morgan said, now having to work a little to maintain his ever-present smile.

Smile and the world smiles with you, his father had told him long ago, *fart and you walk alone.*

Charming man, Morgan's father.

The Sheriff frowned. "Can I tell him when he can expect to hear back?"

He runs you like a pack mule, Morgan thought. *Good to know.*

"Later today," Morgan said. He held up three fingers of his right hand like a boy scout. "Honest injun. I'm meeting Joey for a bite to eat. Need my strength before I wrestle with your brother."

He smiled even wider, showing two rows of almost perfect teeth.

The Sheriff nodded and drove away without another word.

Morgan found Joseph sitting alone in Grumpy's Tavern. He'd picked a corner table, keeping his back turned to the unfamiliar regulars as he chomped his way through a burger the size of a dinner plate.

Not even Joseph is glutton enough to finish that, Morgan thought, cringing as a large dollop of Grumpy's secret sauce plopped onto the table.

"How about you get a doggy bag for the rest of that?" He patted his son's shoulder and sat next to him, keeping far enough back that he wouldn't be in danger of the boy dripping burger juice all over him.

"Ain't you gonna eat?" Joseph spoke through a mouth full of half-chewed burger, and Morgan decided to keep his eyes pointed toward the storefront window and the traffic outside. Safer that way.

"Nope, not feeling all that hungry anymore," he said.

A stick-skinny waitress in a catsup-stained apron appeared moments later with a check and a to-go box, as if she'd been waiting for the slightest excuse to get Joseph on his way. The fine folks at Grumpy's might just be living up to their name, but Morgan thought their special attention was just a result of Joseph just being Joseph.

The boy was about as charming as a rug burn.

"I got it," Morgan said, picking up the slip and rising to give Joseph a little more quality time with the horrendous burger.

The woman at the register was large, with a mass of thick brown hair twisted into a messy bun at the back of her head. She greeted him with a smile, but it faltered when she read the ticket, her eyes flitting quickly to Joseph and back again.

"You're new in town," she remarked, tapping the keys of her antique cash register. "That'll be twelve fifty, hon."

Morgan passed her a ten and a five, accepting his change with a polite nod.

"You plan on settling here, or just passing through?" Her smile remained in place, but it looked forced. Her eyes flicked back to Joseph again.

"I'm still considering, darlin'." He turned up his smile to its full, substantial wattage. When her eyes found him again, his natural charm did its work. She relaxed, and her professional smile became a real one. "I'm here on business, but I gotta say the place is growing on me."

* * *

"That Susan's pretty good-looking," Joseph noted on their ride to the dump. Crumbs fell from a week's growth of beard. He'd left Grumpy's with a quarter of the burger in his to-go box and had finished it before they'd turned off of Main Street.

"She is a fine-looking woman," Morgan conceded, then fell silent, hoping to discourage Joseph from further conversation.

Joseph was not to be discouraged, though.

"You think she's about convinced?" He tossed the empty Grumpy's box on the floorboard between his feet, pounded his chest with a closed fist, and belched his appreciation for a fine meal. "'Cause I gotta be honest, you've been working on her a while and I've been holed up in that dump for too long. I'm missin' Florida more every day. I can't tell if you're conning her or courting her."

Morgan didn't like engaging in business discussions with people too stupid to understand them, but he knew Joseph wasn't going to let it go. Either he could answer a few questions as vaguely as possible or let the boy hound him for the next five minutes.

"I've got her on the line, son. Gotta give me some time to reel her in." He faced Joseph for a second, fixing him with the sternest look he could muster. It usually discouraged argument. "I don't know what you're complaining about, boy. You are probably the highest-paid sanitation worker in the State of Washington."

Joseph seemed set on having it all out, though.

"I'd rather be the highest-paid anything else."

"That may be so, but you're working for me, and you'll do what you're told." He was beginning to wish he'd left the boy to carouse in Miami. Anybody else would have been happy to just keep their mouth shut and do the job for the kind of money he was paying the boy. Joseph, however, seemed to think he deserved a higher place in their working relationship. If that was truly the case, he was in for nothing but disappointment.

"I'm not your slave, you know." Joseph pouted out the passenger window. His cheeks were burning red, his bottom lip pooched out like a little kid's. "If I wanna do something else, I will."

"If you think you can find a better offer, be my guest." He turned to regard his son, a sardonic twist of the lips replacing his usual smile. "I'll let you go your own way with no hard feelings."

For a few minutes silence reigned.

It was a relaxing silence, just the wind outside his big truck's window and the steady hum of his tires on the pavement as he drove toward the landfill. He could actually think now, consider his next move.

But it was never that easy when Joseph was in the passenger seat.

"That little red-haired girl in town," he remarked. "She's that Sinclair lady's girl, ain't she?"

Morgan didn't like the new turn of the conversation.

"That she is. Not that it's anything for you to worry about."

"Okay, here's what I don't get ...."

"Joey," Morgan barked, finally out of patience with the boy. "I suspect the list of things you *don't get* is long, but that's just fine. I don't pay you to *get* things. I pay you to do what I say!"

Another short silence followed, and Morgan dared to hope, again, that his son was finished.

"No need to have a fit, Pa. Just askin'."

A few minutes later Morgan pulled into the landfill and let Joseph out. A half-dozen cars and pickups were waiting behind the locked gate, a few of the drivers standing at the head of the line and sourly regarding the handwritten "closed for lunch" sign hanging from the gate. The looks they turned on Joseph were positively evil.

When this was over he might just convince old Ernest Price to keep Joseph on for a while, Morgan thought. Let the boy pay for his trip back to the East Coast himself. Maybe then the boy would appreciate just how good he had it.

Morgan made a tight U-turn, offering the glowering faces in line at the locked gate his best *Howdy Neighbor* smile, and drove away in a pleasant silence.

* * *

Morgan looked back on his last encounter with Susan Taylor, a sweet and delightful woman really, and smiled.

Plan A was indeed taking longer than he'd expected. Morgan had doubted Ernest Price when he'd said trying to deal with the Taylor woman was a waste of time. On behalf of his silent partner, Price had tried for almost a decade to persuade Susan Taylor to sell, and for almost a decade Susan had refused. Morgan's clients normally did not accept *no*, but for almost ten years they'd continued to play softball with the woman.

A delicate situation, they had called it, requiring a *lighter touch*, at least for the time being. They didn't want his hand visible in the Clover Hill purchase unless the situation in Dogwood became critical.

His clients were a secretive bunch, his only contact with them was through a strange intermediary, Mr. Turoc. Stranger in more ways than Morgan would have believed at the beginning of their professional relationship. He had assumed they were foreigners, though it was impossible to place Turoc's accent, and he had been right. With each job he completed for them, Turoc revealed a little more of himself, things Morgan would never have believed if he hadn't seen proof of them. Still, strange or not, Morgan was happy to continue working with them. They paid him well for his occasional services, usually in gold. They paid well enough in fact that, except for a few personal projects, he had worked for them pretty much exclusively for the last five years.

Everything else was on hold now, all personal ventures postponed or abandoned completely, because the Clover Hill situation was heating up rapidly. In the past few months Clover Hill had become critical. Something had happened to bring his clients' full attention to this little slice of Washington State, so Morgan was here now to do what he did best.

Take people's property away from them for fun and profit.

Of all the work he had done for them—securing one of the smaller Florida Keys, which they had graciously allowed him to use as a residence; a particularly harrowing piece of work in Uruguay;

the destruction of a protected ruin in Ireland—the business in Dogwood was the most puzzling. They'd certainly been more cautious than usual in their efforts to procure this property, allowing years to pass with no reward for their efforts, instructing him to work through that useless hayseed Ernest Price.

Well, not entirely useless. He had important local connections, family and friends in local government. Two years ago, Ernest Price had grown tired of Susan's obstinacy and used his connections to try to find leverage against her. Unpaid taxes, safety-code violations, anything his brother, Sheriff Avery Price, could use to force her out. Price had even considered planting marijuana on her land to justify a drug-related seizure, but Morgan had put a stop to that plan. It was far too risky; that would have meant dealing with the federal government and perhaps many years of legal red tape.

Price never found the leverage he was looking for, but he had discovered something that neither Morgan nor his clients had known. Price had contacted Morgan right away, and Morgan in turn had shared the new information with Mr. Turoc. It explained Susan Taylor's refusal to sell out, even at the grossly inflated price they had offered.

Clover Hill and the land around it didn't belong to Susan Taylor. The land he'd been after all those years belonged to her childhood friend, Diana Sinclair.

Turoc had been surprised but not as surprised as Morgan. He knew of the woman, knew her well enough to bypass the usual background investigation they did on their targets.

They'd made other arrangements.

In the course of making these plans, Morgan finally met Turoc face-to-face and learned definitively just how strange, and foreign, his clients were.

* * *

The shock of meeting his boss for the first time had nearly killed him.

Before, he had spoken with his contact over the phone, received audiocassettes with instructions, had on occasion even met with him through his hallway mirror—Morgan had assumed that Turoc and his associates had bugged it and replaced the glass with some high-tech video display. Not that he ever saw much more of Turoc than the suggestion of a face through heavy mist

Morgan wasn't even sure what Turoc's relationship with the others was; associate, consigliere, familiar? The last almost made him laugh. Almost. He was beginning to think anything was possible with this bunch.

Two weeks after his last report on Clover Hill, he'd dropped the bomb about Diana Sinclair and been told to cancel all plans and stay put at the estate on Macaw Island. Morgan had grown restless. He'd already turned Joseph loose. The boy loved Miami and would spend weeks at a time bouncing from club to club and motel to motel. He was about to begin the slow process of reaching his clients on his own when Turoc finally contacted him. He'd been enjoying his morning coffee in the estate's large sitting room when he'd heard Turoc's voice coming from the hallway mirror. He rushed to see what news there was.

"Stay there," Turoc said, and to Morgan's great surprise added, "I'm on my way."

The hazy outline of his head and one abnormally long, spindly arm vanished before Morgan could respond, so Morgan went back to his newspaper and coffee in the sitting room. He fully expected another week or two wait while Turoc made arrangements, then flew to Florida. What he did not expect was to see Turoc waiting for him in the sitting room. Not standing—Turoc didn't stand—but he was there.

Morgan had frozen midstep at the end of the hallway, numb with terror, wanting to turn the other way and run but unable to move his rubbery legs into action.

Turoc had grinned at him, then given a little nod of greeting. "Master Duke, it's a pleasure to finally meet you in the flesh."

There was no mistaking the voice or the strange manner of speech. It was his longtime silent partner, the hazy shadow in his mirror, the—not a man, necessarily—the thing that had kept him so profitably busy over the past decade. Morgan had always suspected Turoc was partially responsible for the success of many of his lucrative personal projects, though he could never detect his silent partner's hand in the deals. Morgan held a respect for Turoc so deep it was almost superstitious.

In those first moments of recognition, Morgan Duke wished he had never heard of Turoc. Better poor and living out of a suitcase and his father's old Studebaker bus than to have to acknowledge the monster in the sitting room.

Then his rubbery legs failed him, his vision began to fade, and he suspected that if he didn't break his neck in the fall he was about to take, he'd die of a heart attack.

He never finished falling though, and the expected heart attack did not come. Morgan simply existed for the next few minutes in a daze of semi-consciousness in which he watched the monster, Turoc, advance on him so quickly that he covered the length of the huge sitting room in barely a second, catching Morgan with those peculiarly long arms before he collapsed. Turoc carried him as effortlessly as if he were a stuffed doll instead of a nearly seven-foot-tall, three-hundred-pound man. He felt a stab of pain on his meaty left bicep, but it faded quickly.

When he'd recovered his senses, Morgan found himself sprawled on his sofa, his head propped on the decorative pillows and his feet dangling off the other end. Turoc's massive, terrible head hovered close by, regarding him with concern and, Morgan thought, a touch of amusement.

"I hope my visit doesn't find you averse to continuing our rather interesting working relationship." He grinned, exposing large, curved fangs. "I think you'll agree it has been beneficial for you, and I know it has been for me and my benefactors."

"You ... you bit me!" Morgan held up his left arm like an accusation. Twin punctures oozed blood through the long sleeve of his white shirt.

"Only a little." Turoc made a gesture that looked like it wanted to be a shrug. "You gave me little choice, dear friend. Your poor heart fairly quailed at the sight of me. I'm afraid you might have died if I hadn't acted."

"What?" Morgan tore open the cuff of the damaged sleeve and yanked it up his arm, revealing the bite marks. Remarkably, there was no pain, and even as he watched, the slow flow of blood stopped entirely and the holes began to heal. "What did you do to me?"

Turoc laughed heartily.

Morgan flinched away from him.

"Fear not, Master Duke. You won't turn into one of me. I like you very much the way you are. I also prefer you breathing however, and my venom can have certain beneficent qualities. I think you'll find your heart stronger than ever now." He backed away in his peculiar fashion, giving Morgan room to rise. "In fact I think you'll find your overall health better than it has been in many years."

With Turoc's retreat across the room, Morgan found the courage to move again. He sat up, and to his surprise he felt much better; stronger, lighter, more aware, his senses sharper. He stood and easily lifted his considerable bulk. Many of the aches and pains he'd accumulated over the years—and grown quite used to—were noticeable now only by their absence.

"I feel ...." Morgan regarded Turoc, took a cautious step toward him, stopped, took another. "I feel great."

"Excellent!" Turoc smiled at Morgan with benign curiosity. "The House of Fuilrix values you more than you know. It would be a great disappointment to lose your services."

For a moment Morgan was at a loss for words. In the last five minutes his entire understanding of reality had been heartily challenged, the limits of his imagination stretched past what he had assumed was their breaking point. He could feel himself tottering on the edge of panic, though he couldn't help but notice that his legs remained strong, his body upright. His heart beat in a strong, normal rhythm.

Morgan's pragmatic nature kicked it.

Really, had anything actually changed?

Turoc waited patiently for his reply, as always one of the most pleasant businessmen Morgan had ever worked with.

So, no, nothing had really changed. In fact, some things that had puzzled him over the years were beginning to make a little more sense. The secrecy, the trick mirror, gold instead of cash.

Morgan didn't know precisely what The House of Fuilrix was, but their messenger, Turoc, was not human. He belonged in this world no more than Morgan belonged on Venus. Space alien, mutant hybrid, extra-dimensional visitor, or non-of-the-above, Turoc could never exist openly in this world.

But he was still Turoc.

No, things had not changed, only clarified. Morgan retreated back to the couch and sat down.

"It's good to finally meet you, Mr. Turoc." He extended a hand, and only flinched a little when Turoc moved far too quickly across the room to shake with him. "I take it we have business to discuss?"

"Indeed."

The discussion was, thankfully, short. Morgan thought he'd be able to take Turoc easier in small doses.

"Take this." Turoc produced a tiny wooden box with a small clasp.

Morgan took the box, turned it over in his hands, opened it. Inside was a heart-shaped locket on a fine chain.

"Do not open the locket if you value your life."

Morgan regarded him, the unspoken question burning in his mind, and he almost asked. Then he decided he really didn't want to know what the locket held. He decided to take it on faith.

Mr. Turoc told him what he was to do with it.

"Keep it safe until you deliver it, and do not be near when she opens it."

Morgan regarded the locket again, then returned his attention to his silent partner.

"It would be best if she were alone when she opened it," Turoc said, keeping his strange eyes, large dusty-gold orbs with vertical slits for pupils, on Morgan's face. "Collateral damage can be so inconvenient."

Morgan's brain was beginning to wind back into action, forming a plan. He didn't know much about Diana Sinclair, but what he did know, he could use to their advantage.

"She's a frequent flier," Morgan said. "She travels between San Francisco and Los Angeles about once a week on a private company jet ... what?"

He'd seen the startled look, the suddenly tensed posture, and the widening of Turoc's eyes.

"She ... flies?"

Morgan had to stifle a momentary urge to laugh.

"In an airplane," he elaborated.

Turoc calmed at once. "Yes, of course. Continue."

Morgan explained his plan, a rough one to start, but a good one.

Turoc nodded. Evidently collateral damage was acceptable as long as it wasn't public. "I have every confidence, Master Duke. You haven't failed us yet."

"But," Morgan said, wanting to make the potential flaws clear, "what if she refuses it?"

Turoc grinned, and Morgan had to look down at his feet. Pleasant he might be, but when Turoc grinned it gave Morgan the willies.

"Tell her it is a gift from Tracy West. She *will* take it."

He spoke the last with such confidence that Morgan didn't doubt him. He was taking a lot on faith that day.

"I'll leave the details to you." Turoc moved to the center of the sitting room and, seemingly from nowhere, produced a short wooden rod, narrow, and about the length of a ruler. "How long until you've acted?"

"Give me two weeks to get set up in San Francisco, then another week or two to catch her at the right time." Morgan kept his eyes on the wooden rod in Turoc's long-fingered hand. The tip glowed slightly.

A magic wand?

Crazy, but not the craziest thing he'd seen that day.

Turoc nodded a final time, then brought the wand in his hand slashing down through the air, drawing a line of black light.

"I'll be in touch."

The line opened in midair, parted like cloth before Turoc, and he slipped through it and was gone. The opening closed, crackling slightly as the black light burned out.

* * *

Morgan's plan had worked perfectly. Three weeks after Morgan's first face-to-face with his partner, Joseph hand delivered the locket to Diana Sinclair as she rushed from her apartment building toward a waiting cab. Joseph made a rather convincing bicycle courier, Morgan thought. He looked and acted the part: smart enough to write down a street address and buckle a bike helmet on front ways, but not much more than that.

Morgan gave him his single line, and Joseph hadn't varied it by a syllable.

"Delivery for Diana Sinclair. Are you Miss Sinclair?"

When she'd been reluctant to take it, he'd delivered the zinger, and it had worked as well as Turoc had promised.

"A gift from Tracy West, Miss Sinclair."

Then she had taken it, her face pale with shock, her eyes wide and staring. Morgan, who had watched from a street-side comfort station not a block away, thought she looked as though she'd seen a ghost. She'd simply stood there for a moment, staring between Joseph—who had pleased Morgan that day by having the good sense to keep his mouth shut after delivering his lines—and the small, lacy gift box in her palm.

Then the taxi driver honked, and she rushed away.

She may or may not have waited until she was in flight to open the gift box, but she had waited until she was in the air to open the locket itself. Morgan didn't know what was inside the locket, but it had done precisely what Turoc had promised.

Her plane had gone down, and ownership of Clover Hill had transferred, just as they had planned.

But it hadn't transferred to Susan Taylor.

It had transferred to Diana Sinclair's daughter.

It seemed that his associate hadn't known about Miss Sinclair's daughter until very recently; or rather, they knew that she once had a daughter but thought the girl had died long before. They never expected her to become a player in this deal.

The arrival of Penny Sinclair finally prompted them to send Morgan in to wrap up the long-unfinished business personally.

They had not ordered similarly drastic measures regarding the daughter. When his curiosity—something he usually kept well in check in his dealings with Turoc—got the better of him and he asked about it, his partner had said simply that they could not have the girl's blood on their hands. Morgan didn't complain. He didn't want the kid's blood on his hands, either. He had done a lot of mean-spirited things over the years, all in the name of business of course, but he'd never hurt a kid.

So it was back to Plan A, try to charm Susan into making a deal, and if that failed, well, he wasn't throwing in the towel just yet. Just because she didn't technically own the land didn't mean she couldn't find a way to sell it out from under the Sinclair girl if he found her magic number.

While Ernest hadn't been much help with Morgan's main objective, he had come through very nicely on the second. A few pulled strings was all it took for him to get Joseph the landfill job. Turoc had been very candid about the need to keep people away from that old carnie trailer, whatever his reason was, and with some help from Ernest Price, Joseph had been able to do just that.

Despite his love of the game, Morgan Duke was looking forward to wrapping up this business. Sure he liked a challenge; he liked putting his spectacular creative problem-solving skills to profitable use. But he didn't like unfinished business.

Unfinished business was bad business.

PART 2

Night School

Chapter 8

Night School

Penny's favorite thing about school on Mondays was that they only came once a week. She tried *hard* to keep that in mind as she trudged through this one.

First and second hours slid by in their usual, slow fashion. Katie's mood was as bad as Penny had ever seen it when they met each other in second-hour Social Studies, but Katie seemed to be taking a little pleasure in her father's new role as *persona non grata* with the rest of the family. Though it had been just over a week since the scene at her birthday party, she showed no signs of forgiving her father.

On Susan's advice, Penny refrained from adding to Katie's abuse of Mr. West, but that didn't mean she couldn't enjoy it.

Third-hour math with Miss Riggs was, as always, her least favorite. While Miss Riggs didn't play any favorites or purposefully fail Penny, Susan's sister always seemed to keep at least one beady eye on her, as if hoping Penny would act out and give her a reason to kick her out of class. After the scene at Penny's party, she was even worse. She watched Penny from bell to bell, not even trying to hide her dislike.

"Doesn't she give you the creeps?" Ellen Kelly said from behind Penny after the bell rang and they rose to leave. "She looks like she wants to bite you."

"You have no idea," Penny whispered back, aware that Miss Riggs was still watching her over a stack of ungraded papers.

Fourth hour was always a welcome distraction from Miss Riggs's unwanted attention. English was her favorite subject, and Mr. Cole her favorite teacher. Mr. Cole was old, bald, and skinny, but easily the nicest teacher at Dogwood School.

Lunch at Sullivan's, Susan's store, followed, but it wasn't as much fun without Katie. Katie's father had strictly forbidden her from going into Susan's shop, so she was spending her lunches with Ellen and Chelsea in the school cafeteria.

Even with Katie missing from their company, life had definitely improved since last fall.

When Penny thought back to the start of that school year, the looks, the whispers, all the small-town speculation about *The New Girl*, the teasing from Rooster's gang, even the hostility from Katie, Penny had to admit things were much better now. She still wasn't a town girl, even though she'd been born there and her family had lived there since almost the dawn of time, it seemed, but acceptance was slowly coming, and she had a few good friends.

Of course, Zoe was in the same boat, but she tended to attract less trouble since most of the kids their age thought she could probably beat them up. Zoe had enjoyed a greatly enhanced reputation since Trey Miller's appearance at her birthday party. New kid or not, Trey was the epitome of cool to most of the boys in school, and his apparent interest in Zoe had done nothing to stifle the fawning of Dogwood's other girls.

Katie seemed to be as well-liked as ever, with the exception of what remained of her old clique, who usually ignored her. Tori, the richest and meanest of the bunch, mostly called the shots for all of them now, and according to Susan all the Main Street businesses were learning to keep an eye out when those girls paid them a visit.

Even the excitement of last fall's kidnappings and the dramatic rescue were becoming old news, barely worth repeating, and it had been weeks since Penny had heard anyone mention the Dogwood Witches.

Life in Dogwood would have been almost boring, if not for their little secret.

* * *

Though Katie was mostly absent during the day, she met them nightly at Aurora Hollow. In fact, she'd become rather manic about their nightly practices, as if determined to rebel against her father's prohibition in the only way she could. They didn't really do anything new that first week. Mostly they read and studied, which Penny guessed was necessary, but it was also almost as boring as regular schoolwork.

One night they studied the difference between *invocation*—magic that required spoken words, usually a simple appeal to an outside source—and *evocation*, magic that relied on inner talent, innate abilities and, of course, lots of practice.

That night started with Penny's least-favorite kind of assignment, a written essay. The page following the invocation/evocation lesson started blank when Penny opened to it, then quickly filled with text instructing them to explain the dangers of invocation and calling up unknown forces. After they finished, their essays faded away, leaving the pages blank again—there was nothing quite as frustrating as watching a newly completed piece of homework disappear from the page only seconds after completing it—and the book rewarded them with two pages on the differences between active and passive spells.

Watching the still-drying ink of their essays sink into a blank page of the book gave them something to think about, though, and Katie was the first to raise the question.

"If it can understand what we're writing, do you think it'll answer questions?"

"I dunno," Zoe said, yawning hugely. "I'm too tired to think of any."

Penny had a head full of questions, even after her last revealing chat with Ronan, but thought she should contain herself to the ones that were relevant to all three of them. But before she could think of one to ask, Katie picked up her pen and began to scribble on the first blank page.

Penny and Zoe leaned in over her shoulder for a look.

Can we ask you questions?

For a few seconds nothing happened. Katie's scribbles stained the previously crisp page, and Penny felt a rising disappointment.

"Maybe you should have used a pencil," Zoe said, then yawned again.

"No, look!" Katie pointed at the ink that had stood out sharply against the white page only a few seconds earlier. Now it had begun to fade, as if aging years before their eyes. A few seconds later it was gone, the page unblemished.

A reply rose to the surface and lingered for a moment before vanishing.

You can.

"Excellent," Katie said, gleefully regarding the newly blank page.

"Yeah," Zoe said, attempting to rub a little liveliness back into her sleepy eyes with the heels of her palms. "Very nice."

Katie either didn't notice Zoe's less-than-enthusiastic reply or was ignoring it.

Zoe had all but fallen asleep the night before, and looked worse tonight. When Penny had asked about it at school she'd admitted she wasn't getting much sleep. Between regular homework, late-night practice sessions at the hollow, and an early-morning alarm to wake her grandma up for medicine, she thought she was averaging four hours of sleep a night.

Penny suggested she take a few nights off and immediately wished she hadn't. The look Zoe shot at her was almost frightening.

"No! What if something cool happens? I don't want to miss anything!"

The way it had been going, she could sleep through their nighttime sessions and not miss anything cool.

This was at least different.

Katie didn't waste a second but scribbled a second question.

Will you tell us how to make more wands?

Again, the fresh ink shone wetly in the firelight, then faded and vanished, but there was no reply.

Instead, the pages began to flutter, though there was no breeze in the hollow to move them, then turn rapidly. They stopped about a quarter of the way through the book, and the blank page facing them filled with writing. It was the same runic language they had seen every time they touched a blank page with their wands to receive a new lesson, but unlike before, the characters didn't dance and rearrange themselves into English.

Zoe began to laugh, and Katie shot her an irritated look.

"Sorry," Zoe said, and she did look it. She also looked ready to burst into fresh gales at the slightest provocation, loopy from sleep deprivation. "I'm just too tired to be upset."

"Why aren't they changing, though?" Katie demanded. "We can't read that!"

This puzzled Penny too, but the answer, something she'd gleaned from the first page she'd read on passive magic, clicked in her brain: "Where in active magic, the practitioner introduces a new element or energy to *actively change* their environment, passive magic is subtler, working within the existing environment to assist natural processes ...."

Penny reached between Zoe and Katie with her right arm extended and touched the page with the tip of her wand.

"... or bring intended order from apparent disorder."

Instantly, the letters began their familiar dance, and a moment later the instructions lay before them in easy-to-read English.

Zoe giggled.

Katie crossed her arms over her chest and looked annoyed.

"Let's call it a night," Penny suggested, deciding that now would be a good time for Katie and Zoe to separate. "It's late and we're all tired."

"Awesome idea," Zoe said, yawning for a third time.

"Yeah, sure," Katie said, though not as enthusiastically as Zoe.

Zoe stumbled to the door, pulled the black wand from her waistband, and opened the doorway to her bedroom. "You coming, Penny?"

"Naw, I'll catch a ride with Kat." She'd been hoping for a chance to talk to Katie alone, and this was as good a time as any.

"'K," Zoe mumbled. "G'nite."

A moment later she was through the door.

"Kat, there's something I need to tell you."

Katie regarded her dubiously for a moment, then seated herself next to the fire pit. "Okay."

"Last week I found an old photo album in my basement ...."

Penny kept it short, telling her about the old snapshots she'd found in the back of the album, some with her aunt in them, then about Ronan's revelations later in the day.

Katie nodded, even smiled a little, though it was clear that her stores of energy were running low, but she didn't seem surprised.

"I was wondering about that," Katie said. "Your family lived here and Aunt Tracy was their friend."

The book was shut away in its chest, hidden in the hole in the old ash's trunk, but Katie held the wand in her lap and regarded it for a moment.

"That's all, really. I just thought you had a right to know before we told Zoe."

Katie looked troubled. "Ronan said that things 'ended badly' last time. Did he tell you what happened?"

Penny had thought she might ask about that, and had prepared a response that was not a lie but slightly less than the whole truth.

"My mom was in a car wreck and my ... father," Penny still had trouble speaking about him; she didn't know anything about him and could only guess the worst from how everyone else in her life loathed the man. "My father left, and the rest of them just kind of went their own ways, I guess."

"But Dad says that our aunts," and now Katie was struggling with her words, and Penny could see a bright blush blooming in her cheeks by the firelight. "Well, he says our aunts ran off, uh, together."

Penny shrugged. "Big deal, they were friends, weren't they?"

Katie rolled her eyes. "You know. *Together.*"

For a moment Penny remained puzzled, then she got it.

"Ohhh!"

Katie plunged on quickly. Apparently Penny wasn't the only one with news she'd wanted to share. "Yeah. I mean, that's what he *says*. I don't know if it's true or not, but that's why he's still pissed. He didn't approve."

Well then maybe he's the reason she never came back, Penny almost said, but bit her tongue. She still had Susan's caution about not trashing Katie's father firmly in mind. She did have her doubts, though, and she wouldn't be sharing them with Katie.

Ronan had mentioned a traitor, someone inside the circle who had betrayed them, and though he'd refused to tell her who it was, she hadn't been able to keep herself from speculating.

They were not happy speculations.

Not Susan, he had said as much. Penny deliberately turned her mind from the obvious choice, the one that meshed too neatly with her other suspicions, and focused on her favorite choice, the mystery girl Janet. Penny didn't even know her last name yet. She seemed to have simply vanished fourteen years before, along with her aunt Nancy and Katie's aunt Tracy.

Until she learned more she wasn't telling Katie or Zoe that part of Ronan's story.

Great, she thought. *As if I didn't have enough to worry about.*

She hadn't finished researching her own family's past: she had to find out if her mother and father actually had been married, and the tattoo nagged at her. Now she would have to search for the elusive Janet, and her and Katie's aunts as well.

Not for the first time, an inner voice cautioned her.

You know there's probably a reason Ronan isn't telling you any of that stuff. Probably a very good reason.

As always, Penny tried to push that voice to the back of her brain and ignore it.

While she was silently distracted by these unhappy thoughts Katie had risen and approached the door.

"Hey, Penny, we should go." Her manic energy seemed to have burnt itself out for the night. She looked as tired as Penny suddenly felt. "It's getting late."

"Yeah," Penny said, bringing her attention to the present once more. "How about we go to my room first and you can take the wand home tonight."

Katie nodded, smiling. "Maybe tomorrow I'll be able to make my own."

* * *

But it wasn't as simple as Katie had hoped. According to the book, you couldn't just pick up any old stick and do magic with it. They put the next night's lessons on hold while Katie puzzled over the instructions, and after a quarter of an hour Zoe sat tottering on the edge of sleep next to the fire, and Penny had to jab her to wake her up.

"You two fill me in tomorrow. I've got to get some ... some ...," her mouth stretched in a huge yawn, " ... some sleep."

Katie threw a distracted wave in Zoe's direction. "Yeah. G'nite."

Penny amused herself conjuring handfuls of her harmless fire and tossing them into the air while Katie's back was turned and her nose almost pressed to the page of the book. The flames died a few seconds after leaving her hands but left bright streaks that lingered in the air.

"Penny, what are you doing?" Katie shut the book in irritation. "You're making it impossible to read."

"You've read it a dozen times already, Kat," Penny said, but threw the fireball she was holding into the crackling flames of the fire pit before Katie could see it. "It didn't look that complicated to me."

"Well, good for you," Katie snapped. "You do it then."

"Sorry, Kat," Penny said. "I just don't know what you're worried about."

Katie kept her back turned and her arms folded, tapping the wand against her arm in her irritation.

"Just try it," Penny encouraged and, though she knew from experience the answers to the next question were almost infinite, added, "what could go wrong?"

Katie chose not to answer this but ceased her distracting tapping. "Fine."

Katie held the wand over her head and closed her eyes in concentration, breathing deeply to steady herself. When she opened them again, a point of light flickered at the wand tip.

Penny watched as it flared and swelled, then rose into the air. It illuminated the hollow more brightly than the fire but burned out after a few seconds.

Penny thought this new trick would be useful, if they could make the light last a little longer.

"See," Penny said, even though she knew the tricky part was still to come. "You've got it."

Katie did seem a little calmer as she approached the ash. She stopped a few feet from it and searched the trunk up and down until she found the spot she wanted, a tiny knothole a few feet above her head. She pressed the tip of the wand into the hole, and Penny saw light spilling from it as Katie made the light come again. This time however she held her focus until the light spilling out around the tip of the wand grew almost blinding.

Penny shielded her eyes and Katie squinted to cut the glare, but didn't look away.

The long seconds turned into a minute, then two, as Katie focused on the pure energy she was pouring into the big tree. Then, at last, the tree itself began to spill light from every crack and crevice.

"You're doing it!" Penny nearly shouted in amazement.

Katie never even heard her. She was watching the tree's upper limbs, waiting for the energy she was pouring into the ash to find the easiest way out. Whichever limb the pent up energy exited through
....

Then brightness pierced the darkness over their heads, and Penny looked up to find Katie's light shining through the tips of a half-dozen upper limbs. As if pruned from the tree, the glowing limbs fell, raining down into the clearing around them. When the last of them hit the ground, the light shining from the ash faded, and Penny turned her happy grin on Katie.

But Katie was no longer standing at the base of the ash with the twisted old wand. She was collapsed on the ground between two bulging roots, her forehead smudged with dirt where it had struck the earth.

She had fainted.

Around them, the harvested ash wood continued to glow for a few moments, then the light faded from them, too.

* * *

Zoe was furious the next morning.

"Why did you let me go home?" Zoe shoved her ugly old bike into the school's bike rack between Penny's and Katie's. "Something cool finally happens and I sleep through it!"

At least she seemed well rested this morning.

"Hush," Penny said, casting her glance around for potential eavesdroppers. "Stop yelling."

"Don't worry," Katie said, clicking the lock on her bike chain. "Next time *you* can do it."

Zoe's frown lingered for a moment, then quivered a little around the edges. "You ate dirt, huh?"

"Totally," Katie said. She lifted her hair away from her temple and showed her bruise. "I told my mom I fell out of bed."

"You should have seen it." Penny locked her bike next to Zoe's.

The flow of foot traffic past them was easing as first bell approached.

"So, what now?" Zoe led them down the path to the entrance, looking over her shoulder at them. Katie kept an easy pace, but Penny had to quicken her stride to keep up.

"We'll start working on them tonight," Penny said. "Later."

Inside, she went to her homeroom, Katie following Zoe down another hallway toward theirs.

By lunchtime, Penny was ready for the day to be over. The intensity of Miss Riggs's scrutiny seemed to have lessened, but the cumulative effect of all the unwanted attention was enough to shatter Penny's already shaky concentration. Every time she tried to focus on her work, she could feel the teacher's beady eyes boring through the top of her head.

"TGIF," Zoe said as they crossed the street toward their usual lunch destination. She stopped a half-block shy of Sullivan's, and Penny walked straight into her back.

"Who's that," Zoe said, as though she hadn't noticed the collision.

Penny glanced around and saw the object of Zoe's attention. She also understood Zoe's unease. The guy made her want to walk the other way, too.

Leaning against Susan's storefront, next to the open front door, was the creepiest man Penny had ever seen: tall and gangly, with a belly that drooped beneath the hem of a dirty T-shirt; a long, greasy head of hair with a teacup-sized bald spot in the back; a scraggly beard; and tiny dark eyes that seemed to watch them keenly.

He smiled, folded his arms across his chest, and looked away.

"Come on," Penny said in a low voice, angry that she'd let him spook her so suddenly and completely. Penny led Zoe the rest of the way, keeping her eyes determinately on the Golden Arts sign hanging on the next door. Before they reached the door, however, another man stepped out of Sullivan's and spoke.

"Joseph, quit loitering out here and find something to do." The man was middle-aged and plump, his bald head deeply tanned. Penny stopped this time, and Zoe walked into her. The man looked tidy and professional in his crisp, spotless black suit, like a banker or lawyer. "Go on down to the café now and get some lunch, son. I'll meet you there."

The man had a slight Southern accent rather at odds with his appearance. Penny had expected a British accent or maybe a yawning Massachusetts drawl.

Joseph nodded once at his father and eyed the girls again before he pushed away from the wall and strode off in the other direction, toward Grumpy's, the restaurant favored by Zoe's grandma and her troupe of blue-haired town elders.

"Well, hello, girls." The man's eyes twinkled down at them.

Penny was momentarily stymied by his unexpected friendliness. "Uh ... hello, sir."

"Susan said you'd be coming along soon." He moved aside and waved them in, looking more like a doorman than a customer. "I'm afraid I've monopolized her time this morning, but you'll have her all to yourselves in a few more minutes."

Penny looked at Zoe, and Zoe looked at her, eyebrows raised.

"After you."

Penny passed beneath the bald man's indulgent smile and into Sullivan's, and Zoe followed.

"Hi, girls." Jenny stood behind the register, ringing up the first in a short line of midday customers. She waved at them before returning her attention to a man with a stack of invoice books.

They found their usual seats on the reading-corner couch, but it took them a moment to realize that the expected supply of lunchtime pastries was missing.

"Looks like we'll have to fend for ourselves today," Zoe said.

Penny thought she could survive without their daily doughnuts. Susan always fretted that she should be feeding them something a little healthier than dough and sugar anyway, but she was curious about the bald man who had so completely distracted Susan from her normal midday errands. Also, she wasn't sure that Susan could survive without her usual maple bar.

They watched the man as he moved—with a speed and grace that was a little surprising for someone his size—down the main aisle and around displays and customers toward the back rooms of the shop. He lingered at the *Of Regional Interest* shelf on the back wall and flipped through a large *Grays Harbor County* photo book with apparent lively interest.

A few moments later, Susan emerged from the back room with two steaming mugs of coffee and an ear-to-ear grin.

"Oh, my," Zoe said as the bald man greeted Susan and relieved her of the cups. "Does Susan have a new boyfriend?"

"I guess she does," Penny said, glancing toward the register counter to catch Jenny's eye.

Jenny was seeing her current customer off when she noticed Penny. Seeming to guess at Penny's unspoken question, she glanced at the large man chatting with Susan, then back to Penny. She gave a slight shrug, as if to answer Penny's unspoken question: *Yeah, he's a bit old for her, but she seems to like him.*

The big man in the banker's suit seemed to be the 'boyfriend' that Jenny had alluded to at Penny's birthday party and Susan had admitted to the next morning.

"She has the love look in her eyes." Zoe winked, then giggled when Penny elbowed her in the side.

Susan led her new friend to the front of the shop and waved at the girls when she saw them.

"Hi, Little Red ..., Zoe." She took a seat next to Penny, and the bald man sank into the comfy old chair by her end of the couch, setting the cups down on the magazine table in front of them. "Girls, this is Morgan Duke. Morgan, this is Penny and Zoe."

"I've already had the pleasure," Morgan said, giving a little bow in Penny and Zoe's direction. He picked up one of the cups and gulped the steaming coffee, sighing in apparent satisfaction. "This is fine, Susan. Hits the spot for sure."

Susan blushed, taking a sip from her cup. She swallowed quickly and wiped her lips with the back of her free hand. Penny had never seen her quite so fidgety.

"I'll take you over to the bakery tomorrow," Susan said, waving vaguely toward the sidewalk. "They make a mean espresso."

"It's a date, then," Morgan said enthusiastically. He drained the rest of his cup and turned to regard Penny and Zoe. "Been a real treat, young ladies."

Morgan Duke placed his cup back on the table and rose from his chair. To Penny he looked like a benevolent giant.

Susan almost jumped to her feet.

"And you," Morgan said, taking her small hand in his large ones and bowing to give it a quick peck. "I'm looking forward to drinking a mean espresso with you tomorrow. We can discuss my proposal in more detail."

Proposal?

Penny could only blink in surprise.

Next to her, Zoe was nearly shaking with suppressed laughter.

Susan laughed. "I've already given you my answer."

"I know," he said, sounding theatrically regretful. "But at least trying to change your mind gives me a good excuse to spend time with you."

He flashed them one last cheesy grin and joined the foot traffic headed for lunch at Grumpy's.

"Proposal?" Penny jumped from her seat to face Susan. "Is there something you're not telling me?"

Susan laughed. "Don't be silly, it's business. He wants to buy Clover Hill for development."

"*What?*" Penny and Zoe shouted together.

"He thinks Dogwood could be a great tourist town and says Clover Hill is a prime location for a resort. I told him I wasn't interested, but he's determined to change my mind."

Penny guessed that Susan hadn't yet told him the whole story about Clover Hill's ownership. The land, the house, even Aurora Hollow, belonged to Penny, held in trust by Susan.

"So is he your boyfriend or what?" Zoe almost shouted, overcome by her curiosity.

"I'm not sure," Susan said, sending a perplexed grin down the sidewalk after Morgan Duke's retreating form. "I'll let you know as soon as I know. Hang tight and I'll get your lunch."

Susan returned a few minutes later with ....

"Sandwiches?" Penny felt her taste buds rise in silent protest.

"I warned you," Susan said, handing them each a ham and cheese in plastic wrap.

"Thanks, Susan," Zoe said, unwrapping hers and taking an enthusiastic bite.

"Better eat on the go," Susan said, regarding her own sandwich with a little less than Zoe's enthusiasm. "You'll be late."

Zoe's sandwich was gone before they left the sidewalk, and, despite her less-than-eager first bite, Penny's was gone before they reached the school.

"Do you think you'll make it tonight?" Penny had an idea Zoe wasn't going to be missing any nights at the hollow soon, but all the early mornings with her grandma had taken a toll.

"*Yes*," Zoe said, a little fiercely, and Penny thought that she still hadn't completely forgiven them for letting her go home early the night before. "*Don't* start without me."

Chapter 9

How to Fly

They met in the hollow that night and stripped the thin layer of bark from the half-dozen narrow limbs the ash had given them the night before, and Penny recounted the previous night's adventures for Zoe.

"Maybe you should have started with a smaller tree," Zoe suggested, and added quickly, before Katie could take offence, "You did excellent … we won't have to fight over wands anymore … but I don't want you to get hurt."

Katie rubbed the bruise on her temple and shrugged. "It's nothing. Besides, the ash just felt right."

Penny secretly agreed, it seemed different, special. It didn't belong here, but here it was, old and strong.

"You're more awake tonight," Penny said, and Zoe shot her an irritable sidelong glance as she set a newly stripped ash branch aside and picked up another.

"I made myself drink two cups of coffee tonight." Zoe made a face. "I don't know how you stand that stuff."

"It's an acquired taste," Penny said, remembering her time at the group home and how she'd had to gag down cup after cup of the instant stuff the staff kept in their lounge to make it through lessons after her first sleepless nights there. "Try it with cream and sugar next time."

"I'll bring some Red Bull tomorrow." Katie finished her last branch and turned to the wand-making instructions in the book while Penny and Zoe caught up. "Now we have to soak them in the creek for a few days. Hey, Red, did you bring the rocks?"

"Huh?" Zoe looked up from her own work to regard them with interest.

"They're in my room," Penny said, pulling the last narrow strip of gray skin from her last stick. She dropped it next to the others, and a second later Zoe's joined them.

"Well, what are you waiting for?" Zoe pulled the black wand from her waistband and practically bounced to the door. It opened into Penny's room before Penny caught up. Zoe followed her through and immediately spotted four glass jars on the table next to the guest bed. She grabbed two of them, regarding the contents with manic eyes, and was back through the wardrobe door into the hollow before Penny had crossed the room.

The caffeine was clearly having the desired effect.

Penny grabbed the remaining jars, cradling them in her arm, and pulled the photo album from beneath her pillow. There was still a bit of catching up to do with Zoe. Might as well bring the evidence. She thought Katie would like to see the photos, too.

Penny stepped back through and found Katie unrolling a nylon stocking while Zoe twisted the lid off the jar clamped between her knees. The second rested between her feet.

"What are you doing with that?"

A second later Katie answered Penny's question by gathering the stripped ash shoots in her free hand and sliding them into the unrolled stocking.

"It's the closest thing to a net that I have," she said, tying a knot in the stocking, then selecting a large rock from the creek's edge. She pushed the stocking below the water and weighed the loose end down with the rock.

"Quartz, smoky quartz, amethyst, citrine, prasiolite, quartz." Zoe plucked stone after stone from the jar, identifying each and setting them aside. Her jaw dropped, and her eyes went even wider for a moment. "Ruthenium!"

She held up a small, narrow crystal that shone like silver in the firelight.

"There!" Katie said. She rose with a smile of accomplishment on her face, then laughed out loud at Zoe's bug-eyed excitement. "No more coffee for her!"

Zoe ignored her. "I've only ever seen that in books!"

"You can have it," Penny said, barely holding back her laughter as Zoe clutched the small crystal to her chest.

They sifted through the jars for the next half-hour, setting aside anything that looked like it might fit the ends of the half-dozen new wands. When Zoe's excitement seemed to ebb a little, Penny decided it was time to bring out the photo album.

Katie flipped through the brief photographic history of Penny's family and stopped at the page that showed her family—mother, father, and aunt. She spent an especially long time staring at the face of her younger father, and Penny thought she might be softening toward him a bit.

Zoe scanned the photos from over Katie's shoulder while Penny filled her in.

"Someone stole their memories?" Zoe turned to regard Penny with something like disgust, then looked back at the photos. "Did Ronan tell you who?"

"No," Penny said. She wasn't sharing the last revelation, that a traitor had helped to break the last circle, until she knew who it was. Maybe not even then.

Katie turned the page, and Penny saw the overlarge, spectacled brown eyes of the mystery girl, Janet.

"Hey, I've seen her before," Zoe said, bending low over Katie's shoulder to examine the picture more closely.

"You have?" Penny regarded Zoe, stunned into speechlessness for a moment, then her brain kicked into gear again. "Who is she?"

Katie had dragged her attention away from the still images to stare at Zoe.

"I don't know," Zoe said, and, seeing Penny's frustration, elaborated. "My grandma has a picture of her with her family photos. I've never met her."

"Well ... can you find out?" Penny couldn't believe she hadn't thought of it before. After all, Dogwood was a small town.

"Yeah. I'll ask her tomorrow," Zoe said. "She was one of ...."

Penny pointed to the end of a wand protruding from the bag slung over the mystery girl's shoulder.

Katie absorbed the images, but her eyes became dreamy, unfocused. "The lady I saw when we made the circle said it was a bond only death or treachery could break. So which of them was it?"

Zoe's eyes snapped to Penny's face, scrutinizing, and Penny felt warmth in her cheeks as she flushed. "The lady in the trees. She told me the same thing."

"The lady I saw was in the water." Katie faced Penny. Now they were both watching her expectantly. "Yours was in the fire, right?"

Penny nodded.

"So, which was it?"

Penny sighed.

"One of them betrayed the others the night I was born. I don't know who. Ronan wouldn't tell me." And because she was sharing everything she knew now, told them the rest ... the part she felt least like sharing. "The *others*, that's what Ronan calls them, they came here to break up the Phoenix Girls. Ronan said the others befriended them, then turned one of them against the rest.

"Last year, Susan told me about the Reds, a family of performers who used to come to Dogwood with the fair, and she told me that the last time they came to town things ended badly."

"You think the Reds are the others?" Katie said, trying to move the story along.

"Yes," Penny said, and she pointed out a snapshot of her mother and father. "And I think my father was one of them."

Katie regarded her with a mixture of shock and sympathy. Zoe, however, seemed unsurprised. "No wonder Susan hates him so much."

Neither spoke the obvious. If Penny's father was one of *them*, then her own mother might very well be the traitor.

* * *

The next day Penny found herself alone in the hollow, Katie still grounded and banned, Zoe stuck at home to watch her sickly grandmother and, they hoped, getting some information about the mystery girl. Unable to do anything with the new wands until the required time in the creek had passed and unwilling to restart lessons without the others, Penny decided to try something she'd wondered about for a long time.

She tapped the book with the tip of her wand, then set the wand aside as the book sprang open in her lap. She thumbed through it until the first blank page presented itself, then wrote.

Will you tell me how to fly?

She retrieved her wand while the book shuffled its pages, and ran the tip of it over the page of indecipherable text that presented itself.

She read the translation with growing excitement.

Ten minutes later, her wand stuffed into her waistband, Penny dashed through the door, out of her wardrobe, and hurried down the steps of her attic bedroom. The house was deserted, Susan at work, and no guests expected. She ran downstairs and through the front door to her bike on the porch. She wondered if she shouldn't take it up into the deserted field but decided there was no point. She probably wouldn't get off the ground anyway.

If she did, however, it would be something very cool to share with Zoe and Katie that night.

Penny rolled her bike down the steps and into the overgrown lawn, mounted it, and took a deep breath to steady herself.

She'd expected something like the levitation spell; she'd levitated herself once but hadn't been able to do anything but bob around in the air.

Flying was a little more complicated.

It was not the person who flew, but an object.

After reading that, Penny had considered books she'd read, modern fantasy and old accounts of witchcraft. The object was always a broom, a rug, something common, something that every household had at least one of. Something big enough to sit on and innocent enough to hide in plain sight.

She pulled her wand out and realized she was about to perform, or attempt to perform, her first invocative magic.

"Animus de aerus, suo mihi obvius opus es supero efficio."

She felt a wind from the east, weak and insignificant. It died quickly.

"Animus de aerus, suo mihi obvius opus es supero efficio," she said again, careful to pronounce each unknown word exactly as the book had shown her.

A sudden, strong gust nearly toppled her from her bike, would have if the tips of her toes had not been touching the ground.

She spoke the phrase a third time, and a heavy, sustained wind blew in from the east, sending stray weeds, wheat stalks, and a large round tumbleweed flying past her. The porch swing thumped forcibly against the house. The tall grass rippled violently around her ankles, and the wild field beyond the gravel driveway moved like a green ocean. After a few seconds, the wind died down, except around Penny herself. Around her, it intensified and began to spin, centering her in the eye of a small but strong whirlwind. Her hair blew around her head, in her eyes, and across her mouth.

It was time for the second phrase, and Penny couldn't remember it.

She felt her toes and the tires of her bike skid through the grass as the whirlwind tried both to unseat her and to lift her from the ground.

What's the next line?

"Animus de ...."

She felt herself slide again, almost lost balance.

"*Animus de aerus, tribuo ventus ut sic besom ….*"

Her hair flew straight up over her head, and she could see again, but her feet no longer touched the ground. She looked down and was stunned to find herself rising into the air. Buffeted by the wind, Penny's bike began to spin, and her with it.

"*Et vinculum eius volo!*"

The wind died as suddenly as it had come and Penny fell, still whirling, back to earth. The bike's tires struck the ground and bounced her from the seat. Her wand spun from her hand, and she hit the ground hard, the bike landing beside her.

For a few seconds Penny couldn't breathe. Her lungs felt flattened, emptied. When they opened again, Penny filled them with a grateful, gasping breath.

She lay in the grass for a few moments, not moving, enjoying the ability to breathe again, then rose slowly, pushing herself up, moving each part of herself individually to make sure nothing was broken. When she was sure she could, she stood, found her wand, and lifted her bike back onto its wheels. The bike seemed all in one piece, too, nothing bent or broken, so she sat on it.

Time to see if it had worked.

Her bike seemed as normal as ever.

She took her handlebars, the right in an awkward grip because of the wand still in her hand, and began to pedal. Across the lawn, into the driveway, kicking up gravel and dust as she pumped the pedals harder. She hit the stonier, uneven ground of the wild field, wobbled, and almost lost her grip on the right handlebar, then leaned back.

Go up, she thought.

And the bike went up, its tires an inch, six inches, a foot, then five feet above the ground. She saw the bare upper boughs of a scrawny bush racing toward her and leaned hard to the left. The bike followed her lead and turned sharply, looping around and pointing her back the way she'd come.

She was flying!

Then she saw the lone figure standing near the top of her driveway, her own bike firmly on the ground at her side, and almost fell back to earth.

Of all the days to get an unexpected visitor.

It was Ellen Kelly.

"Uh-ohh," Penny said

Ellen stared open-mouthed at Penny as she guided her bike back down to solid ground, thumping down so hard she almost unseated herself again, then backed off a few steps as Penny rolled to a stop in front of her. For a moment, Penny thought she'd jump back on her bike and pedal for all she was worth. She could almost hear Ronan's angry reprisals.

I told you this wasn't a game, Little Red!

"Hi," Penny said, a bit breathlessly.

"Uh ...," Ellen's eyes moved from Penny to the bike, then to the wand in Penny's right hand. "Uh ... hi ...."

Penny tucked her wand into her back pocket, out of Ellen's sight, as nonchalantly as she could manage.

"Penny?" Ellen's eyes settled on her face again, and Penny was relieved to see no fear in them. Only wonder. "How did you do that?"

"Kinda like to know that m'self, Little Red," Ronan said.

Penny's and Ellen's eyes turned in unison and spotted him trotting toward them from under the porch.

Ellen screamed, of course.

Ronan continued toward them unconcerned. He was used to it.

Ellen was in motion, backing another step away from Ronan's approach, and Penny reached out and grabbed her arm.

"It's okay," Penny soothed. "He won't hurt you. He's nice."

Probably kill me though, Penny thought.

"I've been called a lot of things in my life, Little Red," Ronan said, turning his full, intense attention on Penny. "*Nice* has never been one of them."

"It talks," Ellen said, her voice barely more than a squeak.

"Indeed it does," Ronan said. "And apparently she flies."

Ronan turned his attention back to Penny. His irritation seemed to be waning.

"And if you can see me, young lady," Ronan said, turning his attention to Ellen and making her flinch, "then you can, too."

A few minutes later Ellen sat on the porch swing, Penny having coaxed her closer to the house rather than letting her pedal as far away as she could. She sipped from a glass of water Penny had brought her and kept a wary eye on Ronan. Ronan stood well away, giving her the space she apparently needed, but also kept turning his gaze to her. He seemed to be sizing her up.

Penny made herself as unobtrusive as possible, sitting on the porch steps. She didn't think she'd be able to stop Ellen from simply vaulting the railing and speeding away if she decided to, but Penny hoped curiosity would win out over fear.

Ellen took another sip of the water, then unexpectedly poured the rest of it over her upturned face. Eyes squeezed shut, she shook the excess water from her hair, then opened her eyes again and faced Penny.

"Thanks. I guess I know I'm not dreaming this now. So unless I'm completely losing my mind, what I saw actually happened?" She looked at Ronan, as if asking for confirmation.

He neither confirmed nor denied what she'd seen, only settled himself on the porch and continued to watch her.

"It was real," Penny said. She tried to gauge Ellen's acceptance by her expression, but she kept her face unhelpfully neutral. "I'll tell you about it if you want, but you have to promise me something."

Ellen's face finally registered a new emotion—uncertainty.

"What do you want me to promise?"

"I want you to not tell anyone, and I want you to try to keep an open mind." Penny grinned at her, as if to suggest that she wasn't asking much.

Ellen sighed. "I won't tell anyone. I just came over to see if you wanted to hang out. I won't blab."

Penny relaxed a little and saw Ronan do the same.

"And as for keeping an open mind ...," Ellen returned Penny's grin with a slightly manic one of her own, "I'm still not convinced I didn't imagine the whole thing, but I'm not convinced I did, either."

"We can work with uncertainty," Ronan said unexpectedly. "Where do you propose we begin, Penny?"

Penny knew exactly where to begin.

"The hollow," Penny said, and Ronan nodded.

"Are we going somewhere?" Excitement and fear fought for control of Ellen's face as she gave Penny's bike a sidelong glance.

"We are," Penny said, trying not to laugh at Ellen's panicked expression, "but we can get there without flying."

She rose and walked past Ellen to the front door, Ronan following at her heels. Ellen followed her inside, on to the second floor, and up the ladder into her bedroom. Ellen's skepticism remained as Penny pulled out her wand and touched the wardrobe door with it.

"Go ahead," Penny said. "Open it."

"Oookay." Confusion overshadowed doubt as Ellen reached for the lever, pushed it down to unlatch the door, and pulled it open.

A light breeze stirred the coats and shirts, and the muffled babble of running water unexpectedly filled the room. A bird chirped from inside the wardrobe.

Ronan leapt past them and through the door.

Penny pushed aside the scant clothing blocking her way into Aurora Hollow and followed him.

After a brief hesitation, Ellen did the same, bending low to avoid the hanger rod.

She stepped through to the other side, and was convinced.

* * *

A few hours later Penny watched Ellen pedal out of sight down her driveway, Ronan following at a discreet distance. Probably to see if she'd keep her promise not to blab, Penny thought. With Susan still at work and the house to herself for a few more hours, Penny decided to spend some time with the photo album. There was still half a day to consider how she was going to break the news to Zoe and Katie that she'd been seen, flying no less, by one of their classmates.

She tried to convince herself they would be ecstatic, excited to have Ellen in on the secret … one of them. But it had been just the three of them for so long, and Penny knew from experience that the longer you kept a secret, the harder it was to share.

Her mother had taught her about secrets, and Ronan seemed determined to continue those lessons.

Penny sat on her bed, pillow behind her back, leaning against the headboard. Her fingers traced the embossed words on the cover of the album–*Book of Memories*–before she finally opened it. She turned to her mother's page and drank in the images. Her mother as a toddler. Another of her at roughly Penny's age. A third of her as a young woman. Then the empty sleeve, the white space that left her mother's page incomplete.

Penny slid the drawer of her bedside table open and reached inside, fumbling over the odd assortment of stuff that had found its way there over the past year, until she found what she was looking for. She pulled out the old, creased photo of her mother and father together, smiling, happy, and slid it into the empty sleeve, where she was sure it was meant to be.

She saw them all together, a short life-story in four parts, with a ghostly reflection of her own face transposed over the shiny plastic.

Suddenly she wanted more from these still images, needed more. Needed to see herself in them, with her parents, like any other girl.

Penny set the album aside and reached beneath her bed, dragging out the dusty old silver-framed mirror, the Conjuring Glass that had caused so much trouble in the Birdman's hands the previous autumn. She lifted it onto her bed and sat cross-legged before it, taking a few seconds to decide which picture she wanted.

She chose the old one, sliding it back out and placing it on the glass so she could see her face reflected next to the smaller, grainier images of her mother and father.

She blinked back tears.

"Wish I could have been there. Wish I could have known you."

The Conjuring Glass shimmered like a pool of disturbed water, and the old photograph sank beneath its surface. A moment later it was gone.

"No!" Penny shouted. She grabbed the Conjuring Glass by its silver frame, then watched in wonder as it changed. There was no swirl of fog, no confusing jumble of images as it attempted to connect to one of the little mirrors linked to it. Penny's face was gone from the mirror, and the glass *became* the photograph.

Or very nearly.

It became the backdrop, a sunny summer day in the town park, the wide Chehalis River flowing lazily in the background. And the river *was* moving. A tree almost out of frame shivered in the breeze. Then Penny heard voices.

"Don't be silly. It won't steal your soul." It was a woman's voice, strange yet familiar. The young woman's joy and enthusiasm, two things she had never heard in her mother's voice, made it strange, but it was Diana's voice.

She backed into the frame laughing, bent forward and dragging someone with her. "Come on, Torin! I warned you this was coming."

Feeble protests in a pleasant, deep male voice followed. "Stop, Di, you know I don't like being photographed."

But protesting or not, he was also laughing, and Penny knew he would give her anything she wanted.

"Stop your whining, Big Red. It's for the baby!"

Penny could see from her mother's profile that she was pregnant. Not far along, but there was a perceptible bulge pushing at the light summer blouse when she straightened up, at last dragging the tall red-headed man into frame.

Mere mention of the baby—*me*, Penny thought—killed all resistance. He stepped into frame, and for the few seconds it took for him to look away from Diana's upturned, smiling face, Penny saw such tenderness in his face that it made her feel like crying.

He kissed her forehead, then the inside of her left wrist, directly over the vivid red tattoo Penny had never seen in this picture before. She could see it more clearly now, a triangle of intersecting knots. Torin straightened and stood beside her.

Her clothes were light, bright. A loose white blouse and a long skirt that flowed past her knees and rippled in the breeze. He wore a dark shirt, snug, and blue jeans so new the creases were still apparent. She wore open sandals; he wore black boots.

He faced the camera, his expression grim, as if bracing for a blow.

"Okay, Susan," he said, apparently speaking to someone off-camera, "let's get this over with."

Diana threw a sharp elbow into his side, and his grunt of pain became laughter.

"Will you two hold still?" Susan's voice was much clearer, much louder, and Penny had to resist the urge to spin around, almost expecting to find her perched on the headboard like the young bird Ronan had called her. She sounded amused rather than impatient, but Diana and Torin ended their mock struggle and faced the camera, clasping hands. This time his smile was almost as wide as hers, and where her old picture had been creased, worn, and grainy, the image in the glass was as sharp as reality, real as the present.

It was the same face that the Birdman had worn the previous autumn.

Penny heard a click, saw a bright flash of white that filled the glass, obscuring them for a moment, and then Susan advanced on them, camera in hand. A second later another figure joined them, identical to her mother except for her clothes—blue shorts and a black tank top—and her expression—not angry, but unhappy.

"Come on. Tracy's waiting for us."

Nancy spoke directly to her sister, did not even acknowledge Torin, then grabbed Diana by the hand and dragged her away.

Torin stood with Susan for a moment, exchanged a bemused look, then followed the sisters out of frame.

My father's name is Torin, Penny thought. *Diana and Torin, sittin' in a tree* ....

She realized how true Susan's memory of the differences between them had been; they were identical, except for the tattoo, but as different as day and night. She wished she'd known her mother before her joy had died and she had become more like ….

A wild idea hit Penny with such force and certainty that it momentarily robbed her of breath.

She remembered seeing that tattoo for the first time in another photograph in the album that lay open at her feet. She remembered thinking *my mother never had a tattoo.*

What she was considering was so out there that it should have sounded crazy, even in the safe, private echo chamber of her spinning head. To prove how crazy it was, Penny spoke the thought aloud.

"It was my aunt Nancy who never had a tattoo."

The Conjuring Glass cleared; the old photograph was again where Penny had placed it. Penny saw her own face reflected at her, mouth open, skin so pale it was almost gray, heavy scattering of freckles brighter now by comparison. Her eyes were the worst. They were puffy and red, wet with tears she hadn't realized she was still shedding, wide and slightly wild with sudden knowledge, for once a true window into her soul.

Chapter 10

The First Magic

"You okay, Penny? You look sick!" Katie drew back as if afraid her friend was contagious.

Penny had stepped through the door and into the hollow a few minutes past the usual meeting time, to find the fire already lit and Katie pacing before it.

"Thanks, Kat. You always say the sweetest things!" Penny was too tired, too frustrated, and too overwhelmed to hide her irritation. The fact that Katie was right didn't help. If she looked anywhere near as bad as she felt, then Katie's appraisal was probably an understatement.

Katie gave her *the look*, and Penny instantly regretted her prickliness.

"I'm sorry. I fell asleep and almost didn't wake up in time." She yawned hugely, as if to prove her point. "I'm just tired."

"It's okay," Katie said, and though she didn't sound okay, the look was gone. She appeared more sympathetic than angry. "I crashed pretty hard today, too. We've been putting in a lot of late nights."

They waited in silence, Penny occasionally throwing more wood onto the fire to keep it from dying while they waited for Zoe. Penny was again forced to decide how to explain the new complication with Ellen, and couldn't really think of an approach that would make her feel less stupid.

Flying around on her bike in broad daylight. It was a wonder no one else had seen.

"One short tonight, ladies?"

They turned and found Ronan sitting only a few feet away, regarding them with keener than usual interest. Penny knew what he was waiting for, and her stomach felt suddenly heavy with renewed dread.

"Ronan," Katie said, almost shouted. "If you don't quit sneaking up on me like that I'm going to put a bell around your neck!"

"You're welcome to try, young lady," Ronan said, unperturbed. He winked at them, and Penny felt her tension loosen a little.

Katie rolled her eyes and faced the other direction.

At last the door opened, and Zoe stepped into the hollow.

"I'm sorry!" Zoe stumbled as she swung the door closed, dropped the black wand as she caught herself, then kicked it almost to the creek's edge when she bent to pick it up. "I forgot to set my alarm. I just woke up."

She gave up trying to recover her wand and sat down by the fire, head hanging, a long curtain of black hair covering her face. There was no coffee to prop her up, and Penny was afraid they might have to carry her back to her bedroom before it was over.

"No problem," Katie said, retrieving the black wand but not handing it back to Zoe. Penny thought that was probably a good idea. "There's a lot of that going around tonight."

"Excellent," Ronan said. "I believe Penny has something she would like to share, now that everyone is present."

Penny wondered if the local pet store stocked muzzles to go with the bell Katie kept threatening him with.

All eyes were on her now: Ronan's expectant, his usual foxy grin a little more on the mischievous side than was typical; Katie's surprised, curious; Zoe's bleary, barely focused.

Where to start? The part where I can fly, or the part where I was caught flying?

Or maybe the part where I realized that my mother and aunt pulled the old twin-swicharoo on everyone, that Aunt Nancy pretended to be my mother, Diana, right up until the day she died in that plane crash.

So then where is your mom, Little Red?

Maybe gone off to look for Big Red.

Who knew? Maybe Ronan did, but if he hadn't told her yet he wasn't likely to.

Probably thinks it's too much for my little brain to handle.

She felt a sudden flair of anger toward him.

"Earth to Penny," Katie said, snapping her fingers in front of Penny's face, making her flinch. "We need you down here, little red one."

Penny felt her anger turn toward her friend and had to struggle to keep her hands at her side. They wanted to leap out at Katie—hit her, push her, replace the irritation on her face with one of fear. She felt warmth flood her body, felt the tiny hairs on the back of her neck rise, and knew she could conjure fire with nothing more than a thought. She would get her wish then, to see fear in Katie's eyes.

Her anger ebbed at once.

"Penny," Zoe reached for her and Penny stepped back.

Even Ronan seemed uneasy now, tensed as if to spring among them.

Penny sighed and sat down.

"I learned how to fly," she said, and whoops of excitement broke the tense silence that had grown between them.

"Are you serious?" Katie shouted, no doubt startling every wild thing from here to town into hiding.

"Very cool," Zoe said, jumping to her feet and gawking at her. She was wide awake now, no coffee needed.

"Excellent!" Katie rushed Penny, almost knocking her down in her enthusiasm, and picked her up in a rib-straining hug.

As soon as her feet hit the ground again Zoe picked her up and twirled her, making her feel like a red-headed rag doll. Also making her feel even worse about what she still hadn't told them.

"Now you can teach us!"

"Whoa," Penny retreated as Katie and Zoe showed every sign of wanting to lift her onto their shoulders and march her around in celebration. "Sit down ... please!"

Zoe and Katie sat but were unable to sit still. They fidgeted and bounced, and Penny knew she'd have to speak quickly before they lost their thin thread of control.

"Someone saw me," Penny blurted, getting it out as quickly as she could and bracing for the worst possible reaction.

When the worst didn't happen, Penny dared to look up again.

Their manic joy had departed, but the anticipated anger at her stupidity was not in their faces. Both watched Ronan and seemed comforted by his calm acceptance.

"Well," Katie said cautiously to Ronan, "you're taking it better than I expected."

"You already knew," Zoe said to Ronan, and when she turned back to Penny her face registered excitement again. "If he's not furious then I guess we're not in trouble."

"So ... who was it?" Katie looked like she was reserving judgment until she knew the whole story.

"If I may offer a suggestion," Ronan said, and found himself at the center of attention again. "Why tell them when you can show them? She's waiting, and she did keep her word."

Penny agreed. She moved to the door on wobbly legs, pulled her wand, touched the door. Then she knocked and stepped back.

A few seconds passed, and tension grew thick inside the hollow.

Zoe and Katie watched the door without blinking, without even breathing, it seemed to Penny.

Then the door opened, and Ellen stepped through, looking more nervous than Penny felt.

"Hi, guys," Ellen said, then noticed Ronan as he leapt to his favorite low limb on the old ash. "Hi, Ronan." She regarded them individually, but briefly, before turning her gaze to the tips of her shoes. Penny didn't think she'd ever seen Ellen this reserved. "So, you're ... uh ... like her?"

She nodded in Penny's direction before facing her feet again.

Then, almost fearfully, "Don't worry, I won't tell anyone."

Penny turned to Zoe and Katie, her eyebrows raised with the unasked question, the one they would all have to say yes to.

Katie's response was immediate, a smile and a nod.

Zoe's took longer. She watched Ellen for a long moment, frowning in concentration. Penny thought she was trying to imagine Little Miss Congeniality fighting off monsters like the Birdman. Whether or not she could, Zoe finally shrugged, then nodded.

"It's agreed then?" Ronan stood above them all, looking more pleased than Penny had seen him for months. Penny knew for Ronan there had never been any doubt. He'd accepted her as easily as he had Katie.

Ellen looked up at his words, her anxiety returning. "What's agreed?"

She took a step backward toward the door, giving the wand in Penny's hand a mistrusting look.

By way of explanation, Penny held the wand out to her handle first.

Ellen put her hands safely behind her back and shook her head. "No … I can't …."

"Can't what?" Zoe asked, raising a sardonic eyebrow. "Can't do this?"

Zoe took the wand from Penny and shot a fireball into the guttering fire. The flames swelled and leapt upward, painting Ellen's startled face with bright light.

"Or this," Zoe said, plucking a stone from the dirt and throwing it into the air. She aimed her wand at it, and it stopped in midair. With a flourish, she pointed the wand at the granite cliff face on the other side of the creek, and the stone flew like a bullet toward it, smashing itself to dust with a loud crack.

"Or maybe this," she said, now grinning mischievously as she pressed the palm of her left hand against one of the willow trees ringing the hollow. The tree seemed to shiver itself to life, and several slender and leafy whips snaked down from the canopy of green above them. They reached playfully for Ellen as she darted and dodged them.

"I can't do *that*," Katie said, sounding impressed.

Zoe withdrew her hand from the tree's truck, and the whips returned to their places in the braided green canopy. Then she advanced on Ellen.

"Zoe, stop." If she was trying to prove a point, Penny thought she was going too far.

Ellen backed away another step, then stopped and stood her ground, her normally open, friendly face contracting into something like anger. "No, I can't, but that doesn't mean I'll let you push me around!"

"That's all I wanted to know," Zoe said, and reversed her grip on the wand, offering it to Ellen. "The only reason you can't do any of those things is because you haven't tried yet."

Zoe's initial indecision seemed to be gone now. She looked eager for Ellen to take the wand from her, and Penny thought she knew why. Ellen had stood up for herself, held her ground and faced Zoe, with no friends behind her and without a wand of her own.

"Just take it," Katie urged. "You won't believe it until you see for yourself."

"You're like us," Penny said. "If you weren't, you wouldn't be on a first-name basis with Ronan."

Ellen turned doubtful eyes on Penny, but took the offered wand from Zoe's hand.

Ellen's eyes widened as her fingers closed around the handle. A low crackle of energy seemed to jump from her hand and into the weathered wood, and the tip flashed once, brightly, before conjuring a wind that filled the hollow, stirring dust and fallen leaves into a vortex then spun with her at its center.

The wand dropped from her hand, landed between her feet, and the wind died at once.

For nearly a minute no one spoke.

Katie watched Ellen closely, almost rude in her interest.

Zoe had a smug smile, its full force aimed at Ellen.

Ronan was curled up and resting on his limb, looking almost smugger than Zoe.

Ellen's hands had returned behind her back. She didn't bend to pick up the dropped wand, but her eyes never left it, either.

Penny guessed it was up to her.

"We belong to a ...," Penny couldn't seem to find the right word for what they belong to.

"A coven," Katie offered helpfully.

"An ancient and sacred order," Zoe stated grandly, but spoiled the effect by bursting into a fit of the giggles.

"Whatever it is we belong to," Penny said, firing Zoe a look designed to convey the seriousness of what she was trying to say, though she couldn't help the smile that surfaced on her own face, "we would like you to join us."

Zoe folded her arms and regarded Ellen with a look that said, *Of course you want to join us.*

Katie smiled and nodded enthusiastically.

"But you need to understand the risks before you decide."

Penny took a seat by the fire pit and motioned for Ellen to do the same.

When Zoe and Katie were seated as well, Penny began to speak.

They took turns, picking up the narrative from one another.

They told Ellen their story.

* * *

The night ended on a hopeful, almost jovial note. Penny forgot for the night that she was angry with their benefactor, and telling and rehearsing all they had been through reminded her of how much she treasured Zoe and Katie. Indeed, all three girls seemed to have gotten past their sleep-deprived grumpiness. The mood in the hollow was friendlier than it had been in weeks. And as their story came to a close with Penny telling about the making of the circle, even Ellen's initial anxiety seemed to have gone.

She relaxed and smiled encouragement as they passed off the story from one to the next, and when the story was finished, Penny thought Ellen had to restrain herself from clapping. She didn't seem to have any doubts left. She'd seen too much that day, felt the possibilities when she'd held the wand for herself.

"Can I have some time to think about it?"

"Time to think about it?" Zoe repeated this as if it were the most ridiculous request she'd ever heard.

"This isn't like joining the cheerleading squad," Ellen said. "And that was more of a commitment than I wanted to make when they asked me."

Katie nodded and said, "We won't push you into it. You know we want you to join … you've already passed the tryouts."

"What is the cheerleading squad," Ronan asked, as if hearing about a potential rival for the first time.

"Popular girls in uniform skirts," Zoe said dismissively. "Waving their pom-poms at boys with padded shoulders."

Ellen nodded her agreement with Zoe's assessment, and Ronan seemed satisfied.

"You *should* take some time," Penny said. "You already know we tend to attract trouble."

"That's not entirely accurate, Little Red," Ronan said. He stood on his high perch above the girls and stretched before leaping down to join them. "Trouble was already coming. This town was lucky you girls were here to meet it."

"I don't know where I'd be right now if you two hadn't saved me that night." Katie sounded uncharacteristically grave. She faced Ellen. "You were at Tovar's show, too. For all we know you might have been the next to vanish."

"When trouble comes again," Ronan said, walking right up to Ellen, who for a wonder didn't try to shrink away from him. All four girls were listening eagerly. "Four ready wands would certainly be better than three. And it *is* coming."

He sprinted for the creek, leapfrogging from the ash's arching roots to the stone ledge on the other side. He disappeared into his cave.

"He's an odd thing, isn't he?" Ellen said, smiling.

"You have no idea," Katie said.

A moment later he emerged with something in his mouth. He leapt the rushing waters of Little Canyon Creek again and stopped at Ellen's feet, dropping a small mirror.

Ellen recognized it immediately and bent to pick it up. "I had one of these, but it disappeared last winter."

Turning safely away from Ellen, Ronan winked at the others. Penny wondered how many homes he'd had to burgle to find them all.

"Keep it with you," Ronan said. "If you need us, whisper one of our names into it. If we need you, we'll do the same."

Penny, Zoe and Katie each held up their own.

Ellen nodded in apparent appreciation. "Like a cell phone without time limits?"

A minute later Ellen stepped through the door and back into her own dark room. She paused just beyond the threshold, turned back to study the others, then shook her head in wonder. She closed the door.

"So," Zoe said, turning back to Penny with an air of getting back to some important and almost forgotten business. "When do our flying lessons start?"

* * *

Back in bed now, just starting to drift off, Penny heard someone whisper her name from her bedside table. She yawned, stretched to turn on her lamp, and found Ellen's face looking at her from the mirror.

"Sorry ... I couldn't sleep."

"It's okay," Penny said, hiding another jaw-stretching yawn behind a hand before picking the mirror up and lying down with it. "Have you decided?"

"No," Ellen said, and Penny thought it pained her to say the word. Penny thought she understood Ellen a little better now than she had earlier that day. Ellen was popular without being a joiner, unconditionally friendly and outgoing to almost everyone. She strived for harmony, even within the chaos of emotion and uncertainty of a teenage girl's life. She didn't like conflict, and she sensed the coming conflict as well as they did.

"No, you're not joining us, or no, you haven't decided?" Penny forced a smile to show that whatever her answer, Penny was okay with it.

Ellen hesitated.

"It's okay to say no to something you don't want, Ellen. If you can't get comfortable with the word *No*, then you'll spend your life always trying to please everyone else and you'll never be happy."

Ellen seemed on the verge of saying something, then closed her mouth.

"It's also okay to say *Yes* to something you want, even if it opens you up to risk." *Listen to me*, Penny thought. *I sound like Yoda.* "Every day you get out of bed is a risk, and sometimes trouble finds you whether you want it or not. That's when you need friends … good friends."

Ellen was silent, seeming to consider Penny's words.

"Whether you say yes or no, we are your friends."

"When you first came here … you and Zoe, no one accepted you. Even Kat was mean to you, but it seemed like it didn't matter to you."

Penny could have corrected her. Of course it had mattered. Those first few months at Dogwood School had been horrible.

"You two had each other even before all that magic stuff."

Penny waited. She sensed the point of Ellen's late-night call was close.

"I've always had a lot of friends, but no one has ever been that important to me." She turned her face away from Penny's. "I've never been that important to anyone."

"Is that why you've been coming around?" Penny asked the question without thinking and instantly wished she hadn't.

Ellen blushed a little, then shrugged.

Penny opened her mouth to say something, anything to ease her embarrassment, and another yawn took control of it.

"I should let you go to bed," Ellen said, and Penny felt her retreating from the subject. She was relieved. The ability to make intelligent, or even intelligible, conversation was quickly deserting her.

"Come by anytime you want."

"Okay," Ellen said, finally looking Penny in the face again. She smiled, then faded from the mirror.

Penny fumbled the mirror back on her nightstand, and sleep took her.

* * *

Late night or not, Penny awoke at just after six the next morning. A quarter-hour of fruitless flopping in bed later, she kicked her sheets aside and rose, grumpily admitting defeat. She knew what was keeping her awake; she'd dreamt about it for the few hours of sleep she'd managed that early morning and could think of nothing else now that she was awake. She briefly considered taking a quick shower and changing into real clothes, but decided she didn't have the patience. It wouldn't matter to the people in the mirror anyway. They were all from a distant past when she didn't yet exist. She could see them just as easily in her pajamas and with her hair in a tangle.

She leaned over the edge of her bed and slid the mirror out from under it. Sitting cross-legged on her unmade bed, she pulled the old photo album from under her pillow and rifled through it. There were so many to choose from that she had trouble picking one to start. She settled at last on the picture of her pregnant mother with her stern, serious aunt.

Penny pulled the photo from its sleeve. "Hi, Mom. Hi, Aunt Nancy."

She placed the photo in the center of the Conjuring Glass, and waited.

Nothing happened.

Penny picked it up, turned it over to see if there was something stuck to the back, something coming between the photo and the mirror, then placed it carefully in the center again.

Again, nothing.

"Why won't you work?" She closed her eyes and focused on her first encounter with the strange mirror's previously unknown ability. "What am I doing wrong?"

She tried to recall as clearly as she could her actions and emotions the last time, if she had spoken to the photographs or the mirror, and the sense of her previous sadness came flooding back into her. Wanting to see herself, her face, in the same frame as her mother and father. Wanting to see what they might look like together if things hadn't gone so badly wrong the night she was born.

Blinking back tears even though no one else had been there to see them.

She felt a blush of embarrassment. She hated to cry, and she had been crying a lot lately.

Penny recalled blinking back tears and wishing she could have known them.

She had wished.

Penny wished again, and the past came alive for her.

Penny watched as small moments in her mother's and aunt's lives played out in front of her. There were no great revelations that morning, but the smaller revelations, the proofs that her family had once lived, were just as important to her.

When the larger revelations came she would share them, and the newly discovered ability of the Conjuring Glass, with the others, but these moments were just for her.

* * *

Penny didn't realize how much time had passed until she heard a knock on the inside of her wardrobe door and snapped her head toward it. Out of the corner of her eyes she saw the numbers on her nightstand clock. It was almost ten o'clock.

The knock came again, and when Penny didn't hasten to answer, the door began to inch open.

Penny slid to the edge of her bed and threw the top sheet over the moving images in the mirror—she was on her fifth photograph now, having watched the previous four several times each before moving to the next.

Her feet hit the floor as Zoe's face appeared through the partially open door, and she manufactured a yawn, as if she'd only just awakened.

Penny didn't understand why she wanted to keep the photographs' stories secret, if even just for now, but the desire was strong and she couldn't deny it.

"Zoe," she scolded, though she was obviously not convincing. Zoe only grinned at her, unabashed. "Call first, okay."

"I have been," Zoe protested. "You weren't answering."

Penny did a quick about-face to the nightstand, where her mirror lay only inches from the glowing digits of her alarm clock.

The time had flown by fast while she'd been lost in her mother's past. Apparently her awareness had flown with it.

"You did?"

"Course I did. I don't just barge in like some people I could name." Zoe's grin wilted slowly as she regarded Penny more closely. "Have you been crying?"

"No," Penny protested lamely, wiping at the corner of her eyes for any telltale signs. They were there, of course. "I have allergies."

Zoe looked unconvinced but let it drop.

"Must have been sleeping hard," Zoe said, throwing the door wide open and stepping through.

In the background, Penny saw Katie on her knees at the creek's edge, bent low over the flowing water, her arm immersed to the elbow and searching for her makeshift net with their ash sticks.

"I thought Kat was still grounded," Penny said, surreptitiously shoving the old photo album back beneath her pillows when Zoe turned to regard Katie.

"Oh, yeah ... she's still grounded." Zoe put a hand over her mouth to stifle laughter. "Her dad's out of town today and Michael talked her mom into letting her out."

"I'd like to have a big brother like that," Penny said, a little enviously.

Zoe went slightly redder in the cheeks and turned away.

"And what about you," Penny said, rising at last. "Aren't you supposed to be a full-time nurse now?"

Zoe was not amused by this. The tone of her reply was crisper than usual. "Grandma's at church. Then lunch with *The Elders*." Zoe had adopted Susan's pet name for the troupe of old town women with obvious delight. "Then Bingo at the Senior Center."

"So you're free for most of the day." Penny somehow thought Zoe getting almost a full day away from her grandma would be a cause for celebration, but Zoe wasn't showing it.

"Yep," she said, then in an obvious effort to change the subject, continued: "Come on, let's go already! We have stuff to do today!"

"Stuff?" Penny stood confused for a moment. She didn't remember any specific *stuff* planned for the day. *She* had planned on spending time in her basement, searching for more treasures like the photo album.

"You know ...," Zoe glared meaningfully at her, her eyes flicking for a second to the trapdoor in her floor and the folding ladder that led to the second floor, where Susan might even now be getting ready for the day. She whispered, though with such force it didn't make much difference. "We're making new wands today, and you're going to teach us how to fly."

"Oh ... that!"

Zoe shook her head. "You're such a scatterbrain sometimes."

She stepped back into the wardrobe and turned around when she was standing in the hollow again. "Hurry up."

"Okay ... okay!"

Zoe pulled the door most of the way closed again to give Penny some privacy, stopping just short of latching it. Penny took quick advantage of it to change into something a little more rugged than her pajamas.

No time for a shower that morning. Apparently they were having a busy day.

* * *

Penny changed and swept a brush through her tangle of hair, then crept downstairs to leave a note for Susan next to the coffee pot, which she regarded longingly before creeping back upstairs. She stepped through the door into Aurora Hollow five minutes later.

Katie had laid the half-dozen ash sticks on a large rock near the fire pit, next to the assortment of crystals they'd selected. A small toolbox was open in her lap.

She met Penny's questioning look with a wide, wicked grin.

"My dad's," she said. "If he knew I had it, he'd be so pissed."

She paused for a second, perhaps to take some undiluted joy in the knowledge, then opened the box and pulled out an assortment of drill bits.

"She's crazed," Zoe said matter-of-factly. "I'm just going to stand back and watch."

"Oh no, you aren't!" Katie fixed Zoe with a look that reminded Penny of Aunt Nancy. "You get to match which crystal will fit which wand best."

Then she turned to Penny, "And you get to sand them smooth so we don't get slivers."

She pulled out a package of sandpaper and flung it at Penny like a Frisbee.

Penny impressed herself by catching it as it spun toward her head, then tore the cellophane off and selected a sheet of the finest grain she could find.

Zoe's seemed by far the easiest task of the three, but Penny wasn't going to complain. Compared to Katie's slow, tedious chore, sanding the already smooth ash sticks to a velvety texture was quick work. Penny and Zoe had finished completely before Katie finished her first.

"Done!" Katie sounded manic with triumph as she fit a light blue crystal, which Zoe had identified as tourmaline, into the hole she'd painstakingly hand-drilled. The fit was nearly perfect; she'd chosen the size of the drill bit to match the crystal, and, when she'd pushed it in all the way, no more than a centimeter of the crystal's tip was visible.

Penny and Zoe waited in growing anticipation.

"What now?" Penny found the expectation a much-needed distraction from her private concerns of the past few weeks.

"The First Magic seals the crystal to the wand." Katie held the wand close to her face, scrutinizing Penny's work, testing the smoothness with her hands, flexing the wood slightly to feel its strength.

"Does it matter what the first magic is?" Zoe was almost trembling with anticipation.

Katie tore her loving gaze from her new wand and regarded them. "It's called The First Magic. It's when a wand takes its first breath."

"She's speaking in metaphors now," Zoe whispered to Penny, then hushed when Katie's eyes narrowed in her direction.

"Go on," Penny said.

Katie nodded, and now her excitement seemed to be turning to nerves.

Penny could tell that Katie had no more idea what to expect than she did.

Katie pointed her new wand skyward, and something began to happen almost at once. Light spilled from between the fingers clenched around the wand's handle, coursing up toward the tip; and the crystal began to glow bright blue. Then the light faded, the glow around the wood dimmed, but the crystal glowed more brightly still, until it was almost too bright to look at. Then, with a bang like gunfire, the blue light expanded in a bubble that filled the hollow, engulfing them all, and just as quickly vanished.

But for several seconds, everything in Aurora Hollow glowed: the trees, the rocks, the flowing water, the girls.

They regarded each other with varying expressions, Penny with near panic, Zoe with wide-eyed and grinning wonder, Katie with clear pride.

"I think it worked."

Chapter 11

The Snake in the Grass

Katie finished a second wand with a deep-orange topaz while Penny searched the old book for the spell that had gotten her and her bicycle airborne the day before. She finally located it, a single page filled with writing, surrounded by dozens of blank pages. Most of the pages in the old book were still blank. Still a lot to learn.

Bright light filled the hollow again, drawing Penny's attention away from the book. She waited for the final echo of The First Magic spell to die out and the bright topaz glow around the hollow to dim.

"I bet that's beautiful at night," Zoe said, then joined Penny in regarding the page before them. She read, bending low over the page when she reached the invocation. "What does that mean?"

"I don't know," Penny said. "I don't speak ... whatever that is."

Zoe passed the tip of her wand over the two lines, but they resolutely refused to change to something she could understand.

"I don't think saying it in English would work," Penny said.

"But we have no idea what it says," Zoe said. "Doesn't that bother you?"

"No," Penny said in perfect honesty. "We've been following this book's instructions for months and it hasn't hurt us."

Zoe remained dubious.

"Kind of looks like Latin," Katie said, joining them to show off her handiwork. "This one's for Ellen."

She passed the wand to Zoe, who nodded in evident appreciation and gave it a little wave through the air. A faint orange trail followed the topaz tip, lingering for only a second. Zoe pointed it at a sapling that stood at the hollow's perimeter, dwarfed by its nearest neighbors. The little tree shuddered, then grew half a foot before their eyes, twisting its way upward through the air and sprouting new branches along its narrow trunk.

She passed it into Penny's waiting hand, then regarded her old one, the black wand they'd taken from Tovar, with something like disappointment.

When the wand touched her hand, Penny knew why. The long, shiny black wood with the tiny jewel point felt different than the old bent wand she used, or the new ones Katie was making. Penny knew which she preferred.

"We can make yours next," Penny said, then pointed the topaz wand at the fire pit and lit a fire. It worked well ... perhaps too well.

Katie flinched from the inferno but refused to let it out of her sight until it had died down.

"Latin," Zoe said, attempting to get back on topic. "Are you sure?"

"No," Katie said, taking the wand from Penny and admiring it one last time before placing it in the chest with their incomplete wands. "I said it *looks* like Latin. Maybe it is and maybe it isn't."

"How do you know what Latin looks like?" Penny didn't doubt her but was curious. She didn't think they taught Latin at middle-school level, even to advanced students like Katie.

"My dad's a lawyer," Katie reminded Penny. "Half the books in his library have Latin in them."

"Well, I guess we should go get our bikes," Zoe said, her desire to get airborne clearly winning out over her apprehension to recite the indecipherable invocation.

Katie nodded and dashed to the door, using her new wand with obvious relish, then stepped back into her bedroom.

"I'll see you guys a bit later," Penny told Zoe, starting for the steep trail to the field above them. "I told Susan I was going out for a walk so she'll be expecting me to walk back."

"See you," Zoe said, stepping through the door to her room.

It took only one trip up the steep old trail for Penny to decide that she preferred traveling to and from the hollow by magic rather than the old way. The door was much more dignified than slipping and falling in the dirt. Much less sweaty, too.

* * *

Penny found Ronan crouched in the grass at the edge of the downward slope to her house, watching intently.

"Hey," she said, keeping her voice low. Susan probably already thought she was weird enough without hearing her talk to invisible animals. "What's so interesting down there?"

Ronan did not turn, did not move so much as an inch.

"Ronan?"

"Quiet," he said. His voice was only slightly louder than a whisper, but the anger in it was evident. "Get down here … hide yourself in the grass. Don't let them see you."

Penny lowered herself and crept to his side.

She could see the house below them, a strange truck parked in front. New and shiny black. No one she knew in town owned a truck like that.

"Who's …," and before she could even finish asking the question, she saw the truck's owner.

He sat next to Susan on the cozy porch swing. Though they sat at opposite ends, maintaining a prim distance between them, the man leaned toward her as they spoke, as if pulled by gravity. For a moment they seemed frozen in place, facing each other, then Susan leaned toward him and their lips met in a short kiss.

The large bald man who had been charming Susan in her store over the past few weeks, Susan's "kind of boyfriend," was now charming her at home.

"What do you know of that man?" Ronan growled as he spoke, and Penny felt her arms ripple with goose bumps. After the initial shock of their first meeting, Penny had never feared Ronan. Now he was scaring her a little.

Penny thought hard to remember the details of her single meeting with him.

"He's a developer … someone who buys land and then builds things on it."

Ronan turned his eye from the pair on the porch to Penny.

"Why?"

"To make money," Penny said. "He tried to buy Clover Hill but Susan wouldn't sell. Now I think he just wants to date her."

She didn't add that she thought Susan already had a large crush on the man. Ronan didn't need to know *that*.

"They aren't from around here," Penny added when Ronan's gaze didn't budge from her face. "I think they come from somewhere in the South."

Ronan's eyes were the exact orange as the topaz Katie used for the last wand, Penny realized, and she wished he would point them somewhere else.

"His son is here, too." Penny suppressed a shiver at the memory. "He's creepy."

"What else?" Ronan's unwavering gaze was unnerving.

"What else do you want?" Penny tried to inject the proper irritation into her voice, something to mask the unease Ronan was causing her. "I only met them once."

Ronan seemed to realize he was bothering her and returned his glare to the man on Susan's porch.

"His name is ... Duke," Penny recalled. "Morgan Duke."

"He works for *them*," Ronan said flatly. "He's a snake in the grass, blending in until the opportune time to strike."

Penny didn't need to ask which *them* Ronan was referring too.

"Snake in the grass?"

"Too archaic for you, Little Red?" A fraction of his usual good humor had returned. "How about spy, saboteur, a foul and malevolent trickster."

"I liked 'snake in the grass' better," Penny said.

"Where were you going?"

"To get my bike. I was going to meet Kat and Zoe back at the hollow."

"Flying lessons?" Ronan actually smiled for a moment. "Go on then, and meet us back at the hollow."

A second later Penny was alone. Ronan had slipped away silently and completely. She steeled herself, then rose and jogged down the hill, trying to hold on to the cover story she'd made up for Susan with all the new and crazy thoughts competing for space in her head.

Morgan saw Penny coming before Susan did and hoisted himself from the swing to greet her like a favorite niece or neighbor kid.

"The charming Miss Sinclair has returned from her morning commune with nature." He chuckled when Penny only gaped at him. "It's a rare child who chooses the great outdoors over idle hours gawking at a television in this day and age."

Penny wasn't sure, but thought he was trying to compliment her.

"Uh ... thanks?"

Susan joined him at the steps, and the look she gave his turned back made Penny sick.

If you break her heart, Penny thought, *I'll break your neck.*

Something of this thought must have shown in her face because Morgan Duke's smile seemed to wilt on his face, and his air of confidence dissipated. He considered her with poorly disguised alarm.

"I think it's the internet that kids are addicted to now," Susan said. "But she *is* rare."

Penny sent Susan a mental thank-you for not referring to her as a *child*. As far as adults went, *Susan* was a rarity. She never patronized Penny. She had always treated Penny like a person rather than a *child*.

"I'm just gonna go for a ride ...." Penny grabbed her bike and backed away from the porch, afraid that Susan would ask her to stay and get to know Morgan. "I might see what Zoe's doing."

"Maybe we'll meet in town." Susan turned her happy face back to Morgan Duke. "Morgan's taking me out for lunch."

If you're looking for a boyfriend, you can do a lot better than him.

Penny knew better than to say what she was thinking. If she couldn't mask her emotions in front of him then it was time to get away.

"Have fun," she managed, then spun her bike around and mounted it.

"Absolutely adorable," she heard Morgan say as she pedaled down the driveway. "Never had a daughter myself but always wanted one."

She pedaled harder, her speed approaching reckless as she turned onto the blacktop and steered toward town.

The road was, thankfully, deserted. When she was far enough away that she could no longer see the marker for Clover Hill Lane, she slowed and scanned the highway in both directions. Still empty.

Before anyone could come along and spoil her chance, she pulled up on the handlebars and guided her bike off the road, flying only inches above the rough, stony ground and up the sharply rising hill.

A few minutes later she heard the sound of moving water and knew Little Canyon Creek was close.

Dodging the trees and shrubs that grew high on the hill, she followed the sound and found the spot where the creek emptied into the river.

She no longer pumped the bike's pedals, but when she wished to go faster, she did. Past more trees, weaving around jutting rocks, then down to the water. For the next few minutes Penny flew inches above the surface of Little Canyon Creek, a stretch she'd never be able to visit on foot. The banks were too steep, too crowded with trees.

She soared inches above the swift, splashing water, avoiding boulders, her shoes and pant legs soaking. She ducked the outstretched limbs of the crowding trees, nearly crashed when she turned a sharp corner too fast and found herself facing the churning white spray of a waterfall. She shot straight up, passing the edge of the falls, shooting from the protective cover of trees like an arrow, and found herself facing nothing but blue sky. Ignoring the impulse to go higher, she dropped down until she was safely hidden again.

Penny didn't think her heart would ever quit racing with the exhilaration, the fear of it. She never wanted it to.

A few minutes later she reached Aurora Hollow, and found Zoe, Katie, and Ronan waiting for her.

* * *

"In the time since you sent Tovar off, I've been doing more than just searching for the stray mirrors he left behind." As always Ronan seemed to consider his words carefully, measuring their need to know with his own internal yardstick. As always, it drove Penny nuts.

"What exactly *have* you been doing?" Katie pressed him. Her voice displayed some of the irritation Penny felt. "And why haven't you told us before now?"

Zoe cut in, drawing his impatient orange glare to her. "Yeah, have you ever considered the very slight possibility that we could actually help? We're not completely useless, you know."

"Are you bulletproof?" he snapped, moving suddenly in Zoe's direction.

She flinched back a step, then moved forward again, determined to hold her ground.

Katie stepped to her right side in a silent show of support, and Penny joined them on Zoe's left.

After a silent moment, when Ronan visibly worked to calm himself, he spoke again, adopting a gentler tone. "The place I've been going is guarded. I can sneak in but it's hard work not being seen. You girls wouldn't be able to."

"Fine," Penny shouted, losing her temper. "We're not sneaky enough for you, but you could at least tell us what's going on."

"I could," Ronan agreed. "And then endure the constant fear that you might go there yourselves."

"But what if something happens?" Katie finally spoke from near Zoe's elbow. "What if you never come back?"

"How could we look for you if we don't know where to start?" Zoe spoke again, though her anger had eased.

"If I were to not come back some night it would probably mean I was captured ... or worse." He paced in front of them now, his agitation growing again. "And if that is to ever happen you *must not* try to find me."

Penny was about to share her thoughts on what she must or must not do. Ronan saw the gist of it in her eyes and lost his temper again.

"I've told you before that this is not a game! You have a serious purpose here ... more serious than you could understand now, and you will not get yourself killed on my account before you have had a chance to fulfill it!"

He paced more quickly, leapt up into the ash, and resumed his pacing on the low limb he usually reserved for lounging.

"Then why bother telling us anything at all if there's nothing we can do?" Penny regretted the words as soon as they had passed her lips. She thought she had just made Ronan's point for him.

"Because the enemy has made his move. He has involved himself with Susan and placed himself within striking distance. You must be on your guard now more than ever."

Ronan had said what he'd come to say, and before the girls could question him again he leapt down from his perch and sprinted back up the steep path out of the hollow.

"So," Zoe said, grinding her teeth in frustration. "We just have to let him do whatever he's doing and just get over it if he never comes back."

Katie shook her head in angry negation.

"No way," Penny said. "Not gonna happen."

"What can we do?" Katie seized on Ronan's warning to Penny. "Who was he talking about? Who has involved himself with Susan?"

Penny was about to answer when Zoe did it for her.

"The bald guy in the banker suit!" Zoe punched her fist into the palm of her other hand. "That guy who's trying to buy Clover Hill!"

Katie looked blankly from one to the other. "Who?"

They told her about Morgan Duke, the well-dressed gentleman with the Southern accent and creepy son.

"So we'll find out everything we can about the Dukes and what they're doing here," Penny said.

"And maybe that will give us a clue about what Ronan is up to," Zoe said.

"I'll ask Michael if he's heard anything about them," Katie said. "My dad always complains that you can't buy a cup of coffee in this town without the Prices getting a cut. Maybe Sheriff Price has mentioned him to Michael."

"Duke is taking Susan to lunch right now. Where in Dogwood could a guy like him take a...," Penny stumbled over the next word, "... a date?"

"In Dogwood?" Katie laughed. "Grumpy's or The Rail. I'd bet on The Rail."

Penny knew The Rail, at the furthest end of West Main Street, but had never been inside. From the outside it looked classier than a typical bar, but it was a bar, so they wouldn't be getting in there to spy on Susan's ... *shudder* ... date.

Penny felt like doing something about the Morgan Duke situation, but for now there was nothing they could do. Not until Katie had a chance to talk to Michael.

"Well," Penny said, feeling that they could at least accomplish something in the time until then. "How about those flying lessons?"

* * *

Zoe's and Katie's first time in the air went about as well as Penny had expected. They were both airborne by that afternoon, which was progress as far as Penny was concerned. The only limitation they found was that each of them could only use her own bike, but as Zoe pointed out, it was probably good that random people wouldn't be able to jump on one of their bikes and fly off unexpectedly.

"I should get home before Dad does," Katie said. "I'm still supposed to be grounded."

"Me too." Zoe put down the wand she was working on. Drilling the tip out by hand was slow work, made slower by her worry about messing it up. She set the wand inside the chest with the others, and Penny slipped the book in on top of them, locking it with the Phoenix key she wore around her neck day and night. After a moment's consideration she removed the key and searched for a safe place to hide it in the hollow.

"What are you doing?" asked Katie. She had been admiring her new wand before putting it to use on the door to go home. Now her eyes followed Penny.

"Looking for a place to hide this." Penny held up the key from the worn leather strap that served as a necklace. "It's not fair that you two can't open the chest without me here."

Zoe and Katie seemed shocked, but pleased.

"You sure that's a good idea?" Zoe voiced Penny's own concern.

"No one ever comes here but us," Katie argued. "It'll be safe."

After a few minutes of fruitless searching, Penny dropped to her knees and hid it under the edge of one of the rocks by the fire pit.

Resisting the urge to fly back to town, Katie opened the door to her room and pushed her bike through. "See you tonight."

A few moments later Zoe pushed her old ugly bike through and into hers. "Later!"

Penny wasn't ready to leave, but she knew Susan would be home by now. Susan was trusting and patient about Penny's frequent lengthy absences, but even she had her limits.

"Penny?"

The voice startled her. She'd been convinced she was alone.

"Ronan?"

He appeared over the edge of the trail and leapt down to her. "Susan is back now. That man just left."

Penny nodded but said nothing. She was still irritated with Ronan for losing his temper and wasn't ready to let him off the hook.

"Holding a grudge?" There was no anger in Ronan's voice now, only a weary kind of resignation.

Penny crossed her arms and said nothing.

Ronan nodded, as if answering his own question. "How did the flying lessons go?"

"What do you want?" Penny moved a few steps closer to the door, hoping to communicate her desire to get away from him as politely as possible.

Ronan sighed.

"I want you to fetch the egg I gave you for your birthday and bring it back here."

Penny blushed, beginning to feel slightly ashamed of her anger, which only made her angrier. She turned her back on him and left the hollow without a word to him, and stepped back through a minute later with the egg in her hand.

"So … what is it exactly?"

"You'll see when it hatches," Ronan said, and winked at her.

Still not ready to forgive him, Penny didn't respond to his playfulness. "So, do I have to sit on it or what?"

Ronan laughed, and Penny felt a pang of renewed guilt at the sound. His laughter sounded forlorn. "Nothing like that. Only intense heat will hatch that egg. Just hold on to it and do what comes naturally."

"Ronan … I …."

"Don't, Penny. I don't blame you for being angry with me. I just hope you'll understand that I'm only trying to protect you." He shrugged. "I've never had children before, never expected to."

The words touched Penny more deeply than she could have expected, and she steeled her resolve to find out what he was doing, where he was going, so that if something did happen they could find him, help him, even if he didn't want them too.

"It's time now, Penny. Open your present."

Penny held the large gray egg in her cupped hands and did what came naturally to her. She felt the prickle of energy running down her arms, into her hands, and the rising heat. She focused on it, not just letting it come but calling it out. Flames rose between her cupped hands, surrounding the egg. She narrowed her focus, concentrating on keeping the flames from spreading, pouring more heat into them.

She felt the heat as it climbed, saw the flames change from bright red to orange. The tingling in her hands grew stronger, turning into an almost unbearable itch, and, though her skin also began to glow red, the flames didn't burn her.

The flames danced between her cupped hands, and the egg began to change. The dull stone began to shine, then to grow slightly translucent. The deeper gray spots that freckled it began to move, grow, shrink, and Penny realized that she was seeing the thing inside the egg now, moving as the heat roused it.

"More heat," Ronan said. "It needs more."

Penny felt the rest of her body begin to cool as she concentrated on increasing the heat of her flames. They danced frenetically in the palms of her hands, dimming from orange to white.

Ronan backed away, turning his face from her cupped hands.

Penny saw a fallen leaf by her feet begin to dry and shrivel, then disintegrate in a puff of smoke. Steam rose from the ground.

The egg began to shake in her hand.

"Ronan … what's happening?" Penny felt faint. A cold sweat covered her face.

"It's hatching," he said. "You've done it!"

The egg lurched in her hand; it felt as if something were kicking from within. A crack appeared at the end, spreading slowly down the middle, widening until Penny could see inside.

Something was looking at her.

She screamed and dropped the egg. It hit the ground, smoking, setting the grass around it on fire.

The flames in her hands flared bright red for a moment, then extinguished.

Penny dropped heavily onto the nearest rock and shook, cold all over. Ronan was beside her a moment later.

"I feel … cold." Penny began to shiver and was grateful when Ronan climbed onto her lap, sharing his warmth. She hugged him to her, knowing how uncomfortable it made him but not caring.

"It'll pass," he said, sounding unconcerned but snuggling more tightly.

He was watching the egg on the ground, intent, unblinking, and Penny turned her attention to it.

It shivered, then rolled. The thing inside kicked again, and the crack in the shell grew, sprouting new fissures.

"Let me go," Ronan said. "You must be the first thing it sees."

Penny reluctantly loosened her grip on him, then slid down to the ground next to the egg. Her body's heat and her strength were already returning, but she still felt shaky.

Ronan retreated further but kept his eyes on the egg.

With one last shudder, the egg shattered. Flecks of stone flew through the air, peppering Penny's face, and a tiny gray hand emerged from the shattered remains of the stone shell.

"What is it?" Penny demanded, resisting the urge to get as far away from the emerging thing as possible.

"A Homunculus," Ronan said. "A rare creature, moderately intelligent, and very loyal."

The tiny hand gripped a piece of the shell and pushed it aside. Penny saw a pencil-thin body and two arms as narrow as pine needles. A disproportionately large foot kicked away more shell, revealing the lower half of its tiny body.

"And what am I supposed to do with it?" Penny flinched as it swept away more of the shattered shell, and the head appeared. Like the hands and feet, it was disproportionately large. Completely bald, the Homunculus's head looked like a sphere of polished granite, with only a small dark line of a mouth, a tiny little speck of a nose, and eyes that took up most of the top half.

The eyes were milky white. Penny thought it looked blind.

"It connects with the first person it sees," Ronan said, his voice hushed now. "It will do anything for that person."

The eyes seemed to search blindly, above and around its large head, then settled on Penny's face. The creature stilled, and for a second Penny was afraid it had died. It looked like a tiny, malformed statue. Then its eyes began to change, shifting from the pure dead white to a pale green. The green deepened and small black dots of pupils appeared, growing and adjusting to the low light in the hollow. When they had achieved the exact bright green shade of Penny's eyes, they stopped.

Penny heard a thought in her head, a thought she knew wasn't hers.

Mine?

The thing moved then, shifted slightly in her direction, and lifted its arms to reach for her; and in that moment any fear of the creature departed. Penny felt only concern for it. She reached down and scooped it from the rubble of its stone shell.

It fit easily in one cupped hand.

It regarded her solemnly for a long moment, then curled up in her hand, hugging its knobbly knees to its chest, closed its eyes, and seemed to sleep.

Penny regarded it as it lay there, motionless, hard as stone, like a tiny statue.

"Now what?" She regarded Ronan. "How do I take care of it?"

Penny felt out of her depths. She'd never even babysat before.

"You don't have to. It'll mature in a few weeks, maybe a month, and take care of itself."

"Until then?"

"Bury it."

"Bury it?" Penny could hardly believe her ears.

"Yes," Ronan said impatiently. "Somewhere where no one will disturb it. It'll dig its way out when it's ready."

"Bury it," she repeated under her breath, then decided, not for the first time since meeting Ronan, just to go with it and do what he said. It was getting late in the day for more aggravation, and Penny still had homework to do.

"And Penny?"

"What?" She tried to keep her voice even and polite as possible, but it was becoming hard work. At least she wasn't shaking anymore.

"You'll have to think of a name for it while it's maturing. It's important, so pick a good one."

And Ronan was off again, leaving Penny alone in the gathering dusk.

Chapter 12

Fishes and Sharks

Monday mornings on the Dogwood School grounds were always chaotic, and the anticipation of the spring vacation amplified the usual unruliness. Students huddled in groups and pairs, making and discussing their plans for the coming vacation.

"We're going to Westport," one young girl said to her morose friend, locking her bike in place beside Penny's. "There's a beach by the campground that's always covered with sand dollars!"

"I get to help with spring cleaning," her friend said, and kicked the tire of her own bike in frustration.

Oblivious to her friend's less-than-cheerful reception to her news, the girl said. "Don't worry, I'll bring one back for you."

The excited girl bounced off toward the school building, her less-than-enthusiastic friend trudging along behind her.

"That would be nice," Zoe said, shoving her bike in on Penny's other side. "I haven't been to the coast in a couple years."

Penny agreed silently. One of the things she missed most about San Francisco was frequent trips to the ocean and the sound of the tide crashing in on the shore.

"Maybe we can talk Susan into taking us this summer," Penny said. "If we're still alive by then, that is."

"Don't be a buzz-kill, Penny," Zoe said, showing much more spirit than she had of late. "Spring break is almost here!"

Zoe shoved her bike into the rack on the other side of Penny's and locked it. Under her breath she said, "You have no idea how hard it was for me to keep it on the ground this morning."

"Actually," Penny said, "I do."

"Zoe!"

They turned to see Trey Miller striding toward them, a gaggle of unhappy girls marking his progress. A few of them directed openly hostile looks at Zoe, but she ignored them as completely as she did Trey's fawning.

"Hi, Trey." Zoe remained friendly but aloof as ever.

He slipped in between them, draping a casual arm over Zoe's shoulder.

Zoe dodged his attempted embrace with an almost athletic artfulness and, retaining her air of obliviousness, gave him an almost curt wave. "Later, Trey."

Penny was almost alarmed by Trey's continued reaction to Zoe's brush-offs. Her constant polite rejections seemed to be shoring up his determination rather than undermining it.

"Talk to you later, Zoe!" Then, almost as an afterthought it seemed: "Bye, Red!"

"You're breaking his heart," Penny whispered to Zoe.

"Oh, shut up," Zoe snapped.

They saw Katie waiting for them at the front entrance, a change from the polite but distant public front she'd kept up since her grounding. She'd obviously been watching for them, and when she saw them she abandoned her perch against the railing.

"Hi, Kat!" Zoe's good mood seemed unaffected by Penny's teasing.

"Over here," Katie said by way of greeting, grabbing them each by an arm and dragging them down the steps and into the schoolyard.

Zoe had no trouble keeping up with Katie's hurried strides, but Penny had to scramble not to be pulled off of her feet.

"I thought we weren't talking in public anymore," Penny said, half-pleased, half-concerned with Katie's abandonment of the "no public contact" rule designed to get her out of trouble sooner instead of later.

Penny heard only part of Katie's mumbled reply, in which the words *bite me* were clear, but got the idea.

Katie dragged them around to the mostly deserted side lawn and behind a large unruly hedge that hid them from a majority of the students trudging up the front steps. Once out of sight, Katie released them, slid her book bag from one shoulder onto the grass, and leaned against the aged brick wall below the school office window, arms crossed and face almost manic.

"I talked to Michael," she said, sparking Penny's interest. "You will not believe it."

* * *

Penny did believe it, but she didn't like it.

"The Prices?"

"Shhhh," Katie warned, peeking around the side of the hedge to make sure there were no eavesdroppers.

Penny took several deep, calming breaths before daring to speak again.

"That's great," she said at last, keeping her volume, if not her anger, in check. "Rooster's dad put him up to it then. That guy's been trying to get my land for years!"

"I don't think so," Katie said. "Michael says they definitely know each other, but Ernest Price isn't even in this guy's league."

Zoe paid keen attention to the exchange, her gaze moving back and forth from Katie to Penny, but was silent.

"They own half of this town," Penny said.

"No," Katie corrected, "Ernest owns half of this town. His brother the sheriff doesn't own squat. He's just another employee."

"Sounds big league to me," Zoe said.

"Ernest Price is small-town rich," Katie said with forced patience, as if explaining that two plus two equals four. "My dad has almost as much money as he does."

"Then why does everyone around here treat him like Donald Trump?" Zoe was clearly struggling to understand the distinction Katie was trying to make. Penny thought she already knew it.

"Because he owns land," Penny said. "He owns the building Susan's shop is in."

Katie nodded vigorously. "Land and buildings."

"Still seems pretty rich to me," Zoe grumbled.

"He's a big fish in a little pond," Katie said, and smiled. "That's what Dad calls him."

"And Morgan Duke ...," Penny prompted, wanting to get to the point before the bell rang for first period.

"I don't know how much money he has," Katie said with a shrug, "but he owns land all over the country ... all over the world. He lives on a private island in the Florida Keys."

"Ohhh," Zoe intoned, clearly getting it now.

"So if Ernest Price is just a big fish in a little pond ...," Penny said, but Katie finished for her.

"Then Morgan Duke is a shark."

Penny stood silent for a moment, absorbing it all, coming to the same conclusion Katie already had.

"Price is working for Duke!"

Katie shrugged, then nodded reluctantly. "Probably."

The first bell sounded. Katie swore under her breath, then bent and grabbed her bag.

"There's more ...," Katie said, but Zoe interrupted.

"More?" Zoe sounded nervous. "What?"

"Later," Katie said, dashing off without a backward glance.

Zoe looked like she might shout after her, but Penny grabbed her arm and tugged her into motion. "Come on ... we'll be late."

Zoe reluctantly followed, and they ran up the now-deserted steps, past the disapproving gaze of the office receptionist, and joined the throng in the hallway rushing to beat the last bell.

* * *

In Social Studies, Katie had reverted to her polite indifference to Penny, offering a single apologetic look when Penny caught her eye on their way to their seats.

Math with Miss Riggs was mostly unchanged. Miss Riggs's unwanted attention seemed a little less focused than during the previous weeks, but when she did glance in Penny's direction, which was still too often for Penny, her dislike was as strong as ever.

Ellen gave her a weak smile and a distracted wave by way of greeting and didn't talk to her during or after class. She gathered her books and fairly ran from the room when the end-of-period bell rang.

Penny gave a silent thanks for Mr. Cole's fourth-hour English when it arrived. Mr. Cole gave her his standard smile as she passed his desk, always a nice balm for Miss Riggs's scorching scrutiny. She took her seat, already looking forward to lunch at Susan's shop, and Zoe arrived a few seconds later. Before the bell could ring and Mr. Cole called the class to order, she leaned in close to Penny.

"So?"

"So ... what?"

"Did Kat tell you anything else?" Zoe seemed frantic with impatience.

"No."

Zoe slammed her English book onto her desk, drawing eyes from all around.

When the bell rang for lunch, she seemed to have calmed a little.

They hurried through the halls and out onto the grounds.

"Hey, there's Kat and Ellen!" Zoe looked from them to Penny, then back to them.

Penny sighed. "Go on. I'll meet you at Susan's."

Zoe dashed off to meet Katie and Ellen without another word, and Penny started toward the street.

"Ooops, sorry, Little Red." Someone had slammed into her from behind, almost knocking her over. She turned to find Rooster standing behind her, grinning happily. A few of his friends stood behind him, laughing in amusement.

Tucker "Rooster" Price had abandoned the Stetson he used to wear and had gained a few more inches on Penny, but he was otherwise exactly the same as the day she'd first met him. He had the same perpetually greasy mullet, the same dirty cowboy boots, and a sweat-stained T-shirt. He took a step closer to her, well inside her personal space, and crossed his thick arms over his pudgy chest.

Penny shot a quick glance at Zoe, who had just joined Katie and Ellen and appeared to be dancing in place like a kid who needs to use the bathroom. In their own little huddle, they didn't see Penny and Rooster.

"Not so brave without the gang to back you up," Rooster said, grinning unpleasantly down at her.

"I don't need help with you," she said. If he took another step toward her she was going to kick him where boys don't like being kicked.

His grin widened a little and he unfolded his arms, his hands clenching into fists.

"Hey, little bro!"

Penny and Rooster turned in unison to see his older brother James, tall and lean but with the same hostile eyes and unpleasant grin, standing beside his car in the senior parking lot. It was no surprise that his was the newest and best in the entire parking lot. His black Charger had been the envy of the school since the end of Christmas break.

Rooster seemed to deflate a little at the sight. He lowered his fists and forced them to relax, but when he turned back to Penny his cocky grin was still in place.

"You should watch where you're going, Little Red. You don't want to go bumping into the wrong people."

He turned and walked back to his friends.

Resisting the urge to jump on his back, grab a handful of that greasy hair, and ride him around the school grounds like an upright pigmy bull, Penny continued to the sidewalk.

She had to pause before crossing, giving an approaching car time to pass her on the otherwise deserted main street. It slowed as it passed her, and she recognized the black Charger. Loud rock music blasted through the open windows. James Price gave her a quick disdainful look. The man in the passenger's seat watched her without blinking, his unpleasant scrutiny making her skin crawl.

It was Joseph Duke.

He faced forward again as they passed.

"Come on, James, show me how fast this thing can go."

The Charger sped away, chirping its tires as it rounded the bend in the road leading out of town.

Penny watched them go out of sight, not wanting them anywhere close by when she finally stepped out onto the road.

* * *

"Hey, kiddo!" Susan's spirits seemed too fine for a Monday, Penny thought, but that was just Susan.

Penny glanced surreptitiously at the table in the reading corner, to see if Susan was sticking with the new lunch menu.

Sandwiches again, but Penny saw two chocolate doughnuts sitting on a second plate next to them. Penny sat down and tore into her sandwich with genuine enthusiasm, grateful for Susan's ability to compromise.

"Hi, Susan. Hi, Jenny!" Zoe practically sprinted to Penny's side, the light of unshared news shining in her eyes. She saw her lunch and forgot everything else. "Thanks, Susan!"

Zoe tore at her sandwich with indecent enthusiasm.

A few seconds later, Susan glided up to them and sat next to Penny.

Penny surprised herself by not cringing away from Susan's lightning-quick embrace.

"I hope you're not making any plans for spring break," she said, beaming at Penny. "Morgan is taking us to Long Beach for the week!"

Penny felt her jaw drop as she tried to formulate a reply.

Zoe spluttered and choked on her first bite of doughnut.

"*What?*" Penny managed at last.

Susan's smile faltered, then faded. Clearly this was not the response she had expected.

"I thought you'd be excited," Susan said, looking a little deflated.

Zoe was concentrating hard on the next bite of her doughnut, as if wishing she could get up and go somewhere else, but not quite daring to.

"I ...," Penny managed but got no further.

"Don't you like Morgan?" Susan tried but failed to hide her disappointment.

"I ... uh." Penny realized she had hesitated too long.

"Well, I like him." Susan rearranged her face into a weak smile. "And I know he likes you. He was really hoping to get to know you a bit better next week."

Penny felt a slow blush warming her cheeks and prayed that she wouldn't burst into flames during Susan's peak business hour.

Zoe had risen to her feet and wandered to the magazine rack.

Coward, Penny thought.

"It's not that, it's...." But what was she going say? That Morgan Duke was just playing with Susan's emotions? That he was working with Price?

That wasn't a conversation she wanted to have in public.

"Well, what is it?" Angry thunderhead lines creased Susan's forehead.

Penny's blush deepened.

"Well, you haven't known him *that* long."

Susan stared blankly at her for a moment, then burst into laughter.

Of all the reactions Penny could have predicted, this was not one of them.

"Little Red," Susan said, and Penny felt the tension between them ebb. "We would have separate rooms. One for the girls, one for the boy. It's been a few years since I've had a boyfriend, but I'm not going to be a total pushover."

"Susan! A little help, please?" Jenny called from the counter, nodding at a growing line and rescuing Penny from the uncomfortable conversation.

"Just think about it, okay?" Susan gave her another quick squeeze. "We'll talk about it tonight."

Then she was off, leaving Penny alone with her mixed thoughts.

* * *

Thoughtfully, Zoe had not broached the subject of Susan's planned spring vacation with real-estate shark Morgan Duke.

They crossed the street in a rush, falling in behind the students streaming toward the school. Zoe spoke hurriedly, almost frantically, while they walked.

"Duke's son, the creepy one, he works at the town dump now." Zoe's expression was almost triumphant. If there was any spectacular revelation to be gained from this knowledge, however, Penny was missing it.

"Okayyyy ..." Penny waited for the conclusion, if one was forthcoming.

"Ernest Price owns the property the dump is on," Zoe said. "He leases it to the town for almost nothing."

"That's very generous of him," Penny said sarcastically, still not getting the point.

"Come on ... it's like having a brother as sheriff. The city council wants to keep him happy so he doesn't raise their lease."

Penny paused in midstride, then rushed to catch up. Now she was beginning to understand. Ernest Price had been using the same tactic to try to bully Susan into selling Clover Hill, only Susan had not given in.

"Mr. Price made the city council hire Mr. Creepy?"

"I doubt it," Zoe said. "He probably only had to ask. But yeah, we think Mr. Price got him that job."

They slowed now, putting a little more distance between themselves and the nearest lunchtime stragglers. Once again they would be the last in the building, though, and they'd have to run to make it in time.

"But why?" Penny felt like she was still missing something. If she was, so were Katie and Zoe.

"I don't know. Maybe to keep him out of trouble or out of the way."

They slipped inside a few steps behind the last of the lunch crowd, and the door swung shut behind them.

"Michael says there have been a lot of complaints about him."

"What kind of complaints?" Penny was grasping for any missing detail that might shed a bit of light.

"Nothing he can get in trouble for," Zoe said. "Rudeness, tardiness, giving people the creeps."

Penny couldn't think of anything else to ask, which was just as well. She made it through the door of her next class just as the bell rang.

* * *

They met at the hollow almost immediately after school, while Katie's dad and Susan were still at work and Zoe's grandma was enjoying an afternoon nap. Ronan was, thankfully, absent. Penny wanted to warn him about Duke's plans to lure Susan out of town, but she didn't want him to guess that they had been investigating the Dukes behind his back.

"You have got to tell Susan!" Katie almost shouted in her alarm at Penny's latest news. "He's up to something ...!"

"I know, Kat," Penny interrupted, not wanting Katie to build momentum and launch into a full-blown rant.

Of course I have to tell her, Penny thought.

But I don't want to.

She could already imagine the look of hurt, the betrayal in Susan's eyes. She didn't even want to be there to see it, let alone be the one to cause it.

Zoe maintained a distracted silence, working on her new wand while Penny filled Katie in on Morgan Duke's plans for Susan.

"Almost finished," Zoe said in a painfully obvious attempt to break the tension.

They turned to find her fitting her prized silvery Ruthenium crystal into the tip of her new wand and twisting it into place.

"What do I do now?" Zoe asked Katie, finally satisfied with her work.

"Just point it at the sky," Katie said. "It'll do the rest."

Katie turned back to Penny, not content to let the subject drop. "Tonight?"

"Okay," Penny said. "I just hope she believes me."

"Why wouldn't she?"

"Because she *likes* him, and she knows I don't."

"Maybe Michael could back you up," Zoe said, resigning herself to the debate now that she had nothing else to distract her from it. "She'd believe him."

"No!" Penny spoke more sharply than she'd intended. She made herself calm down before elaborating. "Susan's already going to be embarrassed. I don't want her thinking the whole town knows."

And with those words she convinced herself that it would have to be her, that it would have to be that night. Better a small hurt now than a big one later. She cared for Susan, and she owed her the truth … or at least as much of it as she could safely share.

"Go on, Zoe." This time it was Katie's turn to provide a tension breaker. "Try it out."

"Okay … here goes," Zoe said, and steeled herself as she pointed her new wand skyward.

The First Magic spell worked and Zoe's new wand filled the hollow with an ultraviolet black light that they could hardly see but that made everything within glow like the interior of a discotheque.

"That was awesome," Zoe said, and laughed with pleasure.

* * *

Penny was waiting for Susan when she walked through the door, a fresh cup of jasmine tea in hand—Susan's preferred after-work drink—and lasagna cooling in the kitchen. It was not going to be a pleasant night for either of them, but it was going to be harder on Susan. Penny would do anything she could to make it a little easier.

"Hi, Susan," Penny said, stepping from the kitchen as Susan shut the door.

Susan jumped, startled by the unexpected greeting. Penny was almost never around when Susan came home from work, and, if she was, she was usually upstairs. It wasn't her habit to greet Susan at the door.

"Penny, you startled me." She laughed and kicked her shoes off, then regarded the tea with surprise bordering on suspicion. "Thanks."

"Dinner's done, too ... lasagna." Penny gestured over her shoulder into the kitchen. "It needs to cool down but it'll be ready soon."

"Okay," Susan said, taking the tea from Penny's hand. She sniffed it with obvious enjoyment, but the look she turned on Penny a moment later was dubious. "What are you softening me up for?"

"What?" Penny endeavored to sound innocent but knew that the hot blush rising in her cheeks wasn't helping her case. "I just wanted to do something nice for you."

"Hmmm," Susan considered her for a second longer, unconvinced, then made her way into the living room. "Well, whatever it is, give me a chance to get off my feet and relax for a few minutes before you spring it on me."

Indignation won out over embarrassment. Penny crossed her arms and followed Susan. "Maybe I was just trying to be nice."

Susan set her handbag down next to her recliner and settled in slowly. She gave Penny her dubious look again, then smiled.

"Thanks Penny. It smells great."

Penny relaxed a little.

"I hope you made enough for three, though." She winked at Penny and took her first sip of the jasmine tea. "I invited Morgan over for dinner tonight."

"He's coming here ... tonight?"

"We were going to make tacos, but lasagna is fine ... great actually." She winked at Penny. "Especially since I don't have to cook now."

Penny settled into the sofa across from Susan's recliner, suddenly at a loss for words.

"Oh, Penny, just give him a chance." There was a plea in Susan's voice that made Penny's task even more unpleasant. "I know he's a little old for me, but he's sweet, and I like him."

Penny turned her eyes away from Susan's agonized face, chewing her lip, trying to pick her next words with as much care as possible.

She *hated* this!

"Are you afraid he'll make me choose between you?"

Penny's head snapped up and saw true concern on Susan's face.

"No," Penny said, and, though that wasn't the point, knowing it made her love Susan even more.

"Why don't you like him, Penny?"

Anger flushed her face, and for the second time that day Penny was terrified that her inner fire within would overwhelm her.

"He's working with Mr. Price."

For a moment Susan regarded her with unblinking eyes, her fair face paler than usual. Then slowly the pleading expression melted away, shifted into a guarded, neutral one.

Penny couldn't hold that gaze. She looked down at her feet and had to clench the edges on the couch cushion to stop herself from running from the room.

"How do you know that?" Susan's voice was cold, without inflection.

Penny tried to speak but couldn't. Her mouth was too dry, her throat locked up. She could barely breathe.

"How do you know that?"

Penny swallowed, cleared her throat, whispered.

"Penny...?" Susan was clearly struggling to control her anger.

"Kat's brother," Penny croaked. "Michael overheard the sheriff talking about some land deal his brother was working on with Morgan."

Penny dared to look up and wished she hadn't. She stared down between her feet again.

"Kat knew Mr. Price wants our land, so she asked Michael what he knew about the deal. He didn't know anything, but ...," and Penny's power of speech abandoned her again.

Penny heard the creaking of springs as Susan rose from her recliner, the soft patting of her feet on the floor, but didn't look up. Then Susan's feet were in front of Penny's, almost toe to toe, and Penny tried to brace herself ... for what she didn't know.

Shouting?

Denial?

Penny flinched back as Susan grasped her arms, firmly but gently, and guided her to her feet.

Penny closed her eyes.

"Penny," the anger was still in her voice, but now mixed with another emotion Penny couldn't readily identify. "Look at me."

Penny looked into Susan's face. Her expression was less guarded now, the hurt plain in her eyes.

Susan bent down and wrapped her arms around Penny.

"Thank you for telling me," she said.

The embrace was short, and when Susan released her the neutral expression was back in place, but the lines on her brow were as deep as Penny had ever seen them.

Penny could almost pity Morgan Duke. Almost.

"Would you set the table? I need to call Michael."

Penny nodded and rushed toward the kitchen, relieved to escape the tension that had built up and still lingered in the room.

Susan's hand settled on her shoulder before she made it to the foyer.

"Set it for three," Susan said. "We have company on the way."

* * *

"Good evening, ladies," Morgan Duke said, hamming it up with a deep bow to Susan and Penny.

"Come in, Morgan," Susan said. She had her emotions under control. Her greeting was pleasant, inviting. She stepped aside and allowed him in, and gently closed the door behind him. The strain of maintaining this pleasant front showed in the rigidness of her smile, which looked almost painful. Penny thought her jaw might cramp up if she didn't relax it soon.

Morgan swept in between them, bending a little to favor Penny with his wide, patronizing smile. "Young Miss Sinclair, always a pleasure."

Get bent.

"It's good to see you," Penny said, now smiling so widely she thought her own jaw might cramp.

Morgan sniffed the air theatrically as he rose, then grinned.

Penny wished he would stop smiling. Just once, she'd like to see an honest emotion on the man's face. She thought that tonight she might get her wish.

"Is that lasagna I smell?"

"It is," Susan said, returning his fake grin with interest. "Penny is treating us tonight."

"It smells fine," Morgan said, turning that infuriating grin on Penny again. "I can hardly wait!"

"You don't have to," Susan said, taking his arm and guiding him into the kitchen.

Penny barely picked at her food, but Morgan demolished his first helping enthusiastically before settling back in his chair and patting his large gut.

"So," he said at last, winking roguishly at Susan. Penny wanted to vomit. "Have you discussed your spring break plans with the young lady?"

Susan, who Penny now saw hadn't touched her dinner at all, sipped from her water glass, then nodded. "Yes, Morgan, we've discussed it."

"Good!" He clapped his hands together and leaned even further back in his chair to regard them both. "I've made the arrangements already. You two will have a nice condo on the beach, full service, and I'll be right next door."

"I do have one question," Susan said. She picked up her water glass to take another sip and Penny saw it shaking slightly.

Morgan saw this, too, and his own manufactured cheeriness faltered.

Penny grinned, a real grin this time.

"Ask away," Morgan said.

"How much is Ernest Price paying you to work me?"

Morgan's eyes widened at the mention of his silent partner.

"And is our vacation purely business or were you planning on having a little fun with me too while we were away?"

Morgan Duke gaped in astonishment. He seemed frozen in place.

The dash of cold water that hit him a second later broke the paralysis. He spluttered and coughed, shoved himself away from the table and sprawled onto the floor as his chair tipped over.

Penny would not laugh—she knew that this was hurting Susan—but she did enjoy the stunned look on Morgan's face as he rose from the floor.

"Come on now, Susan, don't do this."

"Don't do what?" Susan shouted at him. Her chair flew out from beneath her as she jumped up to face him. "Don't do this?"

Susan snatched Penny's water glass and gave him a second dousing.

His face and the pink dome of his head shone with moisture, and the shoulders of his immaculate black suit were soaked.

"Or what about this?" Susan lunged for the utensil drawer and yanked it open, nearly spilling its contents.

For a second Penny was certain she was going for the carving knife, and the look on Morgan's face suggested he was thinking along the same lines.

She withdrew a nicked wooden rolling pin by one handle and pointed it at him like a sword.

Or a wand, Penny thought.

Susan was awesome in her rage, and slightly terrifying.

She regarded Morgan over the formidable shaft of the rolling pin, eyes narrowed and head tilted.

Morgan watched Susan in pure terror, beads of water still running down his face.

"Susan, just … calm down. Don't do anything …."

"Crazy?" Susan raised a sardonic eyebrow at him. "Haven't you ever heard what they say about a woman scorned?"

"Mr. Duke," Penny said.

He reluctantly turned his gaze to Penny.

"I would get out of here now if I were you."

Keeping his eyes on the business end of Susan's rolling pin, he sidestepped toward the hallway. Once in the hall, he dashed to the front door.

"Ladies," he said, regaining a measure of bravery as he put some distance between himself and Susan. "I did try to do this the easy way."

He slammed the door behind him, and a few seconds later they heard him racing away down the gravel path to the highway.

Susan dropped the rolling pin onto the floor and turned to Penny.

"I'm sorry, Little Red." Her fury was spent now. She looked drained. "I'm just not hungry."

She straightened her chair, sagged onto it, and began massaging her temples, as if fighting off a headache.

Even after all the time with Susan, whose emotional freedom she was still getting accustomed to, Penny was surprised to find she could now give comfort as well as accept it.

She wrapped her arms around Susan's neck, and they held each other in silence.

PART 3

The Crimson Brand

Chapter 13

Cutting Her Roots

Morgan Duke sat on the small deck beneath the awning of his camper, his home away from home, brooding over his failure of the night before and trying to ignore his son. Never in all of his years, in all of his jobs and deals and cons, had he been so badly shaken.

So humiliated.

The boy stood opposite of him, leaning against Morgan's black truck. The new BMW motorbike Morgan had bought him stood a few feet away, the morning sun reflecting off its chrome and glass. He'd supplied the boy with this minimal transportation so that he, Morgan, could spend less time ferrying the kid around, but he wished he hadn't now. The boy's visits to Morgan's solitary little patch of Grays Harbor County—one of Ernest Price's many land purchases made possible by his continued working relationship with Morgan—were becoming too frequent.

Joseph, the smug young pup, was obviously pleased, *too* pleased. Morgan understood why, of course. He'd taken the boy to task too often in the past few months, held him in check and confined him to the task of babysitting a ruin, and he was growing ever more restless.

Soon, Morgan thought. *You'll get your wish soon, Joey.*

Morgan's first and best tool, his charm, his ability to finesse, had failed.

Failed spectacularly, he had to admit, if even only to himself.

That *woman*, that fawning little blond pixie of a woman had shown reserves of insight and courage that Morgan had not thought she possessed. He wondered how long she'd known about his arrangement with Price and how much she knew. He wondered what that would mean for her. Whatever happened, Morgan hoped it would be bad.

That is Turoc's decision, Morgan thought, and felt his anxiety ease a little. Sometimes he had to remind himself that he was only middle management in this strange enterprise.

Do not take it so personally. It's only business.

Wise advice, but hard to follow. Morgan was furious beyond words.

"Joseph, why are you still here? Don't you have a day job?"

Joseph waved the comment off. "Whatcha gonna do, fire me?"

"Son, you do not want to tempt me!"

Joseph ignored this. He could afford to. He knew they would soon have need of his particular skills.

There was still one sure way to compel Joseph's cooperation, though.

"No, as much as the Prices would rejoice to see you gone, I have no intention of firing you."

Joseph smirked. Morgan would have liked to slap it away.

"However, tardiness would be proper cause for, say, a dock in pay." Morgan smiled, a genuine smile nothing like the manufactured front he kept up in his day-to-day business. It was a smile that none of the good folks of Dogwood would have recognized but that Joseph had seen before. The smile, and his words, wiped the smirk from Joseph's face.

"You wouldn't ...."

"You bet your butt I would, boy," Morgan said, leaning forward in his chair toward Joseph. "If you mess this job up a dock in your pay will be the least of your troubles. The boss is not happy."

Mention of *the boss* finally got Joseph moving. He knew no more about Turoc than Morgan had until the start of this business in

Washington, but it was enough for the kid to be wary of angering him.

Maybe the boy wasn't a complete idiot after all.

Joseph stomped toward his bike but turned to Morgan before mounting it.

"How much longer, pa? Can you at least tell me that?"

"Not much longer at all, son." He thought that Turoc was tiring of this business as well. Morgan hadn't told him about Susan's final act of obstinacy, the insult that would force the endgame, but Turoc had an uncanny way of just knowing about things.

Joseph seemed satisfied. He mounted his bike, kicked it to life, and sped away, guiding it off-road and over the hill toward the landfill without a backward glance.

Morgan closed his eyes and sat back in his chair, trying to empty his head, to calm himself before Turoc arrived and they planned the next step in this frustrating dance.

Morgan had a feeling, a happy one, that things in Dogwood were about to heat up considerably.

* * *

"Wake up, Morgan."

The voice cut through pleasant dreams of sailing the Gulf of Mexico at dusk, enjoying the setting sun and cool ocean breeze, enjoying some well-earned rest and solitude.

More insistent, bordering on impatient: "Master Duke."

Perhaps not complete solitude. Perhaps as a bonus for successfully completing what was proving to be a much more difficult job than he usually involved himself personally in, Turoc could use his impressive skills of persuasion on the lovely Miss Taylor, make her forget about Dogwood and the little red-headed brat and leave with Morgan.

A disturbing possibility occurred to Morgan, as they often did when his defenses were down and his mind wandered, that Turoc was doing the same to him.

That venom of his had many uses, many powers, as Morgan well knew. To heal, to control … to kill.

"I grow impatient, Master Duke!"

The glorious gulf sunset turned dark, forbidding, and the azure waters around him boiled with sudden and frightening life. They tossed his boat, tossed him from the pilot's seat, and he landed hard, waking up in the gravel and dust beside his camper.

Turoc hovered over him, his terrible horned head and slitted golden eyes only inches away.

"Do I have your attention now?"

Yes, he knew.

"Are you trying to give me a heart attack?" Morgan shouted, his anger temporarily trumping his fear of the creature he served. He put a hand to his chest, but his heart beat as regularly, as strongly, as it ever had. Morgan knew he would die someday—hopefully a far-distant day—but it would *not* be of a heart attack.

"Your pardon, Master Duke," Turoc said, bowing his head as if in apology, "but I fear the time for good manners and friendly persuasion has passed."

I've been put on notice, Morgan realized.

Just as he'd thought, Turoc was ready to finish this deal, and he was giving Morgan one last chance to end it in the way he wanted.

"Agreed," Morgan said, trying to maintain a modicum of his dignity while lifting himself from the ground. It was not easy.

Turoc waited for him to brush the dust off of his normally immaculate suit, black slacks and jacket, a white shirt that he'd have to change now. No tie today. He had had no plans to go into town today, so he had dressed casually.

"You're aware of the situation with Miss Taylor?"

"Very aware," Turoc said, curling himself beside Morgan's chair.

Morgan resumed his seat, about to pose the question that had occurred to him while still half-asleep.

Turoc seemed aware that the question was coming and shook his head. "I'm afraid my powers of persuasion will work no better against Susan Taylor than yours have. There will be no happily ever after with or for her."

Morgan had not been prepared for that answer, and his expression must have plainly said so.

"The lovely Miss Taylor and many of her old friends," Turoc explained, "have been long inoculated against many of my most useful talents."

"Stay out of my head," Morgan said. He wanted to sound assertive but fell far short. He sounded feeble, fearful. "If you value my trust, then stay out of my head."

Turoc made no reply, only continued to watch him.

"How much longer will you need Joey at the landfill?"

"My work at the *landfill*," he pronounced the word carefully, as if it were something exotic, "is nearly complete. My little friends will begin soon, and they are marvelously efficient workers."

Morgan nodded, happy for the first time that morning. He had an idea, but it would need Joey's full attention. It would also need Turoc's approval, but Morgan didn't think he would object. Not this late in the game.

"Within the week," Morgan prompted.

"Within the week," Turoc agreed. "You have a plan?"

"I have a plan," Morgan said.

"And your local man?"

"Ernest Price is becoming more liability than asset," Morgan confided. "We've made him a rich man, and he's repaid us with constant failure. I think the time has come to retire him from the game."

"We are simpatico, as ever, Master Duke." Turoc rose, unfurling the coiled length of his serpent's body, towering over Morgan in the time it might take for Morgan to blink, and bowed low, a show of respect that eased Morgan's troubled mind. "As always, I defer to your expertise in these matters."

Morgan returned the bow with a polite nod of his own. "And as always, I thank you for your trust."

"Susan Taylor is a willow," Turoc said, gazing into the empty distance, toward Dogwood. He sounded almost admiring. "She seems fragile, but she is not. She bends in the storm but never breaks. Her roots in this place are deep. If we wish to move her from our path we must cut them, one by one, until she falls."

"That woman," Morgan said. "She found out somehow. She ...."

She humiliated me, he almost said.

"Your anger is misplaced," Turoc said, and backed off a few feet to allow Morgan to rise. "I warned you that the girl might be a problem, and so she has been."

Morgan watched the track Turoc left in his wake, a wide zigzag pattern in the dust and gravel.

"The girl," he mused. "She found out?"

"Indeed, and warned the woman of your intent."

"How much does she know?"

"How would I be privy to that?" Turoc snapped. "However much she may know, it is too much. She and her friends will attempt to stop you if they learn of any new plans."

Morgan considered this for a long moment. "Is she the root we'll cut first?"

"I've already told you that I must not cause her intentional harm. That has not changed."

Morgan sensed that Turoc had not finished—simpatico, indeed—and held his tongue.

"But accidents do happen. If she were to be *accidentally* harmed as a result of your best-laid plans … well, I believe my master would forgive us."

"Collateral damage is always a shame," Morgan said, endeavoring to sound somber while smiling inside. "But you know what they say about making omelets."

"What is an omelet?"

"An omelet is dish best served with cheddar cheese and green onions," Morgan said earnestly.

Turoc smiled, bowed. "Again, I defer."

"As well you should, old friend," Morgan said, returning the gesture. Morgan's spirits were rising now. He would cut Susan's roots to this place, and if his blade slipped and he were to sever the wrong one, *accidentally*, what a shame that would be.

Never in all of Morgan's years in his dirty businesses had he hurt a child, but he was tired of this place, tired of these people, and he had been humiliated. Suddenly the thought of having young Miss Sinclair's blood on his hands was not unthinkable.

In fact, it was almost pleasant.

"Make your plans," Turoc said, turning from Morgan Duke and slithering toward the rise on the other side of the country road, a road Morgan was also tired of. The constant dust was killing his sinuses. "Your son will be released from his current obligations soon."

Morgan stood in the comfortable shadow of his camper's awning and watched Turoc go, looking forward once again to a day alone to nurse his ego.

Turoc, his partner. As close to a friend as he had in his business dealings. Turoc, the monster.

Fifteen feet or more long, with a trunk as thick as a tree's, a head shaped like a blunt arrowhead, gold slitted eyes, and curved horns above them.

If Morgan had to guess what normal creature Turoc most reminded him of, he would have said a horned rattlesnake, like the ones common in the desert states. That was essentially what he was, a giant sidewinder, except that no normal sidewinder grew to fifteen feet in length and had arms, or spoke perfect English in a vaguely European accent. No *other* sidewinder in this world could do magic.

Turoc left his sidewinder's tracks across the road and paused at the other side. He pointed the magic wand he always held in the upper right of his four long, spindly arms toward a large boulder embedded in the hillside, and it rolled away, revealing a dark passageway. He dove into the darkness of the passage and the boulder rolled back into place.

Morgan sighed and took his seat again.

He liked Turoc … well, mostly liked him, but, as always, handled him best in small doses. His long familiarity with the monster had not led to true acceptance and probably never would.

He hoped that when this was over it would be a very long time before they had to work together again.

Chapter 14

Into The Fire

The rest of the week dragged on, as all school weeks leading up to a vacation will do, and Susan's sour mood gradually improved from one day to the next. Katie maintained her distance from Penny at school, her father was still showing no signs of relenting in his grudge, but Ellen was beginning to warm up again. She made no reference to Penny's odd habit of flying around on her bicycle and never responded to the offer they'd made her the week before, but at least she was speaking again.

The name Morgan was never mentioned in Susan's presence, and Morgan Duke didn't show up at Sullivan's again until that Thursday. Penny and Zoe arrived for lunch that day in time to see petite little Susan throwing the large man bodily through the front door and out onto the sidewalk.

"That can't be good for business," Zoe whispered to Penny, once Susan was safely out of earshot. But Zoe was grinning broadly, obviously impressed with Susan's newly displayed ferocity.

"I don't know," Penny said. "People will probably be lined up around the block to see who she'll throw out next."

As far as she knew though, there was no more excitement at Sullivan's the rest of that day, or the next. Penny left the school grounds that Friday afternoon in higher spirits than she had known for weeks, and Zoe was, if anything, even more manic than she was at the start of the week.

Their Spring Break seemed to be off to a peaceful start.

When the peace finally shattered, it did so spectacularly.

* * *

They were thirty minutes into their Friday night movie, Susan's choice this time and not one Penny would have picked, but more to her liking than most of Susan's. Susan preferred romantic comedies and dramas, anything with lots of kissing and a happy ending. That night she was in an action-movie mood, much violence and many explosions.

The phone rang, and she reluctantly paused in the middle of a ridiculously destructive car chase scene to answer it.

"Hello?" The look of distracted irritation fell immediately from Susan's face, and Penny was suddenly, intensely nervous. "Jenny, calm down! What...?"

Susan stopped, her eyes going wide, frantic. Jenny had obviously told her *what*.

"Okay," she said after a short but painful silence. "Don't go in. Just stay away. I'm on my way now."

Susan hung up and rushed toward the foyer, pausing to scoop up her handbag from the small table next to her recliner.

"Susan, what happened?" Penny felt a bubble of fear growing in her gut, rising up into her heart.

"There's a fire," she said, "downtown."

Penny jumped from the couch. "Your shop!"

"Not yet," Susan said. Her bag shook in her hand, and when she managed to find her keys, she dropped them. "But it's spreading ...."

She shook her head, unwilling, maybe unable to finish the thought.

"I'll go with you!" Penny ran past Susan to the front door to slip her shoes on.

"No." Susan met her by the front door and shook her head. "I would rather you stayed here."

She slipped past Penny and rushed outside, leaving the door wide open behind her.

"But, Susan ...."

"No, Penny. I don't know how bad it is and I don't want you to get hurt." She paused at the door of her old Falcon. "I'll call you when I can, okay?"

Reluctantly, Penny nodded.

Susan was inside the Falcon and racing away. Penny watched her until she dropped from view down the steep driveway, then looked toward town. She couldn't see downtown Dogwood from her house, not even from her high attic windows, but she did see the faint, ominous orange glow in the distance. She knew if she could see it from that far away, it was bad.

She had barely made it back inside when the mirror in her pocket began to vibrate. She dug it out and saw Zoe's face staring up at her in panic. A second later Katie's joined it.

"Penny," Zoe began, but Penny stopped her.

"I already know about the fire," she said. "Jenny told us."

"It's bad," Katie said. "It started at Homefries and it's spreading."

Katie had confirmed Penny's worst fear. Homefries was a favorite teen lunch spot in the same commercial building as Sullivan's, the little restaurant separated from Susan's shop only by an infrequently used accountant's office.

Penny tried to calm herself.

"The fire station is only a few blocks away," Penny said. "They'll stop it in time."

Katie only shook her head. She seemed incapable of further speech.

Zoe swallowed hard and spoke for her.

"Someone broke into the fire station," Zoe said. "Katie heard it on Michael's scanner. They took an axe to the fire truck's engine and most of the hoses."

"They did what?"

Katie nodded. "And the sprinklers in that building aren't working. Michael went down a manhole to the water main tunnel …. He thinks someone might have turned the water off before they started the fire."

A piercing siren screamed into life, making both the girls in the mirror jump.

Penny felt suddenly dizzy, ready to faint, and realized she was hyperventilating. She closed her eyes and focused on slowing her breathing.

"Penny?" Both of her friends said, sounding frantic.

"Where are you right now," Penny asked, opening her eyes again.

"We're at my house," Zoe said. "In the back yard."

"I'm going down after Michael," Katie said, and vanished from the mirror.

Zoe looked alarmed.

"Wait!" Penny called out, hoping to stop Katie before she made it too far away. "Grab her, Zoe!"

She lost sight of Zoe's face and the view from the mirror became a dizzying swirl of half-lit landscape and buildings. She heard Zoe calling after Katie.

"Stay with her ... I'll be there in a minute!" Penny shoved the mirror in her pocket and ran upstairs to her room. She found her wand in the drawer of her bedside table and ran to her wardrobe. Her red robe, worn only once before, was folded and hidden beneath her oldest and rattiest jeans in the bottom drawer. She'd found the robe, and the larger green one Zoe owned, while exploring the magic doorways in the Birdman's house of mirrors. Those doorways had gone many places, a large room with a desk and walls crammed with shelves of books, a cavern lair lit with candles and decorated with long, flowing red curtains to cover the stone walls, a watery, shimmering mirror portal, and a large closet with a selection of different colored robes. A few of the doorways had gone nowhere at all, simply opened into an empty, humming darkness.

Penny had taken the robe, not because she thought it qualified as high fashion, but because it was a fair disguise, much better than being recognized as Susan's little red-headed orphan if someone spotted her doing magic.

She pulled it out and tucked it under her arm, then pausing only for a moment to visualize the doorway she needed, Penny touched her wand to the wardrobe door, then pulled it open and ran through ....

* * *

... And into the post office's front lobby, the only downtown building that she knew would be unlocked to accommodate night drops but almost certainly would still be empty. The noise of the night's catastrophe assaulted her like a blow to the head: the town siren, shouting from the streets outside, the sound of cars and trucks speeding people away from their homes near the fire, and the fire itself. It roared and crackled like something alive and hungry.

Penny could now appreciate the depth of Katie's fear for her brother; only that could have driven her to follow him into that danger.

She stuffed the folded robe beneath her shirt and hastily tucked it in, shoved her wand down her sock and under the leg of her pants, then ran out into the night to find Zoe and Katie. She hoped that everyone out on the town that night was too distracted to notice her. If anyone told Susan they'd seen her there, Penny would have a hard time explaining how she'd gotten to town so quickly.

She ran past the sheriff's office and courthouse, past the open bay door of Dogwood's small fire department. Three men struggled with a length of canvas hose, hoisting its coiled bulk into the back of a pickup.

"Girl!" One of them shouted in her direction. "Go home! It's not safe out here!"

He turned away without waiting for her to respond and leapt into the truck bed. The other two climbed into the cab, and a moment later they sped toward Main Street. Penny waited until they were out of sight and continued.

She spotted Zoe on the next block, running toward her, then turning the corner in the same direction the firemen had gone. Somehow she ran faster, shouting Zoe's name between ragged breaths. She squinted her eyes against the bright, dancing firelight ahead. Flames licked at the night sky. It looked as if a piece of the sun had fallen and landed in Dogwood.

"Zoe!" Penny was nearly breathless, but Zoe heard at last and, reluctantly it seemed, abandoned her pursuit of Katie and ran to meet Penny.

"She got away," Zoe panted, doubling over, then falling to her knees. "I couldn't catch her."

"It's okay," Penny said, even though the words felt false. She leaned heavily on Zoe for a moment, who was still almost as tall on her knees as Penny was on her feet, and steadied herself. "If we can't stop her … we can at least try to help her."

"I don't have my wand," Zoe nearly cried in frustration. "I left it at home! I'm so stupid!"

"It's okay," Penny said again, and again it felt like a lie. "I'll go after her … you go home and get your wand."

Zoe nodded sharply and scrambled to her feet, nearly knocking Penny over in her rush.

"Zoe!"

Zoe spun around in midstride and nearly fell over again, frantic with worry. "*What?*"

"Get your bike and your robe too," Penny said. "Just in case."

Zoe nodded once, and dashed off for home.

Penny watched her for a moment, then scanned the streets. She found what she was looking for at the curb ten feet away. She checked in both directions, made sure no one was watching. She could see and hear people gathering blocks away, flooding from their houses to watch the unfolding disaster, but the block Penny stood on was deserted. She pulled the wand from beneath her pant leg and pointed it at the iron storm grate. For a moment it resisted, then the rusted iron squealed against the concrete and broke free. She dropped it next to the opening, checked the street around her one last time, and slid inside, into the dark underground.

* * *

Penny had heard about underground tunnels in San Francisco at school a few years earlier and had been briefly interested in them. The rumors about an abandoned underground military base and a colony of aliens supposedly right beneath the city had captured her imagination, but the truth turned out to be a great deal less fantastic. There were service tunnels for utility workers; gas, water, and sewer lines; and floodwater channels.

She supposed that even tiny little Dogwood must have something similar, if on a much smaller scale.

The tunnel was narrow, dark, smelly. Weak light shone down from the opening, and she used it to put on her robe, pulling the hood down as low over her face as she could and still see where she was walking.

Sounds echoed to her, splashing footfalls, grunts of effort, and a shouted expletive, a word she had never heard Michael use before. She walked as fast as she dared in the direction of his voice, keeping her free hand stretched out before her like a blind girl and her wand ready at her side.

Too much time seemed to pass while Penny stumbled through the darkness. The only indication she had that she was making progress was the increasing volume of the activity on the streets above. She knew she wasn't under Main Street—she still hadn't found the intersecting tunnel that would lead her there—but she was closer to the action. Then a distant, weak light ahead alerted her to another's presence.

She paused under the glimmer from another street grate and dug beneath her robe for her mirror.

"Kat," she whispered, and was rewarded when Katie's face, all silhouette and shadow, moved into view.

"Penny?" She whispered. "Where are you?"

"Not far," Penny said, and began walking. "Stay still for just a second and I'll be there."

Katie didn't respond, only looked away from her mirror, peering into the darkness.

Penny didn't wait for her to respond but shoved the mirror into her pocket and hurried toward the distant glow.

She followed it around a corner, the intersecting tunnel she'd been searching for. She saw an open manhole ahead, bright orange light dancing down the slime-covered iron rungs of a short ladder, and just past that, waiting impatiently at the next turn, stood Katie.

Penny sprinted to her, almost banging her head on a low-hanging drainpipe.

"What are you doing here?" Katie was almost frantic with fear.

"Kat, we have to get out of here. Michael knows what he's doing."

"Easy for you to say," Katie snapped, continuing around the corner and leaving Penny to rush after her.

There was another light now, dim and further down the tunnel, but steady and white. Electric light.

Penny grabbed Katie by the arm and yanked her back.

Katie turned, her eyes blazing in the filtered firelight.

Penny put a finger to her lips and whispered. "Fine, we'll stay just in case, but don't let him see us."

"*Who's there?*" Michael shouted from his end of the tunnel, swinging the beam of his flashlight toward them. Penny dragged Katie back behind the last bend in the tunnel before it fell over the spot where they had been standing. A moment later the light vanished, and they heard him grunting with exertion. A high-pitched squeal, the grinding of metal on metal, sounded, and they crept around the corner again to see what he was doing.

Michael had set his flashlight down, angled so that it shone on him and the large handwheel he struggled to turn.

Someone *had* shut off the water to the burning building. The same someone who had sabotaged the fire truck. The same someone who had set the fire.

They watched him struggle with the massive valve-wheel, turning it a little at a time. The pipe next to them rattled briefly as water rushed through it.

Then Michael stopped, leaning against the wheel to catch his breath.

Something rose up from the darkness behind him, one arm held up high.

"*Michael, look out!*" Katie shrieked and started toward him, Penny at her heels.

Michael turned in their direction, reaching for his flashlight, then cried out in pain and collapsed to the ground, silent and still.

"No!" Katie shrieked and stopped.

The thing behind Michael cast aside its weapon, picked up the dropped flashlight and reached for Michael's holstered pistol.

Not a thing, but a man.

A flash of blue light pulsed in the dark corridor, momentarily lighting the startled face sheathed by lank and greasy hair.

Katie's spell missed him, soaring past his shoulder and blasting a chunk of concrete from the tunnel wall behind him.

The man flinched, dropped the flashlight, and turned to run.

There was a second flash of brightest blue and a thin arc of lightning spanned the length of the tunnel, hitting the man between his shoulders. Blue energy played around his body, sparked and sizzled in his hair, and he fell face down in the muck.

Seconds later, they were at Michael's side.

"Is he ...?" Penny couldn't bring herself to finish the question.

Michael lay collapsed on the valve-wheel, his arms dangling, blood running down his scalp and cheek.

Katie placed her head gently against his back, her ear pressed to the cloth of his filthy uniform shirt, and listened. A moment later she sighed in relief.

"He's okay. He's breathing." She stood, then advanced slowly on the spot where Michael's attacker lay. "Try to wake Michael ... I'll cover *him.*"

Penny prodded and shook Michael, careful not to dislodge him from his precarious perch, and at last he began to stir.

Katie rushed to him, but Penny shook her head and motioned her away. Katie nodded and stepped behind Penny and out of sight.

Penny tugged her hood down over her face and stepped back, ready to retreat, but she was too slow.

Michael came to full awareness with a shout of alarm, stumbling to his feet, and saw Penny.

"Who ...?" Michael started to ask, but Penny interrupted him.

Disguising her voice as well as she could, Penny said, "You got him. He's behind you."

Michael turned and found Joseph Duke sprawled out on the mud, groaning as he struggled his way back to consciousness.

"We were never here," Penny said to Michael's turned back. The girls fled down the tunnel, Katie in the lead.

Water now spilled from the grates above them; the sprinklers inside the building and the firemen outside with their one salvaged hose were working. The flickering firelight falling through the grates was weaker now.

They were running blind again. Suddenly, Katie stopped.

"Kat, hurry ...," Penny pleaded.

"*Shhh.*"

Penny hushed, and heard what Katie already had. The clanking of boots treading the metal rungs of the manhole ladder. Someone new was in the tunnels with them, cutting off their escape.

"Michael, where are you?" A man's voice.

Katie cursed and a dim white light glowed at the tip of her wand.

At least we can see now, Penny thought.

"Follow the water," Katie whispered in her ear, pointing to the floor.

The water spilling through the grates had risen to their ankles, flowing in the direction they had been running. "It has to come out somewhere."

"Drain pipe," Penny said and nodded, feeling that they just might get away after all.

They sprinted now, passing the intersecting tunnel before the new person could cut them off, following the water as it rose higher and flowed faster; and sooner than Penny could have hoped, she saw starlight illuminating a wall in front of them and heard the lazy rush of the Chehalis River. They turned a last corner and saw their way out, a narrow drainpipe that led to the stony river shore.

Penny led the way through it, crawling on her hands and knees as the water rushed around her, and finally fell from the other end. She lay, panting, wet and filthy on the stony shore of the river, and was never more grateful to see the sky.

A moment later Katie was lying beside her, wand still in hand and her eyes closed. They lay there for a few minutes, not speaking, only enjoying the clear air and the wide-open sky.

"Thanks," Katie said at last, and sat up, trembling. She looked exhausted but relieved.

"Anytime," Penny said.

* * *

They rinsed off the muck from the service tunnel in the river, then soaked and shivering raced down the shore toward Katie's house.

"Almost there," Katie said.

"What if your dad sees us?"

"He won't. He's probably downtown helping out." Katie said this with an obvious pride that seemed to surprise her.

A few minutes later, Katie changed direction, climbing slowly up a well-traveled dirt path through the stones and weeds, then onto her neatly cropped yard.

"This way," Katie whispered, and Penny crept nervously behind her.

They didn't go to the front, but around back, to the side of the house facing the church and the park beyond it. They stopped for a moment to watch.

Most of the town seemed to have turned out for the spectacle, gathered in the park behind a barricade of cars, trucks, and the town's two sheriff's cruisers.

The firemen had hooked their hose to a hydrant at the corner of the park and school grounds, dousing the nearly demolished east end of the building from Main Street's center line. The flames had mostly died down, but steam and smoke still poured from the shattered windows and collapsed roof. The bakery at the far end was gone, Homefries was gone, the seldom-used accountant's office was intact, but black smoke gushed from its shattered front window and empty doorway.

The little that Penny could see of Sullivan's was a smoke-blackened ruin. The door and picture window lay shattered on the sidewalk, and the blue canvas awning hung in charred, soaked tatters.

Susan's shop, her livelihood, was destroyed.

"Penny," Katie said quietly, and then grabbed her arm to shake her from her shock. "Look."

Penny followed Katie's pointing finger and saw three figures approaching Main Street. They watched the procession in silence, Joseph Duke in the lead, handcuffed and dazed, guided forward by Michael in his mud-splattered deputy uniform. Behind them was one of the men Penny had seen loading the fire hose earlier. With a start of shock, she realized it was Katie's dad.

Then the rest of the town saw them, and the disquieted hum of talk stopped. A woman, Katie's mother, broke from the crowd and ran toward them. Mr. West took the lead and met her before she could get near Michael and his prisoner. For a moment she struggled to get past him, to see Michael, but he restrained her. She struggled for a moment, then gave up and fell into his arms.

There were two figures conspicuously missing from the crowd ... Morgan Duke and Ernest Price.

"I gotta go," Katie said at last, and began to drift toward the park. "There's a side door into the garage ... it's unlocked."

Penny watched her walk away, then scanned the park for Susan. She found the old Falcon first, parked with so many other cars in the school parking lot, and then Susan standing with Jenny, just apart from the crowd, next to Michael's cruiser. They watched Michael approach with his prisoner, and when the men finally reached the car Susan lunged for them. Jenny grabbed her around the waist and held her back as Michael deposited Joseph roughly into the back seat.

Penny could hear her voice rise above the new babble in the park, but couldn't make out her words.

She tore her eyes away from the drama in the park and sprinted to the door before someone spotted her loitering, and stepped through into her bedroom to change out of her wet, filthy clothes.

Five minutes later she was on her bike and flying high above the deserted highway back to town. When she saw the first lights of town below her, she guided her bike down to earth.

"Susan!" Heads turned toward her as she guided her bike through the parking lot and into the park. "Susan!"

The crowd refused to part for her, so she dropped her bike, checked that her wand was still secure in her sock, and shoved her way in.

"Susan!"

"Penny?" She heard Susan before she saw her, but a second later the crowd that would not part for her opened to let Susan through. "Penny, what are you doing?"

Penny found herself hoisted from her feet before she knew Susan meant to do it. A moment later they were outside the crowd again, Jenny trailing behind them.

"I told you to stay home," Susan said, but hugged Penny so tightly it hurt.

"I had to see," Penny said lamely, but Susan seemed unable to scold her any further.

Jenny's eyes were red, puffy, and still wet, as if she'd only just finished weeping. Susan's were dry, but wide and wild with shock.

"It's gone," she said simply. "My shop is gone."

* * *

She was on the way home, her bike safely secured to the rack on the Falcon's rear bumper, when Penny realized she hadn't heard from Zoe since they'd parted back in town.

Susan drove them home in silence, a silence Penny didn't attempt to break, and after a quick and distracted good-night hug, went to her room. The tears she'd kept back all that night broke free now, and Penny fled from the sound into her room.

She was tired, and she was heartbroken for Susan, but before she let herself sleep she had to make sure Zoe was okay.

"Zoe," she whispered into her mirror, but there was no reply. "Zoe?"

She called for Zoe until sleep finally crept up and took her, and fell asleep with the mirror still in her hand.

Chapter 15

Just Like Sisters

Penny arose late the next morning, her body still aching from the night's adventure, the mirror resting beside her on the covers. She picked it up blearily, regarded it, and remembered her desperation to reach Zoe the night before. She couldn't remember why, only that it had been important.

Need ... coffee.

Yes, that was just the thing she needed. And then a shower. She felt filthy.

She opened up the trapdoor to the house below, letting the ladder unfold smoothly on its way down to the floor, but froze with her foot on the first rung.

"My insurance was paid up, so it's not a total loss, but it'll be a while before I'm back in business." Susan was speaking with someone, maybe on the phone since Penny couldn't hear a reply.

Susan should be at work, Penny thought.

And then she remembered. The fire, Morgan Duke's creepy kid down in the service tunnel attacking Michael, Susan's shop destroyed.

"We're meeting the investigators this morning," Susan continued, then paused.

Penny descended to the second floor and followed Susan's voice to her room.

Susan saw her at the door and motioned her in, patting the edge of the unmade bed. She looked tired and was still dressed in her clothes from the night before. Penny wondered if she'd had any sleep at all.

"No, he hasn't confessed." Susan nudged Penny, mimicked drinking from an imaginary cup and raised her eyebrows.

Penny nodded and ran downstairs. She returned ten minutes later with two mugs to find Susan still talking.

"Morgan Duke still hasn't turned up but Sheriff Price is questioning Ernest." Susan barked a short, cynical laugh. "I don't know if Ernest had anything to do with it but he was in business with them. The sheriff says that kid went out of his way to make it look like arson …."

The voice on the other end interrupted her, and she took advantage of the break to drain half her cup in two long, wincing swallows.

"A deal between them went bad. The sheriff is claiming Duke tried to set Ernest up by having his kid fake an insurance fire."

More animated talk on the other end of Susan's phone. Penny wondered who it could be.

"No, it wasn't common knowledge until the sheriff let it slip, but everyone knows now." Susan's brow furrowed, and Penny thought Morgan Duke was very lucky Susan couldn't get to him at the moment. "If he hadn't, I bet he'd be keeping it quiet now. The Prices are taking a hit on this one whether Ernest goes down or not, and there's an election coming up. *Sheriff* Price could end up being plain old Avery Price again."

Interested as she was to know what had happened since the catastrophe, Penny grew bored with her role as eavesdropper. She decided to shower while Susan was occupied. She'd get the full story afterward.

Gathering clean clothes, she noticed the little mirror and decided to give Zoe another try. Zoe didn't answer, so she tried Katie, then Ronan. After half a minute of nothing, Penny gave up in frustration and descended to the second floor to clean up.

A half-hour later, showered and refreshed, feeling almost human again, Penny joined Susan in the kitchen.

"Hey, kiddo," Susan greeted her, sounding more cheerful than Penny had expected. She was finishing a bowl of cereal and working on what must have been her second or third cup of coffee. "I'm headed to town. Wanna go with me?"

Penny did.

Susan allowed her ten minutes to eat a rushed breakfast and chug a second cup of coffee, then they were on their way, her bike once again riding on the back bumper.

"Who were you on the phone with?" Penny was less interested in who Susan was talking to than the information they'd shared, but couldn't think of a way to ask outright without feeling nosey.

"June," Susan said, and as always when speaking about her older sister, any vestige of gentleness left her face and voice. "She just found out about it this morning and called too see how I was doing."

For a moment a new question overrode Penny's desire for information about the Dukes and the Prices.

"Susan, how can you be so ...," Penny struggled to articulate what Susan was being. "*Calm?* How can you not be freaking out right now?"

A quick smile touched Susan's lips, then vanished. "Would you like me to *freak out* a bit?"

"No," Penny said, knowing Susan was dodging the question. "I'm glad you're not freaking out, but it was your business."

Susan sighed. "It still is, Penny."

Susan maintained her calm for the rest of the car ride and said no more about it.

* * *

The stretch of Main Street from the school parking lot to Grumpy's was cordoned off and closed, traffic through town being detoured through the residential district, but the devastated block was still the center of frenzied activity. Susan parked the Falcon between a white car with a Washington State emblem on the door and the words *Fire Marshal* below it in bright red, and the sheriff's car; Sheriff Price was sitting inside, red-faced and shouting into a cell phone. The firemen who had been on duty the night before stood on the center line with a gray-haired man in a gray suit and Michael West, still in his muddied, torn uniform and newly elevated from football hero to supercop.

Standing slightly away from them, Penny saw the old proprietor of Golden Arts, Zoe's favorite shop; a plump, matronly looking woman who owned the bakery; and a scattering of others.

"Going to Zoe's?" Susan climbed from her open door, leaning on it heavily for a moment before straightening up. Her strength seemed to be deserting her in the face of the destruction. "I don't think you'll be allowed near that building. In fact I won't allow it."

"Yeah," Penny said. She closed the door and hurried to Susan's side of the car, knowing she wouldn't be able to catch Susan if she fainted but determined to try.

Susan was pale and shaking, seemed to be moving forward through pure force of will. She shut her own door, perhaps a little harder than was necessary, and strode forward without another second's pause toward the barricade.

Penny watched her for a few steps, then lifted her bike from its rack and pushed it into the park.

The park was not the buzzing center of activity it had been the night before, but it was much fuller than usual. Penny scanned the faces present for familiar ones but found neither Katie's nor Zoe's among them.

Though she was in a hurry to see Zoe, she walked slowly through the park, taking in the full devastation. She couldn't help herself. The light of day revealed far more than she had seen by the glare of electric lights and the dancing orange glow of the flames.

Everything from the bakery to the accountant's office was gone, and Sullivan's was a blackened shell. Golden Arts seemed mostly intact, but with the building itself so badly ravaged Penny doubted that anyone would be buying a new watch or engagement ring there anytime soon.

Penny hated to think how far the fire might have gone if Michael hadn't turned the water back on.

She had to go far out of the way, around Grumpy's and up another block to skirt the closed-off street, but once she was off the grass and cruising along on the blacktop she made good time.

Penny was still a block away when she heard the first warbling notes of an approaching siren. She looked back over her shoulder but the street behind her was empty. She steered onto the sidewalk and continued.

The siren's volume grew, and curious neighbors stepped out onto their porches to see what new trouble was brewing. She peddled past them, looking up and down the street for the source of the noise, and as she turned the corner to Zoe's house, a new, more alarming sound joined the approaching siren.

Crying.

Penny saw Zoe sitting on the porch in the same clothes she'd worn the night before, bent almost double, her face in her hands. She wept into her hands, oblivious to the swelling wail of sirens and the stares of the growing crowd lining her street.

Dread filled Penny's gut. She peddled as fast as she could toward her friend. She didn't think to look as she crossed the street to Zoe's house, didn't see the ambulance, still a half-block away but moving fast, or the sheriff's cruiser, coming from the other direction, that had to slow to avoid hitting her. Forgetting caution in her haste, she flew her bike a few inches above the curb in front of Zoe's house and leapt from it. Unguided, it continued for a few more feet before hitting the ground and crashing onto its side.

"Zoe!" Penny shouted in alarm and ran to her friend, but Zoe didn't look up, only shook her head wildly from side to side. Her weeping had subsided to frame-racking sobs.

Penny heard a brief squeal of tires behind her, and a second later a car door slammed. A new, familiar voice shouted Zoe's name.

A second later Penny had fallen to her knees before Zoe. She took her friend by the shoulders and called her name again, gently this time.

"Zoe ... what happened?"

And now Zoe did look up, and the pain and fatigue in her face started Penny's tears. Zoe's eyes were puffy from weeping, bloodshot and bleary from exhaustion. For a moment she didn't seem to recognize Penny, only stared into her face with pitiable confusion.

"Zoe, is it your grandmother?" Penny recognized the voice behind her now. It was Michael, Zoe's crush. His right hand fell onto Penny's shoulder, his left onto Zoe's.

Zoe's eyes rolled from Penny to Michael, and for once there was no shyness or embarrassment in them.

"She's dead," Zoe said, sounding as if she didn't quite believe it herself. "I tried to save her but I didn't know what to do ...."

Her eyes rolled back to Penny, and the pitiable confusion was gone, replaced with an even more pitiable expression. Comprehension.

Michael stepped away and she began to cry again.

The ambulance rolled to a stop, the siren cutting out midwarble but the lights still flashing panic-red.

Michael led two paramedics past them and inside while Penny sat with Zoe and held her.

After a while exhaustion took the sharpest edge off Zoe's grief and she simply sat, leaning against Penny, leaking silent tears into her hands.

"Penny." It was Michael again, speaking softly. "I need you to move."

Penny, who had been staring into the distance, ignoring the curious onlookers drifting up and down the block, looked up at him. She was about to ask why, then she understood. The paramedics were still inside, waiting to bring Zoe's grandma out.

She nodded, and he favored her with a pained little smile before stepping past them to the front yard. She saw that he still had dried blood on his temple.

"Come on, let's go." Penny was too small to make Zoe stand. All she could do was apply gentle pressure and hope Zoe would follow her lead.

"Where?" Zoe dropped her hands and turned to regard Penny.

But she rose and leaned on Penny as they walked away from the steps. She was unsteady, and Penny knew if she fell, both of them would hit the ground. Penny didn't think she'd slept at all that night. She wondered briefly if Zoe had been up all night long trying to save her grandma, trying to make her breathe again, or crying over her body, and made herself not think about it.

"I don't know," she admitted. "Maybe Susan ...."

But she didn't have time to finish before Susan herself arrived, running through the gathering crowd toward them and scattering the people in her path.

Katie was chasing in her wake, her face a mask of shock.

That must be how I look, Penny thought.

Then Susan and Katie were there, and Zoe found herself in the center of a group embrace.

"I'm so sorry, honey," Susan said. "I'm so sorry for this."

Katie seemed as lost for words as Penny was. She just held Zoe, and when Susan stepped away, Katie moved to Zoe's other side to help support her.

Over Zoe's slumped shoulders, Penny saw the first paramedic backing out through the front door gripping one end of a gurney and guiding it down the narrow steps. She looked away, grateful that Zoe couldn't see it.

Where's Susan?

They needed to get Zoe away from here. Preferably to some place with a bed.

She searched the yard and found Susan standing next to Michael, dragging him away from the crowd of busybodies milling around the sidewalks.

"Do you know what happened?" Susan spoke in a low voice, still guiding him away from the onlookers. Penny could just hear their conversation over the low hum of gossip.

"I'll need to talk to Zoe, but it looks like a heart attack," Michael said.

"Can't that wait?" She sounded angry now. "I think she's been through enough this morning."

"Yes," Michael said. "You're right. She needs to rest, and I need to talk to social services."

Penny grew cold at those words. She remembered her time as a ward of the State of California, the group home. She felt like grabbing Zoe's hand and running.

"Social services?" Susan's voice was weak.

"She has no family here," Michael spoke more softly still, but Penny could still hear him, and if she could ....

She turned to Zoe and found her staring at the ground, the exhaustion and grief on her face now fighting with a blooming fear.

Katie still looked shell-shocked. She held Zoe's hand and patted her shoulder but seemed a million miles away.

"She's staying with me," Susan said, and her voice invited no argument. "With Penny and me."

A moment of silence followed this.

Katie seemed to snap out of her daze. She turned her head to watch her brother and Susan.

Penny saw Zoe's fear slip away. She fixed Penny with her dark eyes again.

"She was …," Zoe couldn't bring herself to say the word. "She was in pain last night so I stayed with her, but she wouldn't let me call an ambulance. She said she could wait until morning and drive herself. When I got up this morning to check on her she …. I tried to save her, but it was too late."

"It's not your fault," Katie said.

Zoe looked down at her feet again, then her eyes closed.

"I'm not letting her go to some damn orphanage or group home," Susan said, her voice at the edge of a shout. "I won't allow it."

Penny turned again and found Susan looking not at Michael but at her. Her eyes were wide, almost insane, her cheeks flushed. When she caught Penny's glance, her face softened.

"Oh, no," Katie gasped.

Standing across the street, staring at the three of them in their huddle, was her father. He watched them, his face pale and neutral, and for a moment Penny thought he was looking directly into her eyes.

Don't you dare! Not now!

He didn't. His eyes shifted from Penny to Katie, and a moment later he was striding through the crowd toward Susan and Michael.

On the other side of Zoe, Katie relaxed visibly.

"I'm so tired," Zoe murmured between them.

She was leaning more heavily on Penny than ever, and Penny was beginning to feel a bit weak in the knees.

Behind the unlikely cluster of Susan, Michael, and Mr. West, Penny saw the shrouded form of Zoe's grandma disappear inside the back of the ambulance. Then the door closed, and Susan was walking toward them, side by side with Katie's father.

Susan wrapped her arms around all three of them and spoke into Zoe's ear.

"Hang in there for a minute. I'll take you home."

"Katie?" It was her father, standing off a little from the four of them. "You should go, too."

"No," Katie said. Her voice was even but defiant. "I'm staying with her."

Unbelievably, her father nodded.

"That's what I meant, Katie." He put a hand on her shoulder. "She needs her friends."

He met Penny's eyes again. He didn't do anything as friendly as smile, but the look he gave her was benign. He took his daughter's hand from Zoe's shoulder and squeezed it, then retreated to Michael's side.

Susan joined him a moment later, leaving the girls alone.

"I tried to save her," Zoe said again, her eyes still closed as if she were talking in her sleep. "I …."

"There's nothing you could have done," Penny said.

"Shhh, let her talk," Katie said.

Zoe whispered something, and Penny had to lean in closer to make out her words.

"What good am I? I couldn't even save her."

Then Susan was with them, her arms around them. "Come on, let's go."

She shepherded them toward the sidewalk and Michael's cruiser.

Sudden, unexpected laughter rippled from a group of onlookers across the street. Penny, Katie, Susan, and Michael turned in unison toward the sound. A pair of girls from Katie's old gang stood at the center. The new queen bee, Tori, leaned heavily on her friend's shoulder making a poor effort to cover up her giggles with a cupped hand.

"Oh my god, look at her *baaaawling*."

Such sudden hatred rose up in Penny that her skin began to prickle with heat.

Oblivious to the looks of shock and disapproval from all around, Tori eyed Katie with malicious glee.

She was also oblivious to the right hook that came at her from the side, until it knocked the grin from her face.

With a shout of pain Tori hit the ground. Ellen Kelly stood over her with clenched fists. She bent down and cocked her fist back for another punch, and arms grabbed at her from all around, pulling her away from Tori.

"Let me go!" Ellen screamed, struggling to get away, to get at the cowering, bleeding girl.

Michael put his arms around Penny, Zoe and Katie, and guided them more quickly toward the car.

He opened the back door for them, looking like a disheveled chauffer, and they climbed in—Katie, Zoe, then Penny. Moments later they were off.

It was a quick trip to Susan's old Falcon, then home.

By the time they turned onto Clover Hill Lane, Zoe had succumbed to her exhaustion. Susan carried her to the spare bedroom on the second floor—a feat Penny found impressive given that Zoe was as tall as Susan—and put her to bed.

Susan waved them away after putting Zoe in the spare room. They met downstairs in time to hear a car pulling into the driveway. When they'd tried to follow Susan out, she'd gently blocked them and redirected them toward the kitchen.

"Why don't you make fresh coffee? We'll be inside in a few minutes." She turned her back on them but paused on her way to the door, and sighed. "It's going to be a long day."

* * *

"So, what now," Penny heard Susan asking from the front porch.

Penny and Katie sat in the kitchen, Penny sipping at a cup of coffee and Katie drinking a Pepsi, straining to see through the curtains to the porch. It had been more than a few minutes—it was fifteen and counting now—but whomever Susan was talking to were finally making their way to the house.

Penny expected to hear Michael's voice. When Mr. West answered, Penny turned to Katie and saw she was just as surprised.

"It's not my area. Jenkins handles the custody cases, but as long as she has somewhere to stay, child protection will probably wait until Monday to open a case."

Penny felt sick at those words.

They aren't going to take her away, she told herself, though she was far from confident.

Katie grabbed her arm but continued to stare through the narrow opening in the curtains.

"Michael called them?" Susan didn't sound alarmed, only resigned.

"Yeah. He had to," Mr. West said. "Don't worry. If you can show she has a good home here, they'll be happy to let her stay here until her parents come for her. Easier for everyone that way."

Her parents ... Penny had forgotten about them.

Easy to do, she thought, redirecting her anger toward Zoe's long-absent mother and father. *They're never around.*

They'll be around now. If the state doesn't take her away, then they might.

They won't, Penny tried to comfort herself, knowing she was being selfish but not caring. *They don't want her or she'd already be with them.*

"Has anyone called them yet?"

"Michael did," Mr. West said. "He left a message."

"What if they don't come for her?"

Mr. West harrumphed. "I think she might be better off if they didn't."

"Markus," Susan admonished.

"I don't have anything against them," he said, "but you know their lifestyle. She needs some stability, and those two have never been stable."

Silence. Penny could almost feel the tension outside seeping into the kitchen.

Mr. West cleared his throat. "If you're sure about letting her stay here ... long term ...."

"I am," Susan said.

"Then you'll need to become her legal guardian," he finished. "Keep me in the loop, Susan, and I'll help out if it comes to that."

"Thank you, Markus." Susan sounded calmer, less likely to snap out or break down. She'd been close to tears again earlier, on Zoe's behalf rather than her grandma's, Penny suspected.

"Are they inside?"

Katie rose at her father's question and left the kitchen.

Penny poured a hurried mug of coffee for Susan and followed.

She stepped out onto the porch in time to see Katie hugging her father.

Susan stepped quickly to Penny's side and relieved her of her burden of caffeine.

Markus West stepped away from Katie and regarded Penny for just a second before speaking again. "Michael's bringing some clothes from Zoe's house. I'll have him bring some for you, too."

He turned away and hurried down the steps to his car, shoulders slumped and hands shoved deep into the pockets of his pants.

"Thank you again, Markus." Susan said. Penny thought she heard a touch of her own disbelief in Susan's gratitude, saw the unasked question in Susan's eyes.

Why so suddenly helpful?

Markus West stopped with his hand on the car door's handle, then slowly looked up at them.

"Seeing them," he nodded toward Katie, but Penny thought the gesture was meant to include her and Zoe, too. "Seeing them today … how they are, just like sisters, it reminded me of how close you all used to be."

He opened his car and slipped inside.

For a moment Penny thought those were his last words on the subject, then his window whirred down, and Penny found him looking directly at her.

"I remember your grandparents, your mother, and aunt taking Susan in, just like she was one of them."

"Dad," Katie said, blushing, clearly unused to her no-nonsense father sharing his feelings in her presence.

He smiled at Katie. "I'm a little ashamed of myself and very proud of you. Loyalty is an underrated virtue."

Before he could embarrass Katie further, he rolled his window up, started his car, and made a U-turn. A moment later he disappeared from sight down Clover Hill Lane.

* * *

Michael arrived an hour later, standing at the open door with two bags slung over his shoulder.

"Zoe's still sleeping," Susan informed him as he handed one bag to Katie. "If you need to see her, could it at least wait until tomorrow?"

"That's fine," Michael said after a brief, distracted glance between Katie and Penny. When Penny tried to take Zoe's bag, he shifted his shoulder away from her. "I've got it."

Penny moved back as he stepped inside. He searched the foyer, then found Susan standing at the threshold to the living room. "I'll just have Kat show me where she's staying and leave this for her."

Before Susan could protest, he was moving down the hallway toward the stairs to the second floor. Katie fell in behind him, and with a quick glance at Susan, Penny strode to keep up with them. She caught up to them on the second-floor landing, where Katie pointed out the spare bedroom.

"Go ahead," he said, and Penny felt herself blushing at the close scrutiny he gave her as she followed Katie past him.

They stopped at Zoe's closed door, and Katie opened it as carefully and quietly as possible. Penny could have told her the caution was unnecessary. Zoe slept in her usual fashion–sprawled out across the double-wide bed like a gangly, dark-haired starfish, her blankets mostly kicked off, snoring extravagantly.

Michael passed the bag to Penny, still scrutinizing her as she set it just inside the door, which she closed again to give Zoe her privacy. She could well imagine Zoe's horror if she found out Michael had seen her in such an undignified state.

When they started away from Zoe's door, Michael moved in front of them, blocking their path.

"What?" Katie crossed her arms and fixed Michael with a look of impatience that only a little sister could manage.

"There's more," he said, and drew something long and slender from inside his jacket.

Zoe's new wand.

The tip glowed slightly as he held it out toward them, drawing his eyes.

He frowned at it.

For a moment Penny and Katie were frozen to the spot in shock, then nearly knocked each other down in their haste to grab the wand from Michael's hand.

"Michael? Girls?" Susan's footsteps echoed up the steps and down the hallway toward them, and Katie, who had been slightly quicker in her lunge toward Michael, hid the wand behind her back. A second later Susan's slightly flustered face appeared around the far corner. "Come back down. She needs to rest."

Michael fixed a pained, unconvincing smile on his face before turning. "Okay, Susan. We'll be right down."

When she was gone, he turned back to Penny and Katie.

"Now is probably not a good time, but sooner or later I'd like the three of you to explain that."

Katie was going slightly red in the face and opened her mouth, as if to tell him to mind his own business.

He shook his head, pressed a finger to his lips, and strode down the hall.

Chapter 16

Homunculi

Ronan approached the junkyard on his usual path, cresting the hill overlooking it from the west just after dark to avoid casting a silhouette against the cotton-candy sunset sky. He expected no trouble; even the garbage man's irritating sniping stopped when the sun went down, as long as Ronan didn't set off any trap lights. He expected an empty maze and deserted ruins. What he saw in the valley below sank his hopes of sweeping up the last of the pesky avian's mess without interference.

Lights and activity.

There was a smell, too, the same as before but stronger now, alkaline and somehow so electric that it crackled like static in his flared nostrils.

"Turoc," Ronan growled, and sank lower into the tall grass.

If it was Turoc, and Ronan was almost certain that stench could come from no other, their situation would get very complicated. He would have to warn the girls, hope for the best but prepare them for the worst, which meant telling them a lot more than he had wanted to.

He could only hope they would be ready to hear it.

"But not tonight," he whispered, not even aware he'd voiced the thought.

Despite the new complications in the junkyard, he had work to do.

He'd expected someone to make the journey long before now, but he'd expected someone who blended in a bit better, someone the red bastard wouldn't miss. Someone expendable.

Not Turoc.

The memory of his last encounter with the old enemy rose from the neglected dungeons of his unhappiest memories, and Ronan forced it back down. He needed to concentrate on the task at hand.

He crept down the hill, frequently pausing to blend in with his surroundings and observe. Turoc's scent lingered, but there was no sign of the monster himself. Not yet anyway.

There were no humans about either, neither the big bald man nor his unpleasant son. The little trailer the garbage man lived in looked dark, abandoned.

The light and activity focused on the center of the maze, the ruins he had planned on visiting himself. He couldn't see what was darting in and out of the burned husk, only got occasional glimpses of running, spindly armed shadows. He couldn't smell them, either. The little monsters mimicked the scents that surrounded them, just a part of their remarkable camouflage. He could hear them, though: plaintive squawks; sharp, chattered replies; and the occasional mad tittering laughter.

These were the things that hatched from the stone eggs.

Homunculi.

Not the most intelligent of creatures. Primitive social structure, a unique spoken language based on intuition and emotion, no written language, but intensely loyal to their master, whoever their master happened to be.

They would be a problem, but Ronan wasn't going to let them turn him back. If anything, the presence of the homunculi made his business more urgent. He had to get close, watch them. He had to find out what they were looking for, or what they might have already found.

* * *

Ronan passed beneath the fence and through a gap in the first wall of the maze, squeezing between an overturned chest freezer and the empty shell of a washing machine, before he saw his first homunculus up close. It streaked past his hiding place, moving like a bald, gray monkey. It had a stout little torso; short, thin legs with large flat feet; and long thin arms with large hands. It ran hunched forward, balancing on its fists as much as its feet. One of those fists was clenched around the tied end of a burlap sack that bounced along in its wake. The contents clanked and rattled against the stony, uneven path.

It ran away from the center of the maze toward the junkyard's wide-open gravel parking lot. Ronan waited until the little monster was almost out of sight, then followed.

He kept close to the junk walls, ready to slip out of sight at the slightest hint of trouble, and followed just quickly enough to keep pace. The homunculi owned this maze now. The only advantage Ronan had left was stealth, and he wasn't going to give that up unless it became necessary.

The shadows deepened as Ronan neared the outer rings of the maze, putting the lights and activity at the center far behind him, and then a new light blazed to life around the next bend, startling a bark out of Ronan.

The homunculus squawked in alarm, and the pounding of its large feet against the path signaled its return.

Ronan was in the open, exposed with no niche in the junk wall to slip through, nowhere to hide. He sighed and closed his eyes, calling on the last trick of concealment left to him. He relaxed his consciousness—not an easy thing to do under stress but he had had a lot of practice—released his grip on the physical world around him, and felt it slip away beneath him. Ronan became as insubstantial as smoke, as ephemeral as a passing thought. His body melted away to mist and settled to the ground.

The little monster came around the corner, skidding in the dirt, its bag left behind and its fists raised as if preparing to fight. For a moment it stared straight through what remained of Ronan, then it turned its large bald head from side to side, scanning the open path. It sniffed deeply, scenting the air.

For a time Ronan existed on a knife's edge, balanced between worlds. A slip either way would be disastrous, either bringing him back into this world or sending him tumbling into the other, out of reach of the girls at a time they needed him most. The balance was not easy; an uncontrolled thought could easily blow him out of this world like a dead leaf in a strong breeze. An unchecked emotion could draw him back into it fully. The longer he balanced, the harder the act became.

At last the monster resumed its journey through the maze, and Ronan focused on the one thought he knew would not fail to gather him again into the body he had worn for so long.

I must return to the hollow and warn the girls.

Ronan stayed still for a moment, settling into his bones and giving the little gray man a chance to get a bit further ahead before resuming the chase.

The maze appeared to end around the next corner, opening onto a large front lot flanked by gently rising hills, one of bulldozed and rotting garbage, the other of recently moved earth on which the garbage man's trailer sat, a blemish on the landscape.

Ronan saw this through a man-sized gap in the maze's tall outer wall and realized how well hidden the garbage man's labyrinth must have been from the other side of that small gap. It would look like nothing more or less than a small mountain of junk.

For a moment the little gray man paused at the exit. It scratched its bald head, then retreated a step, scanning left, then right, like a child contemplating an unexpected and unfamiliar fork in the road home. Though there seemed to be no fork, no path left or right, it gathered up the bag again and scampered toward the right-hand wall. A moment later it disappeared, and Ronan followed.

There were indeed paths to the left and right of the exit, only evident if viewed straight on. They were even narrower than the cramped exit; a man would have to squeeze himself through to continue. They were wide enough to accommodate the homunculus and Ronan, who took up his silent chase again. Their path ended around the next turn, and Ronan readied himself to retreat, sure the homunculus had lost its way and would turn back toward him.

Instead the little gray man approached an old, badly abused refrigerator and pulled it open. The inside was filthy with years of neglect, and completely empty. The little gray man stepped inside, hoisting the bag over its shoulder; and, as the door began to swing shut, Ronan watched the homunculus disappear through the floor. With only the slightest hesitation, Ronan dashed toward the old refrigerator and through the door just before it closed.

* * *

The refrigerator was not a magic door, just a hidden one. Where the floor should have been there was a tunnel that sloped downward perhaps fifty feet before leveling off. Even Ronan, whose eyes were better adapted for the dark than any human's, could barely see where he was going in the near-perfect darkness. There was light ahead, but it was diffuse, the source hidden.

The earthen tunnel was wide and rounded, the soil rich with rot and so compact that it was almost like stone. The familiar stink was strong, masking even the stench of decay that marked this place. The tunnel was a burrow—one of a type he'd seen before.

Ronan continued, weighted down by a dread so intense it felt like physical illness. He hoped his assumptions about the homunculi's presence here were correct. This journey was already a dangerous one; he'd hate for it to be pointless as well. He passed splits in the tunnel, any of which his quarry might have taken. The only reassurance he had that he was on the right path was the weak, distant light.

The path began a gentle but perceptible upward slant, then the light that had teased him from a distance came into view. A chamber loomed ahead, small, but seeming cathedral-like after the dark confines of the tunnel. The light floated inches beneath a smooth, low ceiling. Beneath it, two homunculi were busy sifting through a hill of charred debris. They stood knee-deep in rubble, charred wood, shards of shattered soot-blackened glass, and half-melted trinkets. The gray man Ronan had followed dragged his bag to them and upended it at their feet, laughing at the dismay evident on their wide faces. A moment later he retreated in Ronan's direction, bent low against a rain of flying debris and howling in anger.

Ronan retreated back through the tunnel just ahead of the gray man, the others' laughter echoing down to him. He found one of the side tunnels and backed into it in time to avoid being run over by the fleeing monster, who was still bent low with his hands over the top of his head. When Ronan made his way back to the chamber, the other two were at work.

He crouched low, just outside the reach of the bright, floating light, and watched.

Rubbish and rubble flew in all directions as the homunculi worked. Twice they paused to consider items of interest: a half-melted belt buckle; the pointy steel toe of an incinerated boot. Ronan's breath stopped for a moment and his ears perked up as one of them investigated a cracked, soot-covered mirror. The creature gave a short chirp of excitement and placed the mirror in a wooden crate between them before resuming its search.

Ronan turned his attention to the crate, wondering what other items the little gray men had stowed in it, wondering if he'd be able to steal them without being found out.

Ronan remained in place, knowing that more of the little monsters could come through at any time but also knowing that if he let the box of relics out of his sight that he might never find it again. Unable to move forward and take them, unwilling to retreat.

One of the gray men cocked back an arm to hurl something, and the other caught it by the wrist and snatched the object away. It was a small box, covered with soot, but Ronan saw a gleam of bright red where the homunculus's hand had rubbed the black away.

They fought over the find, almost dropping the box in their struggle. The second one clutched it to his chest and slapped the first across the back of its head, knocking him face first into the debris. Cackling laughter, it rubbed more soot away to reveal a small square of opalescent red stone.

The object was familiar to Ronan. He'd seen it before, years before, and in another world.

The stone began to split, a dark crack that started near the top and spread all the way around, revealing a lid. It was a box, and Ronan remembered where he had seen it.

The gray man opened the lid.

A radiant black light spilled from the open box, mesmerizing the gray man. It stood, frozen in place for a moment, looking like an exceptionally ugly garden gnome. Ronan felt the light tug at him and forced himself to resist it and remain still. At last the homunculus moved, first just the index finger of one hand, curling up from the clenched fist to point at the box. Then the fist began to inch toward the opening, the source of the bright purple light. It put its long finger inside and touched what was hidden within.

It was as if a shadow fell over the homunculus; its gray skin darkened to a deeper gray, then to black. Only its wide golden eyes stayed the same, staring in shock from a head growing ever less substantial, a shadow. Then it screamed, a sound of terror that filled the small chamber and overflowed into the intersecting tunnels. The edges of its body contracted until it was an indistinct blob with eyes, then the eyes vanished, and it drew itself in to a single black point before winking out of existence.

The little red box hovered in the air for a moment. The lid closed, the stone sealing itself into a solid, singular piece again, killing the black light before it fell to the rubble-covered floor.

The remaining gray man struggled to extract himself from the knee-deep wreckage, then bounded to its feet, arms spread wide and its large hands fisted. He leapt around in screeching panic, searching for his companion, then bolted for the opposite tunnel and out of sight.

Ronan knew he wouldn't get another chance like this and acted without pause. Sprinting from cover, he crossed to the center of the chamber in a single leap and caught the bottom of the empty bag in his teeth. He dragged it to the crate and began to search.

His first hurried glance over the contents was not rewarding. Most of the collected items were worthless junk, but the final doorway relic was among the clutter.

He retrieved it, along with a cracked, soot-covered mirror; an old silver pocket watch he suspected of having unnatural powers; and a cloak pin with a blue/black cat's eye gem in the center that conjured a heavy fog when he carefully plucked it up with his teeth.

It's days like this when I miss having hands, he thought. *You really never appreciate your thumbs until you lose them.*

He bagged the pilfered items and turned his wary attention back to the little red box.

It was beautifully fashioned, the Blood Opal it was carved from valuable beyond calculation, but what lay within was perhaps the most dangerous item Ronan had ever encountered.

The Chaos Relic, a remnant of the broken worlds.

An ancient and terrible thing that had lately fallen into the protective custody of the strange man Erasmus and now seemed had fallen out of it.

Now he knew how the lone avian had acquired his treasure trove of relics.

But what of Erasmus?

Ronan retrieved the Blood Opal box from the rubble and dropped it into the bag. He had lingered too long. It was time to go.

No sooner had he retreated into the tunnel than the sound of franticly chattering homunculi reached him, some from far ahead, others from closer behind. They burst into the chamber behind him, barely giving him enough time to slip into the darkness. A moment later he ducked into the first side passage in time to avoid being trampled by two more coming from the other direction.

He waited, wanting them well past him before he resumed his race to the tunnel exit.

A new voice joined the loud, plaintive chattering of the homunculi in the chamber. "Why does it smell like dog in here?"

It was a dry whipcrack of a voice, devoid of any emotion except mild impatience. If Ronan had any doubt about the source of the troubling scent that had lingered in the junkyard these past weeks, that voice would have banished it.

Turoc was here, close enough for his bitter electric scent to overpower the stench of ruin and rot that filled the place.

And now the old serpent had *his* scent.

Ronan broke cover and ran through the darkness as fast as he could, abandoning stealth for speed, hoping the way to the hidden entrance was as straightforward as he remembered.

There must have been many more branching tunnels than he'd noticed on his way in; he heard echoes of shouts through each one he passed. Either they all intersected, or each was occupied. A homunculus burst from a tunnel ahead of him, and he slammed it into the ground before it even had the time to notice him approaching. The end of the bag almost slipped from his mouth, and he clenched down on it harder with his teeth as he put on an extra burst of speed to distance himself from the stunned creature.

Only seconds after leaving the homunculi face first in the dirt, he heard renewed shouting from too close behind that signaled the beginning of active pursuit. Many large feet pounded the ground behind him, and a constant stream of excited chattering told him how fast they were gaining.

Ronan heard a rough whisper of something large and heavy moving quickly over the compacted dirt in an unseen corridor to his right, and a heavy rattling.

He wasn't going to make it out.

Then the ground below him rose sharply, the smell of decay once again discernible above Turoc's scent, and there was nowhere to go but up. Ronan jumped, his front paws hitting the old pitted metal of the refrigerator door, and it swung open to reveal a night growing lighter with the rising moon.

Two homunculi stood outside the door to block his path.

Ronan growled through a mouthful of dirty cloth and tensed his haunches to spring.

Turoc's stench blanketed him, and before he could leap, Ronan felt two long fangs sink into his side.

Ronan screamed and fell. He lost the sack and was dragged backward by the teeth anchored in his body, scraping his ribs, puncturing one of his lungs.

He couldn't move. He could hardly breathe.

And he couldn't escape in his usual way. The fangs burrowing into him, the pain that seemed to flood every nerve of his body, the venom that paralyzed him, all made fading away impossible. He was stuck here now, mind and body, for better or worse. Probably worse.

The fangs pulled free of his flesh and he felt blood gush from the wounds.

"Ronan? Aren't you supposed to be dead?" Rough hands seized Ronan by the scruff of the neck and spun him around. Moonlight fell on the face before him: long, curved fangs; shining golden eyes; and the horns that hooded them. The crimson brand between those horns. The mark of his master. "It *is* you!"

Ronan felt a curse on his lips but didn't have the strength to speak it aloud. Turoc seemed to read it in his eyes, though, and laughed.

"Why are you angry with me? I'm not the one pretending to be dead ... hiding from old friends."

He lifted Ronan by his scruff and brought him closer, face-to-face. "Don't be shy, old friend, speak your mind."

Ronan spoke, a whisper only Turoc could hear, and in a language only his old enemy would understand.

Turoc snarled and flung Ronan back to the ground. "That was quite rude, old friend."

Ronan lay only inches from his dropped bag. He tried to stand, but the effort burned like fire in his every muscle.

"Bring him," Turoc said.

The homunculi jumped down, landing on either side of Ronan. The one on his left, covered to its waste in soot and ash, upended the bag and dumped the contents into the dirt. He ignored the cloak pin, the watch, the mirror, and picked up the Blood Opal box and doorway relic. Then he pointed at Ronan and chittered a command at the others.

Ronan felt himself lifted from the ground again before the pain overwhelmed him and merciful darkness engulfed him.

Chapter 17

Little Gray Man

Penny went to bed early, emotionally drained and physically exhausted, and awoke early the next morning with the rising sun slanting through the open curtains of her window, sliding across her face in dusty bars. She lay there for a few minutes, basking in the warmth of the spring sunlight on her face, her eyes closed, her mind happily blank. Only the gentle squeaking of bedsprings reminded her that she had company. Katie, a much less exuberant sleeper than Zoe, was in the spare bed so often occupied by Zoe. Then Penny remembered that Zoe was just beneath her in the spare bedroom, where she'd been sleeping since noon the previous day. If she wasn't awake by now, she would be soon.

Reluctantly, Penny opened her eyes and turned toward Katie.

Katie had rolled onto her side, away from the slanting shafts of light moving across her bed, and was sleeping as deeply as ever.

"Kat?" Penny's voice was slightly above a whisper, and when there was no response Penny decided to let her sleep.

It was strange having Katie back in her life, beyond the stolen hours late at night in the hollow. Mr. West's change of heart was as unexpected as it was sudden.

Sweeping tangles of hair from her face, Penny rolled onto her side and slid her feet from under the cozy covers of her bed. Cringing a little as the soles of her feet hit the cool floorboards, she stood and walked to the window to close the curtain. She was awake now, but there was no reason Katie shouldn't get a little more sleep.

She gazed down on the vivid colors of Clover Hill, the green of the grass and the mingled white and lavender of the wild clovers. This was her first spring in Dogwood, and though it would be a few more weeks until the abundant trees for which the town was named bloomed, clover was everywhere. While she stood, appreciating the view, a familiar figure appeared. A tall, black-haired figure.

"What's so interesting out there?"

Penny turned, startled, and found Katie sitting up in bed and rubbing the sleep from her eyes. She yawned, stretched, then swung her feet down to the floor, where they quested blindly for her slippers.

"It's Zoe," Penny said, and beckoned Katie to her side. A moment later they were sharing the window and watching their friend make her slow way toward the hollow.

"Think we should go after her?" Katie watched Zoe's progress with mild concern. "She shouldn't be alone now."

"I don't know." Penny was as concerned as Katie, but when she was upset she *liked* to be alone. Zoe might resent their unwanted attention. She was about to say so when she saw something moving through the grass far off to Zoe's right, flanking her. She pointed it out to Katie. "I think Ronan is keeping an eye on her."

"He hasn't been around since last week," Katie reminded her. "Do you think he knows about her grandma?" Even as she spoke, her eyes narrowed. She wiped the dust from the window with her sleeve and pressed her nose against the glass. "That's not Ronan."

"What?" Penny could only make out a small Ronan-sized something parting the grass in tandem with Zoe. Then its path led it to a stunted, skeletal dogwood, and it clambered upward, swinging itself from limb to limb until it was near the top. It watched Zoe for a few moments, and when she paused to turn in its direction, it dropped back into the wild grass and clover.

"That's not Ronan," Katie repeated.

Rather than restate the obvious, Penny simply gaped.

The thing that was not Ronan but that was clearly stalking Zoe was roughly humanoid. It stood a few feet high, had a spindly, hairless body and limbs, a large head, and huge hands and feet at the ends of its short legs and overly long arms. It moved like a monkey through the thinning grass, hunching forward and balancing on its fists as it ran.

Penny stumbled away from the window and ran to her bed, kicking her shoes beneath it, then dropping to her stomach to retrieve them. She pulled them on and ran to the trapdoor to the hallway below without lacing them. She turned to see what was keeping Katie and found her rummaging through her overnight bag next to the guest bed.

"Hurry, Kat! We gotta catch up!"

"Chill out, Penny," Katie urged, cringing as Penny stepped on one of her own shoelaces and nearly tumbled backward over the railing around the trapdoor. "Stop yelling, and close that thing before you fall through it and break your neck."

Penny regarded Katie, nearly weeping in frustration, but did manage to stop herself from shouting again. "Chill out? Did you see that ... thing? We have to ...."

Penny began dancing in place, frustrated beyond words.

"We don't have to catch up," Katie said in soothing tones that made Penny want to scream again. She seemed to read this in Penny's face and rolled her eyes. She at last found what she was looking for in her bag, and held it up. "I have an idea."

* * *

Still slightly pink in the face over her moment of total panic, Penny entered Aurora Hollow via her wardrobe door, her wand ready in one hand, her mirror held tightly in the other. Zoe was still too far away to hear, but Penny figured she had only a few minutes to set Katie's admittedly clever plan into action. She peered into the mirror and saw Katie staring back at her.

"Ready?"

"Yeah," Katie said, then nodded firmly as if to convince herself that she was telling the truth. "Go!"

Penny stuck her wand behind her ear for temporary safekeeping and removed Zoe's wand from her waistband. She clutched it with the mirror in her left hand, retrieved her wand, then threw Zoe's wand and the mirror into the air.

They rose together in an ungraceful arc, broke apart at the summit of their flight, then paused in midair, slowly spinning in place as if dangling from invisible wires.

Penny sighed in relief, then urged them forward with her wand as she began to climb the slope to the flat crown of Clover Hill. They obeyed her direction with only an occasional dip or meander in their gliding journey down the well-worn path. She reached the edge, wishing—not for the first time—that she'd had the good sense to be born with hair that blended a little better into the background, and watched the wand and mirror as they floated down the trail. When they were almost lost to sight, she let the wand fall and encouraged the mirror to rise a little higher, still low enough that the tall grass obscured it but high enough for Zoe to see when she arrived.

With some good timing and luck, they would catch Zoe's stalker by surprise, find out what it was and, more importantly, what it wanted.

A few minutes later the top of Zoe's head came into view, and the rest of her body quickly rose to join it as she crested the last rise.

Her head hung, her face pointing down at the trail and obscured by a fall of long black hair, and just as Penny began to fear she'd miss the mirror entirely, maybe stepping on her wand in her distraction, she paused.

Penny's gaze darted from Zoe to the surrounding field, but she didn't see their uninvited guest.

After a startled step backward, Zoe bent and went to one knee, as if tying her shoelaces, and Penny saw her scoop the small mirror from the air before her. She bent close to it, hiding it behind her curtain of hair. After a few seconds Penny saw her slip the mirror into her pocket and part her hair with her empty hand to search for Penny. When she rose a moment later, Penny saw her wand clutched close to her leg.

Penny readied herself. If Zoe followed Katie's plan, it would happen quickly.

Zoe faced Penny, too far away for Penny to read her expression or even tell if Zoe had spotted her, then she turned right and strode off the trail and into the grass, moving deliberately slowly.

Penny crouched a little lower, aware that her vivid hair made her an easy target for anything with working eyes but unable to do anything about it.

Zoe continued through the waist-high grass, her movements sharp, her posture tense. A few seconds later, the strange gray creature broke through the grass and onto the trail. It paused there and fidgeted for a moment in apparent indecision, hopping once in place to catch sight of Zoe. Then it turned, first one way then the other, and froze when it saw Penny.

Penny's breath caught in her throat. For a moment she thought she was going to faint. Her world went slightly foggy at the edges, and her legs began to wobble beneath her.

She thought she knew what the little monster was now. She'd seen one like it only the week before, tiny enough to fit in the palm of one hand. She knew this one wasn't hers. Hers had green eyes, her eyes; this one's were gold with slits for pupils.

The thing regarded her for a second, its strange face registering surprise, then its thick, pale lips pulled back in a snarl to reveal large teeth that looked as if they'd been chiseled from granite. It growled, a rough, high-pitched sound, like a dog on helium, and charged.

The faint feeling retreated all at once, and her heart hammered in alarm. She remembered with some surprise that she was holding her wand, and pointed it at the charging monster.

The little gray man bounded down the trail toward her in long strides and leaps, dodging the pummeling spells she sent toward it with ease. Her spells gouged divots in the dirt around the little monster. She demolished a small bush on its right and cracked a large rock just as the charging creature leapt over it. She grazed it once, chipping a sliver of stone from its shoulder, throwing it off stride for a moment but not stopping it. She tried a levitation spell, but the little monster was moving too quickly for her to catch it.

Zoe called out somewhere in the distance.

Fighting her panic, Penny conjured a shield just as the thing closed the remaining distance. It bounced back, as if striking an invisible wall.

It shook its head and growled, then faced her again. Its large eyes narrowed, and it snapped at the air between them with its rough stonelike teeth. Then it lowered its bald head and charged again. It struck the invisible barrier between them with enough force to push Penny a few inches down the hill. The shield shimmered momentarily in front of her, and her wand bucked in her hand.

"Could use some help!" Penny cried out, bracing for another charge.

The thing twittered madly in a strange, incomprehensible language, then charged again.

Penny felt this impact all the way to her shoulder, and the shield fell as her wand flew out of her hand. Before she could regain her tottering balance, the little gray man plowed into her and they tumbled backward down the hill and into Aurora Hollow.

She no longer felt ashamed of her earlier panic. It seemed justified now.

Penny heard Zoe call to her as she tumbled to a stop at the bottom of the hill, bruised, dirty, and winded. The little gray man held on to her, chirping madly.

She opened her mouth to call for help and felt blood gush down her chin. Before she could make a sound, the little gray man's hands closed around her throat and began to squeeze. Penny tried fruitlessly to pry the long, gray fingers from her throat, but they were as strong as stone. She could not budge them.

The little gray man thrust its ugly face close to hers and snarled.

She flailed blindly in the dirt for her dropped wand but couldn't find it. The hollow began to darken around her. She felt as if she were cradled in a dense fog.

I'm dead, Penny thought, and the emotion that followed was neither fear nor sadness but anger.

Rage at the creature for stealing her life.

Her skin felt suddenly hot, very hot. Red hot. The animal sneer vanished from the monster's face. Its eyes went round with surprise. Penny was viewing the gray man's face through a bright, shimmering veil of fire.

The stone fingers around her throat loosened, then released, and Penny drew in a deep, painful breath. Her throat felt swollen, pinched shut. For a moment she tottered on the edge of consciousness, the darkness of oblivion settling over her. Then the darkness lifted, the world came back into focus, and Penny could breathe again. She sat up, cringing at the aches and bruises that seemed to cover her from head to toe.

The little gray man waved its long arms, trying to extinguish the flames covering its hands. It howled, not in pain but in frustration, and beat its hands in the dirt.

As her strength returned, Penny's fury swelled. The sheath of fire around her pulsed with each frantic beat of her heart. She forgot about Zoe. She forgot about Katie and Susan. There was only her rage and the creature.

Penny rose, aches and pains forgotten, and cocked her arm like a big league pitcher winding up for a fastball. What she threw wasn't a baseball but a fireball. It hit the gray man in the chest, splattering tongues of flame into the trees behind him. They burned for only a few seconds before dying out, but the flames covering the creature intensified.

He ran in a tight, panicked circle, howled in terror, and scampered toward the hill.

Zoe stood at the top on the path out of the hollow, her wand aimed down as the little gray man scrambled up the dirt steps. She blasted him to the ground.

Penny saw the look of fear on Zoe's face, not of the little gray man but of her, and her anger ebbed away. The shimmering orange heat-haze around her faded. The flames sank into her skin. She felt cold in their sudden absence.

"I didn't know you could do that," Zoe said, looking from Penny to the groaning creature on the ground. She sounded petulant, angry.

"Neither did I," Penny said, and turned her attention back to the monster as well.

It twittered and moaned, sounding like a cross between a monkey and a bird, and rolled in the dirt to smother the flames. Without Penny's anger to feed them, they died out quickly. The little gray man rose into a crouch, its body still smoldering, and regarded its new attacker.

Penny recognized ill intent in the thing's expression, redoubled her search for the dropped wand, and found Katie, holding hers, in the open doorway leading to her room.

Katie dashed past Penny as the thing charged toward the hill.

"No you don't!" A fork of purple lightning arched through the air from the tip of Katie's wand and struck the little gray man in the back. It froze for a moment then fell, spread-eagle and twitching to the ground. A heavy smell of ozone filled the air, and their hair began to dance with static.

Penny approached it cautiously, massaging her sore, swollen throat. Katie stayed at her side, wand pointed at the smoking body.

"Is it dead?"

Zoe skidded to a stop at the last step and braced herself against the trunk of a gnarled willow. "What is it?"

Katie shook her head, then made a sound of protest when Penny took a step closer and nudged the thing with her foot.

"Relax, Kat. I think you knocked it out."

Penny nudged it again, then rolled it onto its back.

"Eww," Katie groaned, keeping her wand pointed at it but averting her eyes.

"It's called a homuncu ... something or other," Penny remarked, wishing she hadn't rolled the little monster onto its back, "and apparently it's a boy."

Its eyes fluttered open. It regarded the canopy of green above it in confusion for a moment, then bared its teeth as it saw Penny standing above it. It grabbed feebly for her ankle, and she jumped back to avoid it, bumping into Katie, who was close on her heels.

Before it could rise again, long green whips snaked down from the surrounding willows and twisted around the little gray man's wrists and ankles, binding him. They hoisted him into the air and more slithered down, wrapping it from waist to knees, binding its legs together. The willows hoisted it higher into the air until he hung above Penny and Katie, chattering down at them in his alien language and looking like a gargoyle in a grass skirt.

Zoe stood at the bottom of the trail, both hands pressed to the narrow trunk of the nearest willow.

"That's a good trick to know," Penny croaked, still massaging her throat.

Zoe's eyes moved from the gray man above them to Penny, but she said nothing.

Penny watched the creature for a moment, worried it might tear free from the limbs, but as strong as it was, they were stronger. It thrashed about over their heads, straining at the willow whips; they wound tighter around him in response.

Zoe passed Penny while she regarded the struggling monster, dropped her wand to the dirt, and sat at the water's edge. She seemed to have lost all interest now that the immediate danger had passed.

"What did you call that thing?" Katie gave the dangling little gray man a quick, furtive glance.

"Ho-mun-cu-lus," Penny said, enunciating to make sure she got the name right. She began to tell them about the egg Ronan had given her for her birthday and the baby homunculus that had hatched from it.

"Tell us later," Katie said, lunging forward and grabbing Penny by the wrist to drag her toward the door. "I saw something when I was looking for Ronan in the Conjuring Glass. I think he's in trouble."

* * *

They stood in her room. Penny could see the outline of the big mirror under the sheet Katie had thrown over it.

"The House of Mirrors?" Penny could hardly believe what she was hearing. She hadn't thought much about the place since leaving it to burn the previous fall. She had no idea the place was still around and standing. "You're sure, Kat?"

"Yeah," Katie said, amazement clear in her voice. "I think all the mirrors in there were linked to the Conjuring Glass, like ours. I saw what was left of the place through a piece of broken mirror."

"And Ronan was there?"

"No." Katie waved an impatient hand, perhaps indicating that Penny should shut up and let her finish. "But I think he *was* there. I was looking for Ronan, and the Conjuring Glass took me there. I think it's in the junkyard."

"The junkyard!" Penny nearly shouted, and Katie slapped a hand over her mouth.

"Can you *not* scream?" Katie gave the trapdoor a quick nervous glance, as if expecting Susan to bust in on them at any moment to ask what all the shouting was about.

Penny slapped Katie's hand away but continued in a lower voice.

"*Of course* ... that's where Ronan has been going, and that creep's son was guarding it ...."

"To keep people away from the House of Mirrors," Katie finished. "I figured that out. Tovar must have had other stuff in there like the mirrors and those doorknobs. Ronan was trying to get them all before someone else did."

"But who was Joseph Duke guarding them for?" It was too much information, too much weirdness to sort out all at once, so Penny decided for the time being to focus on the one small bit of weirdness at a time. "So where was Ronan?"

"I don't know," Katie said, sounding as flustered as Penny felt. "A cave, I think. Somewhere underground. I didn't see *him*. There was a watch and something else. But there was blood in the dirt. *A lot of blood.*"

Penny's blood ran cold. Ronan hurt. Ronan bleeding. Ronan vulnerable and in danger, something she had not truly believed was possible.

"We have to find him, Kat." She barely heard her own words. There was no strength behind them. "We have to help him."

Katie nodded. Her face had gone ashen, her eyes large, and there was a perceptible tremor in her shoulders, but she agreed without hesitation.

Penny sat on the edge of her bed and pulled aside the sheet covering the mirror. The Conjuring Glass reflected her face for a moment, then a swirl of gray mist obscured it. She concentrated on seeing Ronan, but when the mist cleared the glass showed only darkness.

Katie put the tip of the wand close to the glass, and there was light, shining into the Conjuring Glass and out of the little mirror. It seemed to be sitting upright, because the lower half showed them what Katie had described, an old watch on a chain, something that looked like a broach pin, and a large wet spot in the dirt that Penny thought had to be blood. And there had been a lot of it.

But it showed something else Katie hadn't noticed on her first glance—the bottom of a rusted metal door.

* * *

Penny and Katie hid the Conjuring Glass under her bed and hurried back into the hollow to tell Zoe what they'd seen, but she was gone. A quick glance upward confirmed that the little gray man was still securely bound and dangling. He glowered down at them but no longer struggled.

"Zoe!" Katie shouted, but her call went unanswered.

Penny sprinted up the path to the field above and scanned it for Zoe's tall outline. "She's not up here."

Katie pulled her little mirror out of her pocket as Penny stumbled and slid back down to join her. "Zoe!"

Penny bent down over it. "Zoe, Ronan's hurt. We need your help!"

There was no reply.

"Where is she?" Katie cried out in frustration. "Should we call Ellen?"

"No," Penny said, shoving the door closed, cutting off the view of her bedroom. "I think Ellen has already made up her mind."

Katie looked unhappy at the statement but accepted it.

"Are you ready?"

"Not really," Katie said, but she held her wand ready and moved close behind Penny.

Penny concentrated on the image of the rusted door, trying not to puzzle over the odd perspective the mirror had shown them. She touched her wand to the surface of the door the Birdman had thoughtfully abandoned in the hollow, and then turned the knob with her other hand and pulled it open.

Behind her Katie gasped.

Now Penny knew why the perspective seemed strange.

They stared into the inside of a filthy old refrigerator, then down at the missing floor and into the tunnel below.

The drop wasn't far, but the tunnel was narrow, like the drainpipe under downtown, and led deeper into the earth instead of out of it. They could see the mirror, the dull metallic sheen of the old pocket watch, the gemstone sparkle of the broach.

Penny took a deep, calming breath, trying to ward off claustrophobia at the thought of crawling through that tunnel.

She stepped through the door.

Chapter 18

The Rescue

"This is the craziest thing we've ever done," Katie said, an audible tremor in her voice.

And that is saying a lot, Penny added silently.

Penny stood inside the old refrigerator and stared into the opening, her resolve not just weakening but threatening to crawl away and hide under a rock. Before it could, she dropped to her knees and slid head first into the steep mouth of the tunnel, shimmying deeper into it on her elbows and knees. She kept her wand pointed forward wishing she knew how to light her wand tip like she'd seen Katie do.

As soon as she wished it, her wand responded with a weak glow that made her almost wish it was dark again. The tunnel went on as far as she could see, which wasn't far, but she could imagine miles of dark tunnel stretching ahead of her. The hard-packed earth was spotted with blood.

She heard the door close behind her and fought off a wave of claustrophobic panic.

"Why did you close the door?" she whispered. "We want the door *open*."

"No, we don't," Katie whispered back. Her nerves sounded clearly in her tone. "If something else comes back this way, that door would lead it right into the hollow."

Penny reluctantly accepted the wisdom of Katie's words but was unable to move forward. Her limbs seemed frozen in place, and only grudgingly unfroze when Katie prodded her from behind. Panic rode on her back like a monkey, ready to seize her around the throat.

"Penny, you're hyperventilating. *Calm down … breathe slowly.*"

Penny closed her eyes and tried to forget where they were, tried to slow her rapid breathing and pounding heart, to steady her frazzled nerves.

Softly, Katie whispered, "It's not too late to turn back."

"I'm not going back," Penny said, surprised and pleased to feel a new coolness settle into her mind and body, not calm, but almost indifference. A wordless voice in her head told her that she had picked her path and now she had to follow it.

"Okay, then," Katie said, and Penny was relieved to hear a similar resolve in her voice.

For what seemed like a long time, they crawled, Penny illuminating the path ahead and Katie at her heels. They paused at intersecting paths to listen, to search for signs of Ronan's passage and, though she didn't like to admit it even to herself, for more blood or Ronan's lifeless body.

Occasional sounds echoed to them, manic squeaks and chitterings, something that might have been a shout of pain, something that sounded absurdly like a baby's rattle. She could feel the air stirring at each new tunnel they passed, and she knew that there must be other exits to the surface, a comforting thought.

More time passed, and their slow progress continued. Penny was about to suggest that if they didn't find him soon they should use the next intersecting tunnel to turn around and head back to the surface, when something lit the tunnel ahead. She let the light from her wand go out and dropped to her belly so Katie could see what she was seeing.

Behind her, Katie gasped.

There was a bend in the path maybe twenty feet ahead of them, and a glow that threw darting, malformed shadows up the corridor.

They waited for a moment, silent and listening.

The rattling sound came again, and the mad chittering of many gathered creatures.

"Is our guest comfortable?" The voice that echoed up to them cold and crisp, the tone polite but somehow malevolent. A new chill ran down Penny's spine at the sound of it.

More incomprehensible chattering was all the reply the voice received, but he seemed to understand it.

"Good ... good. My old friend and I have much catching up to do." The voice was decidedly chilly now, threatening, like the point of a poised knife. "We have much ground to cover do we not, Ronan?"

"I have ... nothing to say to you, *old friend.*" Ronan seemed barely able to speak, his voice drifting to them in a weak wheeze, but the hate that oozed from his every syllable was clear. "Nothing you do can change that."

"Is that so?" Dark humor infused the cold voice. It seemed eager to take up the challenge.

Ronan screamed, not the howl of a hurt animal, but an almost human scream of pain.

Katie prodded Penny, and they moved forward.

The chittering began again, frantic, alarmed.

"Yes," the cold voice said. "I am aware, but never mind them for now. Patience is my friend too, little ones, as Ronan here could testify."

Ronan screamed again.

Penny crawled faster, heard Katie's heavy breathing behind her as she struggled to keep up.

"Our last interrupted encounter was most dissatisfying, old friend?"

Ronan screamed in reply. Penny could not imagine the torture he was going through, didn't want to imagine it.

They were closer to the bend in the path. The diffuse light seemed brighter, the dancing shadows more frenzied.

"I had promised long ago to kill you myself," the voice said, "so you can only imagine my frustration when I learned that the avians had finished you off in the Bad Lands."

Penny felt the familiar—and now welcome—heat rising from her core, spreading through her.

Ronan screamed, and something inside him seemed to tear loose.

Penny was afraid they were already too late.

"So imagine my surprise to find you here, alive and well. My *happy* surprise."

Ronan's screams became a low, liquid gurgle.

Penny turned the corner, Katie almost on top of her in her rush to get to their dying friend.

The raucous creatures had gone silent, a silence like a held breath.

Penny saw the opening into a large chamber only a few inches away, saw the glowing light globe that hovered in the air above piles of burned wreckage; saw Ronan, bloodied and somehow diminished, in the dirt at the at the other end next to the mouth of another tunnel; saw the glowing golden eyes and shadow of some horrible head in the dark of that tunnel.

She fell through the opening into the chamber, hitting the hard-packed earth and rolling to her knees, wand out and ready. Katie hit the ground beside her, similarly poised.

"And Ronan's lovely screams only served to bring them quicker," the voice that belonged to those golden eyes informed the homunculi gathered in groups on the left and right of the girls, still and silent, but ready to pounce. "So patience, my little friends, has saved us the trouble of going to them."

"No!" Ronan saw the girls, tried to rise, but couldn't. "Run!"

Fresh blood sprayed from his mouth as he screamed and writhed.

Penny pointed her wand at the thing in the tunnel behind him and fired, but there was a sudden shimmering in the air in front of the silhouetted figure, and her fire spells rebounded, hitting the ceiling, the walls, the piles of debris, causing them to blaze.

Beside her, Katie was blasting homunculi to the ground, but though she scattered them, she couldn't seem to hurt them.

The new firelight filling the chamber fell over the thing in the tunnel, and Penny saw the face that went with those golden eyes.

She screamed.

The thing darted out of its concealment and landed in front of Ronan, its long, sinewy body coiled to spring again. Its eyes glowed in the firelight like electrified blood, its smile was all teeth, long and pointed.

Between the shining eyes was a mark, a bright crimson shape that seemed familiar to Penny.

"Aren't you girls a little young for these types of forays?"

It was a snake, the largest Penny had ever seen. Fifteen feet long or more, its underside dusty brown, the harder scales along its back muddy red. Its wide, arrow-shaped head seemed too large for its body, and a pair of horns curved forward out of its flat brow. But unlike any snake Penny had ever seen, it had arms, two on each side of its thick body. One of them held a wand, twirling it like a baton.

"Stop that," the monster said, directing its evil gaze at Katie, who was still attacking his passive homunculi. The end of his tail whipped out, and Penny heard it rattle as it struck Katie across the chest and knocked her off her feet.

It flinched back and hissed in pain as its tail slithered through the flaming debris between them.

"Katie, are you okay?" Penny shouted, not daring to look away from the monster.

"Yeah," Katie said, but her reply was weak, breathless.

Lowering her wand, Penny charged at the monster, dashing between the piles of flaming rubble.

The monster slithered backward in surprise, and the twirling wand in its hand suddenly pointed at Penny. Before he could use it, a spell passed over Penny's head, low enough to toss her hair, and struck the wand from its hand.

A second later Penny was on it, grabbing hold of its loathsome body, her arms just long enough to wrap around and her hands to join.

Penny burned, and the monster in her grasp burned with her.

For a moment the muscles beneath his awful flesh seemed to shiver and roll, then it screamed, and Penny found herself flying backward. She landed hard against the cool earth, winded but scrambling to her feet, and saw the thing rolling in the dirt, its face a mask of outrage and agony. Its body still burned, the hard scales of its back seeming impervious to the heat, but its softer underside blistering. It grasped for its dropped wand and passed the tip down the length of its body, killing the flames that clung to it.

The homunculi waited, poised, eager to join the fray.

The monster faced the girls, surprise and outrage clear on its inhuman face. It rattled as it backed away and slipped into its tunnel.

"Seize them!" It shouted at the gathered homunculi. "I want the red one alive … kill her friend!"

Then it was gone, retreating down the tunnel.

The homunculi started toward them, their golden eyes glowing like their master's.

Penny aimed her wand at the nearest one and almost dropped it in astonishment as her spell exploded off the thing's chest, launching it backward into its companions. One of its arms lay on the ground, like the arm of a broken statue, its fingers twitching.

"Get Ronan," Katie shouted, firing a fork of lightning into the other advancing group and stunning them. They shook the spell off quickly and started toward her again, spreading out to surround her. "I'll hold them off!"

Penny ran to Ronan, leaping debris and dodging one little gray man who tried to head her off. It grabbed her leg, and Katie used a levitation spell to pull it away and slam it against the earthen wall. It fell away, stunned, and left a perfect imprint of its spread-eagled body in the dirt.

Penny fell beside Ronan, and relief flooded through her when he opened his eyes.

She heard a faint rattle deep in the corridor the Snakeman had fled down, and threw a ball of her Phoenix fire after him. It exploded, sending a rush of air, stone, and earth through the opening. From far inside came the deep rumble of collapse.

"Little Red," Ronan gasped, and she bent low over him to listen. "Leave me ...."

"No," Penny shouted and lifted him from the bloody dirt.

He winced in pain.

"You can't help me," he said. "You shouldn't have come down here."

"You can thank us later," Katie said, her voice thick with a false bluster that didn't show on her face. She looked sick with fear, close to tears.

"... Something important," he said as Penny rose with him cradled in her arms.

She lowered her head closer, could smell the blood matting his coat. She was eager to be off for too many reasons to name, but Ronan had fixed her with a look she knew well. Intense and forbidding, inviting no argument.

"In the box." His head rolled against her arm, his gaze sweeping to the ground, and Penny found the small wooden crate he was searching for near the flaming rubble. "The little red box ... the doorway relic. Get them. Hide them."

"Let's go!" Katie screamed from her side of the chamber.

The homunculi concentrated on her now, circling, cautious. Most bore small signs of her handiwork, burns and scorch marks. One crawled toward her, pulling itself forward with its hands and pushing with its one remaining leg. The other leg was nowhere to be seen. Their numbers were smaller now.

Penny shifted Ronan to one arm, cradling him awkwardly, and bent down to look in the box. She found the items he'd asked for at once, but could think of no place to put them.

"Penny!" Katie was growing more anxious.

"Ten seconds," Penny shouted back, and kicked a shoe off, wobbling one-legged in place as she tugged her sock off. She shoved the red box in, unable to stop herself pausing for a moment to admire the beauty of it, then a doorknob ... one she recognized.

"These are from the House of Mirrors," she said, tying the end of her filthy, soot-stained sock through a belt loop on her hip.

Ronan either hadn't heard her or ignored the words.

"Go now," he gasped. "Leave me here ... I'll only slow you down."

"Shut up," Penny said, and dashed through the flaming rubble to join Katie. "You go first. I'll keep them back."

Katie looked as if she might argue, then sent a last fork of lighting at the bravest of the crouching homunculi and sprinted the last few feet to the mouth of the tunnel. She dove in, her wand outstretched and shining bright light into the darkness.

The half-dozen remaining gray men lunged for Penny as she ran toward the tunnel, and she hurled another ball of fire, not at them but at the ground beneath the tunnel. A second later she and Ronan passed through unharmed as the homunculi shied away.

Katie set a brisk pace and Penny fell further and further behind, slowed by Ronan, cradled in her arm.

"Leave me, Penny. Drop me and get away."

"No!" Penny rolled onto her back and propelled herself upward with her legs, shifting Ronan into her left arm and pointing her wand down the tunnel behind her with her right. She made a light to dispel the claustrophobic darkness and again was not comforted by what it revealed.

Two of the little monsters ran toward her, side by side, their heads scraping the ceiling above them. She tried to think of a spell she could use that wouldn't collapse the tunnel on them, and, in her moment's hesitation, they closed the distance and leapt at her.

Reflexively, Penny held her arm up, her wand turned sideways in her hand, to brace herself against the coming attack. The creatures froze in midpounce, their golden eyes widening in confusion, and when Penny straightened her arm, it felt as if she were shoving hard against something semi-solid hanging unseen in the air.

The homunculi flew, squealing and squawking, down into darkness.

I'll have to remember that, she thought, and continued her awkward scramble up the slight incline.

"We're almost there," Katie shouted. "Hurry!"

"I'm coming," Penny shouted back.

Just as she was beginning to believe they would make it out, a muffled crashing sounded above them.

Moments later Katie shouted frustration.

"They blocked the way out!"

"What?"

"They pushed something over the hole. We're stuck in here!"

Below her, Penny heard the sound of the charging homunculi.

* * *

Movement pained Turoc more than he would have thought possible, but the burns would heal, and he *could* move, so he did.

That girl had done something he had only ever heard about in legend, stories from ancient days when his master's oldest enemy still lived and walked the hidden bridges between the worlds. He would never have believed it had he not seen it for himself. Seen it and felt it.

Turoc dragged himself through the rough, dusty ground of the narrow labyrinth, hobbled by his injury but propelled by deadly purpose. He passed the shell of The House of Mirrors, which Ronan had no doubt picked clean before Turoc had even arrived in Dogwood.

The rogue avian who had owned the burnt structure told Turoc and his master much after his expulsion from Dogwood by the very girls Turoc himself had just faced. He had spoken heatedly of the two girls, cursed their existence with his last breath. The girls were as formidable as the Birdman had claimed, but also foolish, and very soon would be dead, trapped in the tunnels that would become their tomb.

Though he was not able to harm the red one—the very blood that ran through her veins ensured that—he was by no means compelled to rescue her from the death she'd earned through her own stupidity.

The avian had told them much while Turoc's venom worked its way into his every muscle and bone: the relics he'd acquired from the old fool Erasmus; his master's drive for more and more human slaves from this world—but he'd not mentioned Ronan. Ronan, whose Shamanic magic had allowed him to cross between the worlds.

Turoc took great joy in the knowledge that Ronan would shortly be out of his path as well, and greater joy in the knowledge that his journey out of this world would be as if through fire.

Ronan had earned his pain.

Turoc spied the open area where the people of this world came to cast their refuse—such a wasteful race. It was empty, but not for much longer. With Joseph captured, the landfill would soon be out of bounds to him and his helpers.

This very day, he thought. *I finish my business in this place this very day.*

The way ahead was too narrow for him—it had never been meant to accommodate him—but Turoc was strong, even if injured and weakened. He shoved his way through the narrower gaps in the junk maze Joseph Duke, the idiot boy, had so carefully constructed, cringing in pain as his raw, blistered flesh tore and scales wrenched free against jagged metal. Edges bent, groaned and creaked with his passage, until at last he forced his way through to the dead end that concealed the homunculi's entrance.

Turoc hissed in pleasure and drew his wand.

He could hear the sounds of struggle in the tunnel below him and knew the girls were close now. Only moments left to stop them. If they escaped, he would again be limited by the blood oath not to kill the red one.

A sweep of his wand brought the wall of rusted metal behind the old refrigerator crashing down, sealing them in and opening his way out of the maze.

Now he could rejoin Morgan Duke in his hiding place and heal before finishing his work in Dogwood, in Aurora Hollow, for good.

The Master wanted this place. It was one of the few stable portals left between the worlds, like the one on Morgan Duke's island. Almost as important, it held great sentimental value. It was, after all, the place where The Master had killed the one he hated most in all the worlds.

The woman and her brat had stood in his way for too long.

The time of gentle persuasion had passed. The time of the fist was at hand.

"Die slowly, little ones," he said, and began to climb over the avalanche of metal.

A streak of movement above caught his eye.

He searched the sky, his wand at hand, and saw them.

Two more girls, flying on the most outlandish besom he had ever seen. The one in front wore green robes that flapped in the wind of her passage, and as she turned and dived toward him, he saw the wand in her hand.

Turoc shouted in frustrated rage and sent a curse at them, but his balance was tenuous, his aim bad, and the girls quickly dove lower to avoid certain death. They passed by him, close enough that he could have swatted them from the air with his tail, but the attempt brought a new molten pain to his seared muscles.

The one in the back half-turned to point her wand at him as they climbed skyward but didn't use it. Her mouth was an open O of shock.

He sent another curse after them, one aimed to knock the doltish expression from her face, but her shield spell sent it ricocheting back toward him. It hit the base of the toppled wall of metal he scaled, shaking it beneath him. His next curse flew wild.

Then they turned sharply and rocketed toward him again.

The girl in front sent a barrage of fire spells, her long black hair flying out behind her as her hood slipped. He blocked the first few with a well-timed shield, but the others pierced the hill of twisted metal below and around him, exploding into flames between him and his attackers. Fires rose on all sides and the cool metal beneath his coiled body began to heat almost at once. He sprang forward, blind to what awaited him on the other side of the blazing wall of pain.

He tumbled down the jagged slope to the ground, the torn edges of metal biting into his flesh, piercing and puncturing him, and landed on the stony earth outside the burning maze, one arm pinned beneath him. He heard bone snap, and screamed with fresh agony.

They came at him again, dropping down at him like arrows. He was weary of this game.

"*Procellium,*" he shouted, aiming his wand not at the girls but at the sky.

Dark gray clouds formed, gathering and reaching to each other with arms like smoke; a wind whipped at him from the east, fanning the flames behind him, then another from the south. Above him the strange besom spun in the crosswinds. A second later the first bright tracery of lightning etched glowing lines through the clouds. The sky rumbled like a waking giant.

The air spun around the landfill in a vortex, growing in strength with each passing second. Above him the girls spun out of control. The one in front clutched the handles of her odd flying machine, and the one in the back held tight to the driver. The vortex closed in on them, spinning them quicker, and then they shot free of it, spiraling away into the distance, still hanging on but abandoning the fight.

The growing tempest fed on Turoc's remaining strength, sapping it. When he could no longer maintain it, he lowered his wand. The wind died at once, the lightning gave another feeble flicker, and the ensuing thunder sounded more like a sigh. The clouds began to drift and thin.

Turoc propelled himself away as quickly as his injured body would allow, vowing to return and pay the girls back for his pain.

* * *

"I can't get through!" It was Katie's turn to panic now. She pounded against the metal barrier with her fist, the sound echoing down the tunnel like the banging of a gong.

Penny cradled Ronan's still, bloody form in one arm and rained spells down on the advancing homunculi. Her continued barrage chipped away at them, a finger here, an arm or leg there, small chips of stone from their torsos and heads. She forced them back until their sheer numbers overcame her defenses, and she sent a fireball at them, scattering them like panicked stone monkeys. The already thin air of the tunnel grew thinner as the flames devoured what was left of their oxygen, and Penny reluctantly extinguished the flames, allowing the homunculi their slow second advance.

They were going to die down there.

"*Penny!*"

Penny turned reflexively to Katie at the sound of the voice but knew it wasn't hers.

Katie quit pounding against the metal and shot Penny an inquisitive look.

"Cover me," Penny said, and dropped her wand to dig the mirror from her pocket. Ronan's limp body began to slide from the cradle of her left arm, and she tightened her grip on him.

Ronan groaned in pain.

Katie's glowing wand tip appeared over her shoulder, lighting the mirror and the face staring at her.

"Ellen?"

Behind her, Katie gasped.

Below, the first pair of homunculi showed their ugly gray faces again, advancing slowly, warily.

"Where are you?" Ellen's eyes squinted against a strong wind that blew her hair back. "We've been calling for you but you never answered!"

"We've been busy," Katie shouted, firing a spell at the advancing homunculi. It was a perfect headshot, striking the right one between its glowing eyes. A small crack opened, the eyes dimmed, and it fell heavily onto its back like a toppled statue, stonelike and perfectly still.

"We're at the landfill," Penny said.

"Where?" The sky, a stormy gray that Penny didn't remember seeing at all that day, moved too quickly past her. "Are you ...?"

"Flying ... with Zoe. We're *at* the landfill but we can't find you!"

A small flicker of hope warmed Penny's insides but was extinguished almost at once.

"Be careful! There's ...," she couldn't think of the proper words to describe the monster they had just faced, "something dangerous out there. We're underground ..."

Katie sent more spells flying past her head, and Penny flinched.

"Underground!" Zoe's voice this time, distant but audible.

"We're in a tunnel," Penny explained. "We were almost out but something blocked the tunnel."

"The ... the Snakeman ... thing?" Ellen said, a little self-consciously.

"Yes!" Hope and dread continued their tug-of-war in Penny's chest.

"It's gone now," Ellen said. "We're coming down."

Encouraged by her success against the still-motionless gray man, Katie continued her assault against any that came within range. A second and third fell, both with cracks in their stone skulls.

A moment later Ellen's backdrop of meandering gray clouds vanished and Penny saw the burning walls of the metal labyrinth. Then Zoe's face appeared in the mirror. "Make some noise so we can find you."

Penny and Katie obliged.

Katie pounded her fist against the crumpled metal that blocked their path and screamed "In here! We're down here!"

With nothing solid to bang a fist against, Penny simply screamed.

The sudden cacophony drove the few remaining homunculi into a startled retreat.

The mirror went blank, and Penny slipped it back into her pocket.

Katie continued pounding and they both screamed. When the homunculi ventured too close, Penny shot spells at them.

"Get outa' here!" The narrow tunnel made targeting the little monsters easy at least, and though every hit she scored damaged them, the minor damage didn't discourage them from coming back for more.

"Leave us alone!" Penny screamed and fired with her wand, scoring a perfect hit between the glowing eyes of the lead monster. It's stone head cracked and it fell on its face.

The other homunculi retreated again.

The minutes passed, and they were beginning to grow hoarse, when some weighty object shifted unseen above them. The ground shook around them, the hard-packed earth over their heads rained dust, and Penny grew certain that the tunnel would collapse before Zoe and Ellen could free them.

The homunculi gathered for a last charge, their high-pitched war cries overcoming Penny's and Katie's.

Penny slid back as far as she could, pressing against Katie. There was no more room for retreat.

Then a loud bang sounded, and daylight flooded the tunnel.

Katie was suddenly gone, and Penny pushed herself backward.

As the nearest homunculus reached for Penny, its chubby stonelike fingers actually brushing her shoe, a hand grasped the back of her shirt and dragged her into the open. She was out, surrounded by Zoe, Katie and Ellen.

Spells flew around her, driving the emerging monsters back into the tunnel. Penny threw a last handful of fire for good measure, then the ground began to shake. A gout of flame and dirt belched from the open tunnel as the entire underground labyrinth collapsed.

They backed away, Penny scrambling to her feet, as the walls of rusted steel around them shifted and tipped. Then they ran. Zoe turned for her bike but Katie grabbed her by the back of her robe to stop her. A second later Zoe's old bike was crushed under tons of twisted, fire-blackened steel.

"This way," Ellen shouted.

They followed her through a narrow gap in the far wall, then through an opening into the wide space beyond the collapsing junk maze. An idle bulldozer sat unoccupied at the foot of a hill of trash. An ugly old camper sat alone on a rise to their right. Ahead, a locked gate barred entrance or exit.

They ran for the trailer, Penny pausing for one last glance back.

The fire had mostly died out, its available fuel consumed, and black smoke rose into the sky.

"Hurry," Zoe shouted, and Penny ran to catch up.

She didn't dare to look down at the still form cradled in her left arm.

They reached the camper, and Ellen drew her wand. Closing her eyes, she pressed its tip against the closed door, then opened it and dashed through. The others followed, Zoe last, and she slammed the door shut.

They were back in the hollow, winded and wounded, Katie coughing and barely able to breath.

"I'm sorry," Zoe said, and the shame in her voice broke Penny's heart a little. "I didn't know you'd gone until Ellen found me."

Ellen sat on one of the boulders surrounding the fire pit, her eyes still wide with shock. "I heard you say my name, but you were gone before I could answer you. I came here but no one was around so I walked until I found Zoe."

"Thank you," Katie said, still wheezing, but finally able to speak. "We would have died down there if you hadn't come for us."

"Ronan?" Zoe turned her streaming eyes to the still form in Penny's arm, and Penny made herself look too.

Ronan was not breathing, not stirring.

Penny was suddenly unable to stand. She dropped to her knees and laid Ronan down in the grass before her.

He was still warm, but the blood had quit flowing from his wounds.

Penny laid her hand down on his chest, felt the heart inside it beat ... beat ... beat ... then stop.

A voice in the wind seemed to come down to them, and they all looked up into the green canopy, searching.

Thank you for coming for me.

When they looked down again, Ronan was gone.

Chapter 19

Closing the Deal

The next few days were calm, if not restful. Zoe mourned her grandmother and they all mourned Ronan. Katie and Ellen became more or less permanent fixtures of the big house on Clover Hill, spending nearly as much time there as Penny and Zoe themselves, and Susan ran herself frantic playing mother hen to the whole brood. She had been hysterical with worry after their return from the landfill; she had awakened to an empty house and no notes of explanation, but Penny and Katie had been able to pass off their minor injuries as a fall down by the creek while looking for Zoe.

Susan, who had seen examples of Penny's grace first hand, accepted the fabrication without question, but they still had to convince her that Penny was in fact not bleeding to death. While Ronan's body had vanished after his heart stilled, his spilled blood had not.

At the end of the second day, Zoe received the phone call she'd been expecting. Her mom and dad would be there by the end of the week to attend the funeral. The arrangements had been left to local friends, the Town Elders, but they promised they would be there. What would happen to Zoe remained uncertain, an unspoken source of anxiety for Penny who couldn't imagine life in Dogwood without her best friend.

Zoe and Penny had not returned to town since the day of the fire, but they got a steady stream of news from Michael, who came by regularly to keep Susan up-to-date on the local drama involving Ernest Price and Morgan Duke.

The two had been out of town on shared business, a ruse to keep Ernest out of the way while Joseph Duke, who short of actual torture seemed unlikely to talk, did his dirty work. At least that was the sheriff's story, Michael said. Whether or not Michael believed the story was another source of speculation for the girls.

Ernest's story—or confession, depending on how you looked at it—was that Morgan Duke had been employing him for the better part of a decade to buy land in and around Dogwood, with the eventual goal of transforming the small town into an upscale tourist town, and that Susan's refusal to sell a key piece of property had finally prompted Duke's visit.

The name Price, which had once been synonymous with God in Dogwood, was now mud. Michael had mentioned as an aside on his last visit that Sharon Price, Rooster's mother, had broken down in hysterics while grocery shopping and had been escorted out by management.

"I didn't even know Rooster had a mom," Penny said in an attempt to tease a smile out of Zoe. "I thought his *papa* just found him under a rock somewhere and brought him home."

Mrs. Price and her boys were now 'vacationing' somewhere on the coast, but Ernest had had to stay in town for continued questioning from state authorities.

"Not looking good for Avery Price," they overheard Susan saying over the phone. "A few more months and he may have to find honest work again."

Zoe had asked Katie if Michael would run for sheriff, to which Katie had replied "Nawww … he wouldn't," as if the prospect was nothing short of ludicrous.

Penny thought differently—he was something of a local celebrity after his heroics the night of the fire—but kept her opinion to herself. Prolonged Michael-talk tended to make Zoe go red about the cheeks and find another room to hide in.

Zoe seemed to be doing better. She'd stopped blaming herself, at least. She vacillated between dread of the coming funeral and the possibility of having to leave Dogwood where she finally had some good friends, and excitement over seeing her mom and dad again.

Penny kept her opinion of Zoe's mom and dad to herself.

She understood that her instant dislike of them was mostly selfish, since they were coming to town and she was afraid they would take Zoe with them when they left, but some of it was not. They had missed many important things in Zoe's life, her birthday being the least of them.

What kind of parents just left their kids and ran away?

That line of thinking always brought her mother and aunt to mind—their identical appearances and dissimilar personalities, and awakened a dreaded certainty in Penny that she had never even known her mother, that it had been her aunt who died in the plane crash, that her mother was still out there, somewhere.

It was Susan's words—"you remind me a lot of your aunt Nancy ... Di was the outgoing one"—and the tattoo on her mother's wrist in those pictures. The tattoo Penny had never seen.

Of Morgan Duke, there was not a trace. Somehow he'd gotten the news of his son's arrest before Ernest, and had flown. When Ernest escorted his brother and a contingent of state police to the secluded spot where Morgan had set up camp, the truck and camper were gone. Gone south toward Mexico, was Sheriff Price's assessment. A man with his connections and wealth would find a way to cross the border and set himself up like a king.

The girls had their doubts but didn't share them. They were just little girls ... who would take anything they had to say seriously?

"I don't think King Cobra is finished here yet," Penny said during a discussion of the topic in her bedroom, where the four girls spent most of their time when away from the hollow.

"It wasn't a cobra," Ellen informed her. "It was a sidewinder ... I've seen pictures."

"Have you ever seen pictures of one with arms?" Penny asked, a little grumpily. All of the waiting, waiting for Zoe's parents to come and take her away, waiting for the newest monster in her life to come back and try to finish them all off, waiting out spring break closeted in her room while half of her classmates were looking at the ocean only an hour west of here, was playing a jagged symphony on her nerves.

Ellen only shrugged in response.

Penny later Googled "sidewinder" on her new laptop and had to admit, at least to herself, that Ellen was right.

What they all agreed on, even Ellen, to whom all of this was new, was that the monster sidewinder was still close, and if it was, so was Morgan Duke.

They didn't think they'd seen the last of him.

* * *

The first official news regarding Morgan Duke arrived via televised press conference that Monday evening. Sheriff Price stood on the steps of the town building that housed the courthouse and jail, Michael on his left and the state Fire Marshal on his right. The sheriff had never been particularly cherubic, but that night he positively glowered down at the gathered reporters and television cameras.

He waited for the smattering of unwelcome questions to die out before beginning.

"The fire of last Friday night has now been positively identified as an act of arson. The perpetrator, Joseph Duke of Miami, Florida, is in custody but refuses to cooperate in the ongoing investigation. Authorities are now seeking Morgan Duke as a material witness and possible accomplice."

A barrage of new questions flew at him and he stoically ignored them all until silence fell.

"I would urge Morgan Duke to turn himself in and cooperate with both state and local authorities ...."

"Joseph Duke is known to have been employed at the Dogwood landfill," a particularly bold reporter shouted from the crush of people crowding the courthouse steps. "Is there any connection between the Friday night fire and the reported disturbance at the landfill the following morning?"

Sheriff Price seemed taken aback by the question, his startled expression suggesting he hadn't thought the events at the landfill were public knowledge. He quickly arranged his face into a passable imitation of his previous composure.

"As Mr. Duke was already in our custody at the time we have no reason to suspect that the *disturbance* was anything but an accident."

"Ernest Price is a known business associate of Morgan Duke's," another shouted, emboldened by the last question's unexpected success. "Will there be an investigation into what some people are calling very shady business or Ernest Price's possible complicity in the arson, which some people speculate ...."

"*This press conference is finished,*" the sheriff bellowed, turning his back on the shocked crowd below him and stalking into the building.

From the seat of her recliner, Susan aimed her remote control at the television, looking almost pleased, and turned it off.

"He should put in his application at the landfill now," Susan said.

Penny and Zoe sat at opposite ends of the couch facing her, Penny with *The Aikido Student Handbook* open on her lap, Zoe with her head lolling on her left shoulder, eyes mostly closed, on the verge of total collapse. They had spent part of the previous night and most of that day at the hollow, trying to prepare for the fight they were sure was still coming, but mostly just moping. Penny had never fully realized how much they had counted on Ronan's counsel and encouragement. Without him there to guide them, if even only in spirit, everything seemed hopeless.

Ellen was learning the basics quickly enough—having her own wand was a bonus in that regard—but wasn't yet ready to join the circle. They all learned the spell that Penny and Katie had used in the tunnel beneath the landfill to break open the homunculi's heads, and Katie had given Zoe an unused bike to replace the one crushed in their retreat, slightly older than Katie's but much newer than Zoe's old one. Katie had also attempted to translate the passage from their book that allowed them to fly. It was very close to Latin but not, and they could only guess that it was an invocation to some natural force or another. The one word she *had* positively identified was *Besom*, an Old English word that referred to a witch's broom.

"Penny?" Susan stood in front of her, snapping her fingers. "Earth to Penny!"

"Huh?" Penny flinched, startled out of her reverie. She hadn't seen Susan rise. She suspected she'd been on the edge of sleep too.

"Do you have any thoughts about dinner?"

Penny shrugged and looked to Zoe for ideas, but Zoe was currently flopped on her end of the couch and snoring lightly.

"Frozen burritos it is," Susan said, and marched to the kitchen.

Penny checked the clock above the television, a charmingly antique thing that she suspected had been with the house for a long time, and saw it was just past seven. They were meeting Katie and

Ellen back at the hollow that evening around eleven. She would rather have had a full night's sleep for once but knew the evening practice was more important than ever now.

At least let Zoe sleep for a while, she thought. *She needs it more than I do.*

Penny followed Susan into the kitchen to help. If she was very lucky, she might be able to talk Susan into letting her brew a half-pot of coffee to wash their burritos down.

* * *

Penny and Zoe arrived at the hollow before Katie and Ellen, Penny slightly revitalized by the one cup of nasty reheated coffee that Susan allowed her, Zoe still dragging despite the extra sleep she'd stolen before and after dinner. As always, Penny scanned the lower limbs of the old ash for Ronan and, as always, felt a stab of grief when she remembered that he wouldn't be there.

The captured homunculus was still there, however, dangling from the tightly wound willow limbs and totally immobile, turned into a statue. Penny supposed that meant he was asleep. She envied him a little.

Katie had wanted to kill the thing outright, had been aiming her wand right between its eyes, but Penny had convinced her not to. She just didn't feel right attacking something helpless.

Penny started a fire in the pit and sat while Zoe busied herself with the book. She was watching the door expectantly when an unanswered and forgotten question recurred to her.

"Hey, Zoe, did you ever find out who Janet is?"

The mystery girl from her old photo album had slipped her mind in the wake of last weekend's events, but now that Penny had remembered her, the curiosity burned as strongly as before.

Zoe shrugged without turning to acknowledge her. "Never got a chance to ask."

"Ask what?" Katie popped through the door and into the hollow, Ellen on her heels. They both looked a little livelier than on the previous nights, almost optimistic, in fact.

"Nothing important," Penny said, wanting to steer the conversation away from the topic of things Zoe had never had a chance to ask her grandma. The woman may not have appreciated

Zoe's company, or anything else about her for that matter, but Zoe still mourned her. "What are you so happy about?"

"Snakes are reptiles," Katie said, apropos of nothing it seemed.

"Yesssss," Penny said, hoping Katie would reveal the relevance of her statement without too much of a windup. "So are iguanas and geckos."

"And what do all reptiles have in common," Ellen asked, bobbing up and down with excitement.

"Oh, I don't know," Zoe said, clearly more interested in a bit of lint on the knee of her jeans, which she picked off and examined before casting aside. "They're green and slimy?"

"They're cold-blooded," Katie said, a certain deadly triumph in her voice.

If there was a point, Penny wasn't seeing it.

Zoe, however, regarded Katie and Ellen with a growing interest. Her entire demeanor seemed to change. She didn't look happy at the news but somehow was satisfied with it.

"I'm sorry," Penny said at last, returning the others' triumphant looks with a puzzled one of her own. "I don't ...."

And then she did get it. The others could see the light of understanding in her eyes.

Snakes are reptiles, and reptiles are cold-blooded.

Their monster had a possible weakness, if they could only learn how to exploit it in time.

Katie pointed her wand at the water rushing by and closed her eyes, but nothing happened.

"*Procellium*," Zoe said, and when the others regarded her with confusion she explained. "When we were trying to find you that ... thing ...."

"Sidewinder," Ellen said, then blushed and mimicked zipping her lips.

" ... Attacked us," Zoe continued, giving Ellen a pointed, sour look. "It made a storm. Almost blew us off my bike."

Ellen nodded but kept her mouth shut.

"It pointed its wand into the sky and shouted *procellium*." Zoe shrugged. "Maybe we can make it snow on him."

"Worth a shot," Penny said, then pointed her wand skyward and said, "*procellium!*"

The sensation that followed was one of the strangest Penny had ever experienced.

Her body and mind separated in an instant of horrible vertigo, and she fell upward, upward into the sky, toward the sun, and her scream of panic became the wind.

"Penny!"

Someone shouted her name, and she strained to see through the distance to the ground below.

Did someone down there know her?

Something touched her arm, but she was alone and incorporeal in the sky. She *was* the sky.

"Penny! Wake up!"

Now the voice was next to her, the arm tugging on her ....

And she opened her eyes, looking into three startled faces above her.

"What happened?" She tried to sit up but felt weak and woozy.

Ellen and Zoe helped her to her feet.

"You went all rigid," Katie said. "And your eyes rolled up into your head. Then you passed out."

"Did ... anything else happen?" The memories that had deserted her flooded back. She remembered what she'd tried to do and was desperate to know if anything had happened.

"The wind blew a bit," Katie said.

"What was it like?" Ellen guided her to a seat by the fire, and Zoe pressed her wand back into her hand.

Penny explained the sensation as best she could, the feeling of separation from the earth and her body, the feeling that she had become the sky, forgetting herself and everything else.

"Hmmm," Ellen seemed to consider this for a moment before venturing a guess. "Maybe the trick is not forgetting who you are while you're ... up there."

They each tried it in turn, Ellen first, who experienced nothing more than an odd queasy feeling; then Zoe, who didn't fall down like Penny, but did no more than rustle the higher boughs of the hollow's trees. Katie tried last, and with more success than Penny had hoped for: a strong but short-lived breeze and a slight darkening of the sky as the thinnest smudge of cloud coalesced above them, but nothing like she had described from the night of their rescue.

After a few minutes to rest, Katie described her experience.

"There's a balance between the earth and sky," she explained. "Like a teeter-totter. You have to find it. It kind of saps you, though."

She yawned hugely, as if to illustrate her point.

"If I keep practicing, maybe I'll get better."

"Maybe," Penny said. "But how much practice do you think it'll take?"

After a short debate Katie conceded Penny's point, and they agreed to try to find something they could learn a little quicker. After another half-hour of wasted effort, Zoe was able to create a thin scrim of ice that broke up too quickly on the surface of the creek.

"How did you do it?" Ellen demanded.

"I don't know," Zoe snapped.

"Maybe it's time to ask the book," Penny suggested, eager to avoid any more bickering.

"Already did," Katie said, and indeed the book was open in her lap. "If there is a freezing spell it isn't in here."

She shut the book and shoved it inside the chest.

"Maybe instead of making the air colder, we need to remove the heat." Ellen seemed to be grasping at straws.

"What?" Penny said.

"There's this little thing called Thermodynamics," Katie said, ignoring Penny and speaking directly to Ellen. "I'm pretty sure the Zeroth Law might have something to say about that."

"Who?" Zoe looked as lost as Penny felt.

Ellen tilted her head down slightly and narrowed her eyes at Katie. "I have an air conditioner in my house ... been using it all summer, and the Physics Police haven't shown up to arrest me yet."

Penny shook her head and sidled up to Zoe.

"Let the science nerds work it out," Penny whispered in Zoe's ear.

Zoe shrugged and endeavored to look interested, though her eyes began to glaze over at once.

Katie folded her arms across her chest and rolled her eyes.

"An air conditioner doesn't make cold air," Ellen explained, as if she were a teacher lecturing a science class. "It removes the heat from warm air. The coil absorbs the heat from the air that the fan blows through it, so if we can just figure out how to absorb ...."

Ellen lost steam then, shrinking back a little at the expression on Katie's face.

"And how are we supposed to do that?" Katie asked.

"I don't know," Ellen said, throwing her hands into the air in frustration. "I'm the noob here, you figure it out!"

It sounded like nonsense to Penny, but she was willing to give anything a shot. She imagined her wand siphoning heat from the air around her, and to her surprise, it actually worked. After her first attempt, the handle of her wand warmed up until it was uncomfortably hot, but the temperature inside the hollow became almost wintry. They all huddled a little closer to the fire.

"Time to call it a night?" Zoe followed her suggestion with a long, languid yawn, which the others mimicked.

They agreed and went back through the door, Katie and Ellen first, then Penny and Zoe.

*   *   *

Penny knew as soon as she stepped out of her wardrobe and into her room that there was no more time to prepare for the fight. An unsteady orange light that shone through her window told her that the end game had already started.

The wheat field that Susan jokingly referred to as "Price's back forty," the piece of land that Susan had years ago grudgingly allowed Ernest Price to lease from her, was blazing, and the fire was racing up the hill toward the house. Zoe saw it too; she leaned heavily against Penny as she peered through the window.

"Susan," Penny whispered but was unable to finish her thought aloud. She seemed to have no breath. It felt like someone had punched her in the stomach.

Zoe tugged on her arm. "We have to tell her!"

Penny felt her paralysis break with Zoe's panic and they rushed down to Susan's room.

She pounded on the door, then threw it open and rushed it.

Susan sat up with a startled grunt, and when she found Penny and Zoe staring at her, confusion became irritation. "What in the world are you two …."

"Fire," Penny blurted, and Susan stopped in midrant.

"The field out back," Zoe said.

Understanding dawned in Susan's eyes. Anger followed it.

"Let's go," she said, rushing to them in a T-shirt and a pair of cut-off shorts. "Get to the car and I'll meet you there."

She shoved them out ahead of her and hurried them down the hall.

"Wait, what are you doing?" Penny nearly fell down the first flight of stairs, and had to grasp the railing to keep her feet and the pace Susan forced on them.

"Calling the fire department," Susan said, slapping them on the back to hurry them along the landing between floors. "Then I'm calling Michael. If Morgan Duke is up here, we're going to get him!"

Penny almost felt bad for Morgan Duke.

Almost.

Penny saw Zoe stuffing her wand into a pocket of her pants, tugging the hem of her shirt over it, and hurriedly followed suit. In her rush she'd forgotten she was still carrying it. She felt in her other pocket for her mirror and pulled it out, holding it discreetly in her closed hand. The second she was out of Susan's sight she would call the others.

They reached the foyer, and Susan squeezed between them to open the door.

"Straight to the car and wait. I'll be right out."

"You ain't going anywhere," Morgan Duke said from the other side of the threshold. He grinned down at them, and as Penny reached down for her concealed wand, he raised a gun and pointed it at them. "Nothing funny now. We're just going to have a nice sit-down chat, the four of us. If you behave, no one's going to get hurt."

"You're lying," Susan said, moving in front of the girls and herding them behind her body with a backward sweep of her arms.

His grin widened, and he nodded.

"Probably I am," he said, "that's what I do best. But you're going to do as I say anyhow."

Susan backed away from him as he stepped inside, pulling the door closed behind him.

"Go back up to your room," she whispered back to them. "Don't come down for anything."

"Not at all," Morgan said. "It would be downright unsociable to leave these little ladies out of the conversation."

Beside her, Penny felt Zoe shift, and saw her uncovering the handle of her wand. Penny grasped her mirror even tighter and whispered so low that not even Zoe could hear her. She only hoped it would work.

"*Kat.*"

"Into the sitting room," Morgan directed them, emphasizing his directions with a wave of his gun, and when they were inside he motioned them to the couch.

"Why are you doing this, Mr. Duke?" Penny spoke loudly, and her shaking voice betrayed her fear. "We never did anything to you."

Morgan simply regarded her for a moment. When he did speak, all of the false good cheer had left his voice.

"Oh, but you did. You and Miss Taylor." He motioned toward Zoe with the barrel of his gun. "Even your little friend here. You did everything to me."

He backed toward Susan's recliner and settled his bulk into it with obvious relief. Penny noticed now that Morgan Duke looked bad, thinner somehow, the normally healthy russet of his well-tanned bald head and face paler, almost jaundiced; and there were dark patches beneath his bloodshot eyes. He caressed his left forearm and winced in pain, but retrained his pistol on the three of them before they could move.

"Miss Taylor has stood in the way of my business for a long time. Longer than I've ever allowed anyone else to, and you ...," he aimed his gun directly at Penny, and for a moment her heart seemed to stop. She was certain he would pull the trigger. "You somehow found out what I was up to and went squealing to her."

His voice, the quivering of his jowls, were oddly indignant, hurt, as if she'd somehow betrayed him. He looked to her like a jumbo-sized baby on the verge of tears.

"But I'm trying to get past all of that," he said, a measure of his false cheer returning. "I'm finishing up my business here tonight."

"You set the fire," Susan said, and Penny prayed that Katie was hearing it all and would know what to do. "What good is my land to you now? What good will it be burned flat?"

"None," Morgan conceded. "But it ain't about that now. It's about closing the deal on my terms. It's about not letting a couple little slips of girls like you meddle in it!"

He rubbed at his left arm again and muttered.

Beside Penny, Zoe had slipped her wand out, unnoticed by either Susan or Morgan. She flicked her eyes toward Penny, then at Susan's back.

Penny thought she knew what Zoe wanted and hoped with all of her might that her friend knew what she was doing.

"In another couple of minutes I'm going to leave. You won't." His discomfort seemed to be growing, but he pressed on. "You like this crappy plot of land so much, you can die on it."

He turned his attention to Penny. "There's so much more I'd like to say but time is short."

His face cramped again in discomfort and his gun hand twitched.

"Now!" Zoe used her considerable volume, startling them, but Penny was ready. She grabbed Susan around her waist and threw her to the floor, landing painfully on top of her, and a second later there was an explosive crash that filled the living room like thunder.

"Zoe!" Penny scrambled off of Susan, desperate to find her friend, hopefully still alive.

Zoe stood where she had, her wand in her hand, staring at Morgan Duke with shocked, round eyes. A second later, Penny saw why.

Zoe had fired her spell at Morgan's gun, and her aim had been exquisite. Whether Morgan had fired or not, Penny couldn't tell, but the bullets in his gun had exploded. A mess of bent, jagged metal clattered to the floor. Morgan stared at the hand that had held it, or what was left of the hand. The fingers were bent and bloody, sticking out at sickening angles from the meat-slab hand.

A single sob escaped Morgan's trembling lips, then he screamed and ran through the room, to the foyer, without another glance at the girls, cradling his ruined right hand in the crook of his left arm.

"Wow," Penny whispered.

"I think I'm going to be sick," Zoe said, and a second later she was. She shoved her wand back into her pocket and ran toward the kitchen.

Susan began to stir at Penny's feet, then leapt up with her own shout of alarm. She saw Penny and grasped her by shoulders.

"Where's Zoe? Where is she?"

"In the kitchen," Penny said, trying to keep her voice calm. She took Susan's hands and forced them to release their painful grip on her shoulders. "Mr. Duke's gun exploded. He ran away. Zoe's ...."

Zoe's retching sounded loudly from the kitchen, and Penny didn't have to explain anymore.

Susan's eyes fell to the twisted ruin of the gun on the floor and the blood splattered around it.

"Is he hurt?"

"Yeah."

"Good!" Susan grabbed Penny by the arm again and dragged her toward the kitchen. "Zoe, let's go!"

She pulled them out of the house, scanning the front yard for Morgan Duke but not seeing him. They were still on the steps and running toward Susan's Falcon when the sound of an approaching car stopped them. They saw red-and-blue lights flashing on the driveway, then the sheriff's cruiser. A few seconds later it slid to a stop next to Susan's car, and Michael jumped out.

He eyed the three of them, then the blazing field behind the house.

"I got a tip-off that Morgan Duke might be here," he said, covering the last of the ground between them at a sprint, right hand resting on his holstered pistol. "I guess the fire is just a bonus."

"He was here, Michael. He tried to shoot us and his gun exploded in his hand." Susan stumbled a little where she stood, as if only just realizing how close to death they'd all come. "He's hurt, and he's close."

Michael eyed Penny and Zoe suspiciously and said, "I guess you got real lucky."

Penny tried to look innocent, but Michael wasn't buying it.

How much did he know, she wondered.

Zoe blushed and looked at her feet.

"I radioed the fire department on my way here," Michael said, addressing Susan now. "They should be here soon, but you and the girls need to get out of here. I'll look for him."

"Blood," Susan said, pointing at the trail of splotches leading into the field, away from the highway. "Girls, get on your bikes and ride to town ... Katie's house or the park. I'll find you when this is over."

She regarded Michael. "I'm going with you. I won't slow you down."

Michael looked like he wanted to argue the point, but Susan was off, following the blood, and he had to hurry to catch up.

"Straight to town," he shouted at the girls. "And be careful!"

"We will," Penny and Zoe said in unison and ran to their bikes. They made it just past the drop to the highway, just out of sight of Michael and Susan, before they nodded to each other and angled their bikes into the sky.

* * *

They flew high to avoid watching eyes, and from their dizzying height they could see how swiftly the fire advanced. It had devoured Price's field of winter wheat and now raced toward the house.

"They won't get here in time," Penny groaned. "Our house!"

"We need a firebreak," Zoe shouted to her. At their speed, staying too close to each other was dangerous, but Zoe swerved near enough to make herself heard.

"A what?"

"If they had a bulldozer, they might be able to clear a wide-enough path to stop the fire."

"I don't see any bulldozers down there, Zoe!" Then a thought occurred to her, and she almost dared to hope that they wouldn't lose the house. "But maybe we don't need one!"

"What?"

There was no time for explanation. Penny dropped from the sky, falling fast, aiming her descent for the fence that separated her back yard from Price's field. She called on her fire and felt it respond at once. Her skin began to heat up beneath her clothing, the fine hairs on the back of her neck to rise as if charged with static. She directed the growing heat to her wand-hand as the fence came into view, then dropped toward it. She raced above the fence to the edge of the hill, then down toward the highway before bringing her bike sideways in a midair slide and rocketing in the other direction. She pointed her wand at the grass, hoping it would work.

Fire shot in a jet from the tip of her wand, hitting the ground and igniting the grass around it. She poured fire onto the ground in a line, following the fence beyond her house, then continuing into the wild grass. Only when her house was almost out of sight did she raise her wand.

She ascended again and watched her flames work. They burned through the dry grass and wheat, spreading out ten, twenty, thirty feet. The flames approaching from Price's field closed in quickly. Penny hoped she'd been able to do enough.

She wished her flames gone, and they obediently flickered and died, leaving a wide, blackened path in their wake.

Zoe joined her, watching as the flames raced up from the field below toward that band of burnt earth.

"Think that'll work?" Penny was almost giddy with relief.

"I think so," Zoe said, "but we can't wait to see."

She held up her mirror, and Penny could see flames reflected in its surface, but not the flames below them.

"Kat and Ellen are at the hollow. They need our help."

Chapter 20

The Crimson Brand

They raced toward the hollow, high in the dark midnight sky and guided by the light of the second fire of the night, the one in the field high above the house and racing toward Aurora Hollow. This night the exhilaration of flight was tempered by the danger, both behind and ahead of them, the lingering sadness of two lives already lost, and the fear that they would lose more before the night was over.

Penny had hoped she could make another firebreak to protect the hollow, but as they flew over the covering canopy of green, her hopes were dashed. Unlike the fire that had raced through Price's field, the one below was slower, the sparse grass and shrubs not as ready a fuel as the dense wheat, but it was already there.

She had arrived too late.

They circled the hollow and dropped lower, searching for a safe spot to land.

A familiar manic chattering reached them over the roar and crackle of the flames.

Penny stopped high above the ground and waved Zoe to her side.

"Homunculi," she said, pointing toward the hollow with her wand. "The gray men are here!"

Zoe nodded and plummeted straight toward the canopy of willow limbs she'd deftly woven together and they parted for her, allowing her in. Penny followed in her wake, slipping through just as the branches began to close again.

Zoe jumped from the seat of her bike and landed next to Ellen, startling the two homunculi advancing on her, forcing her backward toward the creek. Three of the creatures lay shattered on the ground, and another dodged a spell from Katie. The angry homunculus still wore the skirt of green that had bound it and seemed eager to repay the indignity.

Penny dropped onto the little monster as it lunged for Katie, squashing it into the ground. Identical spells from Katie and Penny stilled it, and Penny slid from the seat of her bike, letting it fall as she dashed to Katie's side.

Katie dropped to her knees and rummaged through the open chest, tossing items—the cup, the book, the now-unused black wand—haphazardly into the grass beside her.

"Kat," Penny dropped down beside her. "What are you doing?"

"Finding this!" Katie rose with the strange doorknob in her fist. The etchings and lines in the brassy metal seemed to glow and squiggle under her grasp, and a short metal spike gleamed on the flat end. "Ronan was risking his life to find these, and you told me what they do."

"Yeah," Penny said, feeling that there were slightly more pressing issues to deal with. "But we agreed not to mess with any of the stuff Ronan brought back. We don't know what it does. It could be dangerous!"

"We *do* know what this does," Katie argued. "We just don't know where it goes."

"Some of them don't go anywhere!" Penny nearly shouted, desperate to stress the point she thought she'd already made.

"I know!" Katie did shout. "If we're lucky this might be one of them!"

"What?"

Ellen and Zoe ran to them and stopped just short, on edge and eyeing the hollow for more gray men.

"You and Zoe got rid of the Birdman by shoving him back through his ...," she seemed unable to find the right word for what they had described to her.

"Yeah," Zoe cut in, then nodded, as if in understanding.

"If it worked with him, maybe it'll work again," Katie said, calmer now.

Penny considered it for a second. "Sounds good to me."

Katie nodded and turned toward the door.

Penny grabbed her arm.

"What now?" Katie was almost hysterical with impatience.

"Let me do it, Kat." She pointed up the path to the field beyond. The flames that had only been crowding the hollow a few minutes before were now embracing it, licking at the trees and tracing their way down the short slope toward them. "It's going to burn down. I think you're the only one who can stop it now."

Katie considered for a second then passed the doorknob to Penny.

"I'll do what I can."

But as she started up the path, another gray man appeared to block her path, then a second and a third. Behind them rose the huge horned head of the monster serpent.

"How nice," Turoc hissed. "I'm not too late for the party after all."

* * *

Silence filled the hollow. Katie paused at the edge of the trail; Penny froze in midstep toward the door, the magic knob seeming to thrum in her hand; Zoe and Ellen stood rooted in place near the fire pit. The girls goggled up at the monster snake and his gray men, immobilized by shock.

The monster and his minions moved closer, the former rising behind the latter, his three arms opening in mock welcome. The fourth arm, the one he'd broken in his fall at the landfill, was gone; in its place was a narrow waving stump.

The three gray men bobbed in place, as if eager to leap down and begin the fight.

"I had hoped Master Duke would keep you young ladies occupied back at the home place," he sighed and shook his head, as if in sorrow, "but I did not count on it. He has been less than effective these past few months."

Katie backed away, joining Ellen and Zoe in a frightened huddle.

Penny took a step toward the door, the knob clutched in her left fist, her wand in her right.

The monster turned his gaze on Penny, and she stopped, wondering for a moment if he was hypnotizing her. She forced her eyes away from his, focused them on the crimson brand between them, and remembered where she'd seen it before.

"It may interest you to know that his last successful job was the disposal of your obstinate mother." He grinned hugely at her, revealing the full, frightening width of his mouth and too many pointed teeth to count. His fangs were long, curved downward, dripping with venom. "A job very well done, in fact. We had hoped Miss Taylor would prove more agreeable when ownership of this gateway passed to her, but alas, it was not to be."

He killed her, Penny thought, struck dumb and motionless at the news. *He killed her!*

"We did not count on your interference, however." His voice turned bitter, angry. "You, young one, came as a bit of a shock to us, since we were led to believe that you had died at birth."

Penny saw her friends shift uncomfortably at this unexpected news. Zoe stepped away from the others, put her hand against the trunk of the closest willow. None of it registered, none of it mattered. Even the eager homunculi were unimportant. Penny saw only the monster behind them. The thing that had killed her mother.

"You killed her." Penny's voice came back, weak, barely a whisper, but the monster seemed to hear her fine. He nodded his head slightly.

"Not in the strictest sense, no. That was Morgan Duke and his idiot child, but I did command it and so must take my share of the credit."

The doorknob dropped from Penny's numb fingers, and before she knew she meant to do it, her wand was raised and pointing at the monster.

Intuition and rage guided her hand as she slashed her wand through the air in the Snakeman's direction. It wasn't a spell, just a lashing out, but the first downward sweep of her wand struck him across his horned head and stunned him for a moment.

He blocked her second attack with a twitch of his wand, fangs bared and growling.

Behind him the flames rose higher, closer.

"You'll have to do better than that," he chided her, and sent a spell of his own toward her.

Penny dove to the side, and the ground exploded where she had stood, leaving a small, smoking crater in the dirt.

"Get them," the monster snake commanded, and the homunculi leapt at them with a coarse mixture of snarls and shrieks. Six more appeared and rushed at the girls.

What happened next was almost too quick, too unexpected, to track.

Two long willow whips reached down, wound themselves around Katie's waist, and yanked her into the air. She vanished through the green canopy above them with a cry of surprise. A third willow limb snagged one of the gray men and hurled it out of the hollow, past the Snakeman's stunned face, into the dark. But even as it vanished squealing into the night, another half-dozen homunculi launched themselves at the girls.

Penny forgot the doorknob, forgot about Zoe and Ellen, who were now fighting the gray men by themselves, and catapulted toward the monster that had murdered her mother.

But you don't even know if it was your mother, a small but compelling voice in her brain said. What about the tattoo?

The same design as the Snakeman's crimson brand.

Penny screamed it to silence and raised her wand.

The monster snake blocked the jet of Phoenix Fire she sent at him. It exploded against his invisible shield, clung to it and continued to burn as he slithered down the steep bank into the hollow, then died away when he dropped the shield. She sent another jet of flames at him, but he dove to the side, and the flames exploded against the embankment behind him. Penny's flames began to spread to the trees and the grass at the hollow's edge, adding to the destruction and chaos, so she let them go out at once.

Before she could dodge aside or protect herself, the Snakeman sprang at her. They collided painfully and tumbled to the ground.

Penny felt his tail trying to coil around her, beginning to squeeze, and jabbed her wand into him. His flesh cooled at once, the coils beginning to loosen.

He snatched the wand from her hand with an angry hiss and hurled it away, bringing his own to bear on her. He pinned her to the ground and pressed the tip of it under her chin.

"I can't kill you, but I can make you wish I had."

Penny reached up, flailing blindly, grasping his cold, long-fingered hand. Another hand slapped hers away and grabbed her hair, slamming her head into the hard-packed earth.

Penny groaned with pain, felt herself slipping away from the action, into darkness.

"Penny!" Ellen leapt onto the monster's back and wrapped her arms around him, trying to break his hold. With a hiss of irritation and the flash of his tail, he pried her loose and tossed her aside.

Penny reached upward again, and her flailing hand found the wand pressed into her chin, poised to deal pain. She tightened her grip on it.

"No," he bellowed down at her.

The wood of his wand began to darken, then to smoke, and a second later it burst into flames.

He tossed the ruined wand away with a cry, then his hideous horned head darted down at her.

There was a sharp, blazing pain in her shoulder, a burning like acid in her veins.

Every tree in the hollow seemed to come to life around them, the narrow whips slashing at the monster on top of her, the thicker branches raining down on him like living clubs.

He cursed in a language almost too strange to hear, tried to block the blows with his thin arms. He bellowed as a second arm broke under the assault and struggled to slither free.

Penny rolled away from him, grasping her torn shoulder, groaning as the monster's venom burned her insides. The same venom that had killed Ronan was now in her. She rose slowly, unable to make her legs work the way they should, and when she tried to walk, they dropped her back to the earth.

"Help … me," she whispered, knowing that no one could hear her.

Zoe stood, rigid as a statue, holding the trunk of the ash tree.

Ellen was on the ground, winded and firing wildly at the last of the homunculi.

Katie was nowhere to be seen.

The monster snake slithered toward the creek. The newly broken arm lay in the dirt, detached and twitching as its cold blood drained away, and the monster dragged itself along with its two remaining arms, heading for Ronan's cave.

A mist rose from the place where Ronan's blood still darkened the soil. It swirled, stilled, shaped itself and solidified into the monotone image of a familiar form. A moment later the mist was gone, and Ronan stood in its place, returned and angry.

"Turoc!" Ronan roared and launched himself at the retreating monster.

Three gray men broke from the group trying to fend off Ellen's spells and flung themselves at Ronan, stone fists raised.

A fifth, smaller homunculus dropped from the trees, carrying a wooden club the length of its own body. It landed in the center of the four homunculi approaching Ronan and scattered them with back-and-forth swipes of its club, growling and chattering madly. The enemy homunculi went down around him, one missing an arm, which writhed nearby in the dirt, another attempting to readjust its boulder-like head, which was now facing the wrong way on its thin neck.

The new homunculus's eyes, Penny saw, were bright, luminous green. It had her eyes.

Penny's homunculus raised the club high and brought it down hard on the head of one of its enemies. The stricken gray man fell to the earth, twitching, and the girls' unexpected ally trampled it deeper into the dirt as it searched out and charged another enemy.

Ellen started to target it as it rushed past, then raised her wand when she saw it plunge into the remaining golden-eyed gray men.

Ronan bit and clawed at the Snakeman's exposed neck but did little damage. The scales there were too hard, the soft flesh beneath too well protected. A swipe of the monster's tail put Ronan on the defensive, but he avoided the strike and leapt to his usual high perch in the old ash.

"Finish them, girls! Send them off!" Ronan shouted before rejoining the fight, leaping down to scatter the gray men.

Ellen saw him and grinned in astonishment, rose to her feet, and turned her wand on the fleeing Snakeman.

If Zoe saw him, she gave no sign. She stood in place, her hand seemingly welded to the tree, but the assault of the trees around them grew more ferocious. They slapped and pummeled the gray men, hoisted them from the ground and sent them flying.

Turoc had nearly reached the water when the great ash groaned, its massive trunk bending forward, and its thickest limb swinging down at the monster, striking like a fist at the back of his head.

The Snakeman collapsed to the ground, his tail giving a final spastic rattle, and was still.

The moment Turoc fell, the pain working through Penny's body began to fade.

She tried to rise again but couldn't.

It's dead, she thought, savagely pleased.

But it wasn't. The tail twitched, rattled. Turoc began to stir.

Zoe and Ellen moved toward him, wands pointed, and Penny felt the temperature in the hollow drop. She shivered.

His movements slowed, then stopped as a thin frost formed along his body. After what seemed a long time, Zoe and Ellen lowered their wands.

Zoe stepped closer to him, her breath a visible fog before her face, and kicked him. She might have kicked a rock. He was frozen solid.

But where was Katie?

"Kat," Penny said, and fear brought some strength back to her limbs. She was on her feet and moving unsteadily toward Zoe and Ellen. "Where is she?"

Zoe pointed out of the hollow, toward the flaming field above.

Ronan dashed off in the indicated direction without a word.

Penny ran unsteadily, and found Ellen at her side a moment later, supporting her and helping her up the steep path. They emerged, searching the field for Katie, Zoe joining them a few seconds later.

They found her, finally, and were not comforted.

*   *   *

Katie stood in the distance, frozen with fear, almost encircled by fire. It raced toward her through the grass, flaring high when it overtook a patch of sagebrush.

"Oh, no! I dropped her right in the middle of it!" Zoe rushed forward, straight toward the fire, and Ellen tackled her.

"Don't," Ellen struggled to hold Zoe down. "Kat! Get out of there!"

Zoe struggled beneath Ellen, rolled onto her back and tried to wrestle for her freedom. "Get off!"

"Katie!" Ronan shouted and dashed through the flames, his fur catching fire and smoldering, but the flames were too intense and drove him back.

"Stop it, you two!" Penny dropped to her knees and struggled ineffectually to break the girls apart. "Zoe, Ellen ... look!"

Zoe and Ellen paused in their struggles long enough to turn to Penny, then followed her pointing finger.

Katie had pointed her wand skyward and closed her eyes. Faintly, they heard her cry: "*Procellium!*"

For a moment nothing happened.

"Let me up," Zoe shouted at Ellen and caught her off balance, shoving her away. Ellen didn't struggle but followed Zoe's cautious advance through the flames. Penny followed close behind, still weak but feeling her strength return.

It was time to give up. The hollow was going to burn; but they had to save Katie.

Then the night sky darkened, the half-moon fading behind rapidly thickening clouds, the stars vanishing. Light pulsed overhead, blinding them, and thunder crashed, shaking the ground.

Penny stumbled, almost fell, then gasped, suddenly chilled to the bone by a cold torrent of rain.

Zoe and Ellen stopped in midstride.

Katie stood amid the dying flames, arms outstretched to the sky, head thrown back, seeming to almost float. Only the tips of her shoes touched the ground. A strong wind arose and whipped her rain-drenched hair around her and blew the hem of her soaked shirt around her waist.

It whipped between Zoe and Ellen, and hit Penny, knocking her back a step. The wind carried a familiar scent, and a whisper of a voice, wordless, like a sigh.

"Kat?" All three of them spoke in unison.

Another flash above their heads seemed to answer them.

Thunder rolled across the wild field again, softer this time, and the downpour eased into a drizzle.

Katie's feet settled back onto the ground, her wind-whipped hair settling on her shoulders and her arms falling to her side.

The tempest ended.

Katie shook her rain-drenched hair out of her face and examined the field. Smoke and steam drifted from the blackened ground, but

Katie's rain had quenched the flames. Her eyes fell at last over Zoe, Ellen, Penny, and Ronan. Her smile was as wide as Penny had ever seen it.

"That ... was ... so ... *cool!*"

* * *

The girls descended, shivering, into the hollow, Ronan at their heels. Dead, shattered homunculi littered the ground, and Penny's green-eyed homunculus stood among them, its club resting on its stone shoulder. Zoe and Katie took aim with their wands, but Penny stopped them.

"No, that one is on our side."

Zoe accepted Penny's words with a shrug, but Katie continued to regard it mistrustfully even as she lowered her wand.

Rain dripped from the willow leaves overhead, hissing in the smoldering coals of the fire pit. The monster lay half-frozen before the creek, still struggling to drag himself toward the cave.

"No you don't!" Penny sprinted to him, rolled him over with her foot, pointed her wand into his face. The others were beside her a second later, Ronan perched on the monster's chest, and four wands pointed down at him.

"Who are you?" Penny stared into his eyes, somewhat dimmer than before but still frightening. She suppressed a shiver, and wasn't sure if it was the cold or the eyes. "Who sent you?"

The monster's breath came slowly. He grabbed weakly at Penny's leg, but she kicked his arm away.

She bent down and pressed the tip of her wand into his throat. "Answer me!"

"I am Turoc," he said at last, then grinned. "Familiar to the house of Fuilrix. Your mother's executioner."

Three more wands moved close to his face, drawing his nervous glance from Penny for a moment.

Penny ignored her friends, bent nearer to the wounded monster. She jabbed the point of her wand into the crimson brand on his forehead, and whispered. "What does that mean? Where did you get it?"

"That is a nasty bite you have there, little red one," he said, and Penny felt the wound on her shoulder throb in pain again. "It must be very painful."

He's doing it, Penny realized. *He's making it hurt.*

Penny's homunculus joined them, stomping up the length of Turoc's body. It threw its club aside as it pushed past a badly singed Ronan and punched Turoc in the face with a large stone fist.

The monster's horned head hit the dirt, one of his long fangs breaking free and tumbling into the creek. The glow in Turoc's eyes dimmed, and the monster fell, unconscious.

"It's good to see your present is coming in handy," Ronan quipped, and limped down to the ground. "Have you named him yet?"

Penny nodded, and cringed as her pierced shoulder sent another bolt of pain through her. "Rocky."

Rocky chattered angrily at Turoc one last time, then turned toward the girls and bared its large stone teeth in a smile.

Ronan chuckled wearily and lay down near the fire pit.

Katie grimaced and averted her eyes. "Well, if you are going to keep him at least find him something to wear."

Ellen tittered nervously, then went silent and blushed red as Katie turned a sour eye her way.

"Worry about that later," Zoe said, cringing a little as she nudged Turoc's motionless body with the toe of her shoe. "What are we going to do with this?"

Katie bent down in front of the door and picked up the doorway relic. "I think it's time we find out where this goes."

* * *

It was Penny who figured out how to use the doorway relic. Growing impatient with the delay and glancing nervously over her shoulder at Turoc's body, she snatched the knob from Katie's hand and stabbed the short spike on the back into the weathered wood of the door. The strange etchings glowed brighter. Ignoring the others' stunned faces, she twisted the knob and pulled the door open.

"I don't think this is a good idea," Ronan said for maybe the tenth time, but since he didn't have any better suggestions he didn't try to stop them.

It was not the library or the cave, not the shimmering liquid surface of the mirror portal, or the closet stuffed with hanging robes. It was as they had hoped, a doorway into nothing. A familiar discordant hum escaped and echoed inside of the hollow, filled Penny's head with nausea.

"Hurry," Zoe groaned, clutching the sides of her head and squeezing her eyes shut.

Working together, they dragged Turoc to the door, mustering all of their courage to keep hold of the cold, scaly flesh. Penny thought her skin might crawl right off her bones if she had to touch him much longer. He began to stir, to struggle ineffectually as they lifted him to the open doorway.

"Stop," he hissed, his voice almost inaudible. "I can answer your questions ...."

Penny paused.

"Forget it," Katie growled, and leaned into him, pushing with all her strength.

He toppled, fell through the open door, but did not appear on the other side as Penny had expected, floating ungrounded in a sea of nothing. When he passed the threshold, he simply vanished.

The hum grew a little louder for a second, and that was all.

"What about these," Ellen asked, staring around at the broken homunculi.

For the next minute, the hum of the nothing behind the open door working ugly magic inside their heads, the girls gathered the dead homunculi and threw them into the nothing to join their master. After watching for a few moments, Rocky caught on to what they were doing and joined.

Katie eyed the helpful creature as if she'd like to toss him in with the others, and Penny asked him to go away for a while. She was only a little surprised when he gave a series of quick bows and chattered at her. She was much more surprised that she could understand the thing's squawks and chitters. Not in words, but as an affirmation in her mind.

Yes. He called her something that meant both Penny, girl, and mine, then, *Rocky will come if you need him.*

He sprinted off into the trees, and Katie relaxed ... a little.

Finally, Penny approached the open door with Turoc's lost arm. She threw it in after its owner, then Zoe swept the door shut and tugged the strange, dangerous doorknob from the wood.

"Did we kill him?" Ellen stared at the door, her face a mask of guilt. "Is he dead now?"

Penny put what she hoped was a comforting hand on Ellen's arm and said, "I don't know, but we did what we had to do. He was going to kill us."

Not exactly true, Penny reminded herself, remembering his instructions to the gray men under the landfill to kill Katie, but not Penny.

Why would she be any different than the rest of them?

The answer to that—and to so many other questions she had—was gone, vanished into nothing behind the door.

"We'd better go," Penny said at last. "We're supposed to be in town."

Ronan rose, almost grinning at them, and limped toward the creek. "You do what you need to do, girls. I for one could use some rest. I hadn't planned on so much activity so soon after returning."

Penny had to admit that he was in rough shape. His fur was singed in places, the bare skin blistered.

"Thanks for coming back," Penny said, "but how did you do it?"

Zoe and Ellen seemed to be wondering the same thing. They regarded him with lively interest.

"Later," Ronan said, and Katie seemed to agree that it could wait.

Katie took Penny and Ellen by the arms and motioned Zoe toward the door.

"Let's go!"

They went.

* * *

They emerged just outside Katie's garage door.

Downtown was silent, deserted. Even the park, which they ran toward to wait out news of Morgan Duke's capture or escape, was empty. The grass gleamed wetly in the glow of the moon, and the streetlamps revealed pavement dark with rain. Even if there had been anyone out at that late hour, Katie's storm had probably sent them running for cover.

"Let me look at that," Zoe said, and pulled Penny's shirt down to reveal her bloodied shoulder.

Penny cringed as Zoe wiped her shoulder with the sleeve of her ruined shirt. "How bad is it?"

"Not too bad," Zoe said, sounding astonished. "You said Ronan … he died from a bite like this?"

"He isn't dead," Penny said, "and his was much worse."

Zoe's doubt was plain on her face.

"It hurt for a while," Penny admitted. "It's okay now."

"We should still clean it," Katie said, regarding the twin punctures. "A new shirt might be a good idea, too. Susan will have a kitten if she finds you covered with blood again."

"How about you guys?" Penny asked, passing a quick inspecting glance over the others, not quite able to believe they had gotten through everything with all of their limbs still attached.

"Fine," Kate said.

"I'm okay," Zoe said.

"I'm soaked," Ellen said, shaking water out of her hair.

They were disheveled, Katie's cheek scratched and red from her trip through the willow boughs, and they were probably covered with bruises, but they were otherwise fine.

"Come on, Penny."

Katie led Penny back to the Wests' house, leaving Zoe and Ellen to wait for Susan or Michael's return.

"I was getting ready for bed when I heard you," Katie said, and it took Penny a moment to realize what she was talking about. "You just whispered my name, and I was about to answer you when I heard *his* voice, so I woke Michael up and told him there was trouble at your house."

Penny could feel another complication coming on. Michael had been looking at them strangely since the night under Main Street and the morning he'd found Zoe's wand. Now Katie had alerted him to a danger she shouldn't, couldn't, have known about.

"What did you say to him?"

Katie opened the garage door and led Penny inside. A moment later she found the lights and turned them on.

"Just that Morgan Duke was at your house and you were in trouble." Katie blushed, she knew Penny had guessed where her story was going. "I don't think he believed me at first."

"But you got him to go," Penny said, "and I know he believes you now."

"So what will we tell him?" Katie betrayed real anxiety.

"Whatever we have to," Penny said. She was too tired for fabrications.

Katie nodded and put a silencing finger to her lips as she opened the door into the house and motioned Penny inside. They passed silently through the kitchen and hallway, Katie taking the lead again to guide Penny through the dark, unfamiliar house, and into the bathroom. Katie shut the door behind them before turning on the lights, pulled a package of bandages and disinfectant from the cabinet over the sink, and reached for Penny's injured shoulder.

"It's okay," Penny said, backing away a step and almost falling into the bathtub. "I can do it."

"Okay," Katie said and sighed. "I'll get you a shirt."

When she returned a few minutes later, opening the door just a crack to pass a folded shirt through, Penny was still wincing from the sting of the disinfectant, still applying the last bandage. She changed shirts and stepped into the hall, alarmed by the sight that met her.

Katie stood in her father's shadow, looking as if she'd just been caught burglarizing the place. The lights were on, and Penny saw Katie's mother moving through the kitchen in a flowery robe.

To Penny's relief though, Markus West didn't look angry, only tired and concerned.

"Are you okay, Penny?" His eyes fell to the blood-spotted shirt wadded in her hand. "Katie said there was trouble at your house."

Penny gave him a heavily edited version of the confrontation with Morgan Duke, attributing her hurt shoulder and bloody shirt to a fall as they fled the house. By the time she had finished, they were seated in the kitchen and Katie's mother had pressed a mug of hot cocoa into Mr. West's hands. She apparently saw the covetous look Penny gave the steaming mug, because she left, then returned a few moments later with one for her and Katie.

"Lynne, sit down. You're making me dizzy," Markus scolded, but it was a light scolding at best. A quickly suppressed grin belied any real reproach.

"I suppose Susan will be around after she's finished murdering that Duke man," she said. "He's lucky Michael went with her."

Markus nodded, almost smiled again, then froze. He set his cup down and put a hand on Penny's injured shoulder, making her gasp in pain. "Where is Zoe? Is she okay?"

"She's okay," Penny said. "She's in the park with Ellen."

"I was afraid something had happened to her," Markus said, and backed off a step.

Penny's shoulder throbbed from the contact, but she tried not to show it. They all had enough to worry about without the adults going to pieces over a minor flesh wound.

"Invite them in, dear," Lynne West said to Penny. She ruffled Markus's sleep-tousled hair and gave him a gentle shove toward the door. "They can wait in here."

* * *

Of Katie's friends, Ellen was the only one who seemed entirely comfortable in the Wests' big living room. Zoe sat scrunched into the furthest corner of the couch she shared with the other girls, eyes pointed down at her clasped hands, as if she was afraid to look at, let alone touch anything. Penny sat next to her, trying her hardest to avoid Markus West's eyes, unable to forget the contempt he had shown for her only weeks before. His eyes, however, kept returning to her, stealing quick glances.

Katie's mother stood in the kitchen again, speaking with Michael over the phone. Her voice was too soft for Penny to make out her end of the conversation, but it was over quickly and Mrs. West returned to find herself the center of attention.

"Susan knows you're here," she said. "They're on their way now."

"Did they catch him?" Markus sat on the edge of his chair, hands clutching the arms. The suspense seemed to be driving him as crazy as it was Penny.

Lynne nodded. "They did ... but...."

She glanced back at the girls before answering her husband. "They had to call an ambulance. He'd lost a few fingers and a lot of blood and ... well, he died while they were loading him in."

"He's dead?" Zoe spoke her first words since her arrival in the West house. She sounded horrified, and Penny hoped she would remember that he was about to shoot them before Zoe's spell exploded the gun in his hand.

Lynne nodded.

"Susan didn't ...," Markus seemed almost afraid to finish his question.

"Oh, dear no, he had a heart attack. They'd bandaged his hand up and were loading him into the ambulance when he clutched his chest and just ... died."

The news hit Penny like a slap, rocking her back against the couch.

Dead?

Lights hit the big picture window, and everyone turned as one to see Michael's cruiser pull into the driveway, Susan's old Falcon close behind it.

A minute later the newcomers were inside, and Susan pulled Penny and Zoe from the couch in a frantic, slightly painful, embrace.

"Susan, the house?"

"It's fine," Susan said, and relief flooded Penny. "The fire was dying out when the fire truck arrived."

Amazement was clear in her voice.

"It burned to the fence-line and just ... went out. Ernest lost his entire field, and there were a lot of smaller fires, but the rain put most of them out before the firefighters could get to them."

Penny's relief was somewhat marred by the penetrating look Michael leveled at her.

Whatever he was thinking, he let it drop ... at least for now.

"I have to go," Michael said, giving Susan a quick hug before walking away. "The sheriff is furious with me for responding without waiting for him."

"The sheriff can kiss my ...," Susan stopped herself before finishing the sentiment and rolled her eyes to the ceiling.

"If he does fire me you should consider putting an application in, Susan." Michael smiled and winked at her. "You gave me a run for my money tonight."

Then he was gone.

"Susan," Markus said, giving Susan a look of false consternation. "I do believe you're spending too much time with that boy. I think he's got a crush on you."

"Markus!" Lynne and Susan scolded in unison. Lynne slapped playfully at the back of his head, and he grinned.

* * *

Penny, Zoe and Ellen spent the rest of the night at the Wests' house, the four crammed tightly into Katie's queen-sized bed.

"You are so spoiled," Zoe said.

"Yes I am," Katie agreed, too tired to argue.

Penny was finally drifting to sleep when the door opened and light fell in upon them.

Michael stood in the doorway, returned from a pleasant early morning at the office.

"Michael, we're trying to sleep." Katie groaned and pulled the sheets over her head.

For a moment Michael said nothing.

"What?" Katie barked impatiently, and Zoe awoke with a snort next to her.

"Morgan Duke had some very strange things to say before he died." They couldn't see his face, only his silhouette, but his voice was hushed and more serious than Penny had ever heard it. "That little talk I was planning to have with you … I think it's time."

Penny's chest seemed to fill with lead.

"Michael, it's," Katie twisted in bed to look at her clock. "It's five in the morning and we haven't slept all night."

"Later then," he said. "The five of us."

He closed the door and left them in an uncomfortable silence.

For the second time that night Katie asked, "What are we going to tell him?"

For a long time Penny didn't answer. Her instinct was to lie, to cover up, to keep the secret, but he'd already seen and heard too much, and Michael was no dummy. He would know they were lying.

So what did that leave?

"We'll tell him the truth," Penny said at last.

"Okay," Katie said, and to Penny's surprise she sounded relieved.

"Do you think he'll tell anybody?" Zoe voiced the fear Penny herself felt, but Katie was quick to answer.

"No, Michael's cool. I think he'll understand why no one else can know."

"Nobody would believe him anyway," Ellen said.

Penny laughed. She couldn't help it.

"He'll keep our secret," Penny said. "We can be very persuasive if we need to be."

* * *

When Michael knocked on Katie's bedroom door the next morning, the girls were ready and waiting for him.

"Katie?" Michael sounded nervous but resolute.

"Come in!" Katie shouted back. Muffled laughter followed this invitation.

Michael opened her door, stepped inside, and looked around. The girls were nowhere in evidence. "Kat?"

"We're in here." Katie's voice came from the closet door, open only a few inches.

Michael frowned, hesitated, trying to decide if this was a necessary confrontation or if he should just try to forget the weirdness his little sister seemed to be mixed up in. He didn't notice Penny, hidden behind the door to the hallway. She pushed it closed as he resumed his grim stride to the closet door.

He swung the closet door open, lifted his foot to take his first step inside, and froze in place.

Behind him, Penny latched and locked Katie's bedroom door.

Michael stood on the threshold between his little sister's bedroom, and something that was most definitely not her closet.

"Well, what are you waiting for?" Katie asked, and had to bite her lips against a burst of nervous laughter. She stood at the creek's edge, Zoe and Ellen on either side of her. Zoe was looking at her feet. Ellen covered a smile with one hand.

"What ...?" Michael poked his head through the doorway and looked up, as if hoping to see the ceiling of Katie's walk-in closet. What he saw was a canopy of interlaced willow whips forming an imperfect green roof through which he could see flashes of blue sky. Beneath his still-raised foot was not the carpet of Katie's bedroom, but dirt, grass, and fallen leaves.

Katie rushed to him, concern on her face. She snapped her fingers beneath his nose, and he tore his gaze from the creekside country clearing he had not expected to find inside his sister's closet. He stared down at her, chagrin and disbelief fighting for room on his face.

"What did you do with your closet?" He looked around again. "How did this get inside your closet?"

"Come in and have a seat," Katie motioned to one of the boulders arranged around the fire pit, "and we'll explain it all."

Penny stood close behind him, her hands raised and ready to give him a push through the open door if his nerves failed him.

Michael put his raised foot down, on the carpet of Katie's room instead of the ground in the hollow, and took a step back, almost bumping into Penny. Then he took a deep breath, and walked through into the hollow.

Penny followed him through, meeting Katie's smile with one of her own, and closed the door behind them.

Chapter 21

The End ... For Now

Friday evening in Dogwood was chaotic, even with a block of Main Street still cordoned off and half of the businesses closed. The park was overrun with families returning from vacation to witness firsthand the devastation they'd only seen on the local news or heard about from family and friends. The townspeople watched the demolition and cleanup of the ruined building, one of Dogwood's oldest, with morbid fascination. The bakery's mobile cart did a roaring trade in doughnuts, coffee, and—Penny's favorite—Elephant Ears, serving the workers and watchers alike.

The people of Dogwood watched the workmen loading construction dumpsters with rubble, speculated on which of the businesses would return and which would close for good, and retold the story of Susan and Michael's capture of the villain Morgan Duke a hundred times over, casting speculative and admiring glances at where Susan sat with Markus, Lynne, and Michael West.

Michael was handling the revelation about his sister and the *Dogwood Witches* better than expected. He had honored Katie's wish that he keep the knowledge to himself, but insisted they come to him first before engaging in any more dangerous forays against horror-movie monsters. Katie had reluctantly agreed to tell him next time something mad and scaly tried to kill them, but Penny had seen her cross her fingers behind her back.

Penny didn't think Michael was going to let it go that easily.

"You're only fourteen," he reminded Katie when her obstinacy continued. "It's not up to you to save the world. You're not some comic-book superhero."

"Well," Ellen interjected, perhaps unwisely given the mood of the exchange, "she can fly."

"Don't remind me," he'd said, rubbing his forehead as if staving off a headache.

In the two days since Michael's inclusion in their secret, he made a habit of checking up on them almost constantly. It drove Katie nuts, but Penny thought that Zoe was secretly enjoying the extra attention.

As if reminding Penny that he hadn't forgotten about them, Michael cast her a dark, meaningful look from his seat between Susan and his father. His attention was stolen away a moment later by the arrival of Ellen's parents.

Mr. Kelly, tall, dark-haired and bespectacled, stopped to clap Michael on the shoulder and shake his hand. To Penny he looked more like a politician than a computer geek, which is how Zoe referred to him.

"He's not a *geek*," Ellen had said. "He's a computer systems analyst."

Mrs. Kelly, tall and blonde, looked more like a model than a town-hall clerk. She caught sight of the girls and waved to Ellen before clasping her husband by the arm and dragging him away from Michael.

As if to balance out the ugliness of the ruin across the street, the Dogwood trees in the park were finally, and all too briefly Penny knew, in furious bloom. Bright pink and dazzling white, adding more life to the park than Penny could have imagined. In three weeks the park, the sidewalks, and even the street beyond, would be covered in their petals.

Penny, Zoe, Katie and Ellen sat apart from the rest of the Friday evening throng, under the big oak near the gazebo, Zoe's old reading tree, and the very spot where Penny had first seen her. None of them had seen Ronan since the night of his unexpected return, but they figured he was holed up in that cave, healing. At least that was what they hoped.

The industrious bustle of demolition didn't interest her, nor she suspected, did it interest Susan. She had lost an important part of her life the night it burned down; it was not a spectator sport for her.

They were there for Zoe.

Zoe watched the road winding out of town with an anticipation that was almost painful to witness. Her parents, whom she had not seen in over a year, would arrive soon.

Penny watched too, with dread and growing anger.

She hated Zoe's parents, not because they had left her here with a grandmother who didn't seem to like her much, but because they were coming back.

Katie and Ellen whispered among themselves, idly passing the time with talk about nothing important. They seemed to be aware of Penny's distress and decided that the best way to help her cope was to not help her.

Penny appreciated that.

Zoe's interest perked momentarily when a familiar car, James Price's black Charger, rolled to a stop at the yellow tape cordoning off the demolition zone. For a moment it sat, idling, then the passenger door opened and Ernest Price climbed out, looking dirty and disheveled. His clothes looked slept in, his Stetson bent out of shape and crooked on his head. He stumbled as he slammed the car door shut and walked a crooked path toward the activity.

"He's drunk," Katie said.

"As a skunk," Ellen agreed.

A man with a bright yellow vest and hardhat rushed to intercept Mr. Price before he could cross the barrier, and the ensuing argument was inaudible but animated.

Zoe leapt up suddenly, bracing herself against the trunk of the tree, and seemed unable to breath.

Penny saw the truck a second later, pulling to the far curb in front of the church. It was big and white and somehow strange without the long trailer that should have been following it. Penny thought it looked like a giant head without a body. She heard the distant chuff of air brakes, then the headlights went dark and the low and mellow rumble of its engine died.

Penny, Katie and Ellen stood too, the whispered conversation stopping.

For a few long moments they could only see the silhouettes of the passengers. Zoe's anxiety grew, became almost tangible. Then both doors swung open at once, and two people climbed from the high cab of the semi: a short, dark-haired woman who descended slowly down from the passenger side; and a tall, muscular man who leapt down from the driver's side. They swept the doors shut, and Zoe's hurried breathing stopped for a second.

"Mom ... Dad." Just a whisper at first, breathless, almost inaudible. "Mom! Dad!"

Heads turned from all around at the outburst, but Zoe was blind to them. She sprinted toward the approaching figures, clumsy in her excitement, almost tripping as she vaulted the curb to the street. She didn't notice Penny and the others rushing to keep up, didn't see Susan and the Wests abandon their spot—marked by a half-circle of folding chairs and a cooler—to follow.

The approaching figures, the short, pixyish dark-haired woman and the tall, muscular man, never altered their pace. They approached their daughter at an easy, almost lazy pace, but when she reached them at last, the man bent down and opened his arms wide.

Zoe threw herself into his open arms, and Penny marveled that he remained upright. He enclosed her in a spirited embrace and swung her from the ground, spinning her through the air.

Zoe's exhilarated laughter overwhelmed the low drone of machinery and the babble of the onlookers.

For a terrible moment, Penny was insanely jealous.

Then she saw Zoe's face as her father lifted her high, as if she were no more than a toddler and not a budding young Amazon, and Penny's jealousy vanished in a bright, hot blush of shame.

She didn't realize she had stopped until she saw Katie and Ellen join the happy reunion, Zoe's father setting her back on her feet and her mother swooping in for her turn.

Susan stopped behind her, put a hand on her shoulder, startling Penny.

"Worried?" Susan asked almost casually, and Penny felt the heat rise in her cheeks as she blushed again.

Had she been that transparent?

"Yes," she said simply, and hoped Susan would let the subject drop.

Susan did, and as the Wests joined them, Katie's father in the lead and looking as uneasy as Penny felt, they walked to join the happy family reunion.

*   *   *

That night was Penny's first night alone in a week, and though she missed Zoe, she welcomed the solitude. She sat on her bed, wide awake, though it was late and she had a funeral to attend the following morning, looking through the old photo album again. The Conjuring Glass sat at the end of her bed, the obscuring fog swirling expectantly it seemed, waiting for Penny to resume exploring the past. Her small mirror sat on her nightstand.

Her table lamp threw a small, bright spot of light over her, glaring off the glossy plastic photograph sleeves.

She flipped the pages again, not knowing precisely what she was looking for until she found it, a photo of the mystery girl. She slid it from the album and examined it.

"Who are you?"

"*Penny?*"

Penny almost screamed in shock, dropping the photo and tipping the album off her lap as she kicked her blankets aside. One of these days she supposed she'd get used to being disturbed in the middle of the night by disembodied voices.

She tripped over her own feet sliding out of bed, landed hard on the floor, and cursed silently. A snort of laughter sounded from the small mirror on her night stand.

Not bothering to get up, Penny reached blindly and grabbed at the mirror, bringing it close to her face.

Ronan grinned at her. "Fancy a chat?"

*   *   *

Penny stepped into the hollow, casting a fire into the stone ring even as she pulled the door closed behind her. She searched for Ronan and found him peeking through the mouth of his cave. When he stepped out, she saw that his fur had grown in to cover the singed spots, as thick as ever. He looked healthy, strong. A moment later he confirmed her assessment by bounding across the creek in a single leap, a leap that carried him straight into Penny.

Unlike Zoe's tall, muscular father, Penny didn't have the size or strength to remain upright. Ronan knocked her to the ground and sat on her chest, laughing with joy and sounding more like the Ronan she had met almost a year ago than he had in a long time.

"I am so very proud of you," he said at last, bumping the furry crown of his head against Penny's in a rare show of affection. "You've all done so well."

"We had some help," Penny said, and returned Ronan's head bump with one of her own.

Ronan grinned, gave a little bow, and jumped from Penny's chest, allowing her to sit up. He settled next to her and turned his head to regard her, and though a trace of his smile lingered, Penny could see he was becoming serious.

"I imagine I missed a few things during my recuperation," he said after a short pause. "I would appreciate you bringing me up-to-date."

He had missed a few things, important things, and Penny had every intention of filling him in, but first ....

"You go first," Penny said, unable to suppress her grin. She was determined to beat the hairy little nuisance at his own game for once. She had been dying to know just how he'd come back after dying so convincingly in her arms. "How did you come back? We saw you die. I *felt* you die."

"Very well," Ronan said, unperturbed. "The body that died in your arms, the one you're seeing now, is only a projection."

"What?" Penny's ability to believe the strange and unusual had expanded considerably in the past year, but this was simply too much. Projected images didn't nip playfully at your pant legs or knock you to the ground when they jumped on you. Projected images didn't leave a wet streak across your cheek when they licked you. "Are you trying to tell me you're not real?"

"Don't be ridiculous," he said. "Of course I'm *real*."

"Then what are you ...."

"This," Ronan said, indicating his restored body with a backward glance over his shoulder, "is only a physical projection into your world."

"My world?" Penny found her capacity for belief stretched a little more. "How many worlds are there?"

"Countless," Ronan said. "Many worlds, and all connected."

Penny glanced at the patches of night sky she could see through the hollow's willow canopy. "You mean like Mars or Jupiter?"

"No," Ronan said, shaking his head. "Those are only planets. The worlds are much more than just different points in the same night sky. They are everything ... all the same, but all a little different, and all connected."

"Are you talking about parallel universes?" Penny had read enough science fiction and fantasy stories to know where he was going, even if she wasn't quite ready to believe him.

"Not necessarily parallel, but universes, I suppose." He seemed to consider this for a moment, then dismissed it with a shrug. "Close enough."

Penny digested this for a moment, or attempted to, then gave up and nodded. Sometimes with Ronan it was just best to take things on faith.

"The *real* me ... well, you might find me a bit frightening." He grinned. "When my body died my consciousness traveled back to the real me. It took some time and not a little effort to rejoin you here, and I feared I would be too late."

"Ohhh-kay," she said, and reminded herself to take it on faith. "So we went into that tunnel and rescued you for nothing?"

"Oh, I wouldn't say that," Ronan said. "Had this body died with me still inside it anywhere other than here, I would have been lost. Aurora Hollow is a thin place, a place where the worlds almost touch. I never could have found my way back if you wonderful girls hadn't brought me here."

"Oh." Penny felt a chill overtake her at the statement. It had been very close then.

"I owe you girls more than my life. I owe you my existence."

Penny had no words to reply.

"Your turn now," Ronan prompted. "Have you girls gotten into any new trouble?"

Penny nodded her assent. "Yeah, you could say that."

There wasn't as much as Ronan had thought. The only unpleasant surprise was Michael's inclusion in the secret, but Ronan accepted it, if only because he didn't have a choice. His pleasure at Ellen's decision to join them eclipsed his annoyance.

"And how about your other new friend?" Ronan asked.

"Rocky!" Penny called out, and what at first appeared to be a piece of the solid stone wall above his cave and leapt out, caught the end of a willow whip, and swung over the creek to land at Penny's side. The homunculus considered Ronan briefly before turning its large green eyes up to Penny.

Ronan goggled for a moment, then burst into fresh laughter.

"Don't pay any attention to mean old Ronan, Rocky," Penny said, patting Rocky's head.

Rocky closed his eyes, a satisfied grin stretching his wide, gray face, practically purring with contentment.

Zoe and Ellen thought Rocky was adorable and treated him like a new pet, but Katie was not happy with Aurora Hollow's newest resident. Penny thought that Katie would come around eventually, maybe when a few months had passed without Rocky trying to strangle any of them, but in the meantime she seemed prepared to tolerate him for Penny's sake. She had, however, insisted that Penny put some clothes on him.

Katie needn't have bothered with that demand. Penny wasn't about to let the little gray man run around naked all the time.

Rocky stood before the still-laughing Ronan in a pair of shorts salvaged from Zoe's old Raggedy Andy doll and a set of crisscrossing rope suspenders. The Phoenix Key hung around his neck, the safest place Penny could think to keep it.

Relatively safe, she amended silently.

Her time in Aurora Hollow was a lot of things, amazing, magical, unpredictable, but safe was not one of those things. Thinking about the old photograph album back in her room and the girls who had once called Aurora Hollow their own, all gone now, dead or scattered, Penny supposed it had never been safe. Probably never would be.

But it was hers. Hers, Zoe's, Kat's and Ellen's, and they had saved it.

Penny knew their victory against the monstrous Turoc was not the end of the danger. She knew there would be more trouble to come, and though she feared losing Zoe, they were still all together … The Phoenix Girls and Ronan.

That peaceful and happy moment was not the end, only a happy interlude, but Penny was willing to take happiness wherever she could find it.

The end ... for now.

About Brian Knight

Brian Knight lives in Washington State with his family and the voices in his head. He has published over a dozen novels and novellas and two short story collections in the horror, dark fantasy, and crime genres. Several of his short stories have received honorable mentions in *Year's Best Fantasy and Horror*. *The Crimson Brand* is his second book in *The Phoenix Girls* series.

Photo by Judi Key

CPSIA information can be obtained at www.ICGtesting.com
Printed in the USA
LVOW13s1849230314

378590LV00001B/141/P